To Alexander !
I hope you enjoy
my the spirit in
yours in
[signature]

MetalMagic

Talisman

Derek Donais

MetalMagic: Talisman

Copyright © 2010 Derek Donais All rights reserved. No part of this book may be reproduced or retransmitted in any form or by any means without the written permission of the publisher.

Published by Wheatmark®
610 East Delano Street, Suite 104
Tucson, Arizona 85705 U.S.A.
www.wheatmark.com

International Standard Book Number: 978-1-60494-354-2
Library of Congress Control Number: 2009935950

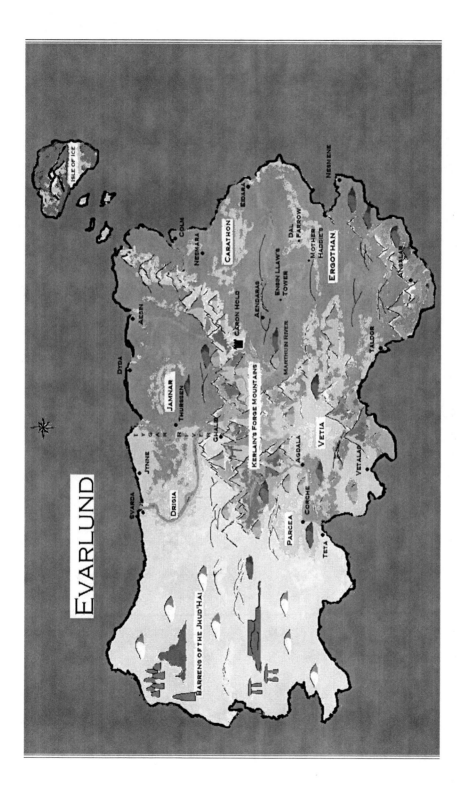

Prologue

FARTHER THAN THE SCOURING WINDS traveled in a winter season, they had tracked Ravien. But no more. It would end here, today.

Despite the frigid gusts tearing at her robes and whipping about her long, ebony tresses, Ravien gave not a thought to the bitter cold. Sholara, Evarlund's sun, was a palely illuminated blur set within a turbulent sea of ivory.

Centered, Ravien awaited the arrival of her pursuers. One way or another, the issue would be settled.

Whether or not she remained standing at the end mattered not. Ravien had resisted for as long as she could, and her endurance was at its end. Once her center was finally lifted, either her once-comrades or the exhaustion of the past, harrowing weeks would surely overcome her. Compared to the unceasing struggle for survival—all she had known of life lately—death would be a welcome release.

In fact, Ravien had been on the run for much longer than mere weeks. For years, they harried and hunted. They would never stop, never tire. They wanted to rewrite history and she was the sole remaining obstacle.

In a way, she had made their goal more attainable. Out here, in the remoteness of the mountains, they could come up with whatever tale they wished to explain her demise. Ravien would do her best to ruin that part of their scheme. She had to.

A ripple in the ether stirred her center and Ravien knew they had arrived.

One by one, globes of glowing blue popped into view about her, obscured partially by the driving snow. They would materialize together, in order that Ravien could not strike at them individually. Singly, or even in smaller groups, she could overwhelm them. Not so with seven.

In an instant they emerged from their gateways and moved to surround her within a barricade of their joined energies. As Ravien had already centered, she could not be easily divided from the magic—

though their plan would certainly not have been based upon the anticipation of such an amateur misstep.

They sported robes similar to Ravien's, though far less tattered:
high-collared, vibrant in color and trimmed with silver and gold. Seven
grim faces stared at her. In most, she saw condemnation. The others
were impassive. Each held forth a glowing sphere of *metanduil*, tendrils
of blue electricity dancing across the silvery surfaces. Within those
spheres, pure energy pulsated, power the group had come to unleash
upon Ravien—and all Evarlund.

For some moments they stood silent, with only the wail of the tempest to disturb the unspoken test of wills.

Jaedha finally offered the challenge. "Submit, Ravien, and be judged
under the Truth!" Even Jaedha's close-cropped, red hair moved with
the flailing gusts and her emerald eyes seemed to bore at Ravien, their
intensity unimpeded by the raging tempest.

She always had been an impulsive one, Ravien mused. "It is not in
me to fear the Truth. Rather, I embrace it."

"And so you shall—"

"Hold, Jaedha!" a thunderous voice cut in. "We will offer one last
moment of counsel to our estranged sister. A decision of this magni-
tude requires…the proper encouragement and support." The winter
gale ripped the words from their mouths, as if Evarlund itself wished
to sweep away all trace of this conflict. Only centered in the magic, did
their voices carry.

All eyes, including Ravien's, oriented to the speaker. Agamund
nodded his shaven head slightly, whether in simple acknowledgement
of the attention or in satisfaction, Ravien could not guess. The inscrutable half-smile he wore offered no further clue.

"I see the weariness in your eyes, Ravien. The burden you carry
draws even at your center. I sense it."

In comparison to Jaedha's gaze, Agamund's was as the light of Sholara to the pinpoint of a distant star. Ravien forced herself to meet it,
nonetheless.

"You do not have to suffer so," he continued. "It is the will of the
Truth. You know this. Why do you still fight us?"

"It is not the way of the Truth to shackle what has been created, to
make a prisoner of free will. That is the way of the Deceiver. Who do
you truly serve?"

"As you well know, I serve all of Evarlund. The *Valir* are the protectors of the realms. We protect them even from themselves, if need be."

"And who will protect them from you? Once you have restored order, in the name of the True One, will you simply leave the realms to maintain it?" Ravien's sarcastic tone belied her true understanding. They did not act according to the will of the Truth. They simply twisted the teachings to their own selfish purposes.

"You know we will. As the *Valir* have always done." Agamund cocked his head and sighed. "You cannot believe your misguided attempts serve the Truth. Were it so, we would have been shown the supposed error of our ways."

"You have been shown, yet you refuse to believe. You invest your faith in half-truths and deception. I ask again; who do you serve?"

"I serve the true cause of peace!" Agamund roared, his pretense at conciliation finally shattered. "Our way will pave the road for a lasting amity among the realms. No longer will the gift of free will be abused. Not by rulers. Not by us—or by you, should you remain opposed to the will of the council." His brow furrowed deeply. "We have reached the end of our patience, Ravien. Choose your destiny."

Her reaction was immediate. Shielding herself, Ravien sent her energy into the earth, delving deeper and deeper, to the mountain's root and beyond.

Vaguely, Ravien was aware of the others striking at her, of their considerable magic brought to bear, combined and amplified by the metanduil. Her shield need only hold until she had accomplished her task. She could feel them forcing it inward inexorably. Still, the barrier withstood. Ravien felt the connection, then, the coupling of her own magic with the essence of Evarlund itself. She grinned in triumph.

Ravien was still smiling when her vision exploded into white-hot oblivion.

❦

The shock waves of the explosions that began late in the afternoon continued throughout the night and well into the hours of Sholara's brilliance the following morning. Days afterward, occasional tremors and aftershocks were felt nearly to the coasts of Evarlund.

Soon after the initial blasts, a fiery plume lanced skyward, radiating light and heat and shedding great clouds of dust and ash. The glow that emanated from the heart of Evarlund's central mountains rivaled the average sunset, even in the farthest reaches.

In the days to come, it was told that a volcano had formed in the midst of the great mountain chain, thrusting itself above the most towering peaks. It was no longer erupting, but ill vapors and smoke belched forth constantly, blanketing the entire range with a murky cloud.

Much quieter, and spoken of only in hushed whispers too soon enveloped by the mists of time, was the true knowledge of its birth.

1

It has to be here!

Jaren fumbled about inside the narrow compartment. He'd watched as Morgaine put it inside last night, and yet Jaren's groping fingers found nothing but rough, dust-covered wood and a few cobwebs. Nearing panic, he redoubled his efforts. *You've only got one chance at this!* Finally, his fingers brushed against something cool and hard. It was cleverly wedged into a crack in one of the boards. Even knowing its hiding place, he'd almost not found his sister's little treasure. He withdrew his scraped and stinging arm and examined the prize.

The weighty little talisman looked unremarkable, though to Jaren, it was the most valuable thing in the world. Roughly the size of a small egg, it was irregular in shape, its surface pocked with dimples, the darker stone infused with silver-hued, metallic ore. It wasn't the material value of the trinket that held the greatest promise, though it was surely worth more than its weight in gold. No, it was the nature of the object itself, for it was *metanduil*.

Magic-metal, it was commonly called—the tool of summoners and conjurers. It was invaluable to them, as none could wield magic without it.

At that thought, Jaren raised his eyes and scanned about apprehensively. He feared discovery at any moment, most likely by Morgaine. He took a steadying breath. His sister would not be back for some time yet, Jaren assured himself, though it had come at a price. He'd agreed to do her share of the farmwork for the entire week, in return for this one chance. Instead of fishing with Iselle, as he claimed, he was at home with Morgaine's talisman. An expensive ruse, but one he'd felt forced to invent.

Jaren had no idea why he increasingly felt the call of the magic, but it could be nothing else. Dream whisperings borne on the wind, their subtle resonance urged him to make contact with it, with the source of a summoner's power. Trying to ignore the pull was futile. Even praying to the True One had not helped—the whispers spoke of Jaren becoming more than what he was, urged him to go where his head told him he did not belong. So, driven in part by this mysterious urging, and because he simply had to try it—the talisman was just sitting there, wasn't it?—Jaren could not let this chance to experiment with the talisman escape. The *Valir* testers would be gone for at least another year or more. Another year of the insistent dream-voices might drive him crazy.

The whispers had awakened something lying dormant within him. They had loosed a sensation of pent-up energy, one that flowed through and emanated from him at the same time. It had to be the voice of the magic. What else could it be?

He blinked. *You're wasting time!* he scolded himself. Taking a deep breath, he forced himself back into the present.

His mouth was dry with anxiety, so he worked his tongue to bring some moisture. It didn't help much. Anxious or not, Jaren would test himself now, though he really hadn't the slightest idea of how to use the magic or the talisman. Feelings and sensations were one thing, but practical knowledge was quite another. Morgaine was very secretive with the magic-metal, and Jaren had managed only the briefest glimpses of his sister with it. Still, he had to try.

He sat on the unyielding wooden floor of their shared bedroom, cross-legged, hands on his knees, with the talisman placed before him. He recreated the image of Morgaine in his mind, recalling one particular, brief observation of her practice with the stone. He'd glimpsed her in this same position, with a fork placed on the floor just ahead of the talisman. Suddenly, it happened. The fork moved—and not just a little. It jumped toward Morgaine. She'd jumped too, startled. Jaren had barely managed to duck out of sight as his sister's wary eyes scoured the surroundings, making sure no one was watching her. But he was sure that Morgaine hadn't seen him.

What to do now? Jaren took a spoon from his pocket and placed it and the talisman in about the same arrangement he had witnessed. For nearly the next hour, he tried everything he could think of to get the spoon to move even the slightest bit, but nothing worked. He focused on the talisman at first, thinking it would be the key to moving the utensil. That failed. Then, he thought to focus on the spoon: another failure. Jaren focused on both at once, then on neither—trying at the same time to calm his racing thoughts—but nothing happened. He even rearranged the objects, tried stacking them, and moved them first closer and then farther apart. In the end, the spoon continued to defy him. He was left exhausted, sweating, and now frustrated as well as fearful. He'd spent all the time he had. There was nothing more to be done. Jaren glared at the tiny objects before him. The talisman seemed larger, somehow, more substantial, and also more inaccessible. The spoon simply sat there, as if goading him.

It didn't make sense. He was sure he could feel something, some mystic strength. It floated about him, through him, teasing him all the while with its whispered promise of exhilaration and release. Jaren was certain it must be the power of the magic. So, why under the eyes of the True One did nothing happen? Was he imagining it all? Was his fervent desire creating this illusion of power? Was it jealousy of Morgaine? Perhaps, Jaren considered, it was all of these and possibly other reasons as well, all driving him to hear and feel something that simply wasn't there. Perhaps it was just as well that Morgaine had been tested and not Jaren. Maybe there was nothing special about him after all.

Jaren straightened his burgeoning shoulders from their hunch and cringed. His back ached with tension, his buttocks were numb from extended contact with the unyielding floor, and his legs were asleep. He ran a hand through his short, dark hair, frowning at the perspiration he discovered. Arching his back, Jaren exhaled sharply in frustration.

"Truth judge you!" he cursed the spoon, keeping a condemning eye on the defiant object while he stretched against the stiffness.

"Did you eat something you didn't like?" called a voice outside the window.

Jaren froze, the breath caught in his throat. Then, recognition brought a brief wave of relief, followed by a twinge of annoyance. The voice was not Morgaine's.

"Iselle," Jaren growled, turning to see Iselle's tanned face peering through the window. "What are you doing here?"

The girl's azure eyes widened at his reaction and the serious look on his face. "I thought I'd come see what you were up to. You know, since everyone thinks you're with me somewhere anyway." The afternoon sunlight played across her wavy, chestnut hair as it bounced with the accentuated movement of her head.

"What do you mean?"

"Well, I was going to help myself to a potato or two from Morgaine's basket, when I heard her talking to your mother. She asked Morgaine where you were. Your sister said she didn't know and that you were probably off with me getting into trouble at the pond. It didn't sound like your mother was too pleased, by the way. Anyhow, I thought that was a good time to leave, just in case they saw me. I figured I'd have the best chance of finding you here..." Iselle's voice trailed off briefly, curiosity replacing the matter-of-fact set to her face. "I should ask what *you're* doing here."

"Since when do I have to explain myself to you? This is my house. I can do whatever I want." As Jaren spoke, he slowly retrieved the talisman, trying not to be obvious.

Iselle apparently hadn't noticed. "Fine. Talk to your fork, too, if you want. I just thought you might like to get out of here for a bit. I doubt you'll get much of a chance for the next little while, if I know your mother and sister. Especially with Morgaine, when she catches you on her side of the room. Have fun with ... whatever."

"Iselle ... Iselle, wait." The frustration had seeped from Jaren's voice. He couldn't stay mad at Iselle for very long. Other than his family, she was one of the people closest to Jaren. He rose, moving nearer the window, and flashed a dimpled smile at his longtime friend, one of the few girls in Dal Farrow who stood just less than a hand's width shorter than he. If trouble were the going unit of measure, she'd tower over him. "Next time, try knocking on the door. People don't like to be spied on. It makes them edgy."

She smirked, and the corner of her mouth rose with its usual, mischievous curl as she peered about the room. "I don't think it was me that made you edgy. Well, at least you didn't curse at me like you did at the spoon. Why did you do that?"

Jaren smiled back. "Come around the front, and I'll tell you."

Iselle disappeared from view, and Jaren heard footsteps withdrawing. *She's come in the window before.* He exhaled in relief. *Good thing she didn't wonder why you asked her to go around front.* Jaren knew he'd have to tell Iselle about the talisman, but he didn't really want to let her in on where it was kept. She had a reputation for "investigating" things. That's all he needed, for Morgaine to find Iselle snooping about, and then he'd be done for. He set the talisman back into its hiding place. As his fingers broke contact with it, Jaren again felt the sensation of power resonating through him, a tingling wave that passed from head to toe. He ignored it, replaced the floorboard of the compartment, and let out an exasperated huff. Gingerly, he stood, threw one last scowl at the spot where the talisman lay hidden beneath the bedroom floorboards, then picked up the spoon and headed for the front door.

Iselle let out a long, low whistle. "She'll wring your neck if she finds out."

Jaren glared at her with an intensity that made her blink. "Well, if I don't tell her, there's only one other person who knows."

"I won't ... I mean, I wouldn't," she pledged, "but you're taking a big chance. What do you think the testers would do if they found out? You might never be allowed to take the trial yourself. The *Valir* are a touchy lot, by the sounds of them."

Jaren didn't answer right away. He could feel her eyes scrutinizing him even more closely. Finally, Iselle spoke again. "It didn't go well, then. That's why you were yelling at the spoon."

"I wasn't yelling."

"Whatever you say."

His face flushed once more, but the anger soon transformed into exasperation. "I just don't understand it. Sometimes it feels like there's energy all around me—inside me—and I'm almost sure it's got to be the magic. But I couldn't do anything with it. And I won't get another chance. I just don't know what I was doing wrong."

"Maybe you can't do anything with it because it's not yours."

He was about to snap back that she didn't know anything about it, but the idea suddenly made some sense. The testers had given the talisman to Morgaine alone. Maybe there was something about the magic-metal that would only let the rightful wielder summon through a talisman. Maybe he really did have some potential. He wanted so much to believe that was true, that there was still a chance!

"It means a lot to you, doesn't it?"

"What?" he responded absently.

"The magic-metal. Do you really want to leave ... everything ... behind?"

"It's not that, it's just—it's just things don't seem to fit anymore. Farming's fine for my parents, but I don't know if it's what I want for the rest of my life. The magic—it's calling me, I know it. How can I ignore that?"

She tried again. "But your family … and your friends. Wouldn't you be ignoring the people that care for you?"

He opened his mouth to respond, but no words came out. Instead, Jaren exhaled wearily and then shrugged. "Well, it doesn't really matter now. I've failed at the only chance I'll have for who knows how long … if I ever earn my own testing."

Iselle offered a resigned, half-smile. "If it's meant to be, it will happen. We all just have to accept what comes."

Jaren studied her for a moment. *Why did she look so sad all of a sudden?* He was about to ask what the problem was but didn't get the chance as another voice cut in first.

"So, here the two idlers are."

Jaren's scalp prickled. This time, it was Morgaine.

2

ALDRAIN KNEW THE FOREST WELL, yet his prey proved elusive. He shifted quietly from behind the concealing brush and scanned the distance, then lifted his eyes to the sky. Not a cloud in sight, and the sun was at its zenith. No breeze rustled the leaves, as not even a breath of wind stirred—typical high summer weather in eastern Carathon. Fortunately, he had at least the shelter of the shade about him. Aldrain wiped strands of sweat-plastered blond hair from his brow to keep the perspiration from running into his eyes.

Small, stinging flies buzzed about, escaping the punishing heat of the direct sunlight, but he dared not slap at them, fearing it would alert his quarry. *I should have listened to Sonja's suggestion*, he lamented. The *Valir* had offered to ward him against the insects with her magic. The prince had shrugged her off. Right now, it seemed like a very bad decision, despite the fact that many thought such uses of magic frivolous, if not even dangerous.

He slipped ahead, confident of his prey's destination. He didn't follow it, but stalked toward the place he had chosen to lie in wait. A copse of trees grew at the very edge of the stream, and it would hide him completely from view. His prey would head to the water from the left, giving Aldrain a perfect profile target.

An occasional dry twig snapped underfoot, and Aldrain froze after each misstep, taking care to make no further noise. By the time he reached the grove at the stream's edge, he had to force himself not to plunge directly into the cool, flowing water. He was soaked with perspiration now, hot and sticky from the stifling air. *Perhaps Sonja could have summoned a cool breeze, too.* He maneuvered into a proper shooting position, partly leaning against an ancient cottonwood. He brought the great yew bow up and nocked an arrow, but did not yet draw the string.

A faint rustling disturbed the undergrowth not far upstream. Almost immediately, a buck emerged from the surrounding shrubbery, close to the spot Aldrain had expected it. Actually, it was even nearer to his position than he had hoped. It wasn't the largest he'd ever seen, but the deer was several years old, based on the spread of antlers it sported. The buck sniffed the air gingerly, easing its head about as it tested for threatening scents. Finding none, it started forward to the streambed.

Aldrain waited, letting the deer get settled, allowing it to dip its head to the water. Ever so slowly, he drew back on the bowstring, cringing at the protesting creaks of the great weapon. He steadied his breathing, letting himself become balanced, and took careful aim—just above and behind the foreleg.

Suddenly, a twig snapped behind him, and Aldrain whirled about, taking a brief instant to assess the threat before loosing the arrow at the shadowy form looming there. The figure swung aside and dove, just avoiding the streaking arrow, which embedded itself deeply into another cottonwood several feet beyond. Without blinking, Aldrain nocked a second arrow and scanned the vegetation before him. Now he'd have time to aim properly. The intruder would not evade a second shot.

"I blooming-well think I'd make a pretty poor meal, Prince Aldrain!"

Immediately, Aldrain let the tension off the bowstring. Glancing back over his shoulder, he saw that the buck had bolted during the commotion. "I may have to shoot you regardless. You made my deer run away."

"Unless your shot improves, it won't matter, Your Highness."

Aldrain strode purposefully forward to the tree his arrow had struck. Ordren rose from the forest floor nearby, the dark man's great bulk casting a shadow to rival those of the trees about them. Aldrain was just above average height, but he appeared as a boy next to the huge warrior. The prince reached up and pulled a shred of wool from the shaft of the arrow. Turning, he made a show of dropping the scrap of material to the forest floor. "If you'd been any slower or clumsier, my father would have to find another companion for me."

Ordren looked down at his shoulder and put a finger through the new hole in his shirt. "Your Highness, it's too hot to bandy words here. Let's go somewhere cooler, like the throne room."

"That's just trading one uncomfortable place for another even worse."

"You must get used to it, sooner or later."

Aldrain scowled, but followed the great man as he wheeled about and led the way. "What made you come out so soon?"

"Your father's orders. He's a bit wary, with the prowlers of late. That, and the last envoy."

"What did they want?"

"That is not for me to know. You can ask him."

"He said nothing else?"

"No. Just to make sure you were all right and brought back."

Aldrain feigned an angry scowl. "I'd be better if I could look forward to fresh venison for my evening meal."

"That's not what's bothering you." Ordren's voice was distant, preoccupied, which explained why he had missed Aldrain's pretense of anger. Even so, Ordren was more accurate than he knew.

"No, and the trespassers we've caught lately can't be the only reason my father sent you out after so short a time." Aldrain swept his jaw-length, straggling hair into a leather tie, cinching it behind his head, then retrieved his bow.

"Again, my Prince, I cannot speak to that."

Aldrain studied the larger man as they picked their way back through the foliage. His body language was worrisome. Ordren seemed tense, as if preparing himself, gathered as a great cat readying to pounce. His eyes panned ahead, narrowed in concentration. Ordren was normally a man of few words, preferring to let his actions speak for him. What he'd related so far amounted to a detailed report, at least for Ordren. He might just as well have told Aldrain something was seriously wrong.

Ordren finally acknowledged Aldrain's scrutiny. "Your Highness?"

"You're still not going to tell me anything else, are you?"

"No, Your Highness."

"Can you at least tell me where the last mission was from?"

Ordren glanced sidelong at the prince, frowning. "They were northerners, tall and grim."

"Jamnites? Were they here about the treaty?"

"No. No Jamnite banners." The big man's face remained stoic.

"Drisians would have no business here, either." In contrast, Aldrain's displayed his increasing annoyance.

"Not Drisians."

"What about *Valir*? If there were more than a few summoners present, it would be significant."

"I did not notice."

"Then who?"

"I could not say."

"Perhaps they were from the northern islands? Though, few live there. Surely too few to send an envoy," Aldrain wondered aloud. Eyebrows raised, he glanced pointedly at Ordren. His companion merely shrugged. The prince shook his head in exasperation, fuming silently.

Aldrain and his escort found themselves nearing the city gates much sooner than normal, their pace quickened due to an impending sense of dread the prince could not readily understand. It built with each passing step, so much so that they were moving at nearly a trot when they passed through the gatehouse and over the bridge, all but ignoring the straight-backed guards who saluted as the pair passed by.

Crowds still milled about the marketplaces and along the narrow laneways, anxious to finish the day's business and head home, unaffected by the near-palpable air of urgency weighing on the prince and his escort. The two waded purposefully and without pause through a din of clamouring voices and a myriad of colors and scents, intent only on reaching their destination.

Aldrain and Ordren found their pace necessarily slowed, lest they begin shoving their way forward. The worst hindrances were the carriages and wagons, the latter burdened with a variety of goods and crafts that precluded any reasonable speed, the former carrying passengers less than eager to bid their coachmen to yield the way—until they realized just who they'd met. Then, they reacted with near-reckless abandon, scattering pedestrians as their horses tamped wildly, frenzied by lashes of the whip.

The spires of the palace disappeared behind the inner curtain wall as the two made what progress they could. They were almost to the gate of the city proper. Aldrain imagined his father's disappointed face. The king would shake his head ever so slightly, so that only Aldrain could perceive the movement. *When will you learn there is more to being prince than fencing, entertaining young ladies, and stalking the preserves?* In those and other words, Aldrain had heard the same message more often of late. He wanted to be king one day, there was no disputing that fact, but he was coming to the realization that it would be a much different lifestyle than the one he'd imagined growing up—and from the one he currently followed.

The angular towers of the inner gates rose before them, and the guards moved to block their way once it was clear the two were headed through.

"Identify yourselves and state your business in the city proper!" came the guards' challenge.

"An unusual welcome for late afternoon," Aldrain called back. "Since when is passage to the inner city barred so early?"

Recognition dawned on the guards' worried faces, and they hurriedly returned to their positions, staring straight ahead. In a much-subdued tone, the guard who had first offered the challenge replied, "Begging your pardon, Your Highness, but we're to question anyone entering the inner city. The orders arrived nearly an hour ago."

The prince's brow furrowed. It had been about the same time that his father had sent Ordren after him. Aldrain's anxious glance at his companion was met with a simple shrug. Aldrain acknowledged the guards' concern, setting their minds at ease for doing their duty. If only someone could alleviate his own worrisome thoughts as easily.

Aldrain and Ordren hurried along the wider, well-kept avenues of the city proper. Far fewer others were about at this hour and in this section of the city. The two passed manicured estates which lined both sides of the lane, as well as the occasional park or public building. Most were shrouded in silence.

The bulk of the palace, darkening as shadows stretched forth, loomed larger as the pair reached the outer wall and were waved on by the guards. These were the elite of the royal guard, and fully familiar with the prince's comings and goings. A faint breeze developed as they entered the barbican, whistling through the gateway from the direction of the palace. The massive citadel of House Draegondor rose a mere two hundred yards before them, across a long expanse of lush, green lawn.

Aldrain was rehearsing in his mind the discussion he'd have with his father, wondering how he could both accede to his father's wishes and save what he could of his freedom. He had just about decided that his cause was hopeless, when it occurred to him that the slight breeze had become a gusting wind. It pressed against Aldrain, impeding his progress, and he felt the stinging of sand grains carried in its flight. A low-pitched thrum resonated, rising steadily in tone and volume. It was like nothing he'd ever heard before. Aldrain turned to regard Ordren, and brightness flashed before him as a massive jolt from behind hammered him to the ground.

Lying flat on the unyielding flagstones, Aldrain struggled to raise his head and search about for Ordren. It took great effort, and still his head did not immediately respond. The ground spun. Aldrain closed his eyes, but that worsened the sensation of vertigo. Eventually, his throbbing head did his bidding, but bobbed weakly about as Aldrain pulled himself to a sitting position. He found his huge friend lying prone as he'd been, shaking the same cobwebs from his head and trying to push himself upright. Casting about, Aldrain confirmed his hunch. No one was about.

If no one nearby attacked them, then what had happened?

Glancing again at Ordren, Aldrain saw the other's eyes widen, and he followed the train of his companion's gaze. Back over his shoulder, Aldrain regarded the palace … or what should have been the palace. He jerked himself around and struggled to his feet, jaw agape. The familiar outline of the palace, his home, had disappeared. Several of the outermost spires remained, but as he watched, one of them tottered and ever so slowly collapsed. It tumbled from view, and a cloud of dust and flying debris rose in its place. Aldrain lurched forward, gradually gaining control of his limbs, though he nearly went down several times in his stricken haste.

If his body was in chaos, his mind reeled equally. Images flashed before his eyes without meaning, without purpose: His father. The deer. His mother. The arrow he'd let fly, speeding toward the tree. Other images rose, jumbled and in random, inexplicable order. Each flickered for an instant before it was replaced by the next. Behind them all, replaying in slow motion, was the scene of the tower's collapse. *How could that even be possible?*

He peered ahead again, praying for the last several minutes to be a figment of his imagination, a result of the day's heat and exertion coupled with his growing anxiety. For an instant, his prayer was answered. The spires and towers still stood, straight and tall and proud, and beneath them sprawled the palace complex. All was intact, the ancient, imposing stonework solid, the gray and white marble gleaming. Only for an instant, the vision lasted. It wavered and evaporated, replaced again by the shocking absence: His family, his home—gone.

A semispherical void now stretched nearly the entire expanse of the palace grounds, as if some giant, round tool had neatly scraped out its contents. Lying about the lowest point of the depression were the ruins of the collapsed tower, the tumbled stone and twisted timbers looking strangely out of place against the smooth-sided perfection of the greater chasm itself.

From somewhere far away, he heard a deep voice swearing an oath to the True One. It brought him back from his stupor.

"Ordren, gather the palace guard—anyone left—and have them assemble at the Plinth at once. Double the watch at the gate, let no one in or out. And keep people back from the...from this. Send for the *Valir*—tell Sonja I want to see her as soon as—" Aldrain stopped himself. What if she were dead, too? What if all of the summoners had perished? He would need them now, perhaps more than anyone else. This attack, or whatever it turned out to be, was some manifestation of magic. Who better than users of that magic to provide answers? "Tell any *Valir* you find that I need them gathered with the others."

"As you command, Your Majesty."

Ordren was gone several minutes before the impact of his words slammed into Aldrain. Harder than the shockwave, they hit: *Your Majesty.* Aldrain was king.

3

ORDREN DIRECTED THE MEN ADMIRABLY. In less than half an hour, the entire remnant of the palace guard—several score of seasoned and loyal men—were assembled and had blocked off the avenues leading directly to the palace. In only one place along the perimeter a large crowd had gathered, securely cordoned off from the royal manor grounds. Doubtless, Aldrain would hear of this from the nobles who'd shouldered in amongst the common folk pressing against the barricade, all eager to learn more about what had occurred.

Obviously, it would be impossible to hide the near-complete absence of the palace and grounds, but Aldrain wanted time for himself to investigate and to search for survivors. They'd found a few, mostly servants, and a small number of guardsmen, all wandering about the ruins, dazed and terrified. Other than those, every single person inside had vanished along with Citadel Draegondor: the king, the queen, and a good many advisors, noblemen, guards, and servants. All were simply gone, just like the palace.

Aldrain felt a surge of emotion and fought it down. This was neither the time nor place to grieve. He had to detach himself—make himself numb to everything but the task at hand. Bowing his head, he steadied himself once more.

"Majesty."

Aldrain turned to face Ordren, nodding acknowledgment.

"Majesty, I have some news that you'll want to hear."

Aldrain's brow rose; *perhaps some answers, at last.* "Go ahead, Ordren."

The other shook his head almost imperceptibly. "Not here, Majesty. Somewhere more private."

If greater secrecy was important to Ordren, that was reason enough for Aldrain. Though, glancing about, he was a fair distance from anyone, here in his position at the ledge of the bowl-shaped crater. The nearest were a couple of regulars down in the ruins, sifting through debris in hopes of finding anything, or anyone, else. Still, when Ordren advised caution, Aldrain knew not to argue.

"Lead the way, then."

They skirted the crater, making for the western edge of the grounds and one of the few standing towers. Ordren spoke in hushed tones as they went. "Count Pacek has been difficult. He may try to force his way to see you."

Aldrain hesitated. Pacek had been a thorn in his father's side for longer than he could remember. It seemed he had wasted no time in finding another target for his bothersome demands.

Ordren must have sensed his displeasure. "The gaol is an option. I can arrange it."

That brought a grin to Aldrain's ashen face. It soon faded, though. "No, Ordren. That would likely just complicate matters. I'll send for him right after you tell me what news you have."

"Not my news, Majesty. Two palace guards wish an audience. They wait inside."

The tower door hung open, and Aldrain could just make out two shadowy forms in the gloom. He blinked as he entered the antechamber, momentarily blind in the darkness. He heard shifting. Aldrain acknowledged, guessing at the cause of the rustling. Surely enough, as his vision returned, he saw the men's arms snap back from rigid salutes.

"Be at ease, men. You've had a hard day"—he exhaled wearily—"as have we all."

The man on the right, a rather tall and rangy fellow, answered first. "Your Highness, we grieve for your loss." The man hesitated, not sure if he should go on. Aldrain gave him a nod of encouragement. "Your father … he was a good man."

"Thank you, men." Aldrain ignored the mistaken form of address. He hadn't been officially proclaimed as king yet, anyway.

"Ah, I'm Rendan, Your Highness, and this is Agnar."

"Very good," Aldrain said, nodding. "And now, if you'd like to perform one last service for the late king, you'll tell me what news you have."

"Yes, Your Highness. Agnar and I were on the morning watch. We were just about to be relieved when the embassy came through. Jamnites, they looked to us, except they carried no banners. Jamnites would have made sense because of the armistice and all...." Rendan observed the crease in Aldrain's brow and cleared his throat nervously. "Anyway, they shooed off the herald and just went in unannounced.

A few minutes later, we heard your father shouting at them, and they were escorted out of the palace." Rendan shifted his feet nervously.

Aldrain's brow furrowed more deeply with the pause. "Is that all?"

"Well, Your Highness...there was something else. Agnar and I were heading home through the inner gate when we passed two of them going back toward the palace. They were holding something under a cloth. It was squarish, like a small box, or chest."

"Did you see if they did go back inside?"

This time it was Agnar who spoke. "Yes, Your Highness. I looked back, just as we were heading down the straightway. They went in. Not long after that, the noise... the thunder hit."

Aldrain nodded—this pair wasn't the first to mention a sound like thunder accompanying the blast wave. He searched Agnar's eyes as he spoke, "That's a pretty fair distance to be certain." Agnar shrugged.

"He's got the keenest eyes of the watch, Your Highness," Rendan interjected. "He can outspy a hawk! And he's a right menace with a bow, besides!" Agnar's shrug turned into an uncomfortable hitch, and he examined the stones beneath his feet.

"Well then, lads," Aldrain said, feeling a small measure of discomfort using Ordren's manner of address with the men. He was barely older than they were, but it elicited a simultaneous nod from the pair. "I don't doubt you saw what you claim. You have done a great service to my father. I will see to it that you get some extra leave time once this...business is cleared up. If that's all, you are dismissed."

The pair saluted and left, beaming with pride. Aldrain wished he felt as elated over their information. It was something, however slight. At least it seemed even more likely that the origin of the implosion—for even now, he could think of no more apt a way to describe it—rested with the enigmatic embassy. Finding out who they were or from where they came might shed yet more light on the mystery.

"Majesty, Count Pacek—"

"Just a moment, Ordren," Aldrain interrupted. He wanted to mull over this new information. "I'll deal with him shortly."

"Your Majesty, he's *here*—with his men."

Aldrain drew a slow breath to help muster all the resolve he could, to fight off a swell of anger and despair, combined. After the day's events, he was afraid he hadn't much left.

Jaren awoke with a start.

A sudden flurry of movement rose in the shadows, and a rustling followed. Morgaine had been practicing again. She'd thrust herself back under her covers at his stirring, pretending to be asleep. She breathed slowly and regularly, trying to emulate the sounds of slumber. It might have worked if he hadn't just seen and heard her an instant before.

"I know you're awake, Morgs."

"I told you not to call me that anymore." The response came after a pause and huff of impatience. "You should be sleeping, especially with all of the extra work you'll be doing for the next few days."

"Yeah, thanks for that," Jaren grumbled. "Our deal was work enough—now I've got even more on top of it."

"You shouldn't make bargains you can't live up to."

"I could live with ours just fine. But you had to go and tell Mom and Dad. I'll remember that, Morgs."

"Don't call me that," she hissed.

"Or what?"

"You'll see," she promised, "not too long from now, you'll see."

He almost ended the dispute right there and went back to sleep, but something caused him to go on. Probably the sting of disappointment over his earlier failure added to the weight of his impending extra chores. Either way, he wanted to take her down a notch. "I know what you were doing."

There was a pause. "Why don't you just tell me, then," she retorted in a haughty tone.

Jaren took a breath—his chance was gone, and there was nothing to be gained by remaining silent. "Playing with your rock."

"What rock? What do you mean?"

"The one you have hidden under the floorboard."

Morgaine was at his bedside before he could blink. The moonlight was dim, but Jaren didn't need to see well. He could feel the burning intensity of her stare. Her long hair tickled his face. "Jaren, what do you know about it?" Her hand closed over his shoulder, uncomfortably tight, but not to the point of being painful.

"I know what I've seen you doing. You can't hide everything from me, Gainey." The grip on his shoulder tightened and he winced. She didn't usually mind that name as much.

"So, you've been pretending to sleep for a while now. You're good at it."

"Better than you, I guess."

"How long?"

"Since the testers came last month."

She paused again, and the pressure on his shoulder subsided. "Well, it doesn't matter anyway. I'm getting pretty good with the *talisman*— it's not a *rock*." In the dim light, he could not be certain, but Jaren would wager a gold mark she'd rolled her eyes, her usual manner with him. "They'll probably take me with them next time, you know. That'll leave you with both our chores from now on." Getting no response, she continued. "Have you ever touched it?" Her tone implied that it would not have been a good thing.

He hoped she didn't feel his recoil at the question. But, with her solid grip, there was little chance she hadn't. "No."

"Are you sure?"

"No, I haven't."

"Do you swear under the eyes of the True One you've never touched it?"

"I'm not telling you again. Let go of me. I want to go to sleep."

"Yes, you have," she ignored him. "But you haven't been able to do anything with it, or you would never have told me you knew anything."

"I told you—leave me alone!"

She snickered quietly. "It doesn't matter, really. You can't use another person's talisman without their permission. There is a bond that protects the stone from unwanted meddlers. That's your first lesson. Soon, I will be able to tell if someone else tried to use it. You're lucky I don't tell the *Valir* you've done just that. They probably wouldn't let you test—at least, not for a long time."

Jaren turned forcefully away, wrenching his shoulder from her grasp. Still, he said nothing.

"Well, pleasant dreams, brother. After your first turn of chores, you're coming with me to the village. We need to get some things for Mom and Dad. So come and find me at breakfast. I should be up by then."

Morgaine must have taken his silence as proof that he was completely defeated, Jaren thought; she had guessed his little game and believed him back in line. Tiptoeing quietly back to her bed, she casually returned the talisman to its place, apparently no longer fearing any designs her brother may have had on it, since she'd told Jaren it was as useless to him as a piece of river rock.

Across the room, Jaren was too worked up to sleep. He was smiling, elated that his hopes were still alive. *Iselle was right!* Not that he would ever tell her, if he could help it. She'd be insufferable for days. Still, there was an eternity between now and the time he might be able to test properly. And that was only if Morgaine didn't report his mischief. Somehow, though, he knew she wouldn't. Morgaine was controlling and bossy, but she wasn't normally cruel. It was still more than an hour before his mind stopped swirling and he at last found sleep.

Bleary eyed, Jaren followed Morgaine the next morning as she made her way down the narrow track to town. He stifled a yawn just in case she turned around. He didn't want her to see how tired he was. She already knew he was in a foul mood, and that was enough. One of the chickens had escaped the coop, and he'd spent a good while trying to catch it. Then, he had tripped on a root and dumped all of the sow's water. Add the list of extra duties his mother had given him for later and it was the worst morning Jaren could remember for some time. He was not about to give Morgaine any additional satisfaction.

Weather-wise, though, it promised to be a beautiful day. A few feathered clouds floated high above, and there was enough of a breeze to keep it from being too uncomfortably hot. At least until later, that was, when Jaren would be doing the rest of his work.

There were few others on the path yet, but before long, it would get busy—as busy as the outskirts of Dal Farrow could get, except, of course, for the high summer and midwinter celebrations. But the latter was half a year away, and the former was almost a month past. That was when the testers had come. It was the best opportunity the *Valir* had to find as many candidates at one time as they could.

The wagon and tent up ahead were therefore a completely unexpected sight. Jaren crashed into Morgaine, as she had stopped dead in her tracks. Clearly, his sister had not expected to see the testers again so soon, either. But what had drawn the *Valir* back?

4

MORGAINE WAS OFF AGAIN AT a hurried pace, heading directly for the tent. The guards posted at the entrance to the makeshift compound paid them little attention. Two youths were nothing to be concerned about, particularly as this was the usual sort of traffic to come in and out. One guard stifled a yawn. *A lot of that going around today,* Jaren thought bitterly as he passed by the man.

Morgaine advanced to a small table set before the great tent to receive would-be candidates. They must not have been expecting anyone so early, as the stool behind it sat empty. It was not altogether imprudent: virtually all of the candidates from the earlier testing had been common folk—many of them farmers—who would have work to do before heading into the village.

After several minutes, a slender man with a long, handlebar moustache emerged from the tent. The dark liquid in the cup at his mouth steamed as he sipped at it delicately. When he noticed them, he placed the cup back onto the saucer that his other hand held slightly beneath his chin, and then he moved over to the table. He had a rather pained expression, as though thoroughly disappointed to have his morning routine interrupted. His shrill voice, however, showed no hint of annoyance.

"Well then, my dear," the clerk said to Morgaine, "can I set you up for testing on this lovely morning?"

"I have already been. And I have been practicing."

The man's eyes opened a bit wider. "Oh, well then. What did you say your name was?"

"Morgaine. Morgaine Haldannon."

"And you've been practicing for a while, then? Recently?"

"Yes, every day since your last visit, sir. I mean, since the *Valirs'* last visit."

"Ah, well, I wasn't with them the last trip here. But, you've been working on your skills for about a month, then, have you?"

"Yes, sir, about that."

The man pulled a thin, leather-backed pad from beneath his dark robes. He pulled a quill from a narrow container that sat on the table and scribbled something quickly on his pad. His lips moved silently as he wrote. Jaren could readily read his sister's name on the man's lips at one point. He also found he wasn't so tired now.

The man rose, glancing briefly at Morgaine. "If you'll excuse me for a moment, then, my dear," he said to her. He disappeared back into the tent, with one last, longing glance at the still-brimming cup.

The two of them were left alone for some time. Time enough for a few others to join their line, the Emmundal twins and Joselle Banath. She looked as if she'd not only come to town expecting to find the testers but also to be the first in line. The ice in her glare nearly stole Sholara's heat. Jaren looked away with a shiver. He'd heard that Joselle received a talisman, too.

The next person to emerge from the tent wasn't the clerk, although the clerk followed her. It was a tall woman in a regal blue gown. She was pale-skinned, with jet-black hair. She emanated an aura of power, and a sense of unease stole over Jaren. She studied Morgaine for an instant, ice-blue eyes looking her up and down from above a hawkish nose, and then motioned his sister forward.

Jaren followed. He'd face the Deceiver himself before he'd let Morgaine out of his sight now, if he could help it. As Jaren moved toward the entrance, one of the woman's eyebrows shot up. His knees nearly buckled, but she made no move to stop him. Jaren was very glad of that. A final glance back revealed that the Emmundal twins' jaws were nearly scraping the ground in shock, and a look of utter contempt twisted Joselle's face. That sent another shiver up Jaren's spine.

"My quarters are on the right," the woman announced from behind them. It gave Jaren yet another start. "The first opening."

The siblings filed through and stood, waiting. A rather large desk took up most of the space in the room, and it bore an ink container and quill, much more elaborate than on the table outside, as well as several neatly arranged rolls of parchment. The desk rested on a large rug made of thick animal fur. For a mobile room, it was expensively, if still sparsely, furnished.

The woman entered behind them, and seated herself at the desk. "I'd offer you a chair," she said, with little sympathy in her voice, "but these field tents leave hardly enough room for the bare essentials." She nodded down at her desk. She eased herself back into the chair, placing her hands on the chair's carved, wooden arms. Cocking her head slightly to the side, she continued, "My name is Andraste. I am one of the summoners assigned to this area. And you are Morgaine Haldannon." She pointedly ignored Jaren, and her smile held little warmth. "Let me get straight to the point, Morgaine. Someone in or near this village has a great deal of potential. We were on our way back to Ansalar when it was brought to our attention." Andraste waited, appearing to measure the response from the girl before her. She remained oblivious to Jaren.

Jaren's lips barely hid a scowl. He wasn't sure he wanted to hear this.

"For the last month or so, we were informed, someone has been experimenting with *Val'tial*." Andraste tilted her head upward, condescendingly. At the same time, her left hand strayed to the circular talisman hanging on a chain at her bosom, fingers tracing absently across the centre-set, amber jewel, then over the runes and the seven-pointed star embossed upon it. She continued, "That's magic, dear girl. In any event, these instances have become gradually more marked—enough to warrant our return." Andraste spoke the final words as if they left a foul taste. "There was no announcement because we arrived at the same time as any message of forewarning would have. So as usual, we have trusted that any who had the inclination or ability would seek us out. And, if any do not, we have all the names recorded. In essence, it is important that we find this particular individual. We will remain until that happens." This, too, appeared unpalatable.

There it was. As Andraste talked, a knot grew in Jaren's stomach. It would turn out to be that they were seeking Morgaine. He knew it. It felt as if the room had become much smaller—and warmer, too.

Morgaine was virtually floating home. Jaren felt as if he were trudging through waist-deep water. His sister was to be tested again tomorrow by a panel of three *Valir*. She and the other four who'd been given talismans would be tested, Andraste had informed them. Actually, she'd informed Morgaine. Jaren might as well have been a snail underfoot, for all the attention he'd garnered. He was too caught up in his misery to notice the others standing in their way before they were face to face with them. Morgaine had obviously been too preoccupied with her own thoughts to see them coming, either.

It was Joselle and several others from her usual group. Her expression had changed little since Jaren last saw her. Joselle angled her head back and glared at Morgaine intensely, fists upon her hips.

"You don't actually imagine you're the one they're after, do you, Morgaine?" Joselle's friends fanned out, one on her right and two on her left. They crossed their arms and tried to look as intimidating as their ringleader.

"I suppose I have as much chance as any of the others."

Joselle's green eyes flashed. "You might as well stay home tomorrow and feed the chickens, girl. You aren't the one they want."

"I think the testers will be the ones to decide that."

The other huffed. "Besides, who'll be left to help your family with the farm work? Face it, Morgaine, you belong with the dirt. Summoning is too high a calling for you."

Morgaine moved to walk past her, but Joselle would not be put off. She stepped directly in the way.

"Tell me you won't go to the trial tomorrow, and I'll let you pass."

"I don't have any choice. They'll send for me if I don't go. But I still wouldn't miss it. Now please move."

Morgaine started forward once more, but Joselle matched her movements, chin thrust forward, her eyes daring Morgaine to try again. The others gathered in closer.

"Joselle, get out of my way."

"Or what? What could you possibly do to me?"

Jaren hadn't noticed earlier, but Morgaine's hand had steadily crept toward her pocket while they spoke. Now it disappeared inside. He wanted to yell at her to stop, because he was almost sure he knew what would be in it. Even though Morgaine had expressed no fear of her brother's attempt to tamper with the talisman, she'd decided to keep it with her today. What if she was thinking of using the talisman against Joselle? It was strictly forbidden; only trained and sanctioned *Valir* were permitted to interfere with others in any way using magic. Jaren had heard stories of people imprisoned for breaking that rule.

A faint whirring noise came from behind and to the side of the ambushers. Then there was a sharp *crack!*, and the girl on Joselle's right put her hand to her head, spinning about and searching the brush behind them for the source of the surprise attack. As the girl rubbed her scalp, a second missile smacked into her shoulder. Sobbing, she let out a squawk and mumbled something incoherent to Joselle, then fled back down the road.

Joselle turned, her immediate victim momentarily forgotten. She ordered the remaining two girls to find the stone-caster, but they just looked at each other doubtfully. A third rock convinced them. It hit the girl nearest to Joselle on the upper leg, making a meaty *thump* as it impacted. It was too much for either of them. They followed their fleeing companion.

Joselle was not bothered in the least. In fact, her face sprouted a smile. She raised her right fist and thrust it forward. A surprised shriek sounded from a dozen yards away, as Iselle's flailing body suddenly burst from the concealment of the shrubbery. Iselle was flung backward several feet through the air, crashing with a crackle of foliage and a muffled grunt back into the brush.

Jaren was torn. He wanted to check on Iselle, to see if she was all right, but Joselle had turned back to face the two of them.

"You see, you don't want to upset me. But, maybe you're right about the trial." Joselle nodded, a dark light in her eyes, and she smiled. "Yes, you'll have to go. But I think there's another way to settle this. You'll just have to fail. I don't know how good you've become with the magic, but I'm sure you are nowhere near my level."

"If you're so powerful, then so what if I try my best? Then I can't possibly be chosen over you."

"Yes, but I still don't think you know your place. You deserve a pot to slop the pigs, not a talisman. So, let's hear your word that you'll fail."

"No. Do what you want. I won't."

"Morgaine, I warn you." Joselle trained her eyes on Jaren, and there was no mistaking the cold look of calculation. "You may be brave with yourself, but what about your dear brother? Surely, you wouldn't want me to harm him?"

"Joselle, if you so much as—"

"What?" she shouted, then lowered her voice again. "We've already been through this, Morgaine. You can't do anything to me. Now, *make the promise!*"

Morgaine's response was immediate. Her own hand came up and thrust forward. Joselle staggered back as if struck by a blow, but she merely offered a black grin.

"You know, I hoped you would try that. I don't think you'll make it to the testing after all."

Morgaine's eyes went wide, and she inhaled sharply. Jaren stood still, gripped with fear. Slowly, his sister sank to her knees. Her chest stopped working, while her lips moved soundlessly. *I have to do something!* Joselle's attention was entirely focused on Morgaine, so Jaren took his chance. He could think of nothing other than to rush at Joselle and to try to knock the talisman from her grasp. He put his head down and ran full force toward her.

Just as he was about to reach Joselle, he hit something else. It felt solid as a tree. Dazed, Jaren collapsed to the ground while the sky spun above him. He could feel invisible coils begin to wrap themselves about his neck and chest, crushing him, making it impossible to draw breath.

His head was cranked to the side, and he could see Morgaine dimly, struggling to raise her arm toward Joselle. Tiny points of light exploded in his vision as he began to lose consciousness. *No,* Jaren screamed soundlessly. *I have to stop her! I have to....*

5

"I WASN'T ABOUT TO WAIT until you decided to make the time for those of us who need answers."

Count Pacek's round face was quite red, though Aldrain couldn't recall a time when it had not been, nor one when he wasn't ranting, as he was now. He'd seen his father handle this noble on enough occasions, though. *Just let him run his course;* the count would say what he wanted and then leave in a bluster. Except, seeing that he'd forced his way through the barricades with his band of soldiers, Aldrain doubted very much that the count would just go on his way without gaining something.

"An account of what's happened is well past due!" Pacek thundered.

"I do not doubt you've had a trying day, my lord, but you are *not* the only one affected. I'm doing what's necessary to keep order until answers are found."

"Order? Perhaps you haven't taken a look around, *Your Highness,* but there is definitely nothing orderly about any of this!" He swept his pudgy arm toward the palace grounds in emphasis. "It's clear that magic was involved. I demand to know what's happened!"

Ordren had inched closer, but Aldrain stopped him short with a hard glance. "I can assure you, Count, that everything is being done to investigate the matter. Perhaps you could spare some of your men for the effort?"

The other harrumphed. "Not until I know who's behind this. They could be after me now, or anyone else of importance. Besides, it seems I need an escort to have access to the grounds."

"Until we've gathered information from every possible source, any additional people simply complicate matters further. That is the sole reason for the delay. I will report to the chamber the full details of what has transpired, as best I can. As chair, you will have your account soon enough."

Pacek scowled. "You will hold an emergency chamber meeting? Today?"

"In the *Valir* guildhall, tomorrow, because I want to be sure that as many nobles as can be managed are present. Messages have already been dispatched."

"I see you're carrying on where your father left off. It would be more appropriate to meet in the council chambers. It is tradition."

"That is my business. The guildhall is one of the few remaining buildings in the inner city that is secure enough, in light of what's happened."

"No business conducted with or near them is *secure*, Your Highness. Your father's fate is proof of that."

Aldrain took an involuntary step forward, "You go too far, Rondul. Do not continue to test me." His voice was low, but laced with iron. The count's eyes had gone wide, but he held his tongue. Aldrain continued, "If you do not remove your men from the area at once, I will have all of you arrested for impeding the investigation. Ordren, please ensure that the count is safely escorted back behind the barricade."

Pacek's expression soured as if he were about to refuse, but after studying Aldrain's face one final time, thought better of it. "Very well," Pacek replied, "but I hope you have learned something about politics from your father. Tomorrow may be a very important meeting for Your Highness. It is difficult to predict where loyalties may rest after so grievous a blow to the state. There may be some call for a … changing of the guard." With that, he wheeled about and strode back through the lines of his men. They fell into step behind him, slowly drawing away toward the barrier.

The man's departure was little relief after all. Aldrain turned to Ordren. "Are any of the greycloaks about?"

"There are a few at hand, Majesty. You would like him followed?"

"I would like much more than that, but I'll have to settle for finding out who he's talking to, and what they're scheming. I don't want to be blindsided at the meeting."

"Very well, Majesty."

"And Ordren, could you please have Sonja report to me? I'd like to hear what information the *Valir* gathered."

"I'll send word to her, Majesty."

Sonja Redsteel was chief among the summoners attached to Aldrain's family. She, in particular, had enjoyed a long history of service to house Draegondor, one that Aldrain was not about to forego now.

Still, it was disappointing that none among his *Valir*, particularly Sonja, had detected anything. Even the slightest of warnings might have saved his parents, and a good many others, on this terrible day.

It was a matter of minutes before Sonja arrived. She picked her way casually through the treacherous footing of the crater, where Aldrain oversaw the search for clues. Her dazzling green eyes and exquisite features were clear even from a distance, enough to turn most men into bumbling fools who would say or do anything to please her. Long, red hair spilled over her shoulders and onto a forest-green dress that did little to hide her pleasing form. Thankfully, Aldrain saw her more as a member of the family, much like an aunt, though she clearly did not look her age—she had been in service before his birth, and the Draegondor heir had grown up with her about. In fact, Aldrain had been turned over her knee on more than one occasion. Thankfully, the last of those instances was some years past. Yet, there were times lately when her timeless beauty distracted even him.

"You requested a report from me, Your Majesty?" she asked in her melodic voice.

Aldrain shook the fog from his head. "Yes. Have you uncovered anything?"

Sonja made a curious, waving gesture with her hand before responding. Aldrain had seen it a few times before, usually when in exclusive audience with his father. She did it to cast a barrier about them, to shield their conversation from prying ears and other, more unnatural means of eavesdropping. "It was a tremendous release of magical energy, obviously, but it was different, somehow. As I have taught you, magical energy—*Val'tial*—surrounds us, permeating living and non-living things alike. Through *metanduil*, we weild *Shar'val*, the positive element, in conjunction with *Shun'val*, the negative."

Aldrain was impatient for an answer, not a review of magical lore. "Yes, I know that. Just tell me what makes this any different!"

She smiled in genuine sympathy. "I was getting to that, Aldrain. The difference is, I can see signs that only negative energy, *Shun'val*, was released here, and in quantities that are truly beyond comprehension."

"You're telling me that someone is able to divide the magic and command its negative essence?"

"And to an extent that has been unknown for many centuries, Aldrain. What happened here is an omen of great dread for all nations."

"But, isn't that impossible? You've told me it can't be done."

"It can't. At least, there has been no one capable of the feat in a thousand years. Aldrain, someone is *An'Valir*—or has attained some of the same abilities."

Aldrain felt cold. *An'Valir*. An individual able to summon without the channeling capacity of *metanduil*. It was a term forgotten by most and dismissed to the realm of mythology by the remainder. Only because of his royal blood had he been educated enough to know anything of the word and its place in history. The last account described a terrible and bloody event. Thousands upon thousands had died in that age, and the *An'Valir* were eventually defeated only through the concerted efforts of a handful of the most powerful *Valir* of the day. And they had given their lives to do it.

Aldrain thought back to the information his soldiers had provided. "Would *An'Valir* need anything else to cause this destruction?"

"What do you mean?"

"A couple of the men told me two people from the latest embassy entered the palace grounds carrying something that could have been a small container of some kind."

Sonja furrowed her brow. "I don't know. As far as I've been taught, *An'Valir* need nothing to command *Val'tial*. And, judging by the damage done here, whoever has this ability wields considerable power. I cannot imagine one such as that needing any sort of tool or device." She shrugged. "But that's just my understanding of it, limited as it is. I don't know exactly what we're dealing with. All I know is that *An'Valir* comes closest to explaining it."

"You must know someone who has more extensive knowledge of this."

"Yes, I'm aware of several brothers and sisters who are more familiar with the histories—mostly advisors to other royal houses, so we must take care in contacting them. I'll try to find something more, though I will have to go into some detail about what happened here." She studied Aldrain's features to see if her meaning registered. "Rival kingdoms will know you are ... weakened."

Aldrain shook his head, "That can't be helped. The news will travel fast enough, regardless. Besides, I have a hunch that we'll not be the only nation to face this threat, and I'd rather word be spread directly to those who can help us sooner than later." Already, the agents of many factions would be running near full-out to relay news of this shocking event, he knew. But the summoners could communicate far faster than they.

"If this is indeed the work of a hostile *An'Valir*," Sonja replied in a distant voice, with a glance at the chasm, "I'm not sure any amount of help will be enough—no matter when it comes."

6

JAREN WAS AWARE OF THE twittering of birds. Unfocused light filtered through his half-closed eyelids, outlining a dark form that loomed over him. Someone's face materialized from amidst the larger blur—a girl's. He started with fright, certain it was Joselle, about to finish him off. He scrambled backward, crablike, scuttling gravel and small rocks from beneath his hands and feet. But the image cleared and became Iselle. She had twigs in her hair, and her face was streaked with dirt.

"It's all right, she's gone."

His ribs were stiff, but he could breathe once again. "What happened? Where's Morgaine?" Jaren croaked. His throat hurt, as well.

"She's over there, catching her breath, too. I don't know what happened. When I crawled out of the bushes, you two were lying on the road. Joselle's gone."

Jaren pulled himself to his feet and walked shakily to his sister. She was seated at the foot of an old, gnarled oak, her head in her hands. Her face was nearly obscured by a cascade of long, dark hair. "Are you okay, Gainey?" He crouched down beside her.

She sniffed, shifting her eyes to the ground and straightening her skirts. "Yes, I'm fine, except for my headache—and my ribs."

"Yeah, I don't feel so good, either. Did you …" he couldn't find the words.

"I don't know. Yes—I think so. Everything's hazy, though." Morgaine stared down at the ground before her. The talisman sat there, much like any of the other rocks strewn about. "I remember trying to reach her with the magic, then … then it all just went black. I must have finally done something, but I don't know what."

He knew her well enough to realize she was afraid—afraid of what had just happened, of what she might have done to Joselle.

"She was okay enough to leave, Gainey" Iselle said. "I saw her run off. I'm sure you didn't hurt her that badly."

"Well, I can't imagine she'd have just left if I hadn't." Morgaine said. "But that's not it. I really wanted to. I *wanted* her to—" She shook her head and tried to suppress another sniffle.

"Morgaine, it's okay," Iselle continued. "Look what she was doing to you. I'm sure you only did what you had to do, whatever that might have been. Jaren and I saw everything. It will be all right."

Jaren added, "They can't blame you—she tried to hurt us. It was the only way to stop her. They have to understand that."

Morgaine lifted her head. Her eyes were moist, and there was a glistening trail down each cheek. She smiled faintly, nodding her head. "We should get back. We've been gone too long already." She brushed off her clothes once more and cleared the frazzled strands of auburn hair from her face. Picking up the talisman seemed an enormous effort for her. Getting to her feet, she quickly put it back into her pocket, as if it was now the last thing in the world she wanted to touch.

She started off, with Jaren and Iselle falling in farther behind.

"You've developed a habit of yelling, lately," Iselle teased Jaren.

"What do you mean?"

"Don't you remember?"

"No, not really."

"Well," she told him with a smirk, "I don't know what you said, if anything, but it was loud enough, anyway. Maybe *you* scared Joselle off!" She giggled at that, and dodged the elbow Jaren sent her way in response.

Jaren knew something was wrong as soon as they entered the yard. Their parents were home. They were speaking with the reeve, Jebdal Asahm. Even from a distance, he could tell it was an animated conversation.

Iselle let out a groan. "I hope he's not looking for me."

Jaren looked sideways at her. "Why would he be here for you?"

"Never mind, Jaren. If I told you, you couldn't deny knowing about it. And you're such a terrible liar."

"Anyone who walks in the Truth should be," he shot back, feigning a superior tone. The response was an exaggerated roll of her eyes.

Morgaine hushed them both. "He's not here for you, Iselle. Father looks ready to strangle him."

Soon, they'd crossed the yard and were just about to the porch. Jaren's father looked over, now noticing the three of them, his flushed face slashed by a scowl. His mother and the reeve followed suit, similar expressions coloring their features.

"Iselle, you'd best be getting home now. Morgaine, Jaren, you go on inside and wait for us," his father directed.

"What's the matter?" Morgaine asked.

"The reeve says you were involved in some trouble this morning, with Joselle Banath. That's all you need to know for now."

Jaren saw Iselle breathe a sigh of relief. She turned to go, giving a sheepish wave to the siblings.

"I'll be coming by your place tomorrow, Iselle," Jebdal advised her. "So don't go making any plans for the day. Someone's been into Master Althow's stables again." Iselle's shoulders sank with the announcement. Perhaps she hadn't gotten away with whatever mischief she'd caused, after all.

Morgaine turned to the reeve. "What did Joselle tell you?"

"Well, that's not really for me to say right now, young lady, not before I've had a chance to ask you and your brother some questions first."

"And that will wait until we've asked them a few of our own, Jeb," their father said.

"Jens, you know the kind of trouble I'll face for holding off."

Jens Haldannon gave his son and daughter a look that meant they were to follow his wishes, and without further delay. The pair obliged, though Morgaine dragged her feet the entire way. Once they were inside and the door had swung shut behind them, Jens focused back on the reeve. "You know as well as I, my daughter did no such thing as what you're suggesting."

"Easy now, Jens. I didn't make the allegation, but I have to investigate it. And it's a right serious matter; I don't have to remind you."

"Mr. Asahm, we are well aware of the implications," Jaren's mother added, "but we still want to discuss things with our children before anyone else has a say in it. You told us yourself that Derone Banath was screaming for justice. *His* kind of justice, we are well acquainted with, and we're not just going to hand our daughter and son over without knowing all of the facts ourselves. The only way we can be assured of that is to do it now."

Pointedly, Jens Haldannon echoed his wife. "We'll have them on their way tonight."

"Well, I guess it won't do any harm to give you 'till this evening. But if they're much later than sundown, I doubt I'll be able to keep Derone from coming here himself."

"Don't worry, Jeb. Morgaine and Jaren will be on their way before then."

The reeve paused before leaving, and issued a heavy, resigned sigh. "I'm just doing my job. Even though it's for Magistrate Banath, it doesn't mean I really want any part of this." He appeared to reconsider his words, then added, "Especially because it's for him."

"We know, Jeb. You do what you have to."

The reeve nodded and left. Jens and Marta Haldannon exchanged worried glances and headed inside.

Neither Haldannon sibling was sitting when Jens and Marta entered. They were standing near the kitchen table, conversing in hushed, but urgent, tones. All discussion ceased as soon as the door opened.

Morgaine faced her parents. "Father, Mother, you know—"

"Quiet down and listen to us, now. We didn't raise you two to be capable of what I think the Banath girl is getting at. The reeve didn't come right out and say it, but I'm pretty sure I can figure out the gist of what he was on about." He studied his son and daughter. "You two have been through an awful lot today, I can tell. Come here."

Morgaine and Jaren rushed to their parents. Morgaine's eyes welled with tears and Jaren's throat tightened with emotion. It felt so good to have strong, loving arms about them after the day's terrifying ordeal. Soon enough, Jens nodded to Marta, and they moved the two back a pace.

"Now, here's what you're going to do. First thing, your mother's going to get some food and water together while you two make up some bedrolls. I'll get some rope and a few other things that you might need on the way."

"On the way to where? Aren't we going to town to see the reeve?" Morgaine asked.

This time Marta answered. "No, dear. That wouldn't do. Derone Banath has half of the town either working for him or working to avoid trouble from him. Either way, neither of you stands a chance of a fair hearing. Besides, something like this happened some time ago down in Cerith Fell, and it's said the girl was sent to Ansalar before the day was over. The *Valir* whisked her away without so much as a word to her family. I don't know whether she ever came back." Marta steeled her expression and gazed at Morgaine and Jaren in turn. "That's not going to happen to either of my children."

"But, don't you want to know what happened?"

Jens replied, "If it's important for you to tell us—but we don't have much time. I think I speak for both your mother and myself when I say that what the reeve told us so far is nonsense. I admit, I've thought you spend a little too much time with that bit of rock since you got it, but what Jeb suggested doesn't come close to what I know my daughter and son are made of." He looked squarely into each of their faces and then went on. "Whatever you did, I know it was because you had no other choice. And, I know it wasn't anything you started. Is that about right?"

"Yes, father," Jaren responded, nodding. His sister stared down at the floor after a barely perceptible nod of her own. "But Morgaine still feels pretty bad."

"I expect she does, son. People sometimes do when they're forced to stand up for themselves."

"But what will happen to you when they find out you sent us away?"

"You let us worry about that, Morgaine," Jens replied, though his worried eyes contradicted the sure set to his voice.

7

ANDRASTE DIDN'T NEED TO TEST the girls to know which of them held true promise. She'd been *Valir* for many years now, many more than her apparent age bore witness to. During that time, she'd acquired a sensitivity to others who had talent for summoning, whether developed or latent.

Actually, two from the village were possessed of a good measure of potential.

Just as she'd shown many years ago: her own rise through the ranks in the Ergothani guildhouse had been rather meteoric, though not dependent only on her own merits, bountiful as they were, even as a novice. Early in her career she'd made the decision that saw a then-young apprentice hurtle past her contemporaries in both power and position. Yes, barely months into her apprenticeship the Master had taken an interest in her.

She'd then made a promise, a vow that she would heed the Master's call. Those summonses had come sparingly, yet not so rarely that she was ignorant of her part in the way of things.

Several weeks earlier, the latest directive had reached Andraste. She knew it was one to obey immediately, and without question, even for one so connected and esteemed as she.

Too late, these poor souls had discovered her secret, and of little use the knowledge was. Andraste stepped over the still bodies casually. She feared no one here. Neither of the two had been a match for her, even together, and they were the most powerful in the group—besides herself, of course. All four of them together would have stood a chance and could probably have bested her. But that was out of the question, now.

Hadn't their eyes nearly popped out as she killed them with a thought? They'd had scant seconds to react. *What went through your mind, Namane, you who always considered yourself my equal? I would assume the ultimate truth was a bitter one to accept, though you didn't have to suffer the knowledge overlong. And you, Kargan, with your pathetic attempts to woo me. Were you finally satisfied to realize that I would claim you, though not as a lover? You found out after all what it was like to truly know me.* Andraste might have laughed if they didn't look so pitiful, frozen in death, as they had writhed together on the floor, faces contorted in agony.

You'll account for yourselves before the True One tonight. As for me, I answer to another.

Some time later, more quietly than death, Andraste made her way past the final two victims and slipped from the tents toward the horse pens. Let the clerks wonder what had happened during the night. She'd destroyed the necessary records and eliminated the other *Valir*. Simple clerks did not warrant the effort. Not when there was still the Master's bidding to be done.

Andraste reached the gate and quietly lifted the wooden bar free, swinging it inward with a faint creak of resistance. Her slim form slid between the larger, dark bulks of the tethered horses, and she soon found a suitable mount. It and two others she untied, leading them noiselessly back to the gate. They made no fuss at being disturbed, as her summoning calmed them immediately.

It was a short ride to her first stop, a stately mansion for these parts, though little more than a mid-ranking official's home by Ansalar's standards. It was wider than it was deep, the second level surrounded by a narrow balcony, supported by thick, sturdy columns. She left the horses in a stand of birch not far from the main entrance to the estate grounds and started toward the building, silently swinging the gate open. A large dog raised its grizzled head as Andraste stalked by, but it let out a whimper and scurried off at once. She reached the base of the large house and peered up at the darkened panes until discerning the correct one.

She rose off the ground, floating up to the second level balcony, then stepped onto the railing and slipped effortlessly down onto the veranda, striding forward in the direction her divining indicated. Finding the door she sought, Andraste turned the brass handle and stepped inside.

The spacious bedroom was well furnished for a country estate. Bureaus lined the walls, and a canopied bed sat against the farthest. Upon it, she could just make out a still form, and she heard the steady breathing of someone fast asleep. *Spoiled child,* Andraste scoffed to herself, *you will learn soon enough.*

She moved to the bed. The sleeping form was one she'd seen earlier in the day: Joselle, or Josette, not that it really mattered. Placing a hand on the sleeping girl's brow, she closed her eyes for an instant and concentrated. There was a low moan, and the form shifted slightly. Removing her hand, Andraste looked down at the girl once again. Joselle opened her eyes, and she sat up stiffly, her disheveled, red hair falling about her shoulders. Her unfocused emerald eyes gazed ahead at nothing.

"Now, my dear, you will dress and meet me on the balcony. Wear something to travel in. Quickly, now." Immediately, the girl obeyed, walking to a dresser and pulling open several drawers.

Andraste waited for her outside, completely assured of the girl's obedience. She would have stopped breathing, if commanded. Such was the power of the summoned suggestion. Another benefit of her arrangement; it was a rare enchantment, known only by the most skilful and talented. Andraste had received the knowledge early, and it had served her well.

A shuffling from behind told her Joselle was ready. She turned to see the girl standing just outside the door in a hooded riding cloak, tunic, pants, and high boots, her glazed eyes still distant.

Soon, the two of them were riding back through the night toward Dal Farrow. After a short while, they approached a modest farmstead.

"Take these," Andraste told the girl, handing her the reins. "Move off of the road and wait for me there."

Joselle did as she'd been ordered, while the woman strode toward the farmhouse. Andraste stopped just short of the porch. She had followed the route she'd divined to the second girl's home, but something was wrong. She let out a frustrated breath, the coolness of the early morning turning it into a trace of steam. The only responses were the songs of night birds and insects.

She didn't need to go inside to know. The other girl was already gone.

Mother Haddie's—it was one place Jaren would never have guessed his father might send them. She was a rough, stoop-backed old woman who lived by herself in the low, rolling hills, several days' ride to the west of town. She didn't come to Dal Farrow often, perhaps twice a year, or on special occasions when a local inhabitant requested her services. As such, their father had reasoned Mother Haddie's was far enough away that word wouldn't reach Dal Farrow regarding their whereabouts, yet close enough that he could come for them without leaving Marta to shoulder the farmwork for too long a time, once things had settled down.

Perhaps the most compelling reason, though, was that just about everyone in Dal Farrow knew how Jens Haldannon felt about the old crone. It wasn't that he had anything against Mother Haddie. Indeed, she'd cured enough of their livestock over the years, and even he himself, when he'd broken his ankle on a hidden root in the fields. He just didn't understand her strange behavior or unorthodox ways, and to Jaren's father, that was a good enough reason to have as little to do with her as could be managed. He didn't mind telling people that, either.

That stance hadn't bothered Jaren one bit. Mother Haddie made him feel uneasy. As far as he knew, she was a healer of some sort. They were a different lot than summoners, the healers were, and probably from everyone else, too. They used a different sort of magic. From what he'd observed, it seemed mostly earthy stuff: herbs, poultices, salves, and numerous other concoctions he knew no words to describe. They all smelled the same to him: bad. Having some of Mother Haddie's cures applied in their house was creepy enough, but now they were going to stay with her. It wasn't something he was looking forward to.

The rain began late the second night after they'd left, starting as a light drizzle and then strengthening into a downpour for several hours, with all of the accompanying lightning and thunder of a typical summer storm. It had slackened somewhat, but it was still coming down hard enough to turn their trek into a miserable affair. Jaren was thankful his father had put an oiled overcoat in each of their swollen packs, along with their other provisions, most of which he'd not yet had a chance to examine. Had the overcoats not provided some measure of protection from the weather, Jaren would have been in an entirely dismal frame of mind, rather than simply apprehensive and a bit on the jumpy side.

After all, it was the first time they'd gone on such a long excursion by themselves. On a few rare occasions, their father had allowed them to take a day hike into the hills to get away from the farm and enjoy themselves. Once, they'd even been allowed to camp out overnight. The occasional howls and strange-sounding night calls had kept Jaren awake the entire evening on that trip. He was hoping to have a more restful sleep this night.

That was, if Morgaine was ever to let them stop again. They had traveled through the first night and slept during the cooler morning hours. Then Morgaine had roused him all too early from his slumber, and they had set off once more. Except for a brief meal, they hadn't stopped all day, and it was now well past sunset.

"How far are we going tonight, Gainey?"

"Father said to make sure we travel a good distance every day before we camp for the night."

"Don't you think we're far enough yet? It's late."

She pursed her lips as if she were considering the idea for the first time. Jaren was sure her missed opportunity with the *Valir* was making her so irritable—and distant. "Fine, I suppose we are. We'll stop at the next place that looks like a good spot."

Jaren scanned about. Under the ample light of the full moon, though obscured by dark rain clouds, he could see quite a few spots that looked good enough to him. The hills to the west of Dal Farrow had gradually become more frequent and increased in slope. There were plenty of copses and sheltered hillsides about that would serve as suitable camping sites. He didn't inform Morgaine of his assessment, however, as he didn't want to hear another lecture about the hierarchy of their family again, and the fact that she was sacrificing far more than he.

He was just bringing his focus back to the fore when he saw the figure. A quicksilver flash of lightning illuminated the distance for an instant, and there it was—a human shape, apparently bundled in dark traveling clothes and a cloak. He, or she, for that matter, looked to be staring directly at them. Jaren blinked and stumbled on a rock, almost pitching him forward, but he caught himself just in time.

He glanced over at Morgaine, but she hadn't noticed. She apparently hadn't seen the figure, either. He looked back again, to the approximate spot, waiting for another flash of lightning. A moment later, it came.

Once more, the jagged line of the hill was outlined for an instant against the silver sky. No sign remained of the figure. Had he even seen anyone? Jaren decided his mind was simply playing tricks. After all, they were alone, miles from home, navigating in the dark through a storm, exactly the right conditions for imagining startling things.

He was still struggling with his thoughts, and whether he should mention anything to Morgaine, when they began scaling a particularly steep-sided hillock. There, the two came upon an outcropping of ancient, grey stone. Several openings appeared in the rock face, one of which looked large enough for them to fit comfortably inside.

Sure enough, they found, it was a deep recess that formed a small cave and, fortunately, it was unoccupied. A few bones and a bit of fur, however, not to mention a thick, musty smell, told them it had recently been home to something. Still, it had room for them and their packs. Space would be tight to stretch out for sleep, but it was out of the wind and rain. That more than made up for any other shortcomings. Besides, huddled together, they would stay warmer, anyway. Furthermore, Jaren didn't think he'd want to be too far from his sister this evening, whether or not he had actually seen someone else and not just a figment of his tired mind and overworked nerves.

They had simply crawled inside and curled up for sleep when Morgaine surprised Jaren with a question. "Why did you want to use my talisman?"

Jaren's tired mind scrambled to come up with an excuse, but he wasn't up to the task. He replied with a sigh, "I just wanted to know if I could make it work."

"It can be dangerous if you haven't been instructed in the proper ways. Even then…" she paused, uncertain how to continue. "You shouldn't have done it."

"I'm sorry, I won't do it again."

Apparently, she wasn't satisfied. "That's just because you think it won't work for you."

Jaren suddenly felt very tired. "Can we talk about this later?" *I think it won't work for me?*

Morgaine sat up. "Yes, that's just like you. Messing about where you don't belong and then pretending nothing happened." Her voice had grown agitated.

"What are you talking about?"

"I'm talking about how you never listen to me! You always have to have your own way no matter what anyone says."

Jaren raised his voice in reply. "Well, at least I don't push everybody around and tell them what to do all the time!"

"This is different! We're not talking about our chores or anything else we used to worry about! It's magic, and it's dangerous!" She was yelling fully now, and Jaren shrank back a bit from the sheer intensity.

He raised his hands in a calming gesture. "Come on, Gainey, calm down. I promise I won't try to use your talisman again—it won't work for me, anyway. Let's just try to get some sleep, okay?"

Morgaine harrumphed loudly, turned away, and lay down again. Even so, he heard her next words very clearly. "That had better be a promise you keep, until you at least earn a talisman of your own from the *Valir*. If we ever get to be tested again..." She closed her eyes and gave a heavy sigh. "I just told you the talisman wouldn't work for you because I didn't want you to go near it again. Please don't," her voice took on a thick hoarseness, "it's just too dangerous."

Jaren's stomach felt as if he'd been kicked. There it was. He really had failed with the talisman. There was no other explanation, now. His mind reeled. It was beginning to look as though his second overnight camping experience was to be as sleepless as the first.

8

THE REPORTS ALDRAIN HAD RECEIVED over the last day were more than worrisome. All five of those implicated were in attendance in the chamber, just as he'd been briefed. They were plotting to dethrone him and place Machim Aesirian, a distant cousin, in power. Machim would be no more than a pawn of theirs—Pacek and the others.

Where the report was short on details, Aldrain could fill in the blanks. They would point to his father's death and the destruction of the palace as an indication of the failure of his rule and, equally, argue that Aldrain was too much his father's son to be trusted with the throne of Carathon. He was sure to repeat the mistakes of his sire and lead the nation into similar disaster. Only one who was far enough removed from the politics of house Draegondor would suffice, though one of the royal bloodline would be accepted more readily by the Carathonai.

Enter Machim. He was not a bad person, as well as Aldrain knew, but he was also not fit for rule. Machim lacked the decisiveness of a true ruler and was too easily cowed by others—very likely the reason he'd been chosen. He'd be a puppet for the schemers.

Aldrain sighed heavily. He could not allow that to happen. He would embrace his birthright, now that a true ruler was most needed. Recent events had shaken the collective nerves of the people enough. It would completely undermine the foundations of the kingdom if the last, legitimate member of the royal family was then simply cast aside. At the very least, unrest would result, and at the worst, insurrection.

Pacek and his followers wanted power, but they did not understand the dynamics of rule. Old alliances between the nobles would fail as they struggled for position within the new arrangement, and the day-to-day business of the kingdom would grind to a halt as conflicts spread like wildfires. Only Aldrain could keep in place the delicate balance his father had managed, as he'd been a pupil—though an oft-reluctant one—of the king's concerted efforts.

Of course, Pacek would have to act through force. They could not remove him from rule without resorting to arms. Aldrain just hoped they thought him too weakened by the destruction of the palace and stretched too thin with the investigation and the maintenance of order to mount an effective defense. It would give him the upper hand if they rushed to move under the assumption that he was not fully in control of matters. From his discussion with the count, Aldrain thought it was more than likely.

"Your Majesty."

"Yes, Ordren?"

"They have planted men within the inner curtain who will attempt to open the gate for their forces outside. They have nearly five hundred gathered."

"Five hundred?" Aldrain asked, surprised. "How could they have mustered so many in such a short time?"

"We hold the walls, Your Majesty," Ordren replied. "We'll not be overtaken."

Aldrain countered, "We need to seize Pacek and the others for this to be ended now."

"The greycloaks are in position," said Ordren. "They will guide our movements against Pacek and his allies on your command."

"How many men do we have in case something else happens— some plot we've not yet uncovered?"

"We have two hundred regulars, and half as many palace guard," Ordren assured him "The additional mobilization you ordered will take a few days, though we may perhaps have several dozen more to call on already."

"That still leaves us vulnerable if they find a way inside the curtain."

"That is unlikely, Your Majesty."

"Yes, just as it was unlikely that I'd wake this morning to find my home and family gone." Aldrain snapped his jaw shut as Ordren dropped his gaze. "I'm sorry, Ordren. I'm just … tired from everything that's happened. You've done a commendable job. I'm sure we'll weather the storm."

"You'd best not keep them waiting any longer, Majesty."

"All right, I'm going inside," Aldrain told him. "Have the men at the gate apprehended. But—send a few additional greycloaks in first, just in case they're expecting our initial move. If they gain a foothold inside, we're going to have a long day of it. Hold off on Pacek and the others until my signal. I'll give word to the palace guard at the doors."

"It is as good as done, Your Majesty."

Aldrain turned to the entrance of the chamber, bowing his head. He offered a prayer to the True One that he manage to hold his warring emotions in check. With a heave, Aldrain swung inward the great double doors to the long, high-ceilinged meeting room. He wanted to make an impression from the start, and the resounding crash of the massive portals achieved that end. Heads spun toward the commotion. A good number of them were visibly relieved when they saw it was Aldrain advancing, apparently comforted to see the new king. A notable few, though, wore smiles of contempt. Count Pacek was at the forefront of this group of about half a dozen, standing to one side of the room in a knot. Aldrain crossed the room to stand before all of the assembled, just over fifty or so nobles, and again as many retainers and aides.

Cerdain, the new speaker, called for those present to be silent, as the arrival of the king signaled the official start of the meeting. "The first order of business is the acknowledgment of our new king," Cerdain cried. "All hail Aldrain Draegondor, Defender of the Realm! May he walk in the Truth and suffer no deception!" Most cheered his words, with the exceptions of Pacek and his party.

Aldrain waited for the murmurs of the crowd to die down. He raised his hand in acknowledgment.

"My friends, thank you for making the effort to attend today. I know more than most the upset that you have endured, and again I offer my appreciation to you for being here." There were some nods of approval from lesser nobles and of acknowledgment from the more influential. "I cannot put into words how important your resolve is now. You may have heard a great many things since yesterday, but know this: the hand of the king remains strong and directed. Your lands and your holdings are safe, secure as they have always been. And, as they will be tomorrow." Aldrain stared directly at Pacek, who avoided his gaze. "I will serve you as faithfully and effectively as my father, may he now walk in the light of the Truth."

There was some applause now, sparse at first, but spreading to all after a short time—all except for the knot of nobles off to Aldrain's right. Pacek exchanged a dark look with several others. He stepped forward.

"You may serve as your father did, proclaiming for the Truth as he, Your Majesty, but may I ask you—to what end?" Pacek pressed. There were a few astonished exhalations, but most simply turned to stare at Pacek in stunned silence. As chamber chair, he had the right to speak first and bring up issues that subjects of the kingdom wished heard. He cast his gaze about the room, trying to meet as many of his peers' eyes as possible before turning back to Aldrain. "We should, all of us, be asking that question. We have arrived where we are today because of your father's misguided attempts to lead this nation." This was greeted with several gasps of outrage, but again, mostly anxious silence. "I know that I am not alone in my belief that your father had too much invested with the *Valir*. He trusted them with more than was proper, and now we have all paid the price!"

A few voices rose in response.

"You come close to treason, Rondul!"

"No more talk of blaming the king for this! Watch your tongue, or I'll see it cut out, I swear on the Truth!"

"He makes a good point! We all know the king's halls were thick with those lying conjurors! And Aldrain would rather be hunting than running the kingdom!"

Aldrain raised his hands in an effort to suppress the growing din. The last claim had nearly pushed him to the brink, already fuming as he was about Pacek's initial words. He glared again at the man. "I wasn't aware that you knew precisely the cause of our present situation, Count. Please, share with us your enlightened knowledge of these events, I beseech you." Aldrain was barely containing his rage. It would not do to lose his composure during his first official act as king, especially one so monumentally important.

"I know as much as is needed, Your Majesty," Pacek stated. "It was your father's heavy involvement with the *Valir* that led to this calamity, and nothing else." Several in his group nodded and voiced agreement, but they were still the minority.

"Count Pacek, might I remind you the *Valir* are present in every nation? Their power is a necessary complement to any governance. Those who think differently are not in a position to rule for long."

"A presence is one thing, Majesty," Pacek retorted with a huff, "but to rely on them to the extent your father did is unacceptable. We will not allow such a thing to happen again."

"You will not allow it? By what right do you issue decrees? When last I checked, I was Aldrain Draegondor, heir to the throne of Carathon!"

Several other nobles cried in agreement and had to be restrained by their retainers from attacking the count, who was in turn being shielded by his comrades. Aldrain turned and signaled to one of the palace guards at the entrance, who then pounded on the door. An instant later, a number of his solders in grey uniforms swept into the room toward Aldrain. He motioned them on toward Pacek and his followers.

Their arrival did not have the effect upon Pacek and his group that Aldrain had expected. Instead, the count sneered in contempt.

"Hear me, subjects of this wretched orphan, entertainer of warlocks and witches! You must choose now: Accept King Aldrain and his scheming conjurors, or ally with me. We support a successor who does not play to the whims of the deceiving *Valir* snakes! One who takes seriously the mantle of power, rather than merely accepting what comes with the carelessness of a pampered royal brat!" Pacek's eyes flashed with venom as he returned Aldrain's fiery look. "But be warned! If you choose the puppet king and his sorcerers' brood, your time will be short-lived! Decide now!"

Utter chaos erupted. A few more enraged nobles joined their fellows in trying to lynch Pacek, while his associates struggled to hold them off. Shouting rang from every corner. Most were crying out their allegiance to Aldrain. Pacek's camp was still a minority, so why was he so brazen in his defiance?

The greycloaks were having difficulty navigating the crowd. Suddenly, the doors behind Aldrain burst open once more, and another knot of soldiers rushed in, all armed with short swords and a few with small bucklers as well. They were not palace guard, nor were they regulars. Pacek screamed something, unintelligible over the din, while directing them wildly toward Aldrain. Instinctively, Aldrain reached for his own weapon, but found nothing at his side. His heart sank. Weapons were forbidden in chambers. He'd left his outside. Cursing, he recalled his greycloaks and braced for the impact of the oncoming soldiers.

Where was Ordren?

❧

"But, my Lord … one more day and I will surely overtake her." Andraste made sure to speak in respectful, if even pleading tones. She conversed with no underling now. All but absolute subjection was out of the question.

"Pray, do not make me repeat myself. I have made arrangements. Your prisoner is needed elsewhere."

"As you command, my Lord."

"She is … undamaged?"

"In perfect health, Master," said Andraste.

A brief pause followed. "Very well. I trust I do not have to emphasize the importance of keeping her that way."

"No, my Master. She will reach the destination unharmed." But it would be so amusing to probe the youth, to find out what real potential she had. It was a distraction Andraste found quite enjoyable, though the host not nearly so. And this one had a great deal of unrealized power. *Fool! Do not think such thoughts*, she berated herself, *not in his audience!*

"Travel north into Carathon. Go to Eidara. At the docks you will meet another of the followers who will take the prisoner."

"Yes, Master."

"Go with all haste to the north, my servant."

"At once, Master."

The swirling, cloaked and hooded shadow-form began to dissipate and was soon gone altogether. Andraste stared hotly at the *metanduil* disk on the floor before returning it to the leather pouch at her belt. She could have the other girl in one single day more. Then, with a little effort, she could arrive at Eidara just as if she'd left now.

No.

One simply did not go against the Master's orders. He would know soon enough, and his reprisal would be swift—her success in taking the other would matter not one whit. She'd seen the result of his wrath before, though luckily never as the object. It was unwise even to question his judgment, let alone move in contradiction to it.

Still, there must be good reason for his commands. As important as she was, Andraste remained merely human. He was the Deceiver, an immortal diety. His resources were boundless and his servants innumerable. Her frustration must yield before the omnipotent wisdom of her lord. Indeed, she would obey, but she didn't have to like it. She at least had control over that. It alone was small comfort, but it would have to do.

9

JAREN CAME AWAKE WITH A start. The clouds had thickened once more, sealing out the light of the moon and stars. They had doused the lantern, leaving it difficult to discern the opening of the cave from the darkness beyond. Still, he peered in that direction, ears straining for another hint of the sound that had awakened him.

Then, he heard it again: a click, as if a rock had fallen against another. What was making the noises?

He cast his gaze in Morgaine's way, but it was no use. He could no more make out her form than the line of the cave entrance. Her breathing was steady, though, telling him she was still asleep. Jaren decided not to rouse her. It was likely nothing but some nocturnal animal, and he didn't want to be teased all the next day about being frightened by a raccoon or some such creature. That had also happened on their last camping adventure.

Instead, Jaren decided to investigate for himself. He crawled from his bedroll and, groping around for the opening, was just about to emerge from the cave when he remembered the figure. What if it was the source of the sounds? He almost went back to wake Morgaine, but his pride ultimately won out over his fear. Besides, who could it be? No one knew they were out here, so there would be no one following them. The figure had just been part of his overactive imagination, stirred up by the excitement of the last few days, that was all.

Still, he found himself holding his breath in anticipation as he emerged into the cool night breeze. He sat for what seemed a long time, until a few patches of starlit sky crossed overhead, letting some of the moon's glow escape.

That little bit allowed a scan of the surrounding country. Above them, the slope continued upward for a few dozen feet, then curved out of sight at its apex. There was no movement on the hill to his left or right. Below, the way they'd come, was a small valley. A dry watercourse formed the floor of the vale, and along its path nothing stirred. Scattered brush and a few lone trees were all he could make out.

He had nearly finished searching the entire range of his view when movement caught the edge of his vision.

He peered down into the small vale. Again, Jaren discerned a stirring as a vague shape, darker than its surroundings, disappeared into some scrub on the near side of the watercourse.

It was definitely bigger than a raccoon.

Jaren's heart raced. What was it? A wolf?

He looked about for some type of weapon. There were a few palmsized rocks, but nothing that would fend off a wolf. He'd need a sturdy tree limb for that, but there were none nearby. The hatchet! His father had packed one with the rest of their equipment, he remembered. Quietly, after one last look back down into the vale to mark the spot mentally, he stole back into the cave.

In the back of his mind, he could hear his father's voice telling him that, as long as they had plenty of their natural prey to eat, and if you didn't threaten them, wolves would never harm you.

Maybe it would be better if it was a wolf, Jaren considered, thinking of the other possibility. That brought a shiver. *You didn't see anyone on that ridge earlier! There was no one there*, he chided himself.

His shaking fingers finally released the leather ties on the pack. He shuffled around inside urgently, until he at last he felt the cool metal of the hatchet's head. Ripping it from the pack, he turned to hurry back outside.

"Jaren…what are you doing?" Morgaine's speech was slurred by sleep and tinged with annoyance.

He had to tell her now. "Something's down in the valley. I think it might be a wolf."

"It won't bother us. Just leave it alone."

"I want to make sure."

"I thought you said it was a wolf." Her voice had lost its sleepiness and now carried more edge.

"I *think* it was a wolf, but I'm not sure. I didn't get a good look."

Morgaine sighed deeply, or it could have been a yawn. "Just wait a minute, I'll come with you."

"I'll just be outside."

"Jaren, I said wait!" Her voice was urgent, though hushed. It didn't matter, however, as Jaren had already left the cave. He heard a muttered curse and the sounds of his sister scrambling about.

In a crouch, Jaren moved down to some brush a few dozen feet below the cave mouth. He heard his sister approaching from behind.

"The next time you—" Morgaine began, but stopped abruptly. "Who's there?" she challenged.

Jaren froze. His grip on the hatchet tightened.

Only a brief shuffling came in answer.

"We're not unarmed. You should just keep moving on, whoever you are." Morgaine's voice cracked, dispelling any of her intended air of authority.

Jaren could see that she wielded their lone hunting knife. It looked very small and ineffective at the moment. A knot of uneasiness settled into his stomach.

"For the last time—" Morgaine began.

"It's just me," a familiar voice broke in from nearby.

"Iselle?" they exclaimed in unison.

Sure enough, Iselle rose from a point just at the base of the hillside below, emerging from a thick patch of shrubs.

"Did you save me any supper? You two may be amateurs at this, but you still led me on quite a chase. I even had to miss a meal or two!"

Iselle refused to turn back, though the siblings hadn't really tried to convince her to do so in earnest, as they both secretly welcomed her company. After all, she was much more experienced in the wilds than they were.

Iselle filled them in on a few details. She'd left not long after Jaren and Morgaine had been discovered missing. "That caused quite the stir!" Iselle reported, while also reassuring the two of them that their parents were all right. "The reeve even had to arrest Master Banath, because he punched old Jebdal square in the nose when he found out you were gone! And in front of a whole bunch of people, too. Said he'd have to sit tight until he calmed down enough to listen to reason. That ought to take a while." She smiled her mischievous grin. "Guess the reeve will just have to wait himself to have his talk with me."

They set out the next morning, the trio winding on through the steepening hills, and their pace slowed. Here and there, outcroppings of ancient, weathered gray stone thrust from the earth, and they entered the deeper forests of western Ergothan. The clouds had disappeared during the early morning hours, and they were glad of the more plentiful leaf cover, for it was growing hot once again. They stopped for brief meals, a sore spot for Iselle, but she more than made up for her grumbling by taking up the lead.

"I've been up this way many times," she told them. "They're like my second home. My father used to bring me up here when he made his trapping runs. Then I just started going on my own."

"Weren't you scared?" asked Jaren.

"Of what?" Iselle replied, raising a quizzical eyebrow.

"Didn't Jaren tell you?" interjected Morgaine, "He's afraid of raccoons."

"I *am not* afraid of raccoons; they just startled me once, that's all!"

"Oh, that's going to cost you," Iselle teased. "Jaren Haldannon is afraid of fuzzy, little forest creatures."

"I meant, aren't there wolves out here?" he tried to switch the subject.

Iselle thought briefly, then replied, "Yes, but only when the raccoons don't chase them away!" The girls erupted into laughter. Jaren stared crossly for a moment, then shrugged and joined in.

Though she hadn't been to Mother Haddie's before, Iselle said she knew generally where it was. After they stopped to camp for the evening, she gave her take on the matter. "We should be close by sunset tomorrow. But, I don't know if we want to walk up to her house at night." Iselle cocked her head playfully toward Jaren, "Now, *she* scares me. We might want to camp nearby and go to meet her in the morning."

They agreed to sleep on the idea, as Morgaine thought it silly to wait, while the younger two insisted they do just that. So, they let the matter drop for the moment and went about readying their site for the evening. Morgaine prepared the food, and Jaren and Iselle went to gather deadwood for the fire. The sun was just beginning to dip toward the horizon, and shadows grew long and thin. As they picked through the underbrush for suitable pieces of firewood, the conversation turned to the subject of the talisman.

"She found out about you using the stone?" Iselle was shocked. "And you're still alive?"

"It wasn't that big a deal. Besides, it's like you said. Only the rightful user can make it work," Jaren lied.

"I think it's a big deal to her. I'd be careful if I were you."

"Thanks for the advice. Just don't go bringing it up any more!" He poked her lightly, grinning.

"Jaren, how can you think I'd do such a thing?" Iselle smiled back. Her grin straightened into a more inquisitive expression. "So, do you still think you've got the touch?"

He frowned. "I don't... I don't know." He didn't feel like telling her the truth now, so he just repeated what he'd already described. "It still feels like the magic is right there... but I just can't reach out and touch it." Masking the disappointment in his voice was tough.

"Well, you found out that you can't make someone else's stone work. You'll just have to wait until you get your own."

He shrugged. "Yeah, I guess so." his frown deepened. "It's easy for you to say, Iselle, you have some freedom. I have to—"

"Quick, get down!" Iselle ordered in a hushed voice, dropping instantly into a guarded crouch.

"What—"

"Never mind what, just get down! Now!" She pulled him down beside her and pointed to the east. Though the horizon was darkening there, he could just make out the figure of a person. Whoever it was seemed to be staring right at the two of them. After a brief pause, the figure pulled something from its back. The thin, curving shape revealed it to be some manner of bow. The other hand reached back to draw an arrow. Casting its gaze back and forth, the figure crouched and struck the arrowhead at an angle against the ground. There was a spark and suddenly, the arrowhead burst into brilliant light.

"We've got to get Morgaine and get out of here!" Iselle cried. The flaring missile arced slowly through the darkening sky. Moments later, the peal of horns and the barking of dogs echoed up through the vales toward them.

Iselle, with Jaren in tow, burst upon the campsite. Morgaine had huddled down, still clutching a frying pan.

"What was that?" she questioned.

"We're being followed!" Iselle answered breathlessly, diving toward her gear and scooping it up frantically into her pack. "Quickly, we don't have much time before they get here!"

"Who are *they*?" Morgaine demanded.

"Does it matter?" Iselle replied. "Just let's get moving!" His sister threw one last, annoyed look at the younger girl and then rushed to retrieve her things.

It seemed an agonizingly long time to gather their few pieces of essential equipment, but finally they were racing for the cover of the thicker trees, leaving everything else behind.

"Stay close behind me," Iselle called back as she ran before them, "I know a few twists and turns of these woods that should throw off whoever that is. Just make sure you listen to me—we may have to go to ground in an instant!"

Morgaine bristled at the command, but she apparently thought better than to argue the point, as it was neither the time nor the place. Still, Jaren recognized the tight-lipped expression she wore. It said she'd not forget to put the situation back to rights once they were safely out of danger. The blare of a horn, getting closer, seemed to suggest that might be some time from now.

Iselle's path led them over a seemingly random route, zigging and zagging up a slope here, then following along the twisting floor of a valley there, and now plodding along a shallow stream, where footing was chancy at best on the slick rocks. There was no discernible logic behind it that Jaren could make out. Perhaps that was the point, he considered.

Another blast sounded in the distance, but it seemed not to have gained on them, though Jaren could not be at all sure any longer. Regardless, their urgency drove them on. Soon, their limbs ached from the strain, and they were all fighting for breath.

As twilight turned to early evening, and they pushed deeper into the wood and higher into the hills, their precious cover proved a great hindrance. The thickening canopy overhead blocked out all but scattered pockets of the moon's illumination, making for even more treacherous going. Branches seemed to reach out, clutching at them with rough, wooden fingers. Boughs slapped and scratched, stinging their faces and limbs. Their pace became necessarily measured; otherwise, one or the other of them would have quickly turned an ankle, or worse. Jaren and Morgaine endured the greatest of the forest's abuse, though Iselle, too, gasped now and then as a branch caught her unaware or a hidden root snagged at her foot.

Still, the horns sounded in the distance. Thankfully, they had become much fainter over the last while—and they could no longer hear the dogs. Jaren's lungs burned, and his body felt on the verge of collapse, yet Iselle pulled them on. Morgaine had developed a slight limp, but she kept on all the same, refusing to call upon the younger girl to stop or to even let up the pace. Pride now spurred his sister on, Jaren knew, as fear was no longer the sole driving force behind her iron will. She would fall unconscious before she let Iselle know she was nearing the limit of her endurance. His was nearly spent, too, and he was ready to admit it. He doubted he had the breath remaining to do so, however.

They struggled on, until Iselle finally pulled them to an abrupt stop beneath a particularly shadowed cluster of ancient oaks. It had been some time since they had last heard the horns.

Brother and sister collapsed to the ground, their chests heaving labored breaths. Iselle sat back against a great, gnarled tree, arms hanging limply at her sides. Jaren could see her shoulders rising and falling rapidly, too. It might at least put Morgaine in a less combative mood to know that she was hurting as well.

After some time, Morgaine raised herself to her elbows and spoke. "So, where have you led us to, Iselle?"

There was a moment of silence before the hoarse answer came. "Away from whoever was chasing us. I think we're safe for now."

"I don't feel very safe out here, in the middle of nowhere without any idea where I am."

"I know where we are." That seemed to melt some of the ice from Morgaine's eyes, though her gaze never wavered. "We're a few hours walk from Mother Haddie's cabin." Jaren's jaw dropped. That meant they'd been running for hours. Then again, it seemed much longer at the time.

"I think we should go there now, instead of waiting."

"I agree," Iselle added.

"I won't hear anything—what?"

"From what I know of the old lady, she keeps a close eye 'round these parts and she may be able to tell who it is that's after us. They may not even know she lives up here."

Jaren simply nodded his agreement. He wasn't sure he could even walk, but he didn't want to spend another minute longer than he had to outside in the dark, exposed.

As it turned out, it took the better part of four hours to reach Mother Haddie's. By then, Sholara was almost an hour in the sky, though she did little to ward off the night's chill. It was all the worse since they remained thoroughly soaked from their efforts. The first hint that they'd arrived was a sweet scent on the air. It seemed a part of the natural fragrances surrounding them, but soon it became a distinctly different, yet no less welcoming, aroma. It was cinnamon, and it was mixed with something else that Jaren couldn't quite put his finger on. Regardless, it sent their stomachs into tumbles, reminding them they'd either run or walked through the entire night and missed their evening meal in the bargain.

They kept to the cover of the thicker trees and, in a crouch, crept closer to the old woman's shack. From their vantage point, everything looked in order, but they weren't about to take any chances. Making every effort at silence, they circled around to get a better view of the front of the cabin. It was fair sized, built with thick, hewn logs that were in good repair, except for a slight stoop in the timbers of a roof that was finished with rough, wooden shakes. A thin finger of smoke curled from a fieldstone chimney set into the middle of the latter. All was peaceful and quiet.

Then it occurred to Jaren: all of the forest noises he'd been hearing had ceased. He wasn't sure for how long, either. Judging from the tense movements of the others, they'd realized it, too. It was then that he noticed the cabin door. It hung at a severe angle, as if smashed open forcefully and left to swing free.

A deep-throated growl from behind froze them in place.

10

ONE OF THE PALACE GUARDS heaved a longsword to Aldrain just as the first enemies reached him. With it, Aldrain had been able to withstand the initial rush until several of his own men forced their way back to him. He'd taken several minor hits, but two of his foes lay unmoving nearby. The enemy began to give ground as more guards reinforced his flanks.

Aldrain's blade darted high and then low as he attempted to lure his present opponent into making a fatal error. The man was a professional soldier, but predictable enough in his movements and not overly committed. Soon enough, the soldier left too wide an opening. Aldrain struck, scoring a deadly hit to the man's chest. The soldier crumpled to the floor in a heap, and Aldrain paused for a moment, glancing back over his shoulder.

The brief scan quickly confirmed his worst fear. Pacek and several of his cohorts had disappeared during the struggle.

"Seal the room!" Aldrain ordered. A pair of his men rushed to each exit to block any further egress. His own group pressed forward, and soon their foes offered up their arms, outnumbered, and with less than half still able to fight. Several of Aldrain's men had also given their lives in the struggle, their motionless bodies joining the others on the floor.

He still had not received word from Ordren.

Aldrain hailed a nearby officer. "Lieutenant Aldar, have everyone detained here, except for those who openly stood with Count Pacek. Take those to the gaol and put them in individual cells. Find out where he and the others may have gone, and anything else you can learn." The man was clearly uncomfortable with the order. Aldrain clapped a hand to his shoulder. "Lieutenant, these men were part of a coup to overthrow Draegondor rule. They are traitors and subject to the law. They are no longer men of office—their lands and lives are forfeit. Do your duty—for me, and for my father." The officer nodded and rushed to carry out his king's commands.

Aldrain hurried from the chamber, reclaiming his own, ancestral blade and handing the other to one of the guards at the exit, where he nearly collided with a frantic messenger who burst through the entryway.

"Your Majesty," he gasped breathlessly, "my apologies! I was ordered to find you in all haste."

"Go on," Aldrain acknowledged, a sickening feeling stirring in his stomach.

"I have word from Commander Ordren. He learned of trouble near the concourse and went to investigate. He is now under attack before the gates. Another force somehow made it inside the curtain and fell upon his flank. He is hard-pressed to stand against them and hold the main gate. He advised that you be notified as soon as possible!"

Aldrain's anger once again nearly escaped him, as his mind reeled with furious thoughts. *Word of Truth! How could all of this be happening? How could I not have seen it coming—any of it?* He breathed deeply to compose himself. "How long ago did all of this occur?"

"Not long, your Majesty, within the quarter-hour. I was briefed soon after the second force assaulted our position, and I came straight to the guildhall."

"Captain Boltun is within, and Lieutenant Aldar will be en route to the gaols. Go first to Boltun and have him send every available man to the gates. Then repeat the message to Aldar. I will take as many as I come across on the way now. Truth speed you."

"As you command, Your Majesty." The messenger was racing into the chamber before the last words left his lips. Aldrain matched the man's pace, speeding out of the guildhall and toward the main gates.

By the time he neared the vicinity of the inner curtain gate, Aldrain had managed to round up nearly two dozen men, most of them regulars. Along the way, he also had some time to think things through. It now seemed as though everything was happening too quickly and too conveniently for his adversaries to be explained by either superb marshaling or uncanny coincidence. In the short span of time since the destruction of the palace, it would have been impossible to orchestrate such well-laid plans involving so many, not to mention significant resources and precise inside knowledge. It was equally inconceivable that a clandestine body had coincidentally planned a coup within days of the annihilation of his father and the Draegondor powerbase.

Dark forces were at work, and they had been for some time.

Aldrain sensed some sinister hand manipulating his circumstances. He uttered another prayer to the True One, as it seemed more and more likely that divine intervention would truly be required to weather this storm.

Finally, they arrived near the gates to the sounds of heated battle. Cries of pain and death rose over the scene, mixed with the ring of steel on steel, as his men struggled to fend off the rebels. They were holding their own, his brave soldiers, though hard-pressed indeed. They faced assault from within the city proper while defending the gates against an outside contingent.

He could see now that Ordren commanded the main thoroughfare and was keeping his force from being surrounded by spearheading attacks directly into the enemy's center whenever they sent men to outflank him. It had been a successful plan thus far, forcing the enemy to reinforce its core at the cost of attacking, but his commander was running out of manpower to maintain his strategy.

Aldrain decided that no better option existed than to locate the enemy command and disrupt it while his forces still held out.

A greycloak brought word that the enemy leaders were located down an alley abutting the concourse. Aldrain retraced for several blocks the path they'd used and was about to lead his troop down a cross lane, when another group of armed men burst around the corner toward them. Cursing his apparent ill luck, Aldrain ordered his small group into a defensive formation just as he realized the newly arrived men were his own.

It was another patrol of palace guard sent by Captain Boltun ahead of the main reinforcements, the wide-eyed sergeant of the company reported. The former would be on their way soon, nearly three score more men.

Soon, Aldrain's bolstered ranks awaited his orders just back of the laneway where the enemy command was positioned. Carefully, Aldrain stole to the intersection, peering around the corner of an inn and down the avenue toward his intended target. The enemy officers were there, indeed, but between them and his company stood a squad of rebel soldiers. There were a number more than in his command, and, for the most part, the lot of them appeared to be hardened veterans as well. As he watched, their captain barked a series of commands and turned in a march toward him. The rest of the troop followed suit.

Aldrain ducked back behind the corner. He had to think of something, and he needed to do it immediately. Already, he could hear the approach of the other company, their booted footfalls striking the paving stones in well-ordered cadence.

"What are your orders, Your Majesty?" the sergeant whispered urgently, sensing the situation was far from good. Aldrain turned toward the voice, his mind reeling to formulate an answer.

11

"I can see why the door would have put a fright into you," Mother Haddie let out a dry cackle. "It nearly fell off its hinges and broke my toe a few days back. Good thing I know a little about healing people. Just wish I was a bit handier." That was followed by another good-natured laugh. "And Dagger, here," she raised a crooked hand to ruffle the glossy, black fur atop the head of her gigantic canine companion—a head that was fully level with her own—"he would scare the breeches off anyone, sneaking up on you like he did. But, these days, you can't blame an old woman for being careful, now, can you?"

The trio shook their heads in response, still unable to pry their eyes from the animal they were sure an instant before was about to tear them to shreds. For his part, the great dog sat on his haunches and looked at them with bright, friendly brown eyes. That made his great, saw-toothed maw no less daunting, though a broad tongue lolled in and out lazily in time with his deep-chested panting.

"Good. Well, now that you know Dagger, and presuming you know who I am, elsewise you wouldn't have come to see me, who might you be? And what do you wish from a crazy old witch like me?"

Morgaine spoke after an awkward silence. "We were sent to stay with you. We're Jens and Marta Haldannon's children, Morgaine and Jaren. And this is Iselle, a friend of ours."

"Ah, yes. Now I remember you two. You were much younger the last time I was out your way—and noisier. Let's see now … yes, it was an ankle your father needed tending, eh? Well, you're to stay with me, are you? It must've been some trouble, for your father to send you all the way out here. And to me! I gathered he didn't have much use for me, other than my talents."

Morgaine and Jaren squirmed a bit under her gaze, but said nothing. Iselle watched and listened with a corner of her lip upturned in amusement.

"And you, young lady. I don't think I've seen you before. You have a sassy look to you. There'll be no mischief played out here, my love. I'm too old for nonsense anymore." Iselle's half-smirk disappeared immediately, and she joined the others in their discomfort at the scrutiny of the old woman. Mother Haddie scanned the faces of the three, her eyes narrowed as if judging their thoughts.

"I was accused of using magic against another girl," Morgaine blurted out, the anxiety of Mother Haddie's silent interrogation getting to her.

"Oh, I see. Did you?"

"No. Well, yes ... I don't know," she stammered in answer.

"Well, which is it, girl? Or do you have yet another answer for me?" The old woman's eyebrows rose in apparent amusement. It didn't seem to put Morgaine at ease, though.

"She was only defending us," Jaren interrupted. "The other girl was trying to hurt us, and my sister only did what she had to do—"

"Let me be the judge of that, boy."

Jaren's mouth snapped shut with an audible click.

Morgaine shot him one of her correcting stares, and then she continued. "I tried to use the magic against her after she attacked us, but I don't know if I did or not. I can't remember ... it all happened so fast. I ... I must have, but I'm not sure."

Morgaine seemed uncertain how to go on, or if she should.

She didn't have to, as the old woman held up a hand, putting an end to his sister's distress. "That will do, child. I believe you. And," she put both hands to the small of her back and stretched, making no attempt to subdue a yawn, "it's about breakfast time, wouldn't you say? I know Dagger gets irritable when he's not had his morning meal on time."

Dagger let out a short, deep-throated bark, then headed for the porch.

"Is it safe to stay here, with whoever-it-is still out there searching for us?" Iselle asked.

Mother Haddie raised an eyebrow. "Safer here than wandering about, love. I have a connection to this place—and the animals that live hereabouts."

Iselle opened her mouth to speak again, but Mother Haddie frowned and placed her hands on her hips, silencing the girl.

"Like I said, sassy. Well, if you must know, I don't just heal people. I make sure the critters are taken care of. In fact, that's how I came upon Dagger a few years back. He was pushing bush for a hunting party when he broke his leg. They left him for dead. Didn't even look for him." She scowled, then looked at the great dog with tender eyes. "I guess Dagger decided to stick around. Anyway, in return for assisting the animals, they look out for me. There are a couple of grizzlies and several wolf packs nearby that will either hide that you've been through or discourage anyone from getting too close."

At that, the old woman nodded and hobbled into the cottage. The trio followed.

The first thing Jaren noticed inside was that the table was already set—for four. He cast a sidelong glance at Iselle. Her raised eyebrows suggested she was wondering the same thing. Morgaine was apparently too preoccupied in her own thoughts to have noticed. The table could have been spread with steaming entrails, and she would have been oblivious.

"Here, boy, make yourself useful and fetch us some water from the stream out back. Take your young girlfriend with you. I'd like to have a moment alone with your sister before we eat, if you don't mind."

He took the worn, wooden bucket from her eagerly, throwing a sly smile at Iselle.

She punched him in the arm as soon as they were outside. "Don't get any ideas," she growled.

On their return, Morgaine appeared visibly more at ease. Her eyes no longer held the pain they had shown almost constantly since the standoff with Joselle. She was actually wearing a hint of a smile. She and Mother Haddie had already heaped the plates with food—some tiny, square-cut potatoes, thin slices of steaming, salted ham, and eggs.

Jaren sat down and started shoveling food into his mouth. He'd forgotten just how hungry he was!

Over the course of the morning, Mother Haddie either entertained them with interesting stories or had them relate the events of the past few days, beginning with the unexpected return of the *Valir* to Dal Farrow. She seemed intensely interested in the latter, though she said nothing more after asking a few pointed questions. She treated all of them kindly enough, if not with a touch of brusqueness one would expect of someone who lived alone and was not used to visitors.

Mother Haddie also revealed that she could be as mischievous as Iselle, as the old woman good-naturedly set Dagger after the girl when she balked at helping with dishes. The dog did little more than bowl her over with his massive head, probably his manner of playing, but the point was made to the entertainment of the rest. Though Iselle was somewhat put out at first, she got over it quickly enough, as was her usual way.

That afternoon, Jaren was sent out with another chore, this time to cut some wood for the fire. Iselle tagged along, while Mother Haddie and Morgaine talked again. Jaren caught enough of the gist of their discussion to wish he'd been asked to take part. They were conversing about magic. He had been tempted to hide out beneath one of the open windows and eavesdrop a while, but since seeing Dagger sent into action after Iselle, he wanted no part of that possibility.

Instead, he stood off to the side of the clearing where Mother Haddie had directed him, fuming while Iselle hacked at a tree with a heavy axe.

"Not that I can't do this all by myself, but you could help out," she said.

It took several seconds for her words to register. "What? Oh, sorry. I just want to know what they're talking about. It could help me, too."

"The old woman seems to know a lot. Maybe she didn't ask you because she knows it's not in you to summon."

Jaren fixed her with a hard look. "Thanks a lot. I really don't need anymore discouragement at the moment."

"Well, you have to consider the possibility that you don't have that talent with magic. Don't you think?"

"I'd rather find out if I do before I give up."

"That's not what I'm saying, Jaren. But if you put everything into wanting this and it doesn't come to be, what will that do to you?"

He sighed. She was just looking out for him, he knew. "I guess it wouldn't be very good." He regarded her again, the light of determination still there. "But I'm not letting go until I know for sure." He paused, a grin spreading across his face. "Maybe I should become a trapper. How's business lately?"

Iselle laughed. "You'd catch yourself in your own trap and starve to death before you landed a single skin, Jaren Haldannon. I think you should just stick to your crops." He frowned, though whether it was because of the barb, the handle of the axe thrust toward him, or a return to his previous train of thought, even he wasn't sure.

After a couple of hours of chopping and splitting, the two had a sizeable pile of firewood prepared.

"Maybe Mother Haddie won't send the dog after you again since you did all of this work for her. There must be almost two month's worth of fuel here."

"Somehow I don't think it will matter. The old bag's got a mean streak, I can tell." Iselle cast a furtive glance over her shoulder as she spoke.

"Well, then, we better get this wood back as soon as we can!" Jaren advised.

Mother Haddie cast a quizzical look at them as they returned, then shook her head as if dismissing whatever thoughts had been roused. The expression had only lasted an instant, and Jaren couldn't quite make it out. The aroma of their supper and the answering growl from his stomach quickly pushed the subject from Jaren's mind.

After they'd eaten and the tidying up was finished—led by Iselle, who literally jumped up to begin the chores—Jaren stepped out onto the small porch to see if he could catch the sunset. The creak of old, wooden boards told Jaren someone had come out to join him. He was surprised to see that it was Mother Haddie.

She didn't speak for a long while, but instead stood beside him, watching the vivid colors swath the horizon as the sun sank lower toward its nightly rest.

"Your sister says you hope to wield the magic as well," she finally broke the silence.

After a moment of considering how to answer, Jaren shrugged. "I guess it almost feels like I should...like I'm supposed to, or something."

Mother Haddie nodded. "Not everyone uses it in the same way. Take me. I don't do much *summoning* as they call it, though I can, to an extent. Mostly, I use the magic to empower my cures and aid in the body's natural healing."

"How did you learn?"

"A crazy old hag taught me." They both shared a chuckle. She turned to face him directly. "You don't have the gift, you know. Not like your sister."

It felt as if he'd been splashed with frigid water. All the air seemed sucked from his lungs. "What do you mean? Are you sure?"

"I can see things about people—what sort of character they have, and usually whether they have magical ability. You want to have the talent. You've convinced yourself you need it. But it won't happen for you, at least not the way you expect. There is something, but I don't quite know what to make of it. It's easy to want to summon so badly that you forget everything—and everyone—else." She fixed him with a compassionate smile.

He sighed in resignation. "You're not the first to tell me that."

"Your gifts are different, though you may come to use magic in an-other way someday, I think. Like I've already said, I can't tell for sure. I do know a man a couple of towns south of here who can use the magic to sing to his crops. Doesn't seem to matter how everyone else's harvest goes; he always has a healthy yield." The furrowing of Jaren's brow in-dicated his disinterest in that route. She breathed her own, weary sigh. "Just know that the lure of *metanduil* is an empty one for you. Better to cultivate your existing talents and friendships to the best of your abil-ity. They'll serve you more in the long term—and in the short term, if I read things right."

"What do you mean?"

"Just that the future is what you will make of it, so be sure to choose paths that you are able to follow. Setting yourself up for disappoint-ment will do no one any good, and it's likely to leave you bitter and alone. And, in the short term, we're going on a journey. You'll want to stay focused on that."

"But…we just arrived. My father told us to come here and wait for him. And whoever chased us here—won't they still be out there?"

Mother Haddie studied the sunset once more. "You leave the wor-rying to me. I want to take your sister to a friend of mine." She pursed her lips. "Pardon my frankness, but much of your problem lies in focus-ing on the future—on what might be. You'd be better off paying more attention to what's going on around you right now. That's just my take on it. Anyway, where we're going is not too far, and from what I guess, I'm sure we'll be back before your father comes for you."

Once more, it seemed, things were moving unexpectedly and not according to Jaren's wishes. They weren't supposed to be staying with Mother Haddie for that long. Also, there was something in her voice that told him they were leaving with her for reasons other than just to take Morgaine to Mother Haddie's friend. Even though she'd dis-missed his concern, Jaren still suspected it had as much to do with the people who had pursued them.

Most importantly, though, she wasn't supposed to kill his hopes entirely. He wanted to scream. What did she know? She was just a mad, old crone who lived by herself with her dog and her roots and couldn't do any real magic. He didn't need her to tell him what was best. Or Iselle, for that matter. They didn't know him as well as they thought.

It was some time before he realized full night had fallen, and that the old woman was gone.

12

ALDRAIN SHOOK HIS HEAD, BEING sure to make eye contact with the sergeant across the way. The others were not completely inside the trap yet. He had decided to use the alley's many hidden nooks and recessed doorways to launch an ambush against the approaching foe, rather than launch a desperate rush and attempt to break through to the enemy leaders—a gamble that had almost no chance of success. His plan was still risky, but there had been little other choice.

After a few urgent, whispered commands, his men had dispersed along both sides of the lane, melting into shadowed alcoves and behind stout doors. So far, it was working. The approaching soldiers appeared completely oblivious.

Soon, the last of the soldiers rounded the corner, and Aldrain raised his hand, concealed by the deep shadows from all but those who knew he was there. He held the gesture for a brief instant longer, then signaled for the attack.

Immediately, cries of alarm and shouts of pain rose up as his men threw themselves at the enemy. They were taken completely off-guard. Still, it turned out to be a hard-fought encounter, as the grizzled veterans put up a stubborn resistance. Eventually, though, they were overcome.

After dispatching the last few, Aldrain ordered his men to disguise themselves as best they could in the equipment of the dead and then hurriedly moved them out in haste toward their original goal. Ordren couldn't hold out much longer.

Aldrain pulled the visor of the enemy captain's helm over his face and held the man's shield before him, trying as much as was possible to block the view of his own armor. It wouldn't take a lot, he knew: *Just a little closer.* The ad hoc disguise needed to pass only briefly, long enough to get them within a short sprint, and then they could dispense with the ruse.

A couple of guards on point ahead spotted his group almost as soon as they turned the corner and continued down the street. *Not much longer—don't let them raise the alarm yet,* Aldrain prayed. He couldn't quite see their expressions, though they had bent their heads and appeared to be holding an animated discussion. Probably, it was an argument about the abrupt return of the troop that had just departed. Aldrain waved to them, as if beckoning. One advanced a couple of steps, but the other called out to his partner. They were at odds about what to do, and the debate grew more heated. The nearest guard indicated that the other should follow, but that one planted his feet, shaking his head vigorously.

Now Aldrain could make out their features clearly. Finally, caution prevailed, and the hesitant guard turned, putting his hands to his mouth. Nothing came of it other than a gurgling rasp, as an arrow took him through the neck. The other stood frozen, wide-eyed, with the realization of his mortal error, before a blade cut him down.

With a loud rallying cry, Aldrain threw down helmet and shield, bursting forward into a full-out run. The man he'd identified as the enemy commander gawked in alarm, torn from a conversation with several others nearby. His eyes, too, went wide with shock as he groped in panic for the sword at his side.

Aldrain bowled into them before the other could free the blade, scattering the officers and landing on his side next to the man. The enemy commander lurched to his feet, drawing steel and crouching in a defensive position just as Aldrain's men caught up, engaging the other officers and the closest guards.

The commander circled, narrowed eyes straining to read Aldrain's movements. They worked around, facing each other, marking each other's movements. His foe seemed competent enough with a blade, taking a balanced stance.

Perhaps Aldrain's overly offensive posture prompted the other man to strike first, or perhaps it was simply overconfidence—Aldrain appeared too young to be an experienced fighter, after all. Either way, the commander lunged forward with a strong attack that Aldrain easily sidestepped. Aldrain countered, landing a solid strike. Maybe the man had been commanding rather than fighting for too long.

A sting to Aldrain's upper arm reminded him not to take that for granted, however. They circled again. This time Aldrain attacked, making contact once more, though superficially. He managed to block the commander's counterstroke and then attacked again. The blade bit deeply. His enemy growled, cursing, and lashed out with his free hand.

Aldrain was able to turn his head at the last moment and take most of the momentum from the punch, but it still sent a few stars across his vision and made him stumble sideward.

Still, the damage was done. Aldrain's opponent began to limp immediately and his injury grew steadily worse as the fight wore on. In the end, though his opponent refused to quit, Aldrain was able to knock the weapon from his weakening grasp. The man called out for mercy, and Aldrain obliged.

He needed answers, anyway.

Able at last to survey the surroundings, he saw that his minor offensive had taken its toll. All of the officers were subdued or down, and in the distance, down the alley, Aldrain observed that the main force, leaderless and left to its own devices, was quickly surrendering to Ordren's men.

Finally, something had gone his way. *Thank the Truth*, the king exhaled.

Jaren was still staring off into the darkened woods when it occurred to him that a tiny point of light had appeared in the distance, though still much screened by the heavy forest cover. A low growl nearly sent him off of the porch in fright. He looked about and found Dagger crouched nearby, staring ahead toward the yet-faint illumination, head down, ears lowered and haunches raised. Jaren couldn't believe that an animal so big could move so silently.

Regardless, the mammoth dog's reaction indicated that Jaren's guess was right. Someone was approaching.

Footsteps creaked on the porch, and Mother Haddie once more peered with Jaren off into the distance.

"They'll be here soon," she stated absently.

"Who are they?"

"The same ones that chased you on your way here."

"I thought your ... friends would keep them away," he said, though he'd feared as much.

She fired an exasperated look at him. "The animals can only do so much. They hurt just like anyone else. Your *friends* seem very determined to get to you." Her last words could have been a growl from Dagger.

"Why didn't you tell us they were still out there, hunting for us?"

Mother Haddie drew a weary breath. "They must have had some help. Dagger and the others gave them some misleading signs to follow. They should have taken at least another day to find us here. I think someone is very interested in your sister, someone with greater magic than mine."

Morgaine, with Iselle right behind, emerged from the cabin. They had dressed in a hurry, and disheveled hair crowned both their heads. How they could even have managed to sleep so soon after their harrowing flight was beyond him.

"What is it, Mother Haddie?" Morgaine questioned. Her eyes followed the others' gaze into the woods, and then opened wider in recognition. "Is that—?"

"Yes, love. Now gather what you need for another journey. And be quick about it. We haven't much time. Jaren, you'd best help them, too."

Their packs were stored together and hadn't been emptied, so it took little time to stock them full once more. Mother Haddie entered the room and ushered them to the back door. On the way, she grabbed a leather belt with several pouches attached and slung it over her shoulder.

The old woman spoke in a hushed, but urgent tone. "Stay close behind me. Dagger will be about, so don't holler if you think you see a shadow moving close by. If we get separated, we're heading for the river. I have a small boat that will take us downstream to Ensin Llaw's stronghold. He's the one I want to take Morgaine to see. In case I have to … to deal with anyone, keep to the path. It heads north about half a mile to the Marthuin River. If I don't find you within the hour, leave without me."

"We won't, Mother Haddie," Morgaine protested, and the others echoed her.

"Don't be foolish child; you'll do as I say. It takes about two days by the current to reach Llaw's tower. I'll meet you there if I've not caught up by the time you leave." She regarded their worried faces. "Don't fret. I'm tougher than I look, and Dagger can take care of the both of us. Now let's go!"

It was something to try and keep up with the fleet-footed healer, despite her age. It was quite a surprise after watching the old woman shuffling about her home. In no time, they had crossed the shallow stream behind the cabin and headed off straight ahead. Mother Haddie passed among the trees with the confidence of one who knew each and every root and limb. The moon was not yet up, so it was good that she did know. A dark form darted across the path before them. At least Jaren thought he saw something. The old woman ignored it completely and kept on. *Must have been Dagger, scouting ahead*, Jaren thought. *Or it was my imagination again.*

Some minutes into their flight, they heard faint shouting back the way they had come. Their pursuers had reached the cabin. Shortly after that, the faint glow increased in intensity. Mother Haddie looked back over her shoulder, and her eyes narrowed in response. She turned away without a word and picked up the pace.

The moon now peered above the horizon, waning gibbous but still offering plenty of dim illumination. They hurried into a clearing, and the line of the path could be seen faintly, a lighter thread running on and into the shadows of the foliage on the far side of the short expanse. They were halfway to the tree line when a howl carried overhead. It sounded like a mix of pain and warning.

Mother Haddie pulled them to a halt, eyes lined with worry. "I'm going back to see to Dagger." She raised a hand to silence any objections. "Head straight down that path and you'll come to the river. I'll meet you there. Go now!" She shoved them forward without another word. Jaren looked back once more, just in time to see her disappear into the darkened wall of trees behind.

He turned around too late to stop and bumped into Iselle.

"What's going on? Why did we stop again?" he asked in a hoarse whisper.

Iselle looked at him irritably.

Morgaine was fishing through a pocket. She soon found what she'd been searching for, and now held it clutched tightly in her right hand.

He didn't have to guess to know what it was. Perhaps their time with Mother Haddie had given her new comfort with the talisman.

"You two follow me." Morgaine turned and started down the path again.

Iselle shrugged and fell in behind her. Jaren took up the rear. Morgaine's pace was not as swift as Mother Haddie's had been, but it was hurried enough.

For some time, they rushed along the route through the forest. The trio heard nothing more from behind, and were glad of that, but the overall silence was eerily disquieting. There were none of the usual woodland sounds about whatsoever, but a low murmur built steadily ahead.

It was the sound of rushing water.

13

THE ENEMY FORCES HAD BEEN composed almost entirely of mercenaries hired by agents of Rondul Pacek months ago, or even longer. Other than their orders and the names of the few men who'd hired them, they knew little else. Clearly, the attack on the palace had been orchestrated by someone as yet unknown, with the full cooperation and aid of a group of his father's subjects operating in secret—led by Pacek—most of whom had escaped. Those who hadn't were minor figures and had no information of real importance.

Pacek had fled to the northwest with his compatriots and a sizeable fighting force. He'd managed to escape the inner city via the same secret passage on his estate that had allowed the mercenaries in, then gathered the troops he deployed outside the city proper and hurried off in the direction of the Stahl Pass. Aldrain's blood boiled at the thought of Pacek's successful flight.

It took nearly all of his resolve not to head off at once in pursuit of the rebellious count, and then what little restraint he had left to follow Sonja's advice and, instead, set out to the southwest. Apparently, a former mentor had sent word to her, claiming knowledge of the forces behind the recent events. The message was vague at best, but it was the single, most promising lead he had, especially since nothing he'd gotten from the prisoners helped to fill in the blanks in the least.

Aldrain's horse trod roughly over a patch of road in disrepair, eliciting pain from a number of his wounds, courtesy of the enemy commander. He could almost hear Ordren chastising him for being hasty and for underestimating his opponent. *Hold your ground. Feel him out. Let him make the mistake of impatience, and then strike when you truly hold the advantage.* He shook his head, which brought another twinge of discomfort. Urgency had necessitated the rather reckless assault, he rationalized.

Speaking of time, he'd determined to spend it as sparingly as possible on this fact-finding expedition. Important as it was to find answers, he'd have little enough of substance accomplished when it was complete. Ordren, as head of the military in Aldrain's absence, was

fully capable of tending to matters on his behalf, but with the recent attempted coup, he was less than comfortable being away from his center
of power. *Just as Pacek said, you're shirking your responsibilities again.* But
that was really nonsense, he reasoned, just his conscience still trying to
get the best of him.

"Nothing is more important than finding out who is behind this,"
Ordren had advised. And, hesitations aside, Aldrain knew he agreed
with his large friend, whether he'd admit it to him or not. And, though
Ordren would have gone in Aldrain's place, the new king had ultimately opted to make the journey himself. He had to hear the information
firsthand, to investigate personally in order to make amends of a sort
with his late parents—in particular to his father—to atone for all of
the resistance and lack of cooperation he'd shown in the past. It was
Aldrain's duty to redress his former behavior by seeing justice done on
whoever was to blame for all of this, if such vengeance were even possible now. For it seemed that his enemies were mighty, indeed.

Sonja had warned that powerful forces were involved, perhaps
the darkest of them all: the Deceiver. Aldrain had shuddered at the
thought. *May the True One save us all from that possibility.* The Lord of
Deceit had not interfered directly in the affairs of men for an age. But
Sonja had said it herself: only negative magic had been unleashed; no
one had been able to accomplish that feat for a thousand years. Who
else could be behind the machination of recent events?

"Sire, we should stop for the night." The officer's voice dispelled his
reverie. "The mounts are tiring, as are the men."

Aldrain nodded. "Yes, see to it, then," he allowed, grudgingly.

The man saluted and wheeled about to organize the making of
camp. Soon, the area was abuzz with activity, as his soldiers hurried
to carry out their assigned tasks. Aldrain's mind had shifted back to its
musings when a familiar voice interrupted once again.

"I thought you might ride the horses to their deaths." It was Sonja.
She had insisted on accompanying him, if not to smooth the introduc-
tion, then to aid in the interpretation of her mentor's eccentricities.

"I'm sure it must look that way."

"You've done your father proud, you know," she stated matter-of-
factly.

"Have I?"

"Aldrain, what happened was planned far in advance and would have occurred whether or not you were in attendance at court. As it happens, your actions resulted in the survival of the Draegondor family and its rightful status as the ruling house of Carathon."

"Perhaps if I'd been more willing to learn, my father could have focused fully on matters of state instead of worrying about what was to become of me," he countered.

Sonja pursed her lips. "Did you know that your grandfather had the same issues with your father?"

Aldrain balked. "Please don't patronize me. It has been a trying few days."

"Think what you will. Your father did exactly as you were doing, and until about the same age. Then, your grandfather died suddenly, and he was thrust into the position you now occupy."

Aldrain raised a dubious eyebrow.

"Believe me, Your Majesty, I had an eerily similar conversation with Aldradein Draegondor, albeit in the midst of some decidedly different circumstances, though they were trying in themselves."

She had been around a long while, Sonja Redsteel. Perhaps long enough to indeed be telling him the truth. Right at the moment, however, he was too fatigued to argue the matter further. "He told me not to debate with you about historical events, since you have firsthand knowledge of so many."

She feigned insult. "I will not be mocked for my usefulness. Find me when you've regained the proper respect for your elders." With an overly dramatized toss of her head, Sonja's red hair flashed as she reined her mount and trotted off toward her tent.

Aldrain inspected the camp as the night deepened. The warm, summer days were accompanied by brisk evenings, a sign that fall was not so far off. The crispness of the air magnified the sounds of the few men still laboring, returning sharp echoes. Once the tour was concluded, Aldrain retired to his tent.

It was a long time, however, before sleep found him.

※

Spurred onward by the noise, Jaren and the others broke into a dead run. Tree limbs and branches flew past in a blur as they raced forward, and the sound increased in volume. It had now become the unmistakable, low roar of flowing water.

Nearing the top of a small rise in the path, Morgaine stopped suddenly, putting her arms out to the sides to signal a warning. She then whirled and motioned frantically for them get down and move back.

"Someone's down there," she whispered hoarsely, panting for breath, once they were halfway back down the slope, "at the boat."

Iselle began to crawl toward the lip of the rise, but Morgaine grabbed her wrist and shook her head. Iselle twisted her hand away and, with a look that said she was not to be trifled with, continued on. Morgaine stared hotly after her, but followed a moment later. Jaren, refusing to be left out, crawled up as well. He reached the top and peered warily down to the river.

The trees continued nearly to the bank, though they thinned considerably, allowing for a better glimpse of the surrounding area. The river itself churned and rolled, the moonlight reflecting brightly off of the roiling surface. The boat, a stout vessel that could comfortably seat no more than five people, lay pulled up on the bank to the right of the path. Standing on either side of the trail at the water's edge was a dark figure. They were facing the water, luckily for the three of them, or they'd probably have been spotted already.

Hidden once more behind the rise, they debated their options.

"We can't go back—they're surely still hunting for us. And we don't know where Mother Haddie is," Jaren said.

"But we can't just leave her," Morgaine argued.

"She told us to," Jaren countered.

"Besides," Iselle cut in, "we have no idea where to look. She's probably headed for the *Valir's* tower right now. If we're captured running around here for no good reason, we'll have wasted the chance she gave us to escape."

"You've had it in for her since she set Dagger on you," Morgaine accused. She looked down at her closed fist. "We can handle ourselves."

"So you've spent a day with a healer and become *Valir*?" Iselle said. "Then what have we been doing, running all night?"

"Come on, Morgaine," Jaren added, "you don't know how many are around or even who they are. There might be *Valir* after us."

"Why would *Valir* be chasing us? They're on our side."

"How do we know that?" Iselle demanded. "We don't know anything. All we do know is that the old woman told us to get out of here. It's past time to wait for her. And she was scared herself. Did you see her face when she went back for the dog? If it scares her, we need to be terrified. The fox doesn't go after the hunting dogs, Morgaine."

Morgaine opened her mouth to respond, but Jaren spoke first.

"Look Morgaine, she's right about getting out of here. We need to go."

"What are we going to do about them?" Morgaine hooked a thumb back in the direction of the river.

"Well, two should be no problem for an all-powerful *Valir*," Iselle quipped, her sarcastic edge apparent.

Morgaine advanced on the younger girl, but Jaren stepped between them.

"Iselle, that's enough," Jaren insisted. She nodded and stood silently, tight-lipped, arms crossed. He turned to his sister. "We can sneak up and surprise one of them, Morgaine, but you might have to … can you handle the other?"

"I think so. Yes." Her fierce commitment had lessened, perhaps robbed of its earlier certainty with the realization of what might be required.

It took little time to devise a plan, for there were few options available other than to sneak up as close as possible and then try to subdue the men. Soon, they were doing just that, worming their way ahead on their bellies toward the river and their foes. Iselle and Jaren had taken the left and Morgaine the right side of the path. The two of them would wait for Morgaine to attempt some type of summoning against the first of their adversaries. She had suggested casting him into the river, and Jaren and Iselle had encouraged her to try that first, rather than something more drastic.

They had covered more than three-quarters of the distance and stopped to wait on Morgaine. Not long after, they heard a muffled cry and saw the farthest figure pulled into the air, as if by an invisible rope. The man somersaulted several times, head over heels, before landing with a great splash into the water. He was immediately swept downstream with the current, thrashing and crying out as he was carried along.

Jaren and Iselle launched themselves forward, closing the distance to the remaining man in seconds. He was casting about, looking for the source of the assault while simultaneously trying to watch as his partner was swept farther downstream. At the last moment, he saw them and tried to brace himself, but Iselle leaped for his legs, wrapping her arms about the hollows of his knees, while Jaren jumped for his upper body. He fell back heavily, taken completely off balance.

Morgaine rushed up then, a cord in her hands. Their captive tried to resist, but winded as he was, he struggled to little effect. With Jaren and Iselle taking an arm each, Morgaine soon had his hands tied tightly behind him.

A startled cry from the rise brought all of their heads about in a jerk. Another figure was rushing toward them now. This one carried a long sword, which was drawn free of its scabbard in an instant.

Morgaine sprang up and fumbled for the talisman once more. She found it quickly, raising it before her, though the oncoming assailant was rapidly closing the gap between them. The soldier lowered his head and ran straight toward her, his sword held high. Morgaine closed her eyes and bowed her head in concentration.

Nothing happened.

It would be mere seconds before impact, Jaren knew. Morgaine's head came up in surprise, eyes wide in panic. He could hear the one they'd captured yelling to his comrade, but Jaren ignored the sound. Pulling a short sword from the latter's belt, Jaren rushed forward.

He reached Morgaine just as did the attacker. The soldier quickly redirected the strike originally aimed for his sister's head. It sliced down at an angle toward Jaren. He raised the short blade in reaction. The weapons connected with jarring force and a metallic ring. The blow was too much for Jaren's wrist, and it gave in, allowing the longer blade to continue downward. It bit deeply into his outer thigh, and he screamed in pain, falling to one knee while clutching his injured leg.

Jaren heard another cry, though it sounded far off and faint. His movements seemed slowed, as though he were suspended in water. He looked up to see the man standing over Morgaine, sword raised. Iselle crashed into him, tearing savagely with her hunting knife, though his leather armor and metal ringmail turned the blade aside easily. He grabbed her by the hair roughly and struck her down with the pommel of his sword. Iselle crumbled limply to the ground. He kicked out and caught Morgaine in the midsection, nearly lifting her clear of the ground and onto her back. Two-handed, he raised the sword once more, point downward for a finishing thrust.

Jaren fell forward, trying to crawl to his sister. His limbs felt heavy and useless. The only thing he could do was watch helplessly as the blade hung suspended over Morgaine, about to descend in a killing blow.

Something hurtled into the man from the side. A great, black blur hammered into him, driving the man heavily to the ground. The sword was jarred free of his grasp, clattering noisily to the rocks.

It was Dagger. He latched himself to the man's throat and landed on top of the unfortunate soldier. The great dog gave a few savage tugs back and forth, and his victim's struggles ceased. Their captive screamed in fear and tried frantically to propel himself away, but failed to make any headway, despite all of his thrashing.

Dagger growled threateningly and started toward him.

"No, boy," Jaren called. "Come here."

The large dog limped painfully. His shaggy coat was matted with blood and crossed with numerous wounds. The man began to sob, muttering incoherently.

Jaren used the dog to help pull himself to his knees. Dagger gave a bit of a whine as Jaren unintentionally touched another apparent injury. "You've had a rough night, too, haven't you boy?" The dog nuzzled his face in response, giving a few anxious licks.

Morgaine began to cough, and Iselle stirred. Jaren lurched to his feet, cringing at the resulting pain in his thigh.

"Morgaine, Iselle, come on! We have to go—now!" He pulled Dagger around to look into his muzzle. "Can you go get our things, boy? Go fetch our bags!" Dagger barked and loped away, though still gingerly, back up the path. "Get to the boat!" Jaren urged the others once more.

His sister hauled herself up, staggered to the small craft, and began to fumble with the mooring lines.

He tossed Iselle's hunting knife to her. "Use this."

"What happened?" Iselle called hoarsely, rubbing her bloodied forehead.

"Dagger saved us," Jaren replied. "Now get moving to the boat!" He turned and saw the dog returning, their packs hanging from his great maw. "Good boy!" he called.

"What do we do about him?" Iselle asked, gesturing toward their captive.

"Leave him. We're going to be gone soon enough. And we can't hide the fact that we were here now, anyway," Morgaine said, glancing at the still form of the dead soldier.

They pushed the boat to the water's edge just as Dagger brought up the last of their belongings. He dropped the bags and turned back to face the forest, sniffing. Suddenly, his hackles rose and he growled.

A dark figure strode casually down the slope from the rise. It was clothed in black from head to toe, but the face was starkly pale. Unblinking, ebony eyes fixed them with a look of contempt, and then nonchalantly surveyed the scene. A chill that was not borne on the night breeze settled into them.

"I see you've been rather busy," the figure said matter-of-factly. The unsettling voice carried a hint of amusement that was far from good-natured.

Dagger's low growl switched to a whine.

14

Jaren suddenly realized what the stranger carried loosely in one hand. It was Mother Haddie's head, held by a clump of blood-matted, gray hair. Horrified gasps from nearby told him the others had noticed it, too. Reading their reactions, the being hoisted the grisly thing level with his gaze. "Foolish, old hag—she died rather painfully." It tossed the gruesome trophy aside indifferently.

Dagger moved toward it, and then stopped abruptly, all the while continuing to whine.

"What do you want with us? Why are you doing this?" Morgaine questioned, her voice rising in panic and grief. Her face had gone nearly as pale as the newcomer's.

"I want you, my dear. Your friends are of no consequence. They may leave—or not. It makes no difference to the Mistress or my Master."

"We're not going anywhere without my sister," Jaren warned. He hobbled forward a step and brandished the short sword, wincing in pain with the effort. The sense of foreboding that seemed to ooze from the stranger increased.

"Goodness, lad, you should see a healer." The being tossed a glance to the side, where Mother Haddie's head lay. "Pity there's not one around when you need tending." A wicked grin spread across its face.

Jaren held his ground. "Don't come any closer!"

"I'm afraid you are in no position to make demands. If you step aside now, you and your companion may go. I just want your sister." It took a threatening step toward them. "But if you continue to defy me, I may change my mind. You've already led us on a merry adventure."

Morgaine staggered forward, her clenched fist held out before her in a warding gesture. "Leave us alone. I don't want to hurt you, but I will."

The response was immediate, cold laughter. "Oh, that's priceless. This has been entertaining, but now it's time to be done." The creature raised its head the tiniest degree, and Morgaine fell to her knees. Her hand opened, and the talisman flew to the other, who easily plucked it from the air. "You think you have the ability to harm me? Using this? This worthless trinket?" It laughed again, mockingly.

Jaren got a glimpse of the being's tongue. It was jet black and pointed, gliding slickly over jagged and broken, yellow teeth that were more like fangs. He shuddered.

Iselle joined Jaren, blocking the man's path to Morgaine.

The figure's look of amusement soured. "Enough of this! If you choose death, so be it. My patience is at its end—"

"Hold!" called a strong, clear voice.

All heads turned as one to observe the newest arrival to the fray. Jaren's mind whirled. He'd seen this one before….Then he remembered: the other night! He'd been the one Jaren had glimpsed in the distance—he was sure of it.

The figure advanced, clearing the trees and the last of the brush to stand beside the path. He, too, was dark-clothed, but wore no cloak. His features were normal, but there was still something about him, some feeling, that suggested he, too, was not merely as he appeared. He fixed Jaren and the others with a brief, concerned eye, and then turned to the black-cloaked man.

"You might as well turn and go; your sport is finished for now."

"Ah, the avatar has come, sooner than usual, this time."

"Not soon enough, fiend." He took measure of the pale-faced horror from head to foot, a disgusted scowl curling the corners of his mouth.

"What, this old rag? I just threw it on. Does it suit me?" The pale stranger, too, frowned. "Why go through all of this again? Just let me have the girl, and we'll save a good deal of time and trouble. No one will have their hopes dashed, and things can go on as they should."

Confused looks passed between the trio as they witnessed the exchange.

The newer man's reply was swift. "Nothing will be as it should, so long as you plague the realms, blacktongue!" He rushed forward, unsheathing a blade in the blink of an eye. The stroke continued straight from the scabbard to dispatch his adversary, who collapsed, headless, in a heap.

The warrior stood over the still form for a moment, head down, long, dark hair falling about his face. He returned the blade to its scabbard and knelt, taking a hand of the dead villain and prying it open. Standing, he turned to them and offered an outstretched palm to Morgaine. He nodded to her in encouragement, and she stepped forward, taking back what Jaren assumed was her talisman.

The stranger nodded somberly. "We must be off now. They know I've come, and they'll be better prepared next time."

"Who are you?" Jaren and the others asked, nearly in unison.

"All in good time," he answered. "Now let's get going." Dagger trotted up and licked the man's hand. He smiled and scrubbed the dog's head. "I guess you'll be coming with us." Dagger barked happily in response and bounded about like a puppy, suddenly unaware of his many wounds.

Come to think of it, Jaren's didn't hurt so badly anymore, either.

It was good that it took two day's time to reach the stronghold of Ensin Llaw, as the three youths needed that long for the truth of things to settle in. Their savior, though vague enough on the details, was apparently a servant of the True One, sent to aid them. The other man, the one he'd named the blacktongue, had been a different story. Jaren recognized that name, for it belonged to terrors and fables told to frighten children. That was, until now.

Their guardian introduced himself as Verithael. He'd accepted the shortened, "Ver," though he'd looked quizzically at them when Iselle first suggested it. Regardless, it stuck.

Ver told them much on the journey about the way of things, matters they had thought just a part of aggrandized history or ancient myth, passed down from parents to youngsters throughout the lands of Evarlund. To hear of these things related firsthand by Ver, considering their recent ordeals, was a bit overwhelming. A good many old legends, it seemed, were more than just that. They were real.

After the evening meal the first night, the group settled down to rest. They had picked a small clearing within sight of the river, the roar of the current reduced to a murmur as the watercourse widened. The glow of the campfire added to the surreal atmosphere, a result of the conversation's subject matter.

"So, was that the Deceiver, then?" Iselle had pressed.

"No, more like me, an agent."

"But what did you mean when you said he used…used…what you said back there?" she pressed.

"Usurped. Unlike the power of the True One, the power of the Deceiver is limited. The Deceiver cannot create; he can only use or misuse, to his own ends. Much too often, he tries to interfere in the balance of things. A common method is to send a malevolent spirit to take over one's body and bend it to his will."

"So that poor man wasn't really bad?"

"The Deceiver generally uses people already False Sworn—pledged to him—as they are easier to master. Regardless, once the body is taken, the original spirit dies. That man probably wasn't someone you would have wanted to know. Still, no one deserves that fate."

"I thought *blacktongue* was a folktale name," Jaren said.

"It is, and it isn't," Ver responded. "Many of the things you now take for make-believe or myth have a solid foundation in reality. It just becomes … forgotten after events have passed. It always seems to happen that way. Perhaps it's just as well. People become unsettled when the truth of it is revealed."

"Being chased across the countryside and having a deadman come after you will do that," Iselle said, recalling another of the beings' folklore names.

Ver chuckled.

"Why does he want me?" Morgaine asked. She'd been silent so far throughout most of their conversations. Jaren guessed Mother Haddie's death had deeply touched her. It had affected all of them, in truth, but Ver's presence had helped a lot.

"For the usual reasons, I suspect," Ver answered. "Power, control—things the Deceiver and his minions crave." He glanced at the others singly after he spoke, his face impassive. His dark eyes settled on Jaren.

"So, was the blacktongue taking us to the Deceiver himself, or simply this mistress he also mentioned?" Iselle asked, incredulous.

"Like the True One, the Deceiver works mostly through others, so I suspect you would be taken to another follower, albeit one higher in the ranks of his servants—perhaps this mistress. But, I am not given all the knowledge you seek, young lady, or authority to reveal all that I possess. Mine is a different charge. I can tell you about the nature of the struggle. The particulars, you'll have to figure out on your own."

"That's not much help," Iselle shot back. Jaren elbowed her.

Ver simply smiled and chuckled anew. "The True One doesn't want to interfere more than is absolutely necessary. You have to find the answers for yourselves. I'm just here for a while to help you on your way, while the odds are stacked against you."

"That's not encouraging, either. So, you could just disappear if you feel we're no longer at a disadvantage?" She got another elbow. This time, Iselle returned the favor. "Jaren Haldannon, you cut that out. I'll ask whatever questions I want. I'm not altogether happy about being caught up in what amounts to a pieces match between good and evil." She glared at Ver. "Why don't you just go and wipe them all out? You said yourself, the True One has unlimited power."

Jaren gaped at her, astonished at the girl's brazen words.

Again, Ver merely smiled. "I wish it were that simple, young one. I truly do. But, while the Deceiver's power is more limited, it is potent nonetheless. As long as he has people willing to sacrifice themselves for him, willing to take up his twisted cause, he cannot be utterly defeated."

Iselle appeared ready to continue her inquisition, but seemed at a loss for anything further to add. She settled on poking a sharp stick into the fire, stirring up the embers. She was in a mood, and Jaren thought it best to keep his distance for the rest of the journey, and from Morgaine, as well, for that matter. She was in a funk also. It was just like girls, he grumbled silently to himself, to store up their frustrations and then let loose the pent-up wrath whenever you said something that displeased them. Since he didn't feel particularly comfortable yet talking to Ver, Jaren spent a good deal of time in silence, mulling things over.

At least he had Dagger to keep him company. Listening absently to the murmur of the water and the crackling of the fire, he reached down and scrubbed the great hound's ears.

15

THE JOURNEY WORE ON GRATINGLY, until finally, their small craft rounded a bend in the river, and there, through breaks in the screening canopy of trees, the imposing structure that was Ensin Llaw's tower appeared. The white, marble edifice towered above the mixed-growth forest surrounding it, and it appeared to be very near the banks of the river itself. Still, it took an agonizing amount of time to reach the place, Jaren was bitterly aware, because as the river widened, the current became much gentler and the waters now meandered serpentine through the wilderness.

Ver guided the boat toward a stone pier that eventually materialized downstream, extending out into the water from the northern bank. The pier itself was the offshoot of a rectangular structure stretching forth from the base of the tower. A crenellated rampart encircled the entire grounds.

An overweight, balding man, dressed in a green robe cinched with a length of leather cord, hailed them as they approached.

"Greetings," he offered, "and welcome to the home of Master Llaw. I am Geldon. I will escort you."

"You've been expecting us?" Iselle asked.

"Not exactly, but … yes," he replied.

"He's been taking lessons from you, Morgaine," Iselle said dryly.

Morgaine seemed not to have heard. She was staring breathlessly at the impressive building before them. Down the length of the pier, a darkened opening beckoned.

The servant helped them disembark, placing all of their belongings onto a wheeled cart. As soon as everything was placed upon it, the cart headed off unaided along the pier to the entrance. The trio glanced about at each other, and Dagger cocked his head to the side, uttering a surprised bark. Soon, he was scampering behind the strange vehicle, nipping lightly at the rear wheels. He stopped, however, and looked back at them with bright eyes and an excitedly wagging tail as the cart continued on into the darkened entrance.

Ver scanned the woods to either side, his expressionless face unreadable.

"If you would please follow me," the green-clad escort requested.

Morgaine was the first to oblige him, with Jaren and Iselle following next. Ver brought up the rear. Once they reached the great dog, Dagger padded in behind, assuming his usual lope.

Jaren had felt gradually better as their journey drew on. In fact, all of his injuries appeared healed, even his deep gash received from the warrior's blade. The others, too, seemed in perfect health, if not in good spirits. It must have something to do with Ver, Jaren guessed. He made up his mind to ask the avatar about it, sometime.

The entry chamber was dimly lit by ensconced torches set at intervals along the smooth, stone walls, which were lined with a number of finely woven tapestries. Soon, the murmur of the water was lost as they traveled farther into the stronghold. Above, the ceiling was hidden in shadow.

Even within this unfamiliar and imposing building, Jaren did not feel the least bit wary. He attributed that to Ver's presence, as well. It seemed to have a calming effect. *Perhaps I should mention that to the girls*, he considered silently. He glanced at Morgaine, who returned his slight grin with a disapproving half-frown. Iselle, too, raised an impatient eyebrow at his unspoken amusement. Maybe you had to be willing to let it calm you. He decided to keep the suggestion to himself for the time being.

They soon came to a heavy door. It swung open with a whisper on their approach. A formal antechamber greeted them within, wood-paneled and carpeted. Immense paintings hung along the walls, and rows of great, wooden bookshelves stood to their left and right, filled with massive, leather-bound tomes beyond count. Directly ahead was an immense table, surrounded by a dozen chairs. Its polished surface reflected the torchlight evenly. The room smelled odd to Jaren. He supposed it was the books. He'd never seen more than one or two in the same place before.

"Master Llaw wishes for you to await him here. I will bring refreshments shortly." Geldon left without another word, disappearing between two of the monolithic bookshelves. The three companions seated themselves, and Dagger lay down not far from the table on a particularly plush, seldom-tread patch of carpet. Ver stood motionless by one of the nearer shelves, in silent contemplation. He appeared to be staring straight through the several massive volumes of history, as if recalling firsthand memories of what was written therein.

Jaren supposed he was. Ver had probably witnessed personally whatever it was, if it had been important enough to be recorded in the first place. Or, perhaps he knew of it innately, being connected so intricately with the unfathomable power of the True One. He shifted uneasily, the thought making him uncomfortable. He supposed he had less to worry about than Iselle, however, as she'd been in enough trouble for the both of them in her short span of years. He glanced at her. She probably wouldn't care. Others' opinions didn't seem to bother her much at all.

Iselle winked, though her flat look remained. Jaren realized he'd been staring at her, unwittingly. At least she hadn't scowled this time. Maybe Ver's presence was having an effect on her demeanor after all.

"A motley lot you are, for sure." The distinguished voice startled them. It didn't sound like it belonged to a frail, old man, as Jaren had imagined. They turned to observe their host, and stood out of respect. His absent gazing momentarily interrupted, Ver acknowledged their host as well. The avatar remained by the bookcase, rather than moving to the table with the others.

Except for the flowing, white hair and a few creases lining his face, the man did not appear as old as he surely was. Indeed, he strode to the table as if he were a hale, young man of fewer than thirty summers.

"Forgive me, but I haven't introduced myself properly. I am Ensin Gaige Llaw, former advisor to the house of Cyrdannon, the ruling family of Ergothan." He bowed deeply, sweeping one hand in a graceful arc before him. Straightening, he continued. "I may not know your names, but I know something of you—except for your studious friend over there." His forehead creased slightly, as he seemed to study Ver before he went on.

Ver did not move from his place, or offer a response, but at least he paid their guest his attention.

The *Valir's* eyes found the dog. "Well, well. Dagger, I haven't seen you in quite some time." The dog raised his head from the large paws on which it rested, and he wagged his tail but did not move. "Never was all that fond of me," Llaw confessed, with a shrug.

"He can be like that," Iselle said.

"Yes, quite," Llaw replied with a laugh, though his smile faded quickly. "Since I don't recall ever seeing him without his owner, can I assume the worst for her?"

After an awkward silence, several hesitant nods confirmed his hunch.

"I see. That is distressing, to say the least. Mother Haddie was a good woman, and the best healer I have ever known. Her talents will be missed in this world." He glanced down at his left arm and worked his hand open and closed a few times, palm up. A look akin to regret came over him.

"I had news that she was bringing someone to see me, but that was about it. Which of you would that be?"

Iselle gestured in Morgaine's direction. "You can't tell?"

Llaw raised an eyebrow. "Hmmm. Yes. Well, usually I can, but lately ... things seem to be out of sorts. I can sense a great deal of potential from someone here ... and, perhaps something else, but it's like nothing I've come across before." He glanced briefly again at Ver. The three young newcomers exchanged anxious looks. "So," Llaw continued, "if you are the one I was meant to see, then you have a talisman?"

Morgaine nodded. "I keep it here in a pouch." She patted her hip lightly.

"A pouch, eh?" He chuckled in amusement for a moment, then composed himself. "I apologize, but it has been some time since I've been around a student. I had forgotten how ... quaint ... one's habits often are in the beginning."

Morgaine was oblivious to anything the man said after *student*. Her eyes had gone as big as saucers and had a faraway look of awe. Jaren found himself biting his lip.

Llaw turned to eye Iselle and Jaren. "If she is to see me, what is your purpose here?"

"He's her brother, and I'm here to keep them both out of trouble," Iselle informed him.

"I'll bet you are well suited to that role," Llaw countered glibly. "And you, my friend, what is your business with these young ones?" Ver had begun alternately observing the discussion and the volumes on the shelves. Llaw fixed him with an especially attentive eye.

"I came across the three of them in the woods. I thought I'd help out, in case the young lady had any difficulties fulfilling her self-sworn duty as protector."

The *Valir* studied him for some time. "You just happened across them and decided to lend your aid? That is most gallant of you, sir. Not many would be so valiant."

"Not many are like me."

"No, I don't suppose so." Llaw inhaled sharply, tapping a finger to his lips as if determined to continue his questioning, but then apparently thought better of it. "In times like these, such unwarranted benevolence is a rarity. I'm sure these three are most appreciative of your concern, especially since Mother Haddie is no longer able to guide them." He peered steadily at Ver's stoic face for a moment longer, as if attempting to read for any hint of reaction. As far as Jaren could tell, a stone would have given more of a hint. Llaw's barely discernible scowl indicated he'd gotten the same impression.

Dismissing the silent duel of wills between them, the *Valir* turned his attention back to the three waiting anxiously before him.

"Ah, but I've troubled you enough for the time being. You must be hungry after your travels. Please, join me at table."

Geldon appeared as if on cue, bearing a silver tray that held a crystal pitcher and glasses. They were each given one and then ushered into an adjoining dining room. The long, carved wooden table was set for a feast. Jaren's mouth began to water as he caught the wonderful aroma of the various dishes, and upon seeing it, had to keep himself from bolting straight for the table. As with the books in the antechamber, he'd not seen so many different foods together at a single setting. Indeed, most of the dishes he'd never encountered before, period. He decided that wouldn't keep him from trying them all.

They ate heartily, listening to Llaw's tales about his exploits while in service to the king of Ergothan. His tales were filled with intrigue, danger, and a good measure of mirth, and the three from Dal Farrow were held spellbound. At one point, however, Jaren noticed Ver sitting quietly, his face impassive, distant eyes staring past the walls of the dining room, to events or times past. Jaren couldn't help but wonder if the avatar had an idea of what was in store for all of them.

16

"THEY ARE GAINING ON US, Your Majesty."

Aldrain muttered a curse that was lost to the cutting wind. The driving rain stung his face.

Two days ago, they had spotted a small army in pursuit. The enemy materialized seemingly out of nowhere, and pressed on after his much smaller troop in an obvious effort to overtake them. At an estimated three-to-one ratio, Aldrain's force stood little chance in a pitched battle. So, they had fled before the larger company, making for the *Valir's* stronghold with all haste. Their efforts had proven fruitless. The foe gained steadily.

How was the enemy doing it? His own men had gone without sleep virtually since the enemy was sighted, stopping only to rest the horses enough to keep them alive and able to continue. Yet, some power seemed to energize their pursuers while simultaneously hindering his force. Half a dozen mounts had thrown shoes, and several had stumbled badly on the rain-slicked, rocky inclines they now traversed, and needed to be put down. Every instance caused them more delay and brought the foe that much closer.

Never in his life had Aldrain witnessed a string of misfortune like this! What more would they be forced to endure?

"How far to the tower?" he questioned the scout.

"Another day, perhaps less if the weather clears, my liege."

"And until they overtake us?"

"Half that, Your Majesty."

"Perhaps we could take to the river?" Sonja suggested.

"We'd be fighting the current. Besides, it would take more than the time we have to construct the watercraft we'd need." Aldrain dismissed the scout. "Lieutenant Bregand, have the men stop to rest the horses."

"At once, Your Majesty."

"Can we afford the time?" Sonja pressed.

"It matters little. We have to stop or risk losing more mounts. Either way, I don't see how we can escape this lot, short of a diversion."

The *Valir* breathed deeply, eyes searching the sky above. "I'll stay behind and delay them."

Aldrain responded immediately. "No. I can't risk losing you. Right now, you're the only magic we've got. We may need you to defend against whatever power seems to be aiding them."

"I think the time for that defense has come," Sonja said.

"No ... not yet."

"Have you another idea?"

"No, but ..." Aldrain cursed again. "How can this be? We're thwarted at every move!"

"Your enemies have been at counsel for much longer than we thought, it seems. They have planned well," the *Valir* said, frowning.

Aldrain's expression steeled. "We will stand and fight. With you to aid us, we can surely overcome the odds."

"We have no guarantee they are not equally supported—or more so. At this distance, I can tell only that they have some substantial magic with them. Alone, I'll be able to find out what exact manner that is, whether *Valir* or in another form."

"Then I'll leave you with a personal guard."

"They would only make it more difficult to hide. I can't cloak others easily if I don't know what I'm shielding them from. Aldrain, I have to do this by myself."

Aldrain was silent for some moments, and then shrugged helplessly. "It seems we are left with no other choice." Looking squarely into her eyes, he continued. "But this is my command: do only what is absolutely necessary. Take no untoward risks. And flee as soon as you've finished. Have I made myself clear?"

It was Sonja's turn to pause. A smile slowly lit her face. "You are your father's son. I hear, Your Majesty, and will obey." But she, too, offered a final word. "Now, if you would listen to my counsel, do not stop from this point on, no matter how many mounts or men you must leave behind. Your safe arrival and the answers that await you are more important than anything or anyone else. You are house Draegondor now. If you are lost, then so is your family's legacy. And chaos will surely follow."

Aldrain nodded, but no further words would come at the moment. Sonja nudged her mount to the edge of the path along which they traveled, then reined in and turned in the saddle to face Aldrain once more.

"Speak the Truth. Suffer no deception," she said.

"I hear the Truth and serve it," he responded. Then she was gone, melting into the woods and the misty gray of the late afternoon rains.

※

A servant set about clearing away the dishes as the guests settled deeper into their comfortably padded chairs, listening to the tales spun by the master of the tower. Suddenly, another hireling rushed to Llaw's side. He bent and whispered urgently into the *Valir's* ear. Concern immediately shadowed Llaw's face.

"Get word to Hronin. Tell him to assemble his men." The servant disappeared in a rush. Llaw turned apologetically to his guests. "I must excuse myself. It appears we have other company. Quaelin here will escort you to your rooms."

Llaw rose and hurriedly exited. Quaelin, a rather tall and gangly fellow, with bowl-cut black hair, bowed and gestured for them to follow. He led them down a few twisting corridors and up a good many flights of stairs, then stopped between polished doors that faced each other across a short, marble-floored hallway. At its termination was a set of ornately fashioned glass doors, opening onto a railed balcony.

"These rooms are yours to use. You may come and go at your leisure." Noticing their interest in the balcony, he added, "The terrace lends a view of the lands to the south. It provides a splendid view of the sunrise over the waters of the Marthuin. If you wish for anything, please pull on the cords you'll find next to your beds. I will attend shortly." Again he bowed, taking his leave.

Iselle ignored the rooms for the time being and headed down the hallway to the glass portals. Morgaine, Jaren, and then Ver followed suit. Dagger simply curled up on a nearby rug.

Beyond the doors, the crisp night waited. The afternoon rain had transformed into a clinging mist with a cool, wet touch. The moon shone faintly through an overcast sky, allowing some light to reach the forested lands below. Approaching in a single-file line were points of illumination—torches—their light glowing faintly through the chill fog. They had nearly reached the tower's battlements. Barely visible on the rampart below stood several shadowy forms.

Jaren heard someone call out, but the specific words were lost to the echoes and their height. The voice held an authoritative tone, however—a challenge to the newcomers, most likely. The call was answered by an even weaker echo, though traces of urgency seemed to carry upon it.

After several minutes of this back and forth, they heard a low, grating noise. Torchlight leaked through a widening, vertical slash beneath the figures on the wall. A gateway: it was opening to admit the newly arrived company. They filed in, the clatter of hooves on paving stones rising sharply up to their place of observation. A number of the horses bore more than one rider.

"Who do you think it is?" Iselle wondered.

"Someone the *Valir* trusts," Ver responded. The others turned toward his voice. It was very nearly the only thing he'd said all evening. He shrugged and left, heading for the rooms.

The three watched the riders dismount and begin to offload some of their baggage, but nothing much of note could be gathered from their vantage point. Weariness overcame curiosity and they retired to their chambers. They found their baggage neatly arranged in the rooms, Morgaine's and Iselle's in one and Jaren's in the other. Ver had nothing, save his sword. It never left his side.

As excited as Jaren was to learn more about the recent arrivals, he still had not caught up on the sleep lost to their travels. He undressed and in moments was slumbering deeply beneath the warm blankets of the luxurious bed.

Ver watched him for some time, and then readjusted his position in the chair. Steepled fingers pressed to his lips, he closed his eyes and rested in his own fashion.

When Jaren awoke, Ver was nowhere to be seen. Jaren dressed hurriedly and exited the room. No answer came from the girls' chambers, so he assumed they, too, had risen earlier. It took long moments for Jaren to navigate his way to the great anteroom where they had first met Ensin Llaw.

A lone figure sat at the dining table, eating the last few morsels from a bone-white plate. He was older than Jaren, perhaps five years or more. His blonde hair, cut to jaw length, was disheveled but still managed to look dignified, and his clothes, while somewhat tattered and worn, were clearly fine garments. His shirt was grey silk, and his trousers dark blue, tucked into high leather boots that bore numerous scuffs. It took only a moment for him to notice Jaren, and he rose in greeting.

"Your master has been most accommodating. Please give him my thanks."

Jaren was about to offer a protest, but the man continued.

"Might you know where I can find *Valir* Llaw? I have some important business to discuss with him."

Jaren shook his head. "No, I don't really know where he is. But I'm—"

"Sorry to interrupt, my lad, but could you go and tell him I wish an audience? It really is of the utmost importance that I see him without delay."

"I have no idea where he is. Or even where to look. As I was about to say—"

The other waved him off. "Very well. When you *do* manage to find him, please convey my message, and my gratitude." He looked a little put off, but, to his credit, he did not scold Jaren. He was obviously a nobleman, and most people of noble lineage, Jaren believed, would tear into you on a whim, even those very distantly down the noble line, like the several families in Dal Farrow with ancient ties to the higher blood.

Jaren nodded his appreciation. "I'll do just that."

After another quizzical glance, the man excused himself and left the room. Jaren sat down and helped himself to several servings from the still-laden platters. He found his voracious appetite had not been quelled by the previous evening's feast after all.

Jaren eventually found the others outside on the grass, enjoying the return of the sunshine. Morgaine was apparently practicing with her talisman, off by herself in a quiet corner of the garden. Iselle, surprisingly enough, was playing with Dagger. Jaren watched as she tossed a stick and the huge dog bounded after it, returning joyfully, his tail wagging in appreciation. Considering Iselle's earliest experiences with the dog, it was a curious development. Ver was nearby, apparently not focused on anything in particular, his eyes staring off in that distant way Jaren had come to expect from him. Regardless, Jaren would bet there was nothing occurring of which the avatar was not aware.

"I met one of the men who arrived last night," Jaren said.

Iselle glanced at him after another toss of the stick. "Who?"

"I don't know. A noble, I think."

She frowned. "It doesn't matter where you go, those better-than-everyone-else fops aren't far away."

"And some are even nearer than you might think."

Their eyes went wide as they turned to see the man Jaren had met at breakfast, standing a dozen yards away, smiling roguishly.

Seeing their alarm, he offered a conciliatory wave. "No harm done. Besides, your description fits a majority of the highborn I know. Furthermore, I must apologize to you," he bowed his head to Jaren, "as I obviously mistook you for a servant. My name is Aldrain Draegondor, at your service."

Jaren had heard that name before. Then it struck him, and he exchanged even wider-eyed looks with Iselle. This was no mere noble; it was the prince of Carathon!

Again, he read their discomfort. "Might I know your names, fellow travelers?"

Iselle, red-faced, said nothing.

Jaren couldn't remember ever seeing Iselle flushed with embarrassment before. "I … my name is Jaren … Jaren Haldannon … Your Highness. This is my friend, Iselle Breit. My sister, Morgaine, is over there." He nodded in her direction. Then, he motioned toward the avatar. "That's Ver, a new companion of ours, and a good friend."

"Well met, Jaren Haldannon. And to you also, Iselle Breit. Tell me, now that I know you aren't servants here, have you seen *Valir* Llaw? I still would very much like to speak with him."

"He should be back shortly," Your Highness. Morgaine had finished with her practicing and approached. "He was giving me a few things to work on and then was called away suddenly."

"You are an apprentice, then?"

It was Morgaine's turn to blush. "Not really … at least, not yet. I was only recently tested, Your Highness."

Morgaine was gazing at Aldrain with an adoring look on her face. She acted like that only sparingly, as when she was admiring Dakken Halburg, back home—she and all the other girls in Dal Farrow, for that matter. Jaren scowled.

Iselle cleared her throat.

"It … it's a very long story. I'm sure you haven't time for such things, Your Highness," Morgaine lowered her gaze.

"Come, now, I enjoy a good adventure story as much as the next fellow. And, by the sound and look of it, you three, or four," he glanced at Ver, "have had quite a journey getting here." His eyes filled with sadness for an instant. "So have we all."

A new voice joined the mix. "I am confident in stating that your separate experiences may share a common thread." It was Ensin Llaw.

All eyes, except for those of the avatar, studied the *Valir*.

"I will explain everything momentarily. I see you've introduced yourselves, but the three of you may not yet know something of our recently arrived, esteemed guest. You now speak with the newly crowned King of Carathon, Aldrain Draegondor."

Their host ushered them back to the comfort of the anteroom, and they seated themselves at the table. "Since I have every reason to believe that your destinies are linked, I will relate what I know of all of your experiences, those you've either told me or I have learned through my own means. Is this acceptable?" Everyone nodded. Llaw then proceeded to inform the Dal Farrow companions of Aldrain's ordeal, much of it gleaned from corresponding with Sonja, it appeared to the king. Llaw then related the events of the others' journey. Most of this information he had gathered during meals and conversations they had shared since arriving.

Finally, he addressed the next topic of discussion, their shared plight. None of them were interested in food at the moment, though their stomachs grumbled in protest, so they declined his offer to break for a proper lunch, and Llaw continued.

"We are, all of us, in grave danger." His dark eyes swept over each person, reinforcing the impact of his words. "Every nation, from Jamnar in the north to Vetia in the south, from Carathon to Parcea, east to west: this new weapon has power like nothing that has existed for a millennium, for at least a thousand years or more. It first came to my attention when I heard rumors of strange happenings on the islands to the northeast. At first, they seemed wild ravings or the product of overactive and superstitious minds, the ramblings of drunken sailors or paranoid merchantmen. But, the signs became too frequent, and all too similar. Then, I learned of the royal palace's destruction in Eidara, and I was certain my greatest fears stood confirmed. I believe we face the threat of *An'Valir*."

17

SONJA RAN ON DESPERATELY, HOPELESSLY, delirious with fright and fatigue. It was out there—stalking her. Never in her life had she been so afraid, so mortally terrified. She wished she'd remained with Aldrain. Then she might have had a chance.

Her ankle buckled and Sonja collapsed heavily. She rolled to a halt on the unyielding earth and laid still, near exhaustion, her ears straining the sounds of pursuit. Wildly, she cast her gaze about, her green eyes flitting here and there in panic. The forest was eerily quiet. No breath of wind stirred, no tree limb moved. The humid air tried to drown her lungs, and she was soaked with sweat. Evergreen needles and other debris covered her, itching and scratching, matting her hair into clumps.

A twig snapped nearby, and she jumped at the sound. Scrambling with every last ounce of strength she possessed, Sonja regained her feet and plunged ahead once more through the undergrowth.

She had known the two *Valir* she'd killed, one very well and the other by casual acquaintance. The former had been under her supervision in Eidara. Only the True One knew how long he'd been leaking information to the enemy. That betrayal fueled her rage, as did the knowledge that one so close had been so obviously instrumental in the deaths of Aldrain's parents, and a good many others, besides. She found new vitality in her anger and pushed on.

Get to the river, she commanded herself. *It's your only chance!*

The other *Valir* had been a liaison between the guild in Jamnar and her company in Eidara. Sonja had only met the woman on a few occasions. She had appeared good-natured and amicable enough, but Sonja now realized that had been part of the ruse. So many things were not what they had appeared.

The hand of the Deceiver was clearly in play. And he had recruited many servants.

A faint sound reached her ears. The thumping of her heartbeat made it hard to discern at first, but it became louder with each passing step: the faint rush of moving water. Indeed, through a break in the trees ahead, she saw the bright reflection of sunlight on the river's surface. She spurred herself forward once more, determined to reach the saving water.

Just a little more, she urged her aching body onward.

Ever so slowly, it seemed, the forest receded and scant yards remained. Jagged rocks pierced the roiling surface of the water, but she would gladly take her chances with them in place of the unnatural horror that hunted her. Just a few more strides would bring her past the last, lone tree, a great, gnarled oak. She could almost feel the cool, exhilarating rush of the water, the freedom of floating downriver to safety—to life.

A tall shadow detached from the twisted trunk. Sonja tried hard to stop, but her footing gave out. Her trembling legs slid from beneath her on the slick ground. She found herself on her back, staring up at the figure.

A low moan escaped her lips.

The black form reached down to clutch the front of her tunic. It hauled her up as though she weighed no more than a child's rag doll. Sonja kicked her feet futilely, suspended as they were above the ground.

"Out for a swim?" grated the voice. A black, pointed tongue lolled from the being's mouth. "I suppose with all that running, you could use a good douse. Sorry to spoil your fun."

The blacktongue pulled her close, so close she could smell its foul reek, feel its hot breath on her face. She turned her head.

"It's not that horrible, is it, pretty one? To be near to one of us?" It chuckled wickedly. "Just say the words, and you can join us. Save yourself the pain and grief."

Sonja cringed and tried to pull away, but the inhuman grip was like iron.

"Would it be that terrible to serve him? No, think on it. Far worse would be to refuse."

"I swear on the Truth, you'll fail. Aldrain will find a way to defeat you, you and your Master." She spat the words.

Mirthless laughter was the response. "So be it, pretty one. If you will not serve…" the black tongue inched closer to her face, and she turned away once more. It caressed her cheek, and her head spun with the touch of the poisonous venom, nausea flooding through her instantly. "You will join the others in death."

"I trust you can tell us more than simply that," Aldrain snapped, scowling. "Sonja had guessed as much."

"But did she know the location of this enemy? Or who it might be?" Llaw countered.

Aldrain shook his head.

"Or what she may have had planned for young Morgaine, here?" the *Valir* added.

Jaren turned to his sister in alarm.

Aldrain looked down at the table. "I apologize. It's just that … you know yourself what we've all been through. I just need answers."

"And so you shall have them, to an extent." Llaw cleared his throat. "It seems a powerful and ambitious *Valir* set out from the coast of Jamnar some years ago, headed to the northeast and the islands that lay beyond. She wasn't heard from until recently, just before all of this began. I, personally, and several brothers and sisters, received a summons to an audience with her. Understandably, we were cautious and, after a hurried counsel, sent our own emissary to reply that she instead meet with us on the mainland. We never heard back."

"Yes, that black man said something about a mistress. But what does that have to do with us?" Iselle demanded. "We're nothing special. What would someone that far away want with farmers and common folk?" All eyes turned to her, and she snapped her mouth closed in response to the scowls directed her way. "You two were thinking the same thing," she accused Jaren and Morgaine, before crossing her arms in a huff.

"Didn't you say that the woman was *Valir*?" Aldrain asked.

"Yes." Llaw replied.

The king went on. "Then what's all this about *An'Valir*? Don't you have to be born with that ability?"

Llaw nodded. "According to everything we know, yes. But I suspect, somehow, that she has discovered a way to circumvent the natural laws and wield power similar to *An'Valir*. Perhaps that's what led her off in the first place."

"That's not supposed to be possible," Aldrain said flatly.

The *Valir* shrugged off the denial. "Regardless of what I have been taught, what even the most studied of my peers has learned, we are clearly dealing with something on a scale far beyond anything known in over a thousand years. It must be either *An'Valir* or an equally empowered individual. That's the only explanation that fits. Whether or not we name it thus, we must deal with the threat accordingly."

"But what about us? What could we possibly have to do with this?" It was Jaren this time. "We're just farmers from Dal Farrow." He never imagined he'd have spoken those words so earnestly.

Llaw continued, "That's simple. Your sister has great potential. This woman is probably trying to recruit—by deceit, threat, or force—a number of *Valir* or potential *Valir*. I suspect that's why I and my colleagues received invitations. Morgaine would be a perfect specimen, because of the latent ability she possesses. Added to that is the fact that your sister is young and impressionable, and has not yet learned to master her abilities. She could be more easily molded to another's designs."

"You mentioned something about the woman's name?" Aldrain looked truly weary.

Llaw gave another solemn nod. "Not her name so much as the title she's assumed. It's descended from a group of Jamnite *Valir*, a society of women who became a sort of fighting summoner, able to combine their magic with conventional weapons training. They became quite powerful and, so it was said, overly ambitious. The sect supposedly perished centuries ago, during the Jamnite civil wars they helped incite." Llaw fixed them with a level stare. "She calls herself the Warwitch."

The name meant nothing to the four of them, but Ver sat back and sighed. He offered no explanation, remaining out of the conversation, with arms crossed, his face inscrutable.

"So, the question remains, what to do now?" the king of Carathon mused aloud.

"What, indeed," Ensin Llaw echoed.

"Wasn't the last *An'Valir* defeated by an alliance of summoners?" Aldrain looked anxiously toward Llaw. "If the guild did the same once again, you could defeat her, couldn't you?"

"The annals I've seen," the *Valir* replied, "record just a handful of references to that time and the victory over Ravien Elluminara—supposedly the last An'Valir—but I am not convinced there wasn't more to it than what is written. And, besides, every single member of that fellowship perished in the conflict. I'm not above dying for the right cause, mind you," he looked suddenly uncomfortable, "but I know for a fact that several of my peers, the more powerful of them, anyway, are very unlikely to submit to such an undertaking—especially without certainty of success." He shrugged apologetically. "I'm afraid there were more *Valir* in the days of yore, and apparently a greater number with the selfless character that is accorded them in the histories."

"I know one with that kind of spirit. And I will not believe she alone among your number possesses that inner strength," Aldrain said.

Llaw nodded. "Perhaps not. But I fear time is running out. I have sent word to my brothers and sisters about this, requesting another counsel. I pray to the Truth that it will not go unheeded."

Aldrain rose. "I need to decide on my own course of action. You are all invited to accompany me, wherever I am headed. Perhaps together we stand a better chance of surviving this threat. I will inform you of my option as soon as I have decided." He wheeled and strode from the room.

It was long after the sound of his receding footfalls had ceased before anyone spoke. They really hadn't thought that far ahead, Jaren admitted silently. What were they going to do, knowing what they now did? He turned to Ver.

"What do you think we should do?"

"That is not for me to decide." He glanced at Ensin Llaw blankly.

"Ver," Jaren coaxed, "we need some help."

Ver retained his reluctant air. "Regardless," he repeated, "I cannot interfere directly in the course of events. Mine is a guardianship only."

Llaw gaped at Ver, the *Valir's* expression a combination of dawning recognition and new respect.

The avatar refused to comment further, though Morgaine and Iselle started in.

"Don't you think telling us about all the things you know is protecting us?" Morgaine pressed.

"What kind of guardian keeps such secrets?" demanded Iselle.

Ver remained silent, unyielding.

Llaw tore his gaze from Ver and focused on Morgaine. "It is more important, now than ever, for you to develop control and discipline over your gift," he explained, "as you will continue to be targeted by the Witch and other dark minions."

Morgaine nodded, though reluctantly. She remained silent, however.

"Time is of the essence, no matter what course of action we determine," Llaw added, "and the better able you are to properly wield magic, the higher your chances of survival." He briefly scanned Jaren's and Iselle's faces before continuing. "And, of those closest to you." With that, he nodded once more and excused himself. He cast a sidelong glance at Ver as he went, shaking his head and muttering something to himself that was incomprehensible to the others, though they clearly heard his disbelieving chortle.

※

Morgaine spent several sessions over the course of the afternoon and evening with Llaw, and her frame of mind improved gradually. She seemed to be moving past the death of Mother Haddie more easily with the adoption of a new mentor. As her spirits steadily rose, however, Jaren's sank. He hadn't warranted so much as a mention in the scheme of things. It was the most telling blow yet. If Ensin Llaw, a *Valir* of high standing, could sense no potential in him, he was compelled to face the reality that he truly did not possess the ability to summon.

Mother Haddie's death seemed to bother Jaren more now, especially because after their last conversation, his thoughts of her had been so negative and condemning. She had simply been trying to help, to show him the truth and save him from the bitter disappointment of chasing a dream that could not possibly come to pass. He became so miserable and sullen that even Iselle avoided him for the rest of the day.

"You look lost." Morgaine had approached unnoticed, as Jaren navigated the swirling thoughts of bitter disappointment and hopeless desire that warred in his mind.

"I was thinking, that's all," he said.

"I know this can't be easy for you," she began, "but I'll try to help as much as I can."

There she went, trying in her own way to fix what couldn't be mended. Jaren shook his head. "No, it's okay, really." He didn't feel like talking. "I just need some time to figure things out."

"Well, let me know if you need someone to listen. I'm here."

That's the problem Gainey, you're always there, even when I want to make my own way. He wanted to tell her that, but he was afraid how it might come out in his current state of mind. Instead, he just nodded. "Thanks. I'll keep that in mind."

Morgaine put an arm on his shoulder and smiled warmly. It was all he could do not to recoil from her touch. She was apparently still too absorbed in her own circumstances to hear the noncommittal tone in his voice. *Good*, he thought, *we won't have to continue this talk.*

"Just remember, Jaren. I'm here for you." She patted his shoulder, rose, and left.

Jaren sat by himself in the garden for some time, watching the shadows lengthen and finally melt into the greater darkness of night, until he was asked to attend once more to the anteroom. Within, he found Aldrain, looking more than a little flustered, and the others, including Ver. Apparently Ensin Llaw had already begun speaking. Perhaps that was the cause of Aldrain's dismay.

"How long until they are here?" the king questioned impatiently.

"Their scouts and a small, advance guard are already nearing positions just beyond the walls. The main force should arrive sometime before dawn," Llaw responded.

"Is there any other way out?"

"Only the river, but I'm sure they will have posted sentries to detect any attempt to reach it."

"Of course," Aldrain reasoned, "they wouldn't have shown themselves before cutting off all routes of escape. There is no other way?"

Llaw shook his head.

"Who are they?" Jaren asked. The others fixed him with impatient stares.

"An army of the Warwitch," Iselle informed him pointedly. "If you'd come earlier instead of moping about, you'd know that already." All attention focused back on Llaw and Aldrain.

Jaren's face reddened.

"How many in total?" asked the king.

"I would estimate almost five hundred, give or take."

Aldrain laughed bitterly. "Not good odds."

"This tower was constructed by potent *Valir* in an age long gone. It is formed into one solid mass of stone and warded to withstand all but the most powerful magic. It has withstood assault and siege before. We should be safe here for the time being."

"I would not count on that." Aldrain's fierce eyes took on a haunted look. "I've seen what the Witch's magic can do to stone. We should leave at once."

⌘

With the arrival of the enemy came a request for parley. So it was that Ensin Llaw, Aldrain, and the others stood upon the battlements between the main gate turrets and awaited the approach of their adversary's mission.

"Please, let either Valir Llaw or me address them," Aldrain advised. "I do not doubt this enemy has wile and means to make one share more than is prudent."

Llaw nodded. "Yes, it would be wise for you young ones not to speak, even if spoken to first. Especially you, Morgaine; we cannot afford to give away anything they might use against us."

Morgaine glanced quickly at Jaren, offering an apologetic smile. He looked away just as swiftly.

Soon enough, a knot of torches detached from the brighter glare of the enemy encampment and advanced slowly toward the wall. The escort stopped some fifty yards from their position, and a lone horse trotted forth. The figure atop the mount seemed one with the night, and the light of the torches avoided it. Regardless, its identity became all too obvious, as a pale face with hollow, black eyes and cruelly grinning mouth gradually became discernible.

Jaren had seen one like it all too recently. He cringed at the thought of the yellowed, sharpened teeth and pointed black tongue. The creature's horse rolled its eyes in apparent near-panic. It was clearly not comfortable with its present rider, though some force compelled it to remain under control. Still, it threw back its head frequently, snorting and flaring its nostrils in protest.

"Greetings from my Mistress, *Valir* Ensin Llaw, King Aldrain Draegondor, and dearest Morgaine Haldannon of Dal Farrow." The titles were announced with open contempt. Jaren was not a little relieved to have his name omitted this time, and by the look on her face, Iselle felt the same way.

"Make your demands, vile one," Aldrain commanded.

"Straight to business, then? Very well—your unconditional surrender. I will take the new king and the girl. The rest of you will be allowed to go where you will. Now, doesn't that sound like a fair bargain?"

"Bargains like that seldom work out, in my experience." Aldrain countered.

"You haven't the strength to take this place, blacktongue," the Valir added. "Be gone with you before I lose my patience."

"You are but a street performer before the power of my Mistress, summoner. And your house will indeed fall, believe me. If not, just ask the king."

"You have our answer. Get you gone," bade Llaw.

"And, what of the rest of you? Surely you have more sense than this tired, old conjuror and vagabond king? Witness what happens to those who resist." The creature raised an arm and a single form appeared from the direction of the encampment, out of the gloom. It shambled closer, and was revealed to be the figure of a woman.

Aldrain suddenly lurched forward against the battlements, a look of horrified recognition blooming across his face.

The woman was clearly dead, though animated through some horrible, unnatural means. She flopped about as if suspended by strings, a human-sized puppet for a deranged child. Her long hair hung in matted, red tendrils, her soiled clothing was in tatters. Glazed eyes stared out in an unseeing gaze. The blacktongue dropped his hand, but the corpse remained standing, motionless.

"What have you done to her?" Aldrain cried in anguish, his throat constricting.

"I did nothing. She chose this end for herself."

"You will pay for this with your life! I promise you that!" The king slammed his fist on the stone, eyes blazing in hatred.

"And this I promise all of you," the being vowed, "you will share her fate and amuse me in death if you do not surrender! You will have until the coming of dawn. Consider well your response."

The horse's hooves clapped sharply on the stones, and it was gone, a black spirit receding into the darkness from which it was born.

The corpse of Sonja Redsteel remained standing for some time after his departure, before collapsing to the ground.

18

UNDER NORMAL CIRCUMSTANCES, THE COMING dawn would have been a marvelous sight to behold. The rising sun flared brilliantly below a few scattered clouds in the eastern sky, bathing the scene in wondrous golds, oranges, and reds. The other three points of the compass showed the skies to be clear, promising of a truly beautiful day.

And all within the tower dreaded its arrival.

Horns sounded from the distant encampment, and through breaks in the scrub and forest cover, the besieged captured the sporadic glint of sunlight on metal as enemy soldiers warily picked their way forward. Their advance was like the coming of the new day: gradual, inescapable.

"What are they about?" Aldrain thought aloud. "They are too few in number, with no siege weapons—what could they be …?" he hesitated, a darkness clouding his face.

Whatever the thought, Jaren recognized it was far from pleasant, and if it caused the king such disquiet, he would rather not know.

"Rather, what are we meant to think of it?" Ensin Llaw pondered, though a glance at Aldrain set his mouth into a pensive frown. He'd shared many conversations with the new king of late, and no doubt had an accurate idea as to what had given the latter pause.

It was surely the same knowledge that had ultimately led Llaw to recommend fleeing his tower.

The group was observing from another high balcony, one lofty enough to offer a generous vantage point. Ensin Llaw had positioned his archers along the wall—perhaps two dozen in total—as a precaution in the unlikely event a conventional attack was launched. The fact that it appeared to be happening did not make sense.

"Maybe they don't want to risk killing us," Jaren offered, "if we have people of value to them. They could be trying to keep us occupied until reinforcements arrive."

Aldrain and Llaw glanced at each other, saying nothing. Their expressions suggested they'd not entertained that thought.

"I doubt that," Aldrain reconsidered momentarily, adding a slight shake of his head. "There were persons of value in my father's palace, too. It didn't stop them from annihilating it completely. No, if we're not willing to surrender, we're meant to die."

Ensin Llaw gestured them back from the balustrade and inside the arched entry to the veranda. "We continue with our plan, then?" he asked, once all six had gathered within.

The response was unanimous. All nodded as one. They'd been given a skeletal account of the dangers that lay in remaining, or as much as Aldrain would speak about, at any rate.

Llaw said, "Then we must be off. I think our presence on the terrace will make them believe, for a time at least, that we've decided to put our trust in the fortress." He gave them an encouraging smile. "All right, this will take but a moment."

He began to summon, arms raised and eyes closed. Minutes stretched on, and Jaren's mind wandered, the low rumble of Llaw's voice washing over him, conjuring the recollection of a familiar bass tone, his father's.

Jens would have the bulk of the summer work finished by now. All that remained would be to watch and tend the crops until the harvest, now not so far away as it had been when Jaren had cast his final glance back upon the village. It would have been hard for them, with no extra help. Then it came to him. *What if father has left for Mother Haddie's already?* But Jaren quickly dismissed the idea. The healer had seemed to think it would be a while before their father came for them. Jaren hoped it was so. The last thing he wanted was for his father to find the remains of the cabin and come searching for them through the wilderness, running into Truth knew what.

Iselle shifted her stance the slightest bit, and his eyes were drawn to her.

He would apologize to Iselle as soon as they were free, he promised himself, to her and to his sister. Of late, he had spent too long in isolated self-pity. He was actually beginning to feel homesick. Jaren suppressed a laugh at the irony of it. Perhaps it was best he had no summoning talent, if little more than a week's absence from home made him yearn for the life he'd left behind. Perhaps it was best to admit the truth and move on.

In any event, his adventure was turning out to be nothing like what he had envisioned—all they'd been doing was running: running to Mother Haddie's, running to Ensin Llaw, and, now, running again—to wherever. Maybe the promise of a farmer's life—predictable and hard, yet safe—wasn't so bad. Few were the times back home that Jaren had passed exhausted into a fitful sleep and woke up no more rested.

But then, why did a little part of his mind persist in crying out against it so? *Just the last of a dying hope*, he reasoned. Time would ease the pain of disappointment. That was the way of it, he guessed. Mother Haddie had encouraged him to stop yearning for what was beyond him and use his real gifts to help those close to his heart. It was time to follow her advice.

Llaw was on the move. Jaren pushed his thoughts to the back of his mind and focused on the others. Swiftly, the *Valir* led them down to the main level of the tower and through the various passageways to the garden egress. It opened directly to the front courtyard. Across the yard lay the main gate and guard towers.

The king of Carathon exited without hesitation, disappearing from sight, leaving the four of them and Dagger with Ensin Llaw.

The *Valir* repeated the gist of their scheme one final time. "Once you step through the portal, my summoning will affect you. You will be undetectable to the naked eye. Follow me across the courtyard and into the right turret. Once outside, keep to the plan, as we may be separated. Stick close to the river's edge. Find your way to the boathouse. Remember, since it's closer to their camp it shouldn't be as heavily guarded, as I doubt they'll be expecting us to head *into* their strength." The *Valir* glanced at each in turn. "Aldrain and his men are going first, to make sure the way is clear. Just remember the plan and all will be well. Ver will stay close by to protect you, should the need arise. Let's hope it doesn't come to that. May the Truth deliver us."

Llaw nodded then, and stepped out into the courtyard after another, final glance at each of them. They followed, one by one.

As each in turn crossed the threshold, their forms became dull and hazy. Jaren was told this would happen, that they would be able to see each other in dim, gray hues. To anyone else, they would be completely unseen. Invisibility! Never in his wildest dreams did Jaren imagine a summoner could do such a thing. His had been visions of calling fire and lightning. *Don't take too great an interest*, he admonished himself, *you'll never be at the other end of it.*

Aldrain and his handpicked troop, seven in all, awaited them. Similarly cloaked by the magic, they appeared spectral in the half-light of dawn, vaporous spirit creatures without fear of the light of day. Llaw moved to the fore and headed off toward the tower.

Jaren wondered as he went what would happen to the men on the walls. Most were turned to face the oncoming threat, but the few eyes directed his way did not shine with inspired courage. More than one face wore a hopeless expression, as if death were imminent. Some were Aldrain's men and the rest hired soldiers in Llaw's employ. All had received the same orders—put up a feint of resistance and then retreat as they would. Jaren hoped they would make it. They risked their lives for his smaller group.

Jaren and the other ephemeral forms drifted across the stones of the courtyard like so much mist. It all seemed so unreal, so far removed from his past experiences.

They reached the turret. Llaw led them through the tight space and around a corner to an obviously neglected door. Thick dust lay on the small ledges of its surface, and the key turned grudgingly with a low, grinding creak, much the same as the hinges then offered. The *Valir* stepped into the blackness beyond. An instant later, a tall sliver of light shone out from the doorway and into the dim chamber, spreading as part of the wall receded. Aldrain and his men slipped through the opening and into the brightness. Jaren and the others went after, Llaw following behind.

They emerged, blinking in momentary blindness, from the side of the turret that faced the river. As Jaren glanced back, the *Valir* waved a hand, and the thick wall slid easily back into place, as if no opening had ever existed. Then, Llaw moved past them once more and gestured for the group to fall in behind as he stole into the woods.

Jaren's stomach tightened into a knot. *May the True One help us.* Taking a deep, steadying breath, he followed.

Even with the growing light of day, it was difficult to discern the others ahead from the shadows of the trees about them. He soon had a dull ache in his head from the effort of concentration it took to successfully follow Iselle's movements as she crept on directly ahead of him. More difficult yet was to spot Dagger, who paralleled their route. It was still hard to accept that such a large animal could move so stealthily, magical cloaking aside. Occasionally, he could spy the fleeting form of

Morgaine farther on, second behind Ensin Llaw. Jaren supposed the
Valir had wanted her closest of all, as she was the most important. He
hazarded several glances behind, trying to pick out Ver's figure from
the brush, but without success. Due to the pressure within his skull,
Jaren soon ceased the attempts.

He began to sweat freely, both from anxiety and the lack of moving air. The cool, night breeze, as weak as it had been, had dwindled to
nothing with the rising of the sun.

Stumbling on a twisted, deadfall limb, Jaren stopped suddenly, frozen in fear. He might be invisible, but, the *Valir* had warned, he could
still be heard. Iselle's hazy form had come to a halt ahead, too, her face
turned toward him. Though he could not discern it clearly, he knew the
look of irritated alarm that was surely etched on it.

A hand grasped his shoulder and he nearly screamed. The firm, yet
unthreatening grip squeezed ever so slightly. Through the corner of his
eye he glimpsed the shadowy face of Ver. The avatar nodded somberly.
Keep going, his eyes said, *carefully this time.*

Jaren did just that. Moments stretched on.

Jaren felt the hand once more, as it applied a downward pressure.
He crouched low in response. A ghostly arm pushed past his face, a
solitary finger outstretched. He followed the line of the digit ahead
and saw the soldiers approaching. As yet, they appeared oblivious, but
it would take some maneuvering—or good fortune—to avoid them
without incident.

The soldiers made no attempt at concealment. Plate armor and
weapons rattled, and limb and leaf underfoot shouted their advance. A
long moment passed, and one of the two men turned slightly around a
stump. He was now heading directly for Jaren.

So much for luck, he groaned inwardly.

Steadily closer, he came. Jaren's feet were frozen. He felt Ver's hand
nudging him to the side. He couldn't move.

All Jaren could do was scream soundlessly for the man to veer
slightly off-course once more. *Please move again,* he cried in silent terror. The soldier was going to walk right over Jaren, and it was unlikely
he'd think it was a root he'd stumbled across. *Please, let them pass by!*
Nearly on top of Jaren, the man staggered, as if he'd temporarily lost
his equilibrium. It was just enough. A brief, puzzled look crossed his
scarred and leathery face as the soldier passed Jaren by, a mere inch to

the side, close enough for Jaren to have counted the hairs on the man's arms.

Jaren's headache had grown worse. He was just relaxing and had begun to rise when the grip on his shoulder returned once again.

Another pair of armored figures approached, these two side-by-side, outer arms spread wide, as if sharing a heavy load between them. As they neared, Jaren saw that was indeed the case. Each gripped the heavy iron handles of a small chest, very solid and weighty in appearance.

The two were straining as if it were even heavier than it ought to have been. Jaren could see it in their flushed, tense faces and bared teeth, as they wore no helmets, unlike their compatriots. They couldn't have looked more physically involved if they were trying to pull out an old, gnarled stump with their bare hands.

Then they, too, were passing by, several yards off to one side. Jaren felt a nudge from Ver, and he started on ahead. Iselle was nowhere to be seen. A sudden feeling of panic stole over him, and he felt cold. *Remember the plan.* He glanced to his right and peered through the dense foliage. *There!* He caught a flash of sunlight from the water. As long as he held to his current course and kept the river on his right, he reasoned, he would make it to the boathouse.

It didn't seem that Ver would let him wander too far from the chosen route, anyway. A shimmering form suddenly revealed itself ahead: Iselle. She was moving ever forward, cautiously, careful not to make a sound.

Their agonizingly slow flight wore on.

Iselle had stopped just ahead. Then Jaren observed why. Jutting from an overgrowth of brush and climbing vines sat a low, blocky, wooden structure. Between it and the river, which had crept within easy sight, was a patch of low ground, thick with cat's tails and swamp grass, an inlet of sorts along the river's edge that had filled in some years ago. He could just make out the rotting remains of a dock, not yet wholly reclaimed by the wilderness after the river receded. The surrounding forest was foreboding in its stillness and silence.

Where were the others? Where was his sister?

Nearby, he spotted a crouched Dagger. But what was the dog doing?

He pawed at the ground just before the wall of reeds that populated the once-submersed depression, dislodging a loose covering of grasses and leaf litter. What was revealed was unmistakable: stark, and out of place. The veiling magic that should have shielded its owner from view had failed.

It was an arm.

19

VER WAS ALREADY ON THE move. He rocketed past Jaren, hauling him after by the scruff of his collar, shoving Iselle forward as well after several long strides. The avatar thrust them up against the boathouse with one arm, the other brandishing his silver blade. He faced the woods, steely eyes scanning.

Iselle called softly to Dagger, and after a reluctant glance at the body he'd uncovered, he obediently came to her, though alert himself, head lowered and ears flattened.

Jaren peered around the corner of the boathouse. Along the wall, he could see the entrance, the door resting ajar. Scarlet spots touched the grass leading to it, and a large, dark stain had crept past the threshold from within. He cringed.

There was no sign of Aldrain or Ensin Llaw or Morgaine.

"Ver," he whispered, "in … in the boathouse …"

"Yes," came the firm acknowledgment. "Don't bother looking."

"How do you know?"

"The reek of death. There are none alive inside."

"What happened to everyone else? Where are they?"

As if in answer, the three of them, and Dagger, began to flicker. Ghostly, ephemeral hues turned instantly to vivid, real-world color and back again—and again, rapidly. Then, as soon as it had started, it was over. They were completely visible once more.

Iselle and Jaren gasped.

"Sit tight," Ver growled. "It takes a measure of concentration to maintain the cloaking, even for one so skilled as Llaw. He may have simply needed to focus on something else." Jaren remembered that same edge to Ver's voice from the first time they'd met him: detached, in control, fearsome. Though he knew the avatar was on their side, Jaren was still unnerved by the promise of danger it carried.

A crashing arose from the brush to the landward side of the building. A blurred figure hurtled toward them, heedless of the limbs and boughs through which it thundered. A battered and torn Ensin Llaw exploded into view, running askance, his left leg dark with blood. He suddenly noticed them, his saucer-wide eyes casting about in near panic. Several diagonal gashes marked his face, and blood flowed from them freely.

"Run! Get to the river! It's nearly here!" he cried with a lurch, almost stumbling to the ground.

"Behind me!" Ver directed. "Protect them!" He moved to face the woods directly where the *Valir* had emerged.

"Where's Morgaine?" Jaren demanded. "What's happened to her?"

"We must flee!" Llaw ignored Jaren, pleading with Ver, tugging at his own clothing. "You can't possibly fight that … that thing!"

He appeared to have aged ten years since they'd last seen him, a mere hour earlier. There were dark, hollow spaces beneath his eyes, and Jaren would have sworn there were twice as many creases in his once near-timeless face.

Llaw sank to his knees and muttered to himself softly, leaning forward precariously on trembling arms. "Nothing I did … it's no use … too powerful …"

Jaren and Iselle exchanged fearful glances.

Dagger began to whine. He backed toward Iselle, brushing her leg, overcome by an urge for the reassurance of proximity. It was not a comforting sight, to witness nearly two hundred pounds of lean-muscled fury reduced to whimpering at her heel.

Then, it was simply there in front of them, the pale-skinned, dark-clad figure that had addressed them scant hours ago. Even Ver could have been startled, though it showed only through a new repositioning of his guard.

"I thought you might try something like this."

To Jaren, the deep, rasping voice sounded eerily like the being the avatar had disposed of days ago. But that couldn't be, could it?

"I brought some friends of yours to help you listen to reason." The fiend beckoned with a casual wave, and immediately several figures pushed their way into the clearing behind it. Aldrain and Morgaine emerged first, each shoved ahead by a pair of large, armored men.

Jaren's headache worsened. It was almost as if he could hear a faint buzzing, it had become so intense. Why did it still hurt so when he didn't have to struggle to make things out anymore?

"I've changed the bargain, *avatar*," the word dripped with acid. "I'll take the Carathonai king and the girl, and the *Valir* as well, in payment for all the trouble you've caused. You and the others may go free. That's a fair compromise, no?"

"Leave them and depart now. I'll brook no deal with you."

"Ever the naysayer," the blacktongue accused with a scowl. "Why do you bother with these creatures, avatar? Surely you can't think them worthy of your True One's attention?"

"I'll not repeat it again. Leave them, and go."

"Why?" It wasn't clear whether the other was addressing Ver's directive or not. "Why aid these foolish mortals? What good can it do? You might save them, but to what end? Your Truth will never overcome the will of my Master. The Mistress, his anointed, will prevail." The blacktongue appeared almost exasperated. "Just turn your back this once. The rewards would be … immeasurable."

Ensin Llaw appeared to have recovered somewhat from his half-crazed state, though he stared incredulously at the two arguing before them. Collecting himself somewhat, he moved in front of Jaren and Iselle. He began speaking in low tones, but it did not sound like his earlier, horror-stricken ramblings.

For the first time, Jaren took notice of his hands. Or moreover, what covered them. Fingerless metal encased them, near half-gloves that continued up his wrists to disappear beneath now tattered sleeves. They glinted brightly, emanating a silvery glow in the dim light of the forest. *Metanduil?*

The avatar's steady voice drew Jaren's attention once again.

"You waste what breath is left in you, lying fiend. I've seen firsthand the prizes won in doing your lord's bidding. His only boon is empty lies and a slow death, deceived. To the Abyss with you!"

Ver launched himself toward the creature, sword flashing brilliantly. This time, however, his foe was equally as swift. A contemptuous sneer twisting its mouth, it lashed out with its own weapon, a cruel-looking, serrated blade. After parrying the avatar's attack, the creature's return blow sliced toward Ver.

Ver matched the stroke. Deftly, he parried it and initiated another blinding strike. It, too, was turned aside.

As the two great combatants circled and exchanged measured blows, Jaren glanced past them. The soldiers clutching Aldrain and his sister struggled to hold them steady as another emerged from the forest and drew forth a wicked-looking, curved dagger. Jaren didn't stop to consider why; there was only one logical conclusion. Sure enough, the newcomer stalked toward Morgaine, raising his weapon. Thrashing wildly, though, she appeared determined to meet her fate fighting to the end. She wrenched one hand free, and it disappeared instantly into the folds of her tunic.

Not Morgaine! Jaren's inner voice wailed, as he reached out in a futile gesture toward the struggle.

Just as the killing blow began to descend, a brilliant flash erupted, momentarily blinding all but the avatar and blacktongue, who remained locked in their dance of death. When the white shroud dissolved from before Jaren's eyes, he saw that the dagger-wielder lay in a smoking, crumpled heap, flesh and armor fused into one smoldering ruin. Simultaneously, a clap of thunder ripped through the clearing.

Ensin Llaw's low, chanting voice became audible through the ringing in Jaren's ears. He peered at the *Valir* with newfound awe. Spheres of liquid light shot forth from his fingers to either side of Morgaine, slamming into the soldiers and hurling them backward.

Taking full advantage of the distractions, Aldrain managed to trip one of his captors with a well-aimed sweep of his foot while slamming his trussed fists under the visor of the other, sending that one staggering.

The furious, yet calculated exchange of blows continued unabated between Ver and the blacktongue, neither feeling pain nor fatigue, though clearly each had received a number of serious hits.

Aldrain fought to dispatch the soldiers, having secured a sword from his would-be executioner.

Morgaine sank to her knees, her face contorted into a mask of hatred as she glared hotly at the blacktongue. She clutched her leather purse tightly in a white-knuckled grip, thrusting it toward the focus of her intense fury.

Llaw had begun to chant once more, his focus, too, trained on the avatar's foe.

Sensing that the tide of battle had turned against it, the blacktongue began to work its way backward, making for the clearing's edge. He threw a second-long glance at the *Valir*, one that held for the barest instant, and yet Llaw lurched backward as if struck. Even so, that minor distraction earned him what would surely have been a mortal wound to any normal man as Ver seized the advantage. Unbelievably, though, the fiend was able to regain his composure and capably blocked another fatal blow.

Still, the creature withdrew steadily. Morgaine maintained her acid glare, while the *Valir* steadied himself and began to summon anew. The blacktongue ducked under a slicing blow from Ver and turned to take flight, but stopped abruptly mid-stride, as if running into a solid wall. The creature glared at the *Valir*, who had stopped his summoning and stared in wide-eyed amazement. The blacktongue lifted into the air, seized and held fast by some invisible force. It tried in vain to shift its gaze from the *Valir* to the only other possible source of his entrapment: Morgaine.

She'd risen to her feet, her arm still upraised, smoldering eyes fixed on the blacktongue, a snarl twisting her features. She gave the slightest twist of her fist, and unseen hands forced the blacktongue around to face her. Now, its eyes widened in realization, and in fear and anguish as well. A high-pitched whine emanated from the being, too low to hear at first, but building in pitch. Dagger was the first to become aware of it, and he backed away, head and ears lowered. Sharp cracking and popping sounds soon accompanied the unearthly wail.

She's crushing him alive! Jaren realized. He looked from one to the other, unsure which expression was the more repulsive: the being's pain-distorted features or Morgaine's snarling leer, laced with satisfaction, even pleasure. Jaren took an involuntary step toward his sister, but stopped short when a louder, wet-sounding snap drew his attention back to the fiend. Though still contorted and twisted, the face was frozen in a lifeless stare. Cold, unseeing eyes bulged from their sockets as the pressure continued to build. Jaren turned away, just in time to see Aldrain place a hand on Morgaine's shoulder. At first, she pulled back, but realization slowly took hold. Her hand dropped, and with it, the blacktongue slumped to the ground, a formless heap.

20

SONGBIRDS TWITTERED UNSEEN IN THE boughs above the river's banks for some time before a lightening of the sky was apparent. Even when the forms about him became more than dark shapes, Jaren barely noticed. It wasn't until the prone figures began to stir, one at first, then a few others, that he came back to his immediate surroundings. He cast about, peering through the dim light into the surrounding foliage.

It had been a near-silent retreat from the scene of the encounter to the river and the beginning of their subsequent journey. Even had the recent ordeal not been enough to quiet them, the final images of Llaw's tower sufficed. Floating downriver, they had witnessed as an intensely glowing orb of light slowly reached above the treetops, enveloping all but the very tip of the massive structure, and then imploded with a deafening boom that shook the stillness of the forest to the roots of the ancient trees.

The *Valir's* tower had been completely annihilated.

Not long afterward, the current of the Marthuin became strong once again with the increasing slope of the terrain, its banks drawing closer together as it coursed more directly east, and their progress had been rapid. None felt in the mood for conversation, and fatigue eventually overcame apprehension as the immediate threat was left behind for at least one night.

Even so, Jaren hadn't managed a decent sleep, free of nightmares. And it wasn't because of the unfamiliar, gentle swaying of the raft. In his dreams, Morgaine kept appearing as a stranger, berating and mocking him. But that was not the troubling part. Each episode ended with her holding him fast, suspended in mid-air, sneering, laughing at his vulnerability and weakness. Heedless of Jaren's cries for mercy, her face a mask of pleasure, Morgaine dispatched him much as she had the blacktongue—and with not the faintest hint of recognition.

Jaren shuddered, and not because of the cool breeze that whispered across the water. He glanced at his sister, moving slowly and flexing the night's stiffness from her muscles beneath her bedroll. Shaking his head, he tried to dismiss the last remnants of the dream.

He couldn't remember the number of times he'd started from his fitful slumber, the final crack of the blacktongue's spine, now his own death knell, thrusting him to startled wakening. At least the ache in his head had lessened somewhat. It was now just an uncomfortable pressure, and it didn't seem to bother him as much when he moved.

Jaren abandoned the idea of further attempts at sleep. He'd get little enough anyway with the others rousing. Ver steered the raft to the north shore, announcing that they would stop for a meal and to stretch their legs.

Jaren quickly busied himself gathering deadfall for the morning fire. At least he hoped they could have a fire. After yesterday's events and last night's dreams, a good, hot breakfast might help settle his nerves. And if they were not permitted a fire, the labor would at least help him to clear his mind and focus on other things.

She was smiling!

Jaren ventured a short distance into the woods. After a brief period of collecting the dry branches and limbs, he straightened from his task and found Ver standing before him. Considering his state of mind, Jaren was surprised not to have jumped and tossed the kindling into the air.

"You have not rested well?" It was more statement than question.

"Not really," Jaren stifled a yawn with his forearm, managing not to stick himself with one of the twigs he carried, "I had some…bad dreams."

"You did well back there. Not many can stand so near a blacktongue and remain…settled."

He hadn't done anything, except cower behind Llaw and Ver. "I wanted to run."

"But you didn't."

He had an unusual look about him, Jaren thought. Then he settled on it. Ver wore what could only be described as a *fatherly* expression—he'd seen it on his own father's face—a mixture of approval and pride, or thereabouts. It was an altogether unexpected expression on the avatar, however. Jaren shook his head and replied, "Only because you two were there. And besides, I had nowhere to go."

"Fear is one thing. Panic is another. It doesn't allow you to think things through rationally, you just act. Remaining calm enough ... well, you'll see. You've done well."

What? What else had he done? Nothing so far as he knew, and there had been no discussion about yesterday's events so far, either.

"Well, you might as well put that kindling to use." A slight smile tugged at one corner of Ver's mouth as he spoke, and he moved off, apparently back to his sentry duties.

Did he ever sleep?

Jaren was still puzzling over the avatar's curious words as he plodded back into the clearing. Ensin Llaw and Aldrain conversed in animated fashion, while Morgaine and Iselle sat off to the side, listening intently. Dagger lay sprawled nearby, uninterested in their conversation, eyes closed, an occasional wag of his tail and the rise and fall of his breathing the only indications he was alive. None of them, perhaps with the exception of the dog, looked to have been successful in achieving any meaningful rest. Dark circles underscored everyone's eyes, most of which were bleary and red.

"—going back to Eidara, to see to the state of my kingdom." Aldrain was composed, but his voice carried an edge.

"Please reconsider, King Aldrain," Llaw wasn't quite pleading, but with much more emotion to his voice, he would be. "This has become more important even than the affairs of your lands."

"If the throne falls, I will be of little help in any of this."

"We have to get Morgaine safely away. I fear if she was not the sole target of the enemy this time, she will be when news of her power spreads. And it will. Anyone able to summon within miles of the clearing will have sensed that release. We must move her quickly!"

"You can do that without me. My men will only attract attention."

Llaw replied, "I do not mean for you to accompany us."

"Then what are you suggesting?" Aldrain's voice was strained, much like his patience appeared to be.

"A distraction, a ... decoy, if you will."

Aldrain measured Morgaine with a glance. "How powerful will she become?"

"In time, and with the proper tutelage, she will be greater than I." Llaw spared a moment for an encouraging nod to Morgaine.

"Unequalled in the six realms?" Aldrain pressed.

"No, but one among the most talented."

Iselle turned her attention to Morgaine, who was oblivious to anything but the two conversing. As Iselle did, she caught sight of Jaren. She shrugged.

Jaren frowned.

"So, if she is not to be all-powerful, why the effort to capture her?" Aldrain reasoned.

Llaw said, "I cannot say for certain, but I assume the Warwitch is attempting to subdue or otherwise dispose of any who might join together against her. It's only logical. Untrained and more easily swayed, as I've already mentioned—and add to that, her incredible potential—Morgaine is an obvious choice for the Witch's initial ... attention. Need I remind you that the guild in Ergothan deemed it necessary to hold a second testing in little more than a month, just to discover her? That would be unheard of, were she a typical candidate."

Aldrain crossed his arms, scowling. "I still find it hard to believe. Despite her potential, as you've described, it would make more sense for the Warwitch to go after the established powers in the lands, and then deal with other possibilities."

"Let me give you another example. As ... effective ... as her ... handling of the blacktongue was," the *Valir* chose his words carefully, and an apprehensive look had flashed in his eyes as he did so, "her manipulation of lightning was truly unexpected. It reflects a level of ability that normally takes the most skilled years to master. I should know, I myself took almost three years to do it. That means—"

"*Valir* Llaw," Morgaine interrupted.

"One moment, my dear," he replied. "It obviously shows that—"

"I didn't call any lightning."

"Her progress in this short time has surpassed ..." Her words finally sunk in. Llaw's mouth worked silently as he tried to shift his thoughts. "Perhaps not knowingly, child, but that strike was not mine. Still, even unwitting command of such elements is beyond most at first, especially with such accuracy."

"It wasn't me. I didn't find my talisman until just before I ..." she looked away, eyes downcast, "until I focused on the blacktongue." Then, her eyes met his again. "I didn't summon against the soldiers. Not at all."

"But, my dear girl, that's impossible." He licked his lips. "If it wasn't you or me, then how ..."

First Morgaine, then Llaw, and finally the other two turned to stare at Jaren. It took a moment for the collective attention to register. What were they looking at? Then, it occurred to him, too. If neither Llaw nor Morgaine had summoned the lightning, then who among them had done it?

"Don't look at me," he countered. "Everyone knows I can't summon." He glanced behind him, fruitlessly. "Maybe ... maybe Ver did it." Where had the avatar gotten to, anyway?

"That is not quite the way I do things." Ver materialized at the opposite edge of the clearing. All eyes went to him. The fatherly expression had been replaced by a knowing look. "So, Master Llaw, what do you make of this?"

He shook his head, his lips moving silently once more. "I ... I cannot ..." he swallowed. "Perhaps with the release of magical energy ... perhaps it drew lightning to us?" He was obviously grasping.

Ver lifted an eyebrow, still leveling the knowing look.

"There was hardly a cloud in the sky," Aldrain said.

Llaw returned his attention to Jaren. "But he cannot summon. He—you—were tested. You have no ability with *metanduil*."

Morgaine's look was unreadable. Iselle's eyebrows lifted high, and her look was anything but knowing.

"Like *Valir* Llaw said, I can't use the magic-metal. So why is everyone looking at me?" Jaren demanded.

"There is another method of summoning," Aldrain offered thinly. "Didn't you say so, Master Llaw?" His face belied the fact that he knew the implication was absurd. More than that: well-nigh an impossiblity.

"Not possible," Llaw muttered, along with something else Jaren couldn't quite make out. The *Valir* scratched his head, shook it in denial, then rolled his eyes up as if accessing some store of seldom-used knowledge. For several moments, absolute silence reigned. Then he spoke once more. "I don't believe I'm suggesting this, but at this point, we have no alternative but to say it. As common, er, knowledge dictates, *An'Valir*—which is what we're talking about here, to state the obvious—have no need of *metanduil* to summon. The ability is born into them. In fact, in one or two of the oldest records, it might even be implied that *metanduil* could somehow block the ability. In all honesty, I haven't the slightest idea. You see, there hasn't been anything written firsthand, or second, or third for that matter, since the last occurrence. Not much to go on."

Iselle asked, "How do you test for *An'Valir?*"

Jaren scowled at her. So did Morgaine, he noticed.

"That, also, is unknown." Llaw paused, frowning. "Well, since there is no need for *metanduil* and the ability is innate, perhaps it's just a question of trying."

Jaren's forehead creased. "Trying what, *Valir* Llaw?"

"I don't know, try to move something. That's a simple exercise in *Valir* testing."

"I have. I can't do it," Jaren huffed.

"Yes, well," Llaw tapped steepled fingers against his lips. Then his eyes narrowed in scrutiny. "Tell me, when you tried to summon, did you use a talisman?"

"Of course, how else was I supposed to—" Jaren's expression brightened for an instant. Immediately, though, he shoved the fledgling hope to the back of his mind. "No. I wanted to summon so much…and every time, I failed. Mother Haddie told me. And so did you. I can't summon. If there's no chance I can summon with magic-metal, what chance is there I can without it?" He shook his head resolutely. "No. It wasn't me."

"My boy, not to trivialize it, but Mother Haddie and I would not know an *An'Valir* from a shepherd. Or a farmer." He chuckled, with a shrug. " At least, not until we had learned to identify the signs. I suppose it follows that sensing *An'Valir* talent, at least when dormant, is different than sensing the ability when it requires *metanduil*. Perhaps when used, it is very much the same, though I wouldn't know about that, either." His face clouded, and he focused on Morgaine. "That would change some things."

Aldrain spoke, and Jaren regarded him. "So instead of just a powerful *Valir*, we also have an all-powerful *An'Valir* in the making?" His tone was skeptical.

"Circumstances would seem to suggest so," came Llaw's shrugging reply. "But until we are able to prove the theory…"

"Well, my decision cannot rest on appearances. How do we find out for sure?"

Again, all eyes fixed on Jaren. He suddenly realized he'd been holding the kindling all this time. He let it drop to the ground and set his hands on his hips. "Fine, let's be done with this nonsense once and for all." His heart lacked the conviction of his words, though. Maybe, just maybe ... *No. Enough of that.* Jaren had had his fill of disappointment and vain hope. It was time to face reality. There was as much chance he was *An'Valir* as there was for Iselle to become a dress-wearing debutante. He didn't realize he'd shifted his eyes to her until she scowled back at the hint of a smirk on his face. *No.*

Llaw directed a question to Ver. "Since you seem to be ... something more than you've let on, perhaps you might shed some light on our dilemma. Have you any suggestions on how to determine the truth of things?"

"You know I cannot." Given the fatherly expression, it could have been a reply to children.

Either way, it earned a barely subdued harrumph from Llaw. He returned to Jaren. "It's up to you. You'll have to settle this, without any help from us."

Perfect. Jaren just had to show them that he was the only *An'Valir* born in a thousand years, without knowing how. And that was with myriad doubts and mounting frustration wrestling for control of his mind against an unruly, unwelcome hope. Exasperated, he was about to throw up his hands when Morgaine spoke.

"When we were cornered by Joselle, and again yesterday, what were you thinking about?" Jaren didn't know what she was getting at. But, some spark of an idea had clearly come to her. "I didn't know what I had done or how. Perhaps it wasn't just me. Maybe it wasn't me at all," Morgaine said.

That last admission had been hard for her, Jaren could tell. She had always been sensitive about the attention he got as the Haldannon's only son. Yet, she was trying to help. He smiled at her, and she returned it, though a little apprehensively.

"I can't remember, exactly," he replied. "I was afraid, angry ... lots of things. I don't think I could say I was thinking just one thing."

Aldrain exhaled impatiently. "Well, short of threatening or beating him to bring back his fear or anger, what's to be done? I need to make a decision, and it would be better to have some idea of why I should choose one direction over another." He gave Llaw a fixed stare. "Why could I not be a distraction heading back to Eidara, anyway? It might be just as likely I'd take them there as anywhere else."

"Your father was a great believer in strong defenses, no?"

"Yes. He always said, 'offense wins battles, sound defense wins wars.' What does that have to do with anything?" Aldrain's brow rose questioningly.

"I might be inclined to think, then, that if threatened, you would act as your father did. Eidara no longer offers the best defense now."

Aldrain nodded, considering. "Caren Hold." He nodded again. "Caren Hold is the strongest of my father's fortifications, built into the side of a mountain. It guards the Stahl Pass north of here." The shadow returned to his features. "But walls no longer protect. Not against...that. The Warwitch will not believe we've put our hopes in walls of stone once more."

"If I've heard correctly, the fortress runs deeply into the mountain itself. She may well believe you intend to see just how destructive her new weapon is—you being your father's son, of course."

There was a long pause before the king spoke again. "Granted, then. But, again, why make the journey—become the decoy—if he is not what you think?"

Spots of color rose in Jaren's cheeks as all eyes turned again to him.

21

ANDRASTE KNEW BEFORE SHE STEPPED from the forest cover that it was the right clearing. She could sense the residue of the recent magical releases—one of which was as powerful as those unleashed in the destruction of the *Valir's* tower, not far to the west.

Furthermore, she could sense ... it, even dead. An involuntary shiver tickled her spine. She'd had considerable experience in dealing with blacktongues over the years; her allegiances all but ensured that, but what she now had to do.... She strode clear of the trees and into the short grass of the enclosure.

She stepped gingerly to one specific, ruined body after peering about at the several other lifeless forms scattered nearby. It seemed that every bone in this corpse must have been shattered: a deliciously painful death, indeed, and one truly worthy of such hideous creatures. The skull apparently remained intact, though, resting at an awkward angle, its dead eyes staring away from her, thankfully. The pointed black tongue, now bloated, extended from the open mouth.

It was a curious thing, with all of the flies at the rest of the bodies, that none came near this one. Of course, she could empathize with them. She would rather not do what she must, either.

She squatted next to the disgusting thing, and a wave of nausea swept over her. Steeling herself, she focused, hesitating. Her Master would not accept feeble, human weakness. It was her task, her charge to see what had truly happened here: if what was suspected were true.

Her orders had changed abruptly. Nearly to Eidara, another of the Master's agents found Andraste. Her instructions were to leave the prisoner in the charge of the messenger and make all haste west, to the tower of Ensin Llaw, there to engage one of her talents. She knew of the man, a competent enough *Valir*, though arrogant and self-assured as the rest. Few individuals could rival her power now, and she doubted he was among that number.

The use of a talent, though: the vagueness had confused her somewhat at first. Little by little she'd pieced it together. Such was the norm, as her communications were brief and little more than simple commands. A truly useful follower was expected to figure things out on his or her own. Those who could not, or who figured wrongly, did not rise to her stature.

Past sight. It was another gift from the Master, one that she truly enjoyed. At least she did under normal circumstances. She could, through contact with another person, see events as they had seen them, as though she were actually there experiencing them firsthand. It was painful for the subject, prodding and poking at their minds until she found the memories she wanted to access. In fact, few survived without some form of lasting trauma. And yet, why she would need to use the gift was puzzling. Surely, any surviving agent of the Master would willingly supply her with information—unless none had survived.

Clearly, that was the case. Whoever was sent to capture the Dal Farrow whelp had failed.

Crouching beside the corpse, she retrained her focus. She'd never attempted past sight with the dead before. Perhaps, with a normal human, it wouldn't work after death. But, with a blacktongue ... well, it must be possible or she would not have been sent.

She clenched her jaw, and her eyelids drew to slits. She inched her hands toward the skull, dreading the touch that must come as part of the ritual. Then her fingers contacted the pale, dead flesh. It felt greasy and all too loose. Her mind began to probe as she closed her eyes, focusing. At once, a feeling of violation entered her, flowing through her fingertips and spreading to the rest of her body in filthy currents, enough to cause her to gasp in revulsion, but not enough to break the link. This was not at all going to be pleasant. It was usually the other way around, the subject bearing the burden of discomfort, while she enjoyed the exercise of power. But, there was no time to dwell on it. Not now. Suppressing shudders, she delved deeper, but not too far; there was no knowing how long the malevolent spirit of this creature had lived.

Images swept through her along the sickening flood of scenes, not a few of which involved horrific instances of torture and death at the hands of the being. A scant few of the memories–fragments, really– must have been from the original inhabitant of the body for, though distasteful, they were not so terrible. She was vaguely aware of her stomach churning. *Concentrate!* More images: darkness and blood.

It appeared: the clearing, the faces, the encounter. She witnessed all of it, staggered by the sensations of agony that accompanied the fiend's final moments. Gritting her teeth, she desperately searched back for the traces of magical flows as her own body convulsed in pain. Andraste had to replay those images several times over, as the answer she sought could be viewed only in the periphery of its vision. Finally, after an eternity of the tortuous process, she found the answer.

It was true, as much as she had known it was impossible.

Andraste thrust herself away from the dead servant, crossing her arms against a sudden chill that did not originate from her contact with the fell creature. She had seen, as reliably as through her own eyes. Soon enough, though, apprehension gave way to calculated desire. If the impossible could become manifest, then why could disaster not become opportunity? She fished the flat, black disc from the secret fold in her skirts, offering prayers to the Deceiver that she be allowed to take up the chase.

Aendaras was a minor city in Carathon, yet by far the biggest Jaren had ever seen. Three days north from the river Marthuin and well removed from the heavier forests bordering its course, the city rose like a solitary mountain above rolling plains that baked in the heat of the day. Scattered copses of trees dotted the countryside, spaced among expanses of wild grasses, fields standing fallow, or tended crops. In the distance, the walls and spires of the place shimmered under the blaze of the early afternoon sun.

"*Stay behind me,*" Aldrain had instructed as they neared the southern gates. "*No one will challenge you, so long as they know you are my guests.*" By the Truth, Jaren had intended to do nothing else, even without the king's directive. The way his sister and Iselle crowded in, they too, had that in mind.

At first, the small party was given no more heed than local farmers hauling baskets of turnips to market, but as they closed within a dozen strides, one of the guards, after a passing glance, snapped his head back to the fore, swatted the other's foot with the butt of his pike, then stiffened woodenly. Irritated, the other glanced first at his comrade, then, seeing his rigid pose, peered at them, too. His eyes grew saucerwide as he snapped to attention, staring straight ahead. Both gave the hand-to-heart salute and held it as Aldrain stepped before the first.

One, then the other, he looked up and down, as if at the pre-duty inspection. Nodding, he addressed them. "Fine work, lads. Not every day you expect a visit from your liege, but I am impressed with your vigilance. I will make a note of your composure and pass it on to your sergeant-at-arms."

If a board could be said more relaxed than a stone, their posture became that much less rigid, Jaren thought.

Aldrain clapped the nearest man on the shoulder. "Carry on with your duties. Truth guide your hand."

"May the king walk in the Truth! Long live the king!" they nearly shouted in response. It brought a lanky, dark-haired fellow in gold-trimmed, red livery huffing around the corner to meet them as they passed beneath the gates. His reaction was identical to the guards', though without the salute. He bowed deeply, right hand to his chest and left hand at his side, his bowl-cut hair falling forward as he bent. "Your Majesty ... w-welcome. I am sorry, we were not expecting you."

"Do not fret, Lagen. I sent no word. However, I will be making my way to the palace. Please have word sent ahead of us. I would like the guest rooms readied for my companions."

"As you command, Your Majesty." He whirled and was gone, in a blur of long arms and legs.

"He's top-rate." Aldrain nodded after him and then faced the group. "One day he'll be chief servant. He also knows his way about the gossip networks in the palace. He's learning under Doman, the current butler, about his duties—*and* rumor-mongering. By the way, even if you're my companions, Doman will set you straight if you don't behave properly." The king chuckled. "Don't say I didn't warn you."

22

EACH OF THEM RECEIVED A more thorough examination down the length of Doman's narrow, hawkish nose than the king had given his guardsmen. He was even thinner than his apprentice, and taller, making his inspection all the more unsettling to all but Ver, who seemed not to notice in the least. Doman was bald save for a wreath of thin, white hair. A protruding Adam's apple was all the more prominent for the haughty thrust of his spadelike chin. An equine face gave the impression that great pressure was being applied to either side of his head, his pinched lips doing little to dispel the image. He expressed his disapproval with a loud *tisk-tisk-tisk* upon completing his scan of the group.

"Your rooms are ready, Your Majesty, as are your … *guests'* rooms." He sniffed dryly. "Would you like dinner at the usual hour, Your Majesty?"

"That would be fine, Doman."

"Quite, Your Majesty. Lagen," he called, his eyes straying to the doorway, through which a sitting Dagger could be observed, though the other was nowhere to be seen, "make sure the animal is tended to— and kept *out* of the kitchen." His cool gaze swept the others. "If you would follow me—and please, do not sit on anything before you've had a chance to bathe," his eyes stopped on Iselle, "or *touch* anything." Not waiting for a response, he wheeled and started off down the wood-paneled corridor.

Iselle stuck her tongue out at his back. Her eyes nearly popped from their sockets as another, barely audible *tisk* echoed from his direction.

Aldrain smiled knowingly. "Better do as he says, or your bathwater may be a bit on the chilly side." He turned down a different passage. "We will gather shortly, after you've refreshed yourselves. I will send for you."

꘎

"He seems like a good judge of character," Jaren teased after—a good several minutes after—the door slid silently closed, and Doman was sure to be gone. If he couldn't see through walls, that was. Given the air of authority he exuded, Jaren wasn't sure the palace itself wouldn't accede to Doman's every notion.

"Funny," Iselle pouted, heading toward a tall, ornate side door. "I'm going to my room. Maybe there's some fine silverware here for you to grumble at."

"I'm sure there won't be any in your room. Either that, or Doman's fastened it in place!"

Jaren had to get a few shots in here and there when he could, though he always ended on the losing side, it seemed. She'd taken many opportunities to goad him about his failure to summon over the last several days. It wasn't helping with his concentration, either. Nearly every time he tried to summon, his mind turned to wondering what her next mocking comment would be. Bundled with his own disbelief and the pent-up frustration that burdened him, it was hardly surprising he'd not shown a whit more talent without using *metanduil* than with it. He was sure Iselle's prodding was an attempt to deal with her uncertainty and apprehension. At least it would account for the sheer volume of her abuse, anyway.

Llaw and Morgaine were equally as exasperating: he, for his continued attempts at guidance and for all his confessions of ignorance concerning things *An'Valir*, and she, for her near-absolute silence. Even though he was apparently fumbling his way, Llaw was obviously the most experienced with magic and therefore the one expected to find a way to bring out Jaren's ability. He'd been summoning longer than the three of them together had been alive. Still, his every suggestion had proven fruitless, and recently all the more desperate, not to mention absurd. Trying to make Jaren angry or afraid to see if that were a catalyst had succeeded, though only in making him angry, if not so afraid. Least favored was the unexpected, invisible poking or the illusion of great, hand-sized spiders crawling all over him. The former did make him upset, but not enough to summon, apparently. The latter had made him scream like a toddler with a skinned knee the first time. That made him angry also, and gave Iselle more opportunity to torment him.

Morgaine's input had ceased since her initial offering. Perhaps she'd reconsidered out of bitterness that he now received virtually all of Llaw's attention, or she simply had come to the conclusion his being *An'Valir* was completely out of the question. She was not hostile, nor was she helpful. Perhaps that was what bothered him the most. If she was helpful, he could be angry at her, too, for adding to his misery. If hostile, at least he could have felt justifiably antagonistic in return. Right now, he didn't know what to feel about her. That soured his demeanor even further.

Maybe Llaw should create an illusion of Morgaine berating you and Iselle taunting you at the same time. You'd summon then, by the Truth! Maybe fire beneath their bottoms—and they'd not sit for a week!

That brought Jaren back to the question at hand. Was he or was he not *An'Valir?* He'd gone around and around in this circular argument since the suggestion was made, from anger and frustration about his true nature, to exasperation over the actions and reactions of the others, and back again. He did feel like yelling. But he held himself in check. It would merely give Iselle another opening to jab at him.

Jaren started at a knock from the main entrance. He wasn't sure how long he had been sitting there. Hopefully, it was not yet Aldrain's summons to meet. He had not used the washbasin that sat steaming on the ornate wooden table across from his enormous four-posted bed. Come to think of it, he hadn't even looked around the room. It was something, to be sure! Gleaming frescoed walls rose above marble tiling on the floor, and ornate furniture filled the chamber. A second knock landed, more forceful.

"Ah … come in."

Morgaine's head peeked through into his room. "Do you have a minute?" she inquired genuinely. It was more warmth than he'd received from her in days.

"Sure."

She hardly batted her eyes at the room—hers must have been equally regal—and strode over to the bed, where she sat beside him.

"I was just speaking with *Valir* Llaw," she offered, with a sympathetic smile, "I'm sure he's not your favorite person right now, nor me." She shifted, as though trying to make herself more comfortable. "I just wanted to tell you I'm sorry for how I've behaved for the last few days, and to tell you why."

"You really don't have to. I've been as ornery as a cornered rock badger."

"Yes, but it's understandable. My actions, I'm sure, are more confusing."

"Well, maybe a little," Jaren lied.

"I've been trying to figure out how summoning has affected me. First with Joselle, then … well, you know. Everyone has looked at me differently since the last time. When I … killed that creature." Morgaine sighed. "I've looked at me differently, too. I had no idea what came over me, why I felt the way I did, why I did what I did. Llaw explained that the magic can be dangerous if not handled properly, if not channeled with the right amount of respect, he called it. Doing what I've been forced to, with very little mentoring and training, he said it should be expected that the darker attractions of summoning have had some influence." She glanced at Jaren to see if he was following.

He gave her an encouraging nod.

"So, I came to find you. I was afraid that I was doing something wrong with the magic; that I was somehow to blame for what happened."

"Morgaine, you don't have to—" he cut in.

"Please, let me finish." She smiled wanly. "It made me think. If I was having trouble properly handling the power when I had at least some guidance, what might happen to you? How much could go wrong?"

"I'll be careful, Morgaine. I promise."

For a moment, irritation flashed in her eyes. "How can you? No one knows what you can or can't do. I've felt the … the pull. It's hard to ignore, even if you know it's going to be there. And you don't know what to expect."

It was Jaren's turn to be frustrated. "What can I say? I have to try, don't I? Otherwise, we'll never know if I have the gift or not. And, yes, I know I have no idea what I'm getting into. I wish … I wish we were back home, and there was no such thing as summoning!"

"We both know that's not true," Morgaine said, after some hesitation, reaching over to give him a one-armed hug.

"Gainey, what am I going to do?" His eyes welled. No. He would not cry. *By the Truth, I will not.*

"As long as we have each other, we'll do what we have to." She turned to hug him fully. He didn't resist.

For a time they sat in silence, the occasional subdued sniffle coming from both sides. Then another knock sounded.

23

THE REST OF THE PALACE was even more luxuriously extravagant than their rooms, though Jaren could hardly believe that. Not a single door or frame was absent a burnished finish, ornate carvings, gilded works, or some combination of these. The plastered walls were brilliantly white, frescoed, or covered with great woven tapestries, many of those featuring exotic animals and representations of places he wasn't sure existed. The polished floors shone brightly, displaying numerous patterns and designs.

He nearly walked right over Iselle, craning his neck to take everything in. She regarded him, arms crossed, and her sly grin in place.

"You'll catch flies with that," Iselle gestured to his gaping mouth.

"This place … can you even believe it?" he managed, in an awestruck mumble.

"And have you seen the silverware? So fine you could just scream."

"No, I think Doman has removed anything that might fit into a pocket," he retorted, giving her an equally mischievous smirk in return, as they started down the corridor.

"What's that? A smile? I thought you'd forgotten how," She teased.

"Only for a while. Sorry I was such a—"

"Hoe-brained sot?"

"Yeah, something like that." He looked at her expectantly.

"Don't worry. All is forgiven."

Jaren arched his eyebrows and scowled.

"What, you didn't think I'd hold a grudge, did you?"

"No, absolutely not. Everything slides off you like water from a duck. Until you can use it, of course," Jaren said.

Iselle's grin widened. "So, what do you think is likely to come of this meeting?"

"I don't know. Maybe Aldrain …," Jaren peered around nervously, to see if anyone had overheard his lack of propriety with the name, "maybe the king will just put me out for all the bother I've caused."

"Hmmm. Doubt it. If anything, it's the dungeon for you."

"Well, you'll keep me company soon enough if your fingers have anything to say about it."

She feigned insult. "Don't think for a second I'm that much of a bandit. You have no idea how … proper I can be, when I want to."

"Right. I can see you now, in your place at the king's royal court."

Iselle's response did not come immediately. "And why is it so hard to imagine that?"

Was there a touch of genuine hurt there? He couldn't remember a time she'd ever worn a dress. The look on her face convinced him to let the matter drop. She was not grinning now. Besides, they had reached their destination.

Aldrain stood at the head of an immense, rectangular wooden table, leaning over it and supporting himself on straightened arms, palms against the gleaming surface. With room for more than a dozen people, it was as intricately carved as any of the doors, with four great, clawed talons as legs. A map was spread before the king, and seated on his left was Ensin Llaw. Beside him was Morgaine. Ver stood nearby, along a dazzlingly white, alcoved wall, motionless, as one of the marble statues filling the niches. He had never slept that Jaren had seen, but did he not even sit down? One by one their heads turned to greet the newcomers, though Aldrain's attention lingered on the map, making him the last to notice the pair.

"Please, sit down. We have much to discuss." The king gestured to the seats nearest him on the right. "I trust you've found everything to your liking?"

"Yes, Your Majesty," Iselle answered, as Jaren fumbled for a reply.

He nodded enthusiastically instead.

They moved to the indicated places and seated themselves, as the doors at both ends of the room swung silently closed. Ensin Llaw's face was a picture of weighty consideration as he studied Jaren, who tried to appear as if he didn't notice. *Just as easily ignore a bloatfly*, Jaren grumbled to himself. At least he hadn't used the invisible prod yet. Jaren almost checked around for spiders, then caught himself. He could feel the man's eyes nearly boring into him, for their intensity. Thankfully, Aldrain began again, making it easier for Jaren to ignore the *Valir's* intrusions, if just barely.

"We've a decision to make," Aldrain said, and he glanced at Jaren. "With less knowledge than we might have wished for. And yet, there is news as well, some encouraging, and some less so." He straightened from the table, eyeing them in turn. "I have been informed that my position is secure enough, that the rebels who would have usurped my rule have fled west, and I have the support of the remaining nobility. So, it seems, my need to return to Eidara is not as grave as I'd feared. However, there is a storm gathering on the horizon. My own summoners tell me, through communication with others in their capitals, that the Warwitch is indeed intending to use the example of my family's destruction to force our hands. She has demanded a great deal, though she just might get what she's after: pacts of nonaggression from each of the six realms; her pick of new *Valir* candidates; and, finally, a good share of our *metanduil* production, delivered at the turn of every season."

Llaw had ceased his scrutinizing. "What does she propose in return?" He very nearly spluttered in outrage.

Aldrain responded, "Our right to exist, and to conduct our affairs as before, more or less."

"The council will not stand for this! I must speak with the *Valir* among your people, as soon as possible. We must convene a meeting immediately."

"They will be available to you whenever you wish, *Valir* Llaw." Aldrain glanced at the door as Lagen entered, a silver tray in hand, and the barest of frowns marked the king's features. "Thank you, Lagen. Please set that down on the side table for now." He gestured with a nod to a small semicircular table behind Jaren and Iselle and continued speaking. "It has also come to my attention that the Jamnites and Ergothani are mobilizing, though to what end, I do not know."

"Isn't that good news?" Jaren queried. "Maybe together, all of the kingdoms can defeat her."

"That may be," Aldrain offered, "but without knowledge of why they are mustering, we cannot assume that is the reason."

"But what else could it mean?" Jaren pressed. "If they're not going to try to stop her, then—," he stopped, and his eyes widened in horror. "They wouldn't be working with her, would they?"

Aldrain raised his hand in a calming gesture. "Although that is possible, at this point, it's too early to know. I highly doubt the Ergothani would ally themselves to her so readily, but the Jamnites … they can be a superstitious lot. At times, they hardly trust their own *Valir*."

Ensin Llaw gave a snort, muttering something under his breath.

"And they can be equally unpredictable." Aldrain scowled, again turning his attention to the servant. "Thank you, Lagen. You may go now. I'll send for you if we require anything else."

The man turned from adjusting the items on the tray and gave a curt bow, and then began for the door through which he'd entered. The edge left Aldrain's voice as he continued to address the group.

Suddenly, Ver stiffened and peered about. The avatar's eyes settled on Lagen and narrowed. In the next instant, the servant bolted toward Jaren's exposed back. Ver launched toward him. Jaren turned, half-rising from his chair. Lagen closed the distance, plunging a short, black blade toward Jaren's chest. Ver would be too late.

Aldrain, too, moved to intercept Lagen.

Jaren inhaled sharply, thrusting his hands out to ward off the blow.

The dagger suddenly veered off at an angle, tracing a line of blue sparks as it slid across some sort of barrier before Jaren. Lagen's strike continued downward, embedding the deadly instrument several inches into the solid wood of the table. He snarled, a purely animal sound, and tried to wrench it free, still glaring blackly at the youth.

Jaren clutched at the assailant, just as Ver and then Aldrain reached him, bearing the servant roughly to the floor. The man struggled fruitlessly against the two of them, his baleful eyes still locked on Jaren. Lagen let loose another inhuman shriek, beyond furious that his quarry had escaped. Aldrain called out, and immediately several armed soldiers burst into the room. Seeing their king wrestling about on the floor, they rushed to Aldrain's aid without hesitation.

Jaren managed to pry his focus from the would-be assassin and peered down at the dagger and the charred area that had spread from its buried tip. He was also aware of Iselle standing beside him, her own small knife now disappearing back into the folds of her tunic. Opposite him, Ensin Llaw and Morgaine stood uneasily themselves, eyes trained on the small blade.

Tendrils of black smoke now snaked up from the scorch mark surrounding the point of contact.

Ver, having let the soldiers escort the still-struggling Lagen from the room, withdrew the dagger from the table, clearly the only person in the room who felt comfortable doing so. "Night scythe," he breathed in a disgusted tone.

Llaw blinked. "Yet another manifestation of legend."

"They exist, all right," Ver said coolly.

"What's wrong with Lagen? Why did he attack Jaren?" Iselle asked. Something caught her eye, and she stooped, picking the object from off the floor beneath the table. "What's this?"

Llaw squinted at the item. It was a shiny, metallic bracelet, inlaid with unfamiliar runes and designs. "May I see that, please?" he requested.

Iselle obliged him.

Morgaine followed the movement. "I don't remember him wearing that before."

Llaw studied the ornate band. "It's *metanduil*. Some sort of … wait. I think I recall something about this, as much as about the blade, anyway. I believe it's a *mal'han*. The carvings seem to be right, if I remember the accounts correctly. It's a tool that bends one to the will of its maker."

Aldrain wondered, "Is Lagen freed of the influence now that it's off?"

Llaw exhaled sharply. "I can't be sure, though if I had to say … no. I doubt it. I seem to recall that the one bonded was damaged somehow in the process. Though, it would be better if we had some firsthand information." He glared accusingly at Ver, who simply shrugged.

"His face," Iselle began again, "it … it looked … wrong." She pointedly did not turn her eyes in Morgaine's direction.

Jaren recalled the brief glimpse he'd had of Lagen during the assault, of Lagen's expression. It had been a reflection of Morgaine's during the final minutes of the encounter with the blacktongue: sneering, full of delight.

The siblings' eyes met briefly, then she looked away and down at the floor.

"It didn't necessarily mean she wants him dead," Llaw continued. "The weapon apparently puts the victim into a trancelike state. Perhaps into a sleep that the Deceiver can enter more easily, but that's just my speculation. The records are too old, and spotty." He directed another intense look at Ver.

Then they were staring at Jaren again.

The king of Carathon spoke. "It seems, my young friend, that we have our proof. And that your secret is out." He gazed solemnly in the direction the soldiers had forcefully ushered Lagen, letting out a weary sigh.

24

"Perhaps your lord needs reminding that he now exists to do my Master's bidding, not the other way around. He's been marked," Andraste said.

The messenger squirmed like a fish clutched in the talons of an eagle. "He wished for me to tell you, it was too dangerous to come here."

"He shows contempt at ignoring the summons, whatever his belief of the danger." She took the man in a measured glare, from head to foot. "Perhaps he has outlived his usefulness."

His shifting increased twofold, and he very nearly fainted in dismay. "Please, my lady, allow him the chance to redeem himself!"

"Very well." She seated herself in the creaky, wooden chair that was one of the room's few pieces of unremarkable furniture, slid it to the table, and removed a writing quill from its ink bottle. *I deserve better than this room and to be suffering these fools!* She forced the thoughts away. It was not wise to entertain such ideas. They had a tendency to linger, and to build. *Dangerous.* Too many others had indulged in similar thinking, only to have it lead to their deaths, or worse, in the end. They were best left unthought. Or, if that were impossible, then shoved to the darkest corner of the mind where they became the barest of whispers and were more easily dispelled. She focused on the smooth parchment beneath the quill's tip and began to write hastily.

Out of the corner of her eye, she could see the messenger becoming more agitated by the moment. Clearly, her response had not calmed his nerves in the least. Be that as it may, it was the closest to kindness he would get from her. He was very nearly vibrating with fear. She finished the note, folded it, reached across the table for the small lamp and the block of wax, and sealed it, pressing her ring into the wax drippings. The crescent and hawk insignia made a clear imprint.

"I don't have to tell you what would happen should this message not make it to your lord, do I?" He flinched as if Andraste had reached out to swat him like some mongrel dog. All the same, his composure warranted the threat. If he decided to abandon his duties and flee out of sheer fear, another note would have to be sent. It had already taken far too long to get the man here. "Now go." She held up the letter. He took it gingerly and backed toward the door. "And please, remind your lord that the next time I request his presence, I will accept no substitute." She accentuated each of the last three words icily to make her point. It achieved the desired result, because he flinched with every one as though slapped. He turned and fled, nearly tearing the doorknob from its place.

Andraste glared after him, scowling. As much as she hated to admit it, she might need his lord's resources now that the group had reached Aendaras. The chained one had failed, after all. She was of two minds about that. Most importantly, the Master might be displeased at the failure, though she doubted it. She could hardly be faulted, with such precious little time to prepare. Even so, what others maintained about events seldom interested the Master. His opinion was the only one that mattered. *Ah, but that leads back to the dangerous way of thinking, doesn't it?*

Her attempt had failed, and she'd simply have to move on to the next. At least breaking the poor soul had been enjoyable. Andraste had not had the pleasure of undertaking that ritual before. She hoped she would again, at some point. The music of his screams was still fresh in her mind.

Andraste could do little now but wait for them to move. It was frustrating to no end. She hated to wait. Glancing about the pitiful room, she barely contained a grunt of disgust—such abhorrent adequacy. If she hadn't been instructed to keep a low profile, she might have had a modicum of comfort. Perhaps that was why she'd enjoyed preparing the chained one. It had given her a chance to vent. *They'll all pay for this,* she promised silently, *especially the boy and his sister.*

Now, there had been a surprise. So unexpected a find, he was. The Master had been well pleased with her report concerning him. And things were so much better when the Master was appeased, as difficult as that could be. *Watch yourself,* her inner voice cautioned again. Indeed, a summoner with high potential was one thing, but *An'Valir!* Should she deliver that prize ... a wave of delightful anticipation enveloped the *Valir.* Perhaps she would be raised even above ... her. It galled her that another servant, a one-time rival, had surpassed her. But the other had been given a truly magnificent gift, one that tipped the scales greatly, and she had readily exploited that gift. Except for the Master himself, she was powerful beyond all others. *Though, if I can bring the whelp to heel, that will change!*

Andraste took a deep, steadying breath. There was no use getting ahead of herself. Now was the time for planning, not dreaming. She set about writing another note. *But what a sweet dream it was!*

❧

Ensin Llaw set himself to discover the link to Jaren's magic, a determination that had brought no end to the questions. No, he hadn't taken the time to concentrate. Yes, he had feared for his life. No, he couldn't remember exactly what he was thinking, except that it was probably the same as his first answer. No, he wasn't aware he'd used his hands in a warding motion. He was simply trying not to be stabbed. Yes, he'd wanted Lagen to stop, very much. No, he couldn't remember anything else important, but, yes, he'd tell Llaw if he did. There had been a great many other questions, as well, but they were, to Jaren, even more inane and did not warrant another thought.

Llaw mumbled to himself and scribbled notes furiously on parchment, between brief, yet intense periods of scrutinizing Jaren over the curious, rounded spectacles that seemed not to want to rise with the rest of Llaw's face. He had to push them up from the tip of his generous nose with a spidery finger, when he was aware of them at all. Jaren caught something barely audible about "the three selves," but that was the limit of what he could glean. He wondered what it meant.

Soon after the inquisition and subsequent recording of whatever he'd made of the answers, Llaw had gone to contact the other *Valir*, in hopes of putting together more of a polished explanation of what Jaren had done. He was not to be disturbed, Llaw mentioned in no uncertain terms, except by Jaren.

Jaren thought he'd seen a stiffening of Morgaine's spine at that.

Another *Valir* came to claim the items Lagen had carried. This one was a younger man, tall and graceful, garbed in robes of emerald green with gold-embroidered sleeves and breast. His flowing, blonde hair trailed after him as he padded off on slippered feet.

"Several decisions remain for us," Aldrain gathered them back to seats at the table once they were alone again and settled. Ver returned to his place along the far wall. "Given the events of the day, I am convinced both of Jaren's abilities and of others' dark ambitions for him."

"It seems that *Valir* Llaw's original plan is still our best option. I will move north to Caren Hold with a small force. I want to send the impression that we're in a hurry to get there, while Llaw heads west with Jaren and Morgaine and a small escort."

Iselle's eyes narrowed. "You mean, I'm not to go with them?"

"Enemy agents will be looking for youths. If you don't come with me, we'll have to drag other people along to make appearances." He regarded the siblings. "As it is, we need to find another of your age, a boy."

"Won't they see Morgaine and Jaren, and know anyway?" Iselle demanded. "So what difference is it if I'm with them, too?"

"Llaw can make things appear differently, if you recall."

Iselle set her jaw. "No. I'm not leaving them."

"He will have his hands full enough trying to keep them safe, without a third charge to worry him." Aldrain scowled at Iselle's apparent disdain for Llaw's abilities. "Whatever happened before, he is a very powerful man. It would take a stone to be undaunted by the likes of a blacktongue." Aldrain nodded. "Now that he knows what he's up against, there should be no more surprises."

"All we've been dealing with are surprises, and you promise that's not going to continue?" Iselle was giving no ground. "Besides, I don't need anyone to protect me."

Jaren raised his eyebrows. Iselle shot him a dark look.

"You are a fierce one, I'll give you that." Aldrain put a reassuring hand on her shoulder, and his voice took on a soothing tone. "You'll be doing your part to help support the rumor that Jaren and Morgaine have gone to Caren Hold. Appearances can be maintained to an extent, but if we're to pull this off successfully, we need more than that."

"Fine," Iselle relented, "but I want to know where they're going, first."

"All I know for now is that it's west. Llaw will have the rest of the details. If he's decided for himself yet, that is."

Iselle opened her mouth to speak again, but held her tongue. *Maybe it won't be her straying fingers that get her in trouble here, after all,* Jaren pondered. It was only Iselle's return scowl that made him realize he'd been grinning at the thought.

25

LLAW'S INSIGHTS HAD CAUSED JAREN to once more consider his sense of the magic. Why did it have to be so difficult to grasp? The *Valir* had mentioned "the three selves." That was all very good, but Jaren had no idea what the phrase might mean. Different parts of himself? He was aware of the magic. Perhaps that was his spirit or mind that wished for connection to the power. He had been faced with danger and reacted: at least it appeared so now. What self might that represent? His body? Was it related to the warding gesture that Llaw had asked about? And what about the third self? There were still so many questions without answers. Perhaps he'd have the opportunity to ask Llaw about it during the journey.

That brought a frown. Hopefully, there would be no further need for the other *tests*. Jaren was quite tired of those, and, to his thinking, they had added absolutely nothing of value to the search for truths. Though at one point, when he'd challenged Llaw about it in a huff on the road to Aendaras, the *Valir* had simply stated, "Knowing that something *isn't* a cause is as important as knowing it is." Jaren wasn't so sure he agreed.

At a creak from the side door, Jaren sat bolt upright. At least it wasn't the main doorway. The guards stationed there should prevent any intrusions. Though, after the earlier attempt on his life, Jaren wasn't convinced of his safety. He peered through the gloom, his eyes narrowed to slits.

"Relax, it's just me," Iselle's voice drifted to him in a whisper. "Can't sleep either?"

"Would it matter if I could?"

"No, probably not." She sat on the edge of his bed.

Jaren said, "Sounds like we'll be parting ways."

"Has Llaw said anything about where he plans to take you?"

"No. Well, he let something slip about going around to the north of the mountains, but nothing else."

"If he means to go around the mountains, then he's going to Drisia, or beyond?"

"Like I told you, I don't know. What's west of Drisia?"

"Nothing good, that I know of. The Barrens is a desert with even less water than trees, so I've heard. And people called Judai, or something like that."

"Well, wherever we're going, we won't find out right now. You okay?" Jaren couldn't see her face well enough in the dim light of the moon to read her expression.

After hesitating, Iselle answered, "I just wanted to wish you luck. You'll need it. Don't worry, though, Morgaine will keep you in line. She might be stubborn, but she has good sense enough."

"And I don't?"

Iselle shrugged. "Like I told you, good luck. And be careful. You don't want to drop a big rock on yourself or anything. If you can do that, I mean."

He didn't have to see her to know her salty grin was in place.

"Okay, I will. Now go get some sleep."

"You, too." She rose from the bed, and then hesitated.

He still couldn't see her face. Suddenly, though, there it was, right above his. She kissed him on the cheek abruptly and spun away without another word.

Jaren still had trouble quieting his mind for some time after she'd gone, but now he wasn't thinking so much about summoning.

The first light of dawn crept across the wall of Jaren's room, though he wasn't sure he'd slept at all. A silver tray of dried fruits and breads had been laid at the threshold of the outer door, and the guards on either side barely registered his presence as he retrieved it. He'd eaten hurriedly, packed his few remaining belongings into the now-worn pack, and knocked on the side door. There had been no response. Iselle must have risen earlier and was already gone. He set a swift pace and made his own way to the rear of the palace.

A red and gold liveried servant barely older than Jaren appeared and offered an escort. Through the well-manicured grounds and past several outbuildings he led, and Jaren followed, until finally they came to a broad square flanked on either side by two-story residences. Probably those of the servants, he guessed. The fellow bowed deeply and then darted off.

The enclosed space was abuzz with activity. The clattering of hooves, the rattle of weapons and equipment, and a multitude of voices competed for mastery over his hearing. Servants rushed here and there, armored soldiers checked tack and harness on mounts. Jaren counted thirty horses before he lost his place due to the bustle and gave up. Finally, he spied the others. Weaving through the milling bodies, both human and animal, he reached the group.

"Poor time to sleep in," Iselle said.

"You've been here yourself for all of five minutes," Aldrain offered in a chuckle. "Your horse is being readied over there," he told her, adding a gesture, "if you want to make sure it's being done to your standards."

Iselle glared at Aldrain before she headed off in the direction he'd pointed, to a spot several dozen yards away. Jaren couldn't tell if she was actually put off or not, nor whether it was due to the king's comment or from her resentment at having been divided from her companions. Then again, in a short while, it wouldn't matter. It would be different, not having Iselle around: a lot quieter, no doubt, but not nearly as entertaining. Though, most of the time, Jaren acknowledged, he was the one who provided the sport for her. He glanced about. Aldrain had vanished into the center of the mob.

"All rested, then?" Ensin Llaw asked.

"Well enough, I suppose," Jaren replied.

"Ah, that's good. We've some ground to make before nightfall."

Jaren glanced at Morgaine. Her face was unreadable, though her rid-rimmed eyes surely mirrored his own, and Iselle's, for that matter. Something else was different, too.

"I have a theory to share with you, whenever you'd like to hear it," Llaw added. He seemed to be in good spirits. "Perhaps we'll have the chance to test it out on the road."

Jaren grimaced, turning away and pretending to stifle a yawn so the *Valir* didn't see. *As long as it doesn't involve hitting me or covering me with insects, or any other bothersome things.* "I'm looking forward to it," he lied, studying his sister.

That's it! She's nearly as tall as Llaw!

Morgaine was standing not far from the summoner, and indeed, she was less than two hands shorter. She noticed his interest. "An illusion," she explained, guessing at his wonder. "You look taller, too."

"Yes, well, we couldn't have you two appearing as you did and make a convincing show of being nothing but ordinary travelers—all adults, mind—heading west, could we? Unfortunately, I can't make the reverse work the entire time for the king's company; my reach isn't so great. But, I think the king has found an answer to that problem."

Llaw's tone indicated he wasn't too pleased with the solution, either.

Jaren followed his rather aloof nod to where Aldrain's escort sat astride their mounts. Between them sat another figure, clad in the same dark, cowled riding cloaks they'd each been given. Beneath the shadows of the hood, he could just make out the lower features of a sun-darkened face, a boy's face.

"Who is he?" Jaren asked in hushed tones. There was no response at first. Jaren looked back and found Ensin Llaw fussing about with the packs on his horse, presently oblivious to anything else.

"A thief," Morgaine answered after a moment, her voice equally subdued. "He's the perfect companion for Iselle."

"What's he bringing a thief along for?"

"He probably couldn't find anyone else willing to go," his sister added.

Jaren shook his head. "It looks like they're keeping a close eye on him." They were. One of the soldiers flanked the boy's horse, near enough to grab. "What, did they get him from the dungeons?" Jaren joked.

Morgaine looked at him flatly.

"You're not serious?" he said.

"I think so. He was sentenced to lose a hand for stealing, so I've overheard from the servants."

Jaren blinked. Sure, just the sort of influence Iselle needed. Well, it didn't matter anyway, the king knew what he was doing and Aldrain wasn't about to listen to his concerns at any rate, Jaren was sure.

Good luck, she had wished *them*.

The cowl shifted toward him, and Jaren caught the flash of dark eyes from within the shadows. He thought the faintest of smirks had creased the boy's lips briefly, and had he winked? It was over so quickly, Jaren couldn't say for sure. He looked down at the ground self-consciously. When Jaren raised his head for another glimpse, the boy had moved off, his escort close behind.

Iselle led her horse near, choosing not to climb into the saddle yet.

"At least we'll be riding instead of walking." She noticed Jaren's eyes were still following the young thief. "Kind of mysterious, isn't he?"

Jaren shook his head, coming back from wherever he'd been, and forced himself to look away from the retreating figure. "What? Oh, him. Yeah … I think you'd best keep clear of him. He's probably dangerous."

Her eyebrows lifted mischievously. "Oh, I think he's harmless. Maybe he'll have some new tricks to show me."

At that, Jaren's head swiveled immediately to Iselle, his eyes narrowed. "What? The only thing he could teach you …"

She flashed a knowing smile.

Jaren appeared disgusted. "Sure, whatever you say. When you land in the dungeon beside him, don't come begging to me to settle your debts."

Iselle laughed. "I'm going to have fun with this." Her face then darkened. "Still no word on where you're headed?"

"I overheard something about Ghalib earlier," Morgaine offered.

"You've been overhearing quite a bit this morning," Jaren declared.

"And all you've been doing is sleeping in," she countered. "It's surprising what you can learn when you're awake." She wore a smug look.

There was a brief moment of awkward silence, which Iselle finally broke after a glance toward the stables. "I can't believe I'm saying this, but I will miss that dog."

Jaren and Morgaine shared a look, then regarded Dagger. He sat happily beside a young girl who was obviously the child of a servant, for she was garbed in much the same fashion. The girl realized they were watching and gave a nervous half-wave, then went back to playfully rubbing behind the huge canine's ears.

"After your first encounter, I thought you'd be glad to be rid of him!" Jaren quipped.

"Yes, well, I was just trying to be nice. He did lose his owner very suddenly, you remember." Iselle, her voice having grown thick, turned her face away and cleared her throat.

Jaren ended the silence after another brief pause. "Well, I'm sure the girl will keep good care of him. And, he is a big dog after all."

Iselle nodded, and was about to speak when the king's voice cut in. "Well, we've wasted enough light already." Aldrain had approached through the bustling throng, unnoticed by all. He straddled a black charger, a stallion, whose glossy, dark coat shone in the early morning light. Aldrain had opted to don a suit of gilded plate armor overtop his usual mail, with the gold dragon, namesake of his house, emblazoned on the breastplate. "If we are to gain sufficient ground this day, we must ride now. It has been a pleasure to share your company," he regarded Jaren and Morgaine sincerely, "and I promise to do all that I can to see you again, safe and secure once more. Go with the Truth in these troubled times. Should you meet any among the Jhud'Hai, don't look them in the eyes until the greeting is finished. May the True One guide and protect you!"

They bade the king farewell, and Iselle, too. Jaren wasn't certain if his friend's misty eyes were caused by their parting or if she was still thinking about Dagger. Casting a hard glance toward the young boy in accompaniment of her group, Jaren hoped it was the former.

Aldrain's final words had not come as a shock, but the news was far from settling. Jaren peered at Ensin Llaw uncertainly. He really was leading them into the Barrens. Well, he supposed, there were few places less populated and as expansive to navigate. Not to mention that it was supposedly a treacherous wasteland, full of poisonous snakes and worse. It should prove difficult for anyone to find them there, even if they were actively searching. He only hoped it would not be equally as difficult to find a way back, when the time came.

And, who are these Jhud'Hai?

26

TWENTY-FIVE OF ALDRAIN'S SOLDIERS, ARRAYED as he was, rode in escort behind the king and his two charges. They would leave the city by a different gate than Llaw's little band, with as much of a show of themselves as possible while at the same time making a pretense at stealth by taking a lesser-used gate. The intended impression was that they were hoping to slip away with the sought-after siblings in tow.

The *Valir* and his party, Jaren, Morgaine, Ver, and two warriors handpicked by Aldrain himself for bravery and skill at arms, would leave by the main gate. A merchant and his retinue, by all appearances they were heading for markets to the west. The soldiers were outfitted to appear as normal mercenaries. Both were unshaven, several days of stubble darkening their faces. One had short, dark hair and eyes and was stockier in body; the other was fair-haired and thin, though ruggedly so. Worn leather and mail armor beneath heavy riding cloaks would convey the intended impression, it was hoped. As long as you didn't look too closely at their weapons, or their eyes, for the former were a little too fine for warriors-for-hire, even with dirt and grime rubbed over surfaces and into grooves, and the latter too filled with the promise of death. Still, Jaren felt much better having Cadin and Rheen along, not to mention Ver. They wouldn't have survived this long without him.

The avatar joined them now, from his chosen spot at the edge of the enclosure where he could see all comings and goings. His horse was a bay stallion. A mount like Aldrain's would have suited him more, but they were trying to keep up appearances. Ver appeared as comfortable in the saddle as he did walking about.

Along the route, tradespeople opened their shops, preparing for the day's business. The flow of citizens in the streets had steadily increased once they left the palace grounds. Most were Carathonai, average in height and dark in complexion and hair, much the same as his own people, the Ergothani. A few hailed from elsewhere, though not many of these could Jaren readily identify.

Jaren was quite sure that the taller, fair-haired folk, mostly hard looking and somewhat aloof, were Jamnites, or other northerners. Most of these were tradesmen, he observed, already hard at work in the shops as they passed. Mainly they worked in smithies or with leather, as far as he could tell.

Other than these, only Vetians were vaguely familiar to him, with their tanned skin, oiled dark hair, and, for the men, peculiar moustaches and pointed beards. The women wore outlandishly colored dresses, nearly indecently low cut and high enough to expose knees, their dark hair gathered into hundreds of tiny braids, each intertwined with beads, shells, or numerous other oddities. These people he knew only from stories that his father had told him. They were supposedly master sailors and had visited lands far from the six realms.

As they moved farther from the palace, the streets became narrower and more choked with people. Shouts and calls from those selling their wares trailed after them, or were cut short with a look from either Cadin or Rheen. People milled about, slowing their progress, though neither of their guides did much to steer clear of anyone. They directed their mounts straight ahead, to the muttered curses and hard looks from a few. These too, though, were abandoned with a glance from their escorts.

Occasionally, Jaren observed other people on horseback navigating the crowds in much the same way. Apparently, keeping your course with little regard for anyone else was the thing to do in the city. It seemed quite rude. If you bumped into someone in Dal Farrow, you either apologized or you heard about it later, one way or another. It was a small community, after all. Jaren sighed and shook his head.

None of them, not even Ver, noticed the dark figure skulking in the shadows of an inn they passed near the outer gate. In fact, no one seemed to pay the stranger any heed. Any who did glance that way or who strayed too near felt a sudden chill for no apparent reason and quickly hurried on after a brief shudder. Catlike eyes glowered malevolently after the party from the darkness of a drawn cowl. A woman hurrying down the street nearly tripped over herself trying to avoid the spot, her eyes wide in wonder at the sudden feeling of disquiet.

She quickly bustled off, not daring to glance back at the source of her apprehension.

The fearsome eyes remained locked in place and didn't so much as blink until Jaren and his group had disappeared through the gate.

On the second day of their journey, one of the scouts had alerted Aldrain to the fact that they were being tracked. *Good,* he'd thought then. *The plan is working.* He wasn't so sure it was so fortunate now. They still had two days' ride ahead before Caren Hold and they'd be hard-pressed to make the fortress before they were intercepted. He had a fair idea of whom it was that followed them—Pacek. Aldrain scowled. Had circumstances been different, he would have welcomed the opportunity to meet the man on the field. Ten-to-one odds, though, had dampened his enthusiasm for such an encounter at present.

The king glanced ahead to the northwest, at the ridge of mountains that grew steadily in height, if only gradually. News of Pacek had not been the only unsettling word. A rider heading south had met up with them, one of his men from Caren Hold, who spoke of an army on the move from the northwest, just beyond the mountains: Jamnites. And, so far, there had been no word of their intentions. It was a sizeable force, indeed, numbering in the tens of thousands. Still not enough to take the Hold, but it was sufficient to cause alarm. At least the army would not clear the pass before they reached their destination.

Yet, that was not the most troubling of all. By far, the most disconcerting news was the announcement of a third force, this one equal to or greater than the host approaching the northern reaches of the Stahl Pass. The Warwitch, too, was on the move. Why would she need an armed host when she had such weapons of utter destruction at hand? Surely, they were equal to the impact of a conventional army. She had landed on the coast, not far from Colm, ignored the city and instead headed straight for Caren Hold.

Three groups, all meant to pen him in? Their appearance at the same time, with the same apparent destination in mind, was too much to be ruled a coincidence. Even so, he didn't know enough about the Jamnites to determine whether or not they shared the same objective as his known foes.

Aldrain sent the rider back to Caren Hold, with orders to initiate contact with the Jamnites at all costs. He needed to know their intentions. An unexpected, fleeting hope dared whisper in his ear. *Could it be the Warwitch has used up her deadly weapons?* He doubted it, but, perhaps she was without them for a time. For all he knew, they could take years to produce. It didn't make sense, then, why she would have used one on Llaw's tower if they were at all scarce. She could simply have had it surrounded and stormed in the usual fashion. He wouldn't wager on the possibility that the Warwitch held no such devices in reserve, not with what was at stake. Ten thousand Jamnite spears at his side would help, even if she was carrying one of the fearsome weapons.

Aldrain prayed they were not marching against him.

He heeled in lightly, causing his mount to drop back in the line. Soon enough, Iselle's white mare was even with his own. She offered him a slight nod, and then stared ahead, sullenly. *By the Truth, this one has fire!* Only a handful of nobly born ladies would look at him that way. She was so much like Ismene, his younger sister. She had been gone a long time, so long that Aldrain sometimes couldn't conjure an image of her.

The king willed the distressing thoughts away. It was becoming an all-too-common practice of late.

Turan, the young thief, had been riding along Iselle's opposite flank. Apparently, they'd been conversing. The youth cast his eyes downward and reined his mount in lightly, dropping back down the column.

"I see your spirits have not improved much," Aldrain said.

"That would have been simple enough to avoid," came the terse reply.

Fiery indeed! Aldrain decided to try another approach. "In time, you'll realize I only acted in everyone's best interests."

Iselle was unmoved. "High-born people are always claiming that, except that it always works out to be in *theirs*. Why should this be any different?"

Aldrain barely managed to suppress an amused chuckle. She wasn't much for diplomacy, but she said what she thought. "Yes, well, in any event, we'll be at the Hold by late afternoon the day after tomorrow. Remember what I asked you to do in case something happens?"

She scoffed in exasperation. "I'm to find you. If I can't, I find Delrain. If he is not to be found, I will ride as hard and as fast as possible along the northern path, to the fortress. I'll know it when I see it."

"Good," he nodded, "please make sure to heed those instructions. I would be very hurt indeed, were something to happen to you while under my care."

The defiance in Iselle's eyes lessened greatly. "Thank you, Your Majesty. I will try to do as you ask." She sounded sincere. "When do you think I'll see my friends again?"

"As soon as I can safely arrange it, I promise."

She opened her mouth to speak, her face darkening once more, but appeared to reconsider. Was it the mention of his word? Someone had broken a promise to her, perhaps more than one, and she remembered that. It would go a long way to explaining her animosity toward anyone in authority. Ismene had acted that way some time ago. Their father had made a vow to her, and then had been unable to follow through with it. Aldrain didn't know what the promise had been, but it was important enough to his sister at the time. After that, she'd—

Enough! Recent events had brought old wounds too near the surface; too little time had passed, and Aldrain hadn't had the chance to grieve properly since losing everything, and everyone, else.

He became aware that Iselle was studying him with a quizzical eye.

"If you'll excuse me." Aldrain paused. "I don't know how comfortable I'd get around Turan. The best influence on a young lady, he surely is not."

Her head rose in affront. If she were a cat, her back would have been up, tail waving in warning. Just to spite him, he was certain, Iselle eased off on her reins and, slowly, fell back toward the boy. Shaking his head, Aldrain turned and trotted to the head of the line once more.

27

Shouts of alarm stirred Aldrain from a troubled sleep. He dashed to fetch his sword and raced from the tent, nearly bowling over a runner who'd just arrived to give him word of the disturbance.

"Your Majesty, we have visitors."

"Who is it?" A hint of annoyance at being caught off-guard reflected how truly unexpected these newcomers were. He'd had no word of any new developments.

"I'm not sure, Your Majesty. But I think there are *Valir* among them."

And so there were, indeed. Sitting mounted in the saddle, and illuminated in the pale, orange hues scattered by the watch fires, were five dark-cloaked figures. They waited just inside the palisade that encircled the camp, surrounded by his men. Their horses' flanks heaved, breath steaming in the chill of the early morning hours, and they tramped uneasily on the grassy earth. One of the figures had thrown back the obscuring cowl, revealing a raven-haired woman of stunning beauty. He'd seen her before on a number of occasions. She was head of the *Valir* council in Carathon. Her name was Jhennain Earlsen.

"Greetings, Your Majesty. I trust we haven't caused too great a stir. Unfortunately, we were unable to reach you in Aendaras before you departed, but we wanted to catch you, nonetheless. There are matters of great importance to discuss."

She was swinging herself out of the saddle before he'd even given the nod to his soldiers to stand down.

The three newly-arrived Valir had joined Aldrain inside his tent. In attendance with Jhennain were were *Valir* also, Methas Kobol, a Vetian, and Aesin Bartaq, also from Carathon and a member of the council. The former was stocky, typical of his people, and dark skinned. Close-cropped black hair capped a round face and showed sprinkles of white, as did his moustache and beard. Bartaq stood several hands taller than his counterparts, and his regally white, shoulder-length hair added to the air of authority about him. He had a piercing gaze and a hard set to his strong jaw—the look of a fighter more than a summoner, to Aldrain's mind. Had it not been Jhennain who spoke first, Aldrain would have thought him in charge, for his ability was also of some renown.

Aldrain had two more chairs brought to the sitting room and motioned for the trio to be seated, after the formalities of introductions and welcomes were concluded. Once they'd settled, he followed suit, on the other side of a smallish, rectangular table that had been hastily cleared of several maps and his field notes. The dim light of the oil lamps made the occupants appear larger, a somewhat surreal effect. Or perhaps it was the intensity of their faces. All three bore expressions of severe determination, even resignation.

Resigned to what, Aldrain was curious to discover.

Jhennain spoke first. "We will cut to the heart of the matter, if it pleases Your Majesty," she began. At his nod, she continued. "For some time we have been investigating the activities of a rogue *Valir* named Rhianain Othka. You may be more familiar with her self-acclaimed title, the Warwitch. Her reach has become great, indeed, it seems. Her power has grown equally so, as you know firsthand. Again, I offer the apologies of our guild, as well as my own. Had we known sooner—"

He acknowledged with a wan, though sincere, smile. "What happened cannot be changed, though I appreciate your kind words. Please, continue." He willed away the grief that threatened to surface. At least the darkness should help with that. His father had often counseled that to feel emotion was human, to show it, unwise, especially when acting in office.

Jhennain went on, "Through her manipulation of magic and the metal of summoning, she has somehow gained at least partial abilities of *An'Valir*. It seems we will soon enough discover the full range of her development. Rhianain leads an army toward you."

Aldrain replied, "We learned of the host some time ago. And of two more, one on our heels, much the smaller of the three, and another about to traverse the Stahl Pass."

By her response, at least one of these was a new revelation. "Have you any detailed knowledge of the smaller group?"

Jhennain hadn't known of Pacek. It was the rogue noble, Aldrain was certain now, as his scouts had caught a glimpse of the count's banner in the distance. "A noble from the lands about Eidara who has caused considerable trouble, but he's the least of our worries at the moment."

"You are certain the third force is a Jamnite army?" questioned the *Valir*.

"Yes, but we're not certain of their intent. Have you any information?"

The dancing shadows accentuated the lines of worry creasing Jhennain's face. "Not as yet. We are expecting two more of our order from the north, four more in total, but whether or not they ride with the army, we do not know. Since Rhianain's landing, our communications have been … compromised."

Aldrain raised an eyebrow at that. Three of the more notable *Valir* in the six realms sat before him, and they were having trouble utilizing magic to communicate with their own kind. It did not bode well. "I am confident we'll make the fortress before either of the larger forces, and we should be able to keep ahead of Pacek, as well. The trouble is, once we're there, we may be hemmed in, especially if the Jamnites are not friends."

"Thodan and Wendl are from Jamnar. I could not say if they've ever made passage through the Stahl, or what familiarity they have with the mountains on your border, though we should be able to get a message to them if we must. There are other methods." The distasteful look that followed belied her disapproval of obviously more conventional means. Clearly, they were not used to being thwarted.

Winds of change, Aldrain mused.

Jhennain leaned toward the king slightly. "Has Ensin Llaw taken the young ones west?"

"They are being escorted as we speak, hopefully, to someplace safer than here." Few places, if any, in the six realms could be termed safe any longer. If the Warwitch knew of them, and if her reach was grown as far as they feared, the list would shrink to none.

The winds of change reach all of us.

The *Valir* appeared pensive for a moment before speaking. "Good. Llaw can be trusted to look after them, and their training, for now. The boy may require additional attention, later."

Of course, the *Valir* would not leave someone of Jaren's potential power in relative obscurity and with only one mentor for long. He would eventually become more than one lone *Valir* could manage or control, if it came to that. Aldrain felt a pang of regret for the boy. His life truly had changed, and whether for good or ill was yet to be seen. Regardless, Jaren had started down a long and difficult path.

Jhennain's expression hardened anew. Her silent companions displayed somber acquiescence.

"Which brings us to the purpose of our mission: Have you heard of the last *An'Valir?*"

Aldrain gave a faint nod. "As much as any event from that time, but who's to say what actually happened so long ago?"

"Our libraries are more fully comprehensive than most. In any event, you should then be aware of the conclusion to that event, no?"

Now it began to make sense. Even had he not seen where she was headed, she'd soon enough made it quite clear. Three of the most powerful summoners of the age were here, and four more were on the way. A sudden chill swept through Aldrain, and he knew it wasn't the night breeze. Their grim countenances were all the more understandable.

He was conversing with a trio under sentence of certain death.

Kerlain's Forge was the heart of the six realms and the source of all *metanduil*. The ancient formation was a mammoth cluster of towering, jagged peaks, the tallest white-capped year-round, and perpetually cloaked in iron-gray cloud. Something about the nature of the ore itself, Llaw had informed them, caused the thick, slate-colored veil to remain constantly overhead.

The closer they'd come, the more forbidding the landscape. When Jaren had wondered aloud how they would ever manage to pass through, Llaw related some of the history of the Forge, and *metanduil*.

"Since it was first discovered countless years ago that the ore gave one the ability to manipulate magical energy, it was sought greedily by the nations. Innumerable wars were fought over claim to the area, but no one realm could ever manage to control the entire range, at least not for long. Factional infighting and insufficient numbers had long since proven the bane of controlling the Forge in its entirety.

"Additionally, the formation of the original order of *Valir*, headed by a council of the most powerful practitioners, went a long way to moderating such unbridled ambitions. Serving as advisors and mentors to the rulers of the lands, this order, which eventually became the present-day guild, effectively served to guide their lords along more peaceful routes. It was even claimed that they forcefully intervened when several of the most ambitious and ruthless of leaders acted against the collective will of the order.

"In any event, down through the years, the borders of the six realms gradually became fixed as they are presently, with each controlling a more or less equal tract of the mountains that are the magic-metal's source. Disputes and minor squabbles still occur, mind you, like the recent struggle between Carathon and Jamnar, not yet a decade past, but major conflict has been by and large avoided for many hundreds of years.

"Throughout this time, groups of miners and large-scale production enterprises have carved out countless pathways, tunnels, and underground networks in their quest to harvest the all-important ore. As vast as the mountain range is, this incessant and often voracious exploitation has left fewer and fewer areas within untouched, leading to the creation of countless paths throughout the region."

Accessible or not, Jaren cursed to himself as he stumbled over a particularly rough section of pathway that apparently was the scene of a minor avalanche, the journey was going to be anything but pleasant.

While they did not plan to pass near the heart of the Forge itself, an immense volcano that dwarfed the surrounding peaks, spewing forth deadly vapors and ash from the bowels of Evarlund, the intent was to navigate a route that circumvented the northern edge of the mountains. They might encounter, with a little good fortune, a temporary mining town or two on their way. Little more than camps these were, really, where they could stock up on provisions or possibly even find a spare bed or two. Llaw couldn't say for sure where these places might be, as they often moved when the supply of *metanduil* diminished enough to be too costly to support them. Most likely, there would be few enough in the more thoroughly exploited fringes.

Good for keeping out of sight, bad for comfort, Jaren supposed. It was becoming very apparent that the two aims were mutually exclusive.

"And," Llaw warned, "the Forge plays tricks with the abilities of even the most proficient summoner, so I expect that neither of you will attempt any use of magic, except when I have been consulted, and then only under my direct supervision or in the direst of need."

Jaren complained about not being able to practice, and Llaw explained that the influence of unrefined ore was somewhat different than worked *metanduil*. Though when asked how it would affect his abilities, the *Valir* was frustratingly silent. "Just please do as I ask for now," was the final answer Jaren received to further probing.

Neither of the soldiers were much for conversation, Ver was busy either scouting ahead or behind, and Morgaine had become sullen and distant once more, so Jaren was forced either to endure Llaw's long-winded, roundabout lectures or to ride on in silence. Often enough, he opted for the latter course.

They had crossed the foothills into the lower reaches of the Forge's northeastern spur, from which sprouted the snaking line of lesser peaks that formed the border between Jamnar and Carathon, and were ascending steadily into the heights when Ver brought warning. The avatar had spotted a small band a day or so behind them. There were more than ten, but less than twenty among them. Until their own party gained the advantage of the heights, the others had been able to pursue them unnoticed. Even so, Ver had managed only chance glimpses, for all his constant vigilance. There was little doubt as to the intent of the trailing band, however. It was tracking directly the route they'd come. They did not appear to be gaining ground, or they simply weren't yet attempting it.

Their pace had been anything but leisurely before, and now Llaw had insisted they make all haste onward. Added to the steep inclines and the treacherous terrain, it made for a miserable development. They were soon forced to leave the horses behind. The mounts could not possibly traverse the increasingly angled slopes of unfriendly rock that frequently shifted underfoot, or the narrow sets of curving stairs they'd begun to encounter, carved into the sides of the ever-climbing mountainsides.

To further dampen their spirits, the dome of steel-gray sky blotted out the sun and cast a pall over everything and everyone. It was much colder now, the wind often screaming down at them through broken fingers of rock or scouring the wider expanses they crossed.

It felt to Jaren that they had come to an alien world, where the dull gray and earthen tones of the mountains blended into the darkened skies above. It was like a fearful dream world of treacherous, hidden dangers. His head throbbed, though Llaw had no answers to give as to why it might have started to ache so. At least they didn't try to travel much after the sun set. That would have proven quickly disastrous, given their pace and the perilous terrain.

Several such dreadful days passed, and luckily, or by design, their pursuers appeared to remain the same distance behind. Still, their hurried trek wore on exhaustingly, the hours blurring together so that a sense of time was virtually nonexistent. At first, they were allowed to practice summoning once they had stopped for the night or during the few brief breaks in the day, under Llaw's watchful gaze, and when he sensed the *metanduil* would have the least adverse effect. Morgaine seemed to be making some good progress, though Llaw's attention on Jaren frequently seemed to overshadow her achievements.

Then, while Jaren was attempting to summon fire, an apparently novice exercise, it happened.

It had taken Jaren almost a full day's worth of concentration and effort to conjure the fire successfully. It was frustrating enough without having so few opportunities to actually attempt the feat, and he had to return to the beginning every time, trying to recall whether he'd felt the proper connections beginning to form or not, and what he'd been doing or thinking at the moment.

Eventually, though, with Llaw's patient encouragement, he'd finally done it. The relaxation and balancing exercises seemed to help, though the *Valir* noted that they were, strictly speaking, not part of the summoning process itself, but they helped beginners to reach the proper state of mind to facilitate the bond between the magic and *metanduil* more readily. So long as they helped Jaren to concentrate, Llaw added, so much the better.

One minute, a small, flickering tongue of flame danced before Jaren in midair, and the next, it had become a searing ray of destruction, slicing into the side of a nearby boulder, causing molten rock to spray forth, scattering everyone in a shower of sparks and stinging debris. Within the rent in the stone glinted dully a concentrated vein of raw *metanduil*, a small portion fused into an irregular nugget.

After that, Llaw had Jaren practice again the breathing techniques and visualization exercises he thought would be less unnerving. The *Valir* sat on a nearby boulder, scratching his head and muttering to himself, often turning his head to study the youth more closely and sometimes shaking his head as if rejecting ideas that occurred throughout his scrutinizing.

Jaren found that, in doing the balancing exercises, he could shut out not only the anxiety he felt but also the whisperings of the magic. The more he practiced, the better he could insulate himself from its insistent voice, and all other worries, and just focus on *being*, or when on the move, simply putting one foot in front of the other.

At dawn the next day, or the pale version of dawn that such wretched country entertained, Ver brought urgent news that shattered Jaren's calm, exercises or not. Their pursuers were now mere hours behind and coming on rapidly.

28

THE RIDERS CRESTED THE DISTANT hill and cantered down the near side, keeping their mounts reined in during the brief descent. This larger band, Pacek's force, would reach Aldrain's position in minutes. *How many horses had died or come up lame to catch us so soon?* His own group should have been able to maintain its lead, but not when the enemy was pursuing with such reckless abandon. He had no spare horses, and so could not so easily afford to match Pacek's progress. The traitor had to have several, well-connected allies in the countryside along the way from Eidara, to have gained such an advantage.

And so Aldrain sat, waiting to spring his own trap rather than be intercepted and forced to the defensive.

Whether it resulted in killing many of their horses or not, Aldrain would have been forced to attempt flight had the *Valir* not shown up. They more than evened the odds, he would bet, even at such numerical inferiority. He glanced back from his perch near the crest of the hill to where his own men sat saddled, reins clutched tight, their eyes hard with the knowledge of what they faced. Clearly, they lacked his familiarity with what *Valir* could do and were understandably apprehensive. How could three people deliver them from two hundred fifty charging cavalry? But these were not normal individuals, not even among *Valir*. All his men needed to do was protect them, and the day should be theirs.

The *Valir* positioned themselves to the rear of the group, along with Iselle and Turan. They may have confided in him their desperate plan to confront the Warwitch, a suicide mission to be sure, but now they faced conventional forces of flesh and blood enemies. They held themselves with a knowing confidence.

Aldrain inched back down the hill at first, then, well out of view of the oncoming force, rose and remounted. He nodded to Jhennain, who returned the gesture and glanced skyward. She was sending her sight to a vantage point high above them. He wasn't sure how it was done, but it had something to do with hardening the air and reflecting light, as Sonja had once related to him.

Sonja.

Aldrain would exact a measure of revenge today. For Sonja, for his family, and for the many others who'd died because of the machinations of his advancing foe. The king glanced down to see his knuckles clenched white upon the hilt of his scabbarded sword.

Moments passed. Jhennain raised her hand, and Aldrain slid his blade free slowly, silently. His men did likewise: all faint whispers singing the promise of death.

Jhennain dropped her hand and nudged her mount to a trot. Her companions followed suit. An instant later, Aldrain urged his own horse forward, twenty-five Carathonaian soldiers mirroring its movement. Theirs was a rather brief, though steep ascent to the hilltop, compared to the long, sloping expanse on the windward side that Pacek's forward men had just begun. The instant before his eyes broke the plane of the hillcrest, he raised his blade and kicked his mount's flanks. The animal leapt to a gallop.

Crossing its apex, he took in the sweep of the hillside below. Pacek's men quickly caught sight of them and began bellowing warnings back down their lines. He eyed the count clearly enough, a short distance from the leading horsemen. His nearby bannerman was an easy mark. Pacek had reflexively signaled for a halt, but momentarily belayed the order. Obviously, he did not fear Aldrain's petty little band, outnumbered as they were, even at a full charge. His men soon began racing uphill to meet the oncoming rush at his self-assured command.

Then, the first bolts of lightning arced past, above Aldrain's head, tearing into Pacek's riders, spewing up dirt, chunks of earth, and remnants of horse, rider, or both. Aldrain hazarded a final glance rearward to the summit of the rise, where the silhouetted *Valir* made their stand behind his line of men. He was glad Pacek had brought no company of archers, for that could have meant trouble. *Valir* were no more indestructible than other mortal beings, after all. It would take only one or two chance arrows to quickly turn the momentum back heavily in Pacek's favor. His last glimpse was of Jhennain, raising her arms to begin summoning.

A horizontal wave of flame surged forth, originating scant yards before his mount and rolling toward the enemy riders, many of whom had simply reined in or already wheeled their mounts and started back down in a rout. Pacek screamed at them in defiance, even daring to swing at several ineffectually with his blade, but the summoned destruction ahead held infinitely more danger than his futile wrath. Several of Aldrain's soldiers, equally thirsting for revenge, had outpaced his steed and crashed into the few lead riders who had not been incinerated and remained willing to meet them. The clash of metal added to the clamor of the battle.

More lightning strikes sliced outward, and more fire swept across, hurtling devastation farther into Pacek's now heavily disordered ranks. Soldiers and mounts burned, lying still or turning in flight; it made little difference, once enveloped by the summoned onslaught. A few still offered challenge, but their numbers dwindled by the second, as magic, Aldrain's soldiers, or second thought took them. Screams of fear and cries of the dying, both equine and human, rose in a collective wail, competing with the thundering hoofbeats of the king's squad as they pressed forward.

In moments, the entire enemy company was in headlong retreat, Pacek among them. Cursing their good fortune, Aldrain flew recklessly toward the fleeing noble, the source of so much senseless loss and fatal division. Even the count's men, once loyal to his father and now cut down by fire and lightning, should not have died this way. *How many had he brainwashed with his anti-Valir fervor? How many eager and dutiful young men had Pacek corrupted to his cause?*

Directing his mount around craters and fallen bodies, Aldrain kept up the pursuit until it was clear that his hopes to apprehend Pacek himself this day were in vain. He'd driven his horse as hard as he could for nearly a third of a league before reining the stallion in, its sides heaving and its breath exploding in ragged blasts. Pacek and his remnant force scattered and disappeared from view over the far hills and thickets.

Turning slowly, Aldrain surveyed the hillside. His men had begun gathering the wounded or stunned into a small group some distance back up the slope. Here and there an animal or human stirred, but not many. There were few cries of pain or fear now. Mostly, it was eerily quiet. Even the insects had ceased their music. Perhaps two hundred of Pacek's men had died outright and a handful of the score or so wounded would live only past the next few hours, until their appointments at the gallows; they had taken up arms against their king.

Progress to the Hold would be slowed as a result of tending to the captives, but not enough to put them behind the arrival of the two approaching hosts. It was less than half a day's ride from here. In fact, though Aldrain could not make out the fortress itself, he knew the mountain into which it was built well enough. He could see it rising abruptly from the foothills at the mouth of the pass at a near ninety-degree angle, a massive, sharp finger of stone set in stark relief to the deep, blue sky beyond.

Though it once held the promise of safety, he couldn't help wondering what would be the cost in lives to hold it, if such a thing were possible now in light of the Warwitch and her destructive power.

The trio of *Valir* conferred in a tight knot at the top of the rise, while nearby, Iselle and Turan gaped fearfully at the scenes of carnage below them. A pity they had to witness such an encounter, but he couldn't have spared the men to keep them safe at a distance. After a final, remorseful glance back in Pacek's direction, Aldrain turned to see to his men and the securing of the prisoners.

⚘

Ensin Llaw stood stone still, arms down at his sides. His face was a mask of concentration, thin beads of sweat breaking out in response to his efforts. Jaren glanced back down the deep, yet narrow gorge. It had taken them a good amount of time to scale the steeply inclined defile, and he also knew that whoever tracked them had gained considerable ground in that time. He had an idea what Llaw was up to, but he wasn't sure just how it might unfold.

Then he heard a faint grating, similar to the grinding of the stone in Harker's mill back home, but much deeper. Just as he thought he could make out some sort of movement at the far end of the chasm below, rocks began to tumble into the space, mere pebbles at first, which simply rolled and clattered down the slope, but then bigger and bigger chunks, until finally, massive slabs of stone cascaded down, choking the passage completely within minutes and sending up a great cloud of clinging dust.

Suddenly Llaw was thrown backward. Hurtling head over heels, he impacted the rock wall behind them with a solid *crunch*. The *Valir* slumped awkwardly to the ground. Blood flowed from one ear, and his left leg was bent at an impossible angle.

"Quickly, take him and move out of sight of anyone below," Ver commanded briskly. "Head straight up the path until it forks. Go right until you come to the bridge. I'll meet you there."

"What happened?" Morgaine managed, in a horror-stricken tone.

"Who could have—" Jaren echoed.

"It doesn't matter! Move, now!" Ver interrupted impatiently.

His voice had taken on such an edge that even Cadin and Rheen nearly fell over themselves to comply.

In moments, they were at the fork, already out of breath and beginning to perspire, despite the chill in the early evening air. They dashed to the right and hurried on as a moaning and still unconscious Ensin Llaw bounced along in the soldiers' arms. Some time later—Jaren was kept too busy remaining upright to take any measure of its passage— the side of the mountain on their left fell away, and they followed a narrow ledge that curved around to the right. Their pace, of necessity, slowed. The scene before them was dizzying; hundreds of feet stood between their path and the nearest cliff side, and below a straight drop promised a sudden, brutal end should they miss their footing along the precipitous route.

A thin, dark silhouette, too regular to be anything but human-made, began to materialize out of the deepening gloom. At last, they reached it, a rope and wood bridge that extended from the near side and disappeared into the shadows beyond. The precarious span of ancient-looking materials swayed uneasily in the expanse, buffeted by the rougher winds away from the great canyon's edges.

Cadin and Rheen set the *Valir* down before the bridge and sank to their knees in exhaustion. Llaw was not a stout man, but neither was he a starving street waif. The pair had kept pace with the siblings all the same.

"How long do you think that's been here?" Jaren wondered aloud, hoping Morgaine would answer. They hadn't shared more than a handful of words since they'd first ascended from the plain, and before that, their conversations had been brief enough.

A moment later, she did reply, though her voice was subdued "Too long, I'm sure. Longer that it would take to hit bottom."

He was glad the floor of the chasm was shrouded in darkness. Soon, everything but a hand before their faces would also be. He shivered in the cold wind. "I hope we don't have to cross it in the dark," he said, though he wouldn't relish crossing it on the brightest of days and even then if it was but newly built.

Suddenly, Ver was beside them. "I've already been over," he announced. "There's not much to it. Just put one foot in front of the other. An added incentive," he offered, "is that there's a small cabin on the other side. Whoever maintains it hasn't been there for some time, but at least it has a roof to cover our heads and walls to stop the wind." He smiled and made a sweeping gesture toward the bridge. "After you, my young friends."

Jaren was about to protest that a friend would not force him to do something that so terribly frightened him, but he knew it wouldn't do any good. There was nowhere to go but forward, now.

Thankfully, the darkness actually helped. It made it possible for Jaren to pretend he was not walking suspended, hundreds of feet in the air, but instead down a dark underground passage. Except for the wind and the swaying; but there was nothing to be done about it. As it turned out, though, the crossing was uneventful, except for a couple of dire-sounding creaks from boards underfoot. Each sent his heart pounding in his chest as if it would break free, but he found solid footing once more.

The cabin was less than plain. A single chair sat in one corner, and along one wall was a cot with straw bedding. On the wall opposite the cot was an ancient iron stove, though, save for the chair and the bed, there was no fuel for it. The shelter was scarcely large enough for four men to stretch out fully on the floor, which Cadin and Rheen did without hesitation. They were asleep within moments. Jaren and Morgaine shared the remaining space, while the injured *Valir* tossed and turned on the slim bed. After several long moments, Ver seated himself in the chair by the lone, dust-coated window. Although cracked in several places, it was mostly whole and let in no more outside air than did the thin walls.

The sound of the wind without was not much subdued by the rickety, old building. An ever-present wail, it did little to help Jaren find sleep. Finally, in desperation, he began working through his relaxation exercises. Even so, it was some time before he drifted off to what became an uneasy slumber.

29

THE NEXT MORNING CAME TOO early. Stepping outside while stifling a yawn and trying to smooth out the kinks, Jaren became aware of the reason the avatar had taken those few extra moments before entering the previous evening. The bridge was gone. All that remained on this side were short lengths of frayed rope, and he could just make out the clinging form of at least part of the structure dangling over the far edge.

Ver lent Jaren a measuring eye as he surveyed the avatar's work. "I've led you from the immediate threat. Now it's up to you; where next?"

"How should we know?" Morgaine huffed. She'd exited the shack immediately behind her brother. "We haven't been making any of the decisions up to now. We don't even know where we are!" She was even more upset than Jaren would have believed. *How much of it was because of him?*

"You're straight south of the Tygar River. Jamnar lies there," Ver offered, pointing north. "And Drisia is over there." His arm changed its bearing to the west.

Morgaine still glowered. "That doesn't really help. Ensin Llaw didn't tell us where exactly we were headed, so how are we supposed to know?"

Ver nodded silently in acknowledgment.

In a conciliatory tone, Jaren said, "Why don't you give us a hint, Ver? You must suspect where the *Valir* was taking us. I mean, other than just 'the Barrens.'"

"You know that's not my way, young one. I'm surprised you would ask me by now."

"Why not?" Morgaine demanded. "What kind of helper are you anyway, if all you do is save us when we or someone else puts us in danger? Why can't you steer us clear of it yourself?"

Jaren still couldn't quite believe what was coming out of her mouth.

Ver fixed her with a considering stare. A low moan floated from the ramshackle shelter. "Could you two manage to fetch some water for the *Valir?*" he asked of Cadin and Rheen. They looked at one another, their hard eyes puzzled. "There's a stream not far down that way." He gestured to a path winding away on the right. Shrugging, they headed off to do the avatar's bidding.

Once they were gone, Ver turned back to the siblings. He sighed. "I can only empathize with you, being forced from your homes and into constant flight and danger. I would be equally unsettled."

Morgaine sniffed.

"But, you must understand the nature of my service. I cannot interfere, other than protecting you through the decisions you or others make. There is no room for negotiation on this," he said, as Morgaine opened her mouth to interject. "It is forbidden. I am to act as a balance only, nothing more."

"A balance to what?" Jaren puzzled aloud.

"To the agents of the Deceiver. I am a guardian. Do you not recall the familiarity of the blacktongues with me? I have faced them before, many times. I will do so again, until the time of my service is at an end."

"When will that be?"

"That…" he shrugged, "that is up to the True One. Then, others will receive the calling and be chosen to take my place. That is the way of it, for all who serve as I do."

"You mean to say there are more of you?" asked Jaren.

"I couldn't say at the moment, but at times, yes."

"Are they all guardians?"

"Some have…different duties. But I cannot offer much more on them." Morgaine stiffened again, crossing her arms. Ver ignored her. "You would know if they were sent to you."

"How long have you been protecting people?" Jaren pressed.

Ver smiled wanly, and his eyes took on a distant cast. After a few moments, he answered. "I cannot really say, my young friend. A long time, not as long as it's been since someone like you was born, but long enough. Long enough to forget some things, but I fear others will be etched in my mind for all eternity."

"Can you make friendships?"

The avatar's smile warmed, though a slight look of sorrow washed over it. "Of course, Jaren, but I will be around for some time, perhaps long after you are gone. I will be called in another direction at some point. That makes friendships somewhat temporary. I suppose, after a while, I stopped getting close to people. Being a servant changes you, from who you once were, and from others even more so."

"Sounds lonely," Jaren observed somberly, but then, after a moment, his voice perked up. "I'll be your friend for as long as you like."

Morgaine looked at her brother blankly.

"I'd like that," Ver replied with a genuine chuckle. He clapped Jaren on the shoulder.

"So, as a friend, you still have no advice for us?" Morgaine's tone had turned from angry to sarcastic. She must have been near her breaking point, to speak to him so.

Jaren gazed at her, dumbfounded.

Ver shook his head regretfully, ignoring her tone. "It is not my place. You were created by the True One to have free will. My role is to see to it that you are allowed the chance to exercise that freedom."

"Well, little brother, I guess it's up to us."

Jaren nodded, offering a weak smile.

Morgaine announced, "If Ensin Llaw was taking us to the Barrens, we should continue that way. Perhaps he'll recover soon enough and be able to guide us after that."

"All right," Jaren said.

"All right then." Morgaine was already heading back into the cabin to collect their few possessions.

She could at least wait for my response before assuming it, Jaren objected silently.

Suddenly, Ver bolted past her. "Leave your things!" he shouted. "Follow the path the others took! Hurry!"

"But what—" Morgaine began in protest.

"There's no time! Go!" Ver disappeared into the shack.

Cadin and Rheen had come running up, apparently overhearing the avatar's shouts while enroute back to the cabin. Water sloshed from a worn, old bucket in the former's hand. It was discarded without a second thought as they, too, raced inside the small structure.

Jaren cast about hurriedly, trying to discern what had moved the avatar to such haste. Morgaine had gone white and her mouth gaped. He followed her line of sight across the expanse of the chasm. Then he saw her. She stood, motionless, eyes fixed on them.

It was the woman summoner from Dal Farrow.

⁊

The advance units of the Jamnite army wound their way down from the pass to the floor of Stahl Vale. The waning light flashed in brief glints along the columns' lengths as hard blade and burnished armor reflected Sholara's last rays. The arrival of the army had been heralded by messengers and scouts scant hours before. Less than a day had passed since Aldrain's own small company reached the fortress just after dawn. Though the news of the approaching host had turned out to be good indeed, it was still unsettling to know they'd almost made the Hold at the same time as his band.

Had the messengers not brought word that the Jamnites were marching *against* the Warwitch, he would have been much more un-nerved. Most importantly, they had brought two more *Valir*, both Jam-nites, and both peers to those who had accompanied Aldrain.

Now, they awaited the final two.

The Jamnites would strain the resources and space of the Hold to its breaking point, to be sure, for it was near impregnable and there-fore was designed for a garrison of no more than a thousand, possibly even less. The caverns and subterranean passages beneath the massive edifice, however, could be made to accommodate them all. Luckily they hadn't brought too great a number of cavalry. The horses didn't like to be kept underground, and there was precious little space to exercise them.

Still, Aldrain welcomed the assistance, complications aside, though the anticipated arrival of the Warwitch carried no small amount of trepidation. A hundred thousand men might not be enough against her power.

The expected *Valir*, both Ergothani, would be hard put to reach them at all if they did not arrive before the new day dawned. By then, the vanguard of the Warwitch should have reached them. She herself was following with the main host, which would likely not arrive until the late afternoon or early evening.

Could they hope to outlast the Warwitch? If not, Aldrain would be forced to flee via the catacombs beneath the Hold, with as many as could make the passage. They would emerge several leagues to the north from a hidden exit nestled deep within towering spurs of rock.

From there, he'd have to make his way to Colm. After that, his course would depend on other considerations.

The most unthinkable eventuality was capitulation to the demands of the Warwitch. They had again received such from a messenger a short time ago. Her conditions for peace were unaltered—save one additional demand, placed foremost on the list. Jaren was to be handed over now as well.

Aldrain's thoughts scattered at the echo of footfalls from the corridor behind. He turned to see one of his runners approach.

"Your Majesty." The youth saluted. "The Jamnite commander wishes to meet with you."

"Very well," Aldrain replied. "I will attend in short order."

He gazed somberly for a moment longer from the balcony far above the vale and rolling emerald country to the south, his own eyes lingering over what was possibly Sholara's final glimpse of Draegondor rule.

❧

The hardness in the Jamnite's one eye more than made up in intensity for the lack of its twin. Judging by the number of purplish scars that crossed his face, the commander was used to pain. Frequent violence, they spoke of, and in good measure. An engraved silver circlet with an eyepiece crowned his bald, battle-scarred head Actually, it was more than a simple eyepiece. It continued down from the inch-wide band to cover his cheekbone, extending nearly back to his ear.

There appeared to be another ore worked into the headpiece. *Metanduil? A little out of place on a warrior—maybe he's just overly superstitious, even for a Jamnite.*

Angrill was tall as well, about a hand more so than Aldrain, and of sturdy build. Much like his men, the commander wore a dark green, open-sided surcoat that reached below his knees. It was bordered with silver silk, and a black hawk was embroidered into the breast. His calf-length, firm leather boots were still covered in dust from the journey. He offered Aldrain a solemn salute.

Aldrain acknowledged with one of his own. "Well met, commander. I am Aldrain, king of Carathon."

"Well met, sire. I am Angrill, First Watcher of Jamnar. I knew your father. He was a fine swordsman. He will be missed on the field of battle."

As close as a Jamnite will likely come to expressing condolences. Aldrain nodded in reply.

"We have heard of the recent events in Carathon. We are here to join you in your struggle against the Witch."

His tone at the last was less than civil. *Typical Jamnite sentiment about things magical,* Aldrain thought. "I thank you for your aid," he added, with a single nod. "It is as likely as not that what befalls us befalls the whole of Evarlund."

"As we believe, also. Our best chance is to strike at her before the Witch can consolidate her power and coerce the lesser nations to heel."

Aldrain wondered if Carathon was was numbered among that inferior group by most Jamnites. Perhaps before the treaty they were, perhaps even now. The Jamnites were a proud people.

"The *Valir* you've brought may be instrumental in that," Aldrain offered.

The commander's mouth drew into a half grimace. "Cousins of the king. Pity, Wendl would have made a great swordsman. Even now, he's not bad for a summoner. Still, royalty must be allowed their eccentricities." It appeared it was all he could do to not to spit on the ground.

"And yet, the beggar cannot be choosy with his alms," Aldrain said, in a conciliatory tone.

Angrill gave a grudging harrumph in acknowledgment.

"You are all welcome. I have cleared the upper barracks for your horses. The soldiers will be accommodated in the levels below. You will, of course, have free reign of the citadel, to tend to your men as needed." He received a slightly friendlier nod at that, but not by much. A stone might be as soft as he. And yet, considering their upcoming struggle, Aldrain hoped all of the Jamnites exhibited the same coarseness.

Aldrain took his leave from the commander, meaning to take measure of his soldiers' preparations. He had ordered nearly fifteen hundred Carathonaian regulars to the Hold, as many as he could spare from the capital with the added uncertainty surrounding the Ergothani muster. There was still no word from them as yet regarding their intentions. Perhaps the *Valir,* whenever they might arrive, could shed some light on that front.

Though his kingdom might be more vulnerable than he would have liked, Aldrain was left with little choice. He needed men here, and he was still left to wonder, if they failed in their struggle, what did anything else matter? What sort of rule could be expected under the heel of the Warwitch? Who was to say that he would not be replaced on the throne or given an advisor of her choosing? Either way, it amounted to the same thing. Their very way of life, all that had been left to him, was in jeopardy.

Winds of change, indeed. He just hoped all was not swept away entirely.

30

SHE HAD EITHER BEEN TOO far away, which Jaren doubted, or she was confident she had them, which was more likely. Those were the only two explanations Jaren could think up to explain the *Valir's* inaction at the cabin. If she were strong enough to withstand Llaw's summoned avalanche, then she surely had the power to reach them from across the gulf. It was more reasonable to assume that she was simply in no hurry because she felt they were already hers.

Andraste, Morgaine had said her name was. He remembered her now, cold and detached. *If any Valir was to turn from the Truth, it would be her.* But why hadn't she simply taken them captive during that first meeting? Maybe she'd feared the others would stop her, then, if she moved overtly. It seemed to fit the way servants of the Deceiver operated, in the shadows, behind the scenes. Andraste must be in service to the Deceiver, he reasoned. Who else could she be working for? In the end, he supposed as he'd been taught, it came down to those two sides: the True One or the Deceiver. She certainly was not for the Truth.

He got a glimpse of Morgaine as they hurried along the rocky pathway at the bottom of a wide defile. They were not running now, but Ver was pushing them hard. Jaren wondered what would cause someone to turn to the Lord of Lies, to become his servant. He wondered also if it had to be a conscious decision.

Could you wander from the Truth unwittingly? If so, what were the signs that it was happening? He shuddered involuntarily with the picture of Morgaine's face back in the clearing days ago, twisted with dark pleasure, and then thought of his own path, just begun. Which way was Morgaine headed at present? Obviously, the magic had an allure, a draw that was deeply tempting. He'd felt it himself. He'd even felt the yearning for it before he discovered his abilities. It was the pull that had caused him so much grief over the past months. But he knew it now, all the same. How could you handle such power and remain true?

He was somewhat relieved by the fact that Morgaine could find mentors to tutor her. They had the same abilities and had undergone similar trials to those she was now enduring through the use of her talents.

But what of himself? What if it were easier for Jaren to cross the line that separated truth from deceit? He had no guide, really, none that knew what he was actually dealing with. For all Llaw's studying, he was apparently still just postulating and making logical assumptions.

And Jaren didn't even have the *Valir* for the time being. The man jostled about, drifting in and out of consciousness, on a makeshift stretcher borne by Cadin and Rheen.

What if they were taken?

Could they withstand this *Valir's* attempts to turn them, should she try, he or Morgaine? He thought his sister might have a harder time of it, as they shared similar abilities, and, therefore, the summoner would likely know how to get to her, directly or otherwise. He wasn't so sure of his own situation, though the idea offered little in the way of reassurance. While Andraste likely had no more knowledge about him than Llaw, if they were taken, he would soon enough face other False Sworn, if not the Deceiver himself, though he'd never heard of such a thing. Of course, he had never heard of *An'Valir* before he was proclaimed one. His blood turned to ice at the thought of coming face to face with the Lord of Lies.

Ver bounded ahead of the others, nimbly picking his way through the scattered bits of rock that obstructed the path, the movement catching Jaren's eye and dispelling his thoughts for the moment. Every so often, the avatar would pause and look back, whether to urge them on or simply to ensure they had not fallen too far behind, Jaren wasn't certain. It seemed hours that they had spent, rushing along the various trails, and Ver gave no indication he would ease the pace of their flight any time soon. Towering cliff walls or vast, dizzying expanses inched by slowly, despite their haste. Jaren clutched his cloak tighter about him and staggered wearily ahead.

Morgaine fell as a small slide of rock gave way beneath her. Jaren lurched to a stop and offered her a hand. She grudgingly took it, but with the next step nearly dropped again as her left foot touched down. She gasped in pain.

Ver observed momentarily, and swiftly rejoined them. Cadin and Rheen set the stretcher down and collapsed, flushed faces dripping with sweat, chests heaving.

The avatar inspected Morgaine's ankle. "I think it's just a slight sprain. You'll be all right to move again after some rest."

"What difference does it make if we can't get away from her?" she managed, through labored breathing. "We might as well just sit down and wait here."

Jaren had never heard such despair in her voice. "Come on, Gainey, we'll be all right. Just a bit farther, right, Ver?"

The avatar glanced at him, and nodded grimly.

The use of her nickname seemed to have had the opposite of the desired effect. "Why don't you just go on with him? You're the one she's after anyway. I doubt she'd even notice me."

"Gainey, you're in danger, too."

"Why, because I'm your sister? Well, I'm tired of being responsible for your messes. Maybe for once you can just try to get by without me."

"What are you talking about?"

"You don't even realize it, do you? You do whatever you want, and always get away with it. Mother and Father have always let you have your way, but I'm stuck looking after you. I get in trouble if I don't do a proper job. Well, they're not here now, and I don't feel like watching my little brother anymore."

"Gainey, calm down and listen!"

"No, I won't calm down! Just when I thought I was going to do something for me—just for me—it all fell apart. You had to ruin it. You couldn't live with me having something special of my own; you just had to have it for yourself. Now look where we are!"

"How could I—I didn't make all this happen!" Jaren was incredulous. "Do you think I chose to be *An'Valir* or whatever I am? That's impossible!"

"Just leave me alone! You and your new *friend*, and everyone else, for that matter! *Just leave me be!*" She was yelling so loud that her voice cracked. Immediately she began to weep, great heaving sobs that shook her from head to toe.

Jaren simply stared. Was that how she really felt? She was his big sister, always there, always around to listen to his hopes and to share her own. No, it had to be her frustration and fear speaking. He didn't believe her anger was really directed at him. He had to believe it wasn't. She was all he had, right now.

Ver scanned the distance behind them with a wary eye. Cadin and Rheen tried to look everywhere but their direction, not doing a very good job at hiding their obvious discomfort.

Time passed slowly, awkwardly, as the interval between Morgaine's sobs lengthened. Suddenly, Morgaine's head lifted. "I'm sorry," she apologized, looking at no one in particular and wiping tears from her red-rimmed eyes. "We should be going now. I think my ankle is okay to walk on." She flexed her foot several times and put some pressure on it.

Jaren caught the slight wince that brought on, but she nevertheless stood up and seemed able to bear the discomfort, able and willing, now.

Ver nodded, and without a word, he slipped off ahead of the group. The soldiers took up their burden and followed once more, Morgaine resuming her place behind them. After a brief pause, Jaren started off, too.

The men had said nothing during the entire tirade, or after, for that matter. Jaren had thought about trying to talk to Morgaine before she'd spoken up again. He wanted desperately to bridge the gap that seemed to be forming between them, but he had no words to begin. He set his jaw and struggled on.

Their progress necessarily slowed as they came to a narrow, high-walled cleft and began to work their way along gradually and with some difficulty, due to the large amount of debris that had cascaded down to the floor of the defile over the years. The sky overhead was a lighter, slowly shifting ribbon of gray above the darker stone of the cliff walls that stretched toward it. Here and there, thin veins of *metanduil* spread through the rock like the bare branches of trees in winter. The ore felt oddly warm, much warmer than the cool stone that contained it, and now and then Jaren even thought he sensed a weak shock when his fingers chanced to contact the raw magic-metal.

Morgaine stumbled often along the jagged route before him, though Jaren had heard little more than muffled grunts in response. She hadn't so much as looked at him since her outburst.

He glanced back the way they'd come, the vertical slash of the defile shrinking into the distance, another dreary, gray stretch of stone left behind. He'd just begun to turn away, but a sudden glint from the periphery drew his eyes once more.

"Ver! She's back there!"

Instantly, the avatar was running, sliding past him and then hurtling on toward the female *Valir*. Her shadowy form was now clearly visible. She stood motionless once more, just outside the entrance of the cleft. It was the midmorning light, reflected from her burnished armor that had alerted Jaren. Shoulder and breast plates, inscribed with metanduil symbols, framed her silhouette.

What Valir wears armor? Jaren wondered.

Cadin and Rheen followed Ver, heedless of his command to continue on. Morgaine and Jaren stood transfixed, watching the confrontation unfold.

The *Valir's* arms came forward, and Jaren waited fearfully for something to happen. Seconds passed, yet still nothing occurred. Jaren caught the echo of a shrieked curse, a piercing female voice. Apparently her summoning, too, was affected by the presence of so much *metanduil* ore nearby.

Jaren felt a sudden surge of hope. If she could not bring her power to bear, then maybe there was a chance for them, after all!

Ver was halfway to her by now, the others not much farther behind. She stood still, as if in contemplation of her next move. She had precious few seconds before they reached her, and unless she was immortal, it would mean her end.

She lowered her arms then, and her head as well. The strip of iron sky above began to swirl, and suddenly arcs of lightning lanced down into the narrow canyon. Tendrils of blue and white pulsing energy coursed across the drab, gray stone with an ominous, crackling sound. Great showers of sparks rained down intermittently, apparently caused by the lightning's contact with the *metanduil* ore. Down, the spidery arcs streamed. Ver continued on, ignoring their descent, though Cadin and Rheen froze, peering panic-stricken at the deadly web of electricity.

Suddenly, feelers of lightning knifed into the soldier's blades, turning them instantly white hot. The pair hadn't even the time to shout out in alarm before they fell lifeless to the rocky floor, tendrils of smoke rising from their ruined bodies. Ver had cast aside his own blade, and now reached the *Valir*. Both hands reached for her neck, but her arms were instantly there to block him, and he instead wrapped his hands about the bracers covering her forearms.

Now, the feelers of electricity flowed toward the two combatants. As their struggles intensified, the tendrils closed in faster. Soon, they were both enveloped in a knot of twisting light, a blinding tangle of arcs that slithered over them and coursed into the space about them.

Unbelievably, neither appeared harmed by the shroud of electricity. Then, abruptly, the air about the struggling foes exploded in a ball of blue fire. Separated by the blast, Ver and Andraste were thrown violently against the canyon walls. Several veins of *metanduil* near at hand were instantly transformed into flying liquid death. Droplets of the silvery metal splashed about, some falling harmlessly, others alighting on the still forms of the avatar and *Valir*, hissing as they seared flesh. A wave of heat reached the siblings and rolled past, but they were far enough to avoid the more dangerous fallout.

"Ver?" Jaren called weakly after several moments. "Ver?" There was no movement. Silence reigned until a low moan rose behind them. Ensin Llaw stirred weakly on the stretcher.

The noise of a clattering stone brought them back to regard the scene of the struggle.

Andraste had pulled herself up to a sitting position. Slowly, her head pivoted toward them. She rose unsteadily to her feet, bracing herself against the nearby wall. Then, she started forward.

31

No sooner had the vanguard of the Warwitch arrived than it launched itself at the Hold in utter abandon. Trailing units were still arriving as they threw themselves, wave upon wave, crashing into the solid rock of the citadel like the tide falling upon a rocky shore. It had availed them nothing.

The fortress's foundations, hewn from the base of the mountain itself, were all but invulnerable to normal assault, and the Witch's advance legions, try as they might, could not hope to breach the solid stone. Three walled and heavily fortified ramps formed the sole admittance to the great edifice, each climbing diagonally from the base of the citadel in a zigzag fashion, the last ending at an enormous gate set into the curtain wall proper, far beyond the reach of even the tallest of siege towers. Access to the first ramp was achieved only via a long drawbridge, which formed its lowest section and extended onto the floor of the pass when not raised, as it was now. It was operated by a massive work of pulleys and gears housed deep within the mountain. Above the curtain wall rose the spires and turrets of the fortress: thick, towering fingers of stone quarried from the heart of the mountain itself.

In all of its considerable history, no weapon or manner of siege craft had breached the Hold. It could not be undermined. It could not be stormed and scaled while even a few score of men defended its walls.

No conventional weapon could defeat it. Nonetheless, it remained to be seen what scheme the Warwitch had wrought.

With the arrival of her main force, the vanguard had withdrawn reluctantly, until the last few units grudgingly broke from the futile assault and retreated, still under a hail of arrows from the citadel walls. They encamped barely out of arrow shot from the fortress, orange watch fires springing up over the rolling expanse below like stars winking into sight across a darkening sky.

Many among the defenders, Carathonai and Jamnite alike, had been heartened by the seemingly ineffectual tactics of their enemy. Those with experience, grizzled veterans and officers with years of campaigns under their belts, however, knew better. They sat, puzzled, conversing in hushed tones or silently contemplating what such useless struggle might mean. Their greenhorn fellows, meanwhile, sang colorful songs of battle and clapped each other on the backs, until their sergeants-at-arms chased them to barracks with scowls and curses.

Amid all of this activity strode Aldrain, past the numerous kettle fires spaced throughout the barracks, headed back to his quarters for the night. The base of the central tower loomed before him, massive and dark except for dim light washing through a few of the lower, arched windows. He was approaching the great oaken double doors of the entrance when a shadow detached from within the darkened recess. His blade rang free in a flashing of polished metal, singing out a challenge to the unknown figure that stood statue-still before him.

"Peace of the True One favor your blade, King Aldrain." The voice was female. He'd heard it recently: Jhennain.

"It seems I'm as jumpy as a deer in my fath—, in the royal preserves," he replied.

She drew back the cowl of her dark cloak, her raven hair spilling about her shoulders. "We are all on edge of late, my king. We stand at the twilight of this age, perhaps. What the coming night will bring, who can say?"

"Perhaps," he acknowledged grudgingly. "But I have faith in you and your brothers and sisters. You may yet deliver what strength of arms cannot."

"Even should we successfully meet the challenge of the Warwitch tomorrow, there will be much change. The knowledge to do what she has done, the once inconceivable and impossible, has been learned and exploited. I fear others may eventually choose to tread the same path." The *Valir* sighed heavily.

"Then we must learn from this lesson well, severely though it was taught us. We must be vigilant for the signs that may have been ignored. She could not have done what she did in too short a time, and without the spread of rumors."

"Yes, there were indications. But none of us gave heed to the stories, in the beginning, or for even some time after that. They were too outlandish and absurd to be believed. Rhianain was always recounting her achievements with a good measure of embellishment and ensured they were spread far and wide. It was only just before the demise of your parents that we realized the truth of what she'd done. By then, it was beyond us to do more than react in haste." Jhennain's voice held genuine regret.

"Well, no longer, then. Never again can we afford to disregard the warnings, however far-fetched they may seem. Not if it can mean the destruction of everything we hold dear." Aldrain took measure of her features. Even her beauty was marred by fatigue; dark circles had formed beneath her eyes, and lines of worry etched her face. "You are prepared, then?"

"As much as is possible," she nodded. "None of us have but read about what we are trying to accomplish here, which brings me to the point of my visit. Should we fail, what are your plans?"

The king sighed. "I'll have no choice but to retreat into the mountain, through the passages and north to Colm. From there..." He paused. "Will any of you be able to return and assist us?"

"I cannot say, though I would think not. If we cannot overwhelm her, then we may not even be strong enough to escape her. Certainly, not all of us."

"If I knew I could detect the weapon before it was unleashed, I might make a stand of it," Aldrain said. But, not to know and remain would be a gamble, in the least, with thousands of lives in the balance."

Jhennain nodded gravely.

"I will maintain both courses as possibilities, as I mentioned before, and make the decision when the time comes."

"Agreed, Your Majesty," she offered with another solemn nod. "Your confidence is appreciated, as are your prayers."

"Let's hope the True One is listening tonight."

"And sees fit to grant us whatever advantage is possible."

They took their leave from one another, the *Valir* melting back into the shadows and Aldrain heading into the tower. He drew a torch from its sconce. His footsteps trailed off into faint echoes about him as he ascended the narrow, spiral stairs. "The twilight of an age," the *Valir* had said. His eyes searched the unyielding blackness above.

So much was at stake. Everything he had left.

❦

A high, piercing wail rose up within Jaren's mind, distant at first, but building to a screaming crescendo. *No!* How could Andraste still be alive? He was dimly aware of Morgaine stumbling toward the approaching *Valir* drunkenly. She dropped to her knees, head down. She had given in to her despair, utterly. Morgaine had given up.

So should you, his mind reasoned. Jaren closed his eyes.

No! I will not! He raged against the voice of defeat within himself. The fury built, much like the soundless scream had. Images of all those who'd died, sacrificing themselves in vain, flashed before his eyes: Mother Haddie, Cadin, Rheen, and who knew how many other warriors who'd fought in their aid, including Ver. Finally, he saw Morgaine's face. But hers was a tortured visage, at the same time filled with regret and loss. It was what would become of her should Jaren, too, give up.

The burden was upon his shoulders. What could he do?

The image of Morgaine's face contorted to become that twisted look of pleasure at what she had done to the blacktongue, at the power that beckoned sweetly to be released against any who stood in her path.

Now, it called to him.

I will not! He railed inwardly again, both at the whispers of despair and in revulsion to the urging pull.

Jaren's eyes opened to find the *Valir* only yards from him, a wicked smile twisting her mouth. Her clothing hung in tatters, and she was badly burned, much of her hair incinerated. Her metanduil pendant shone with a dim, cool light, the amber stone within appearing as a lidless, staring eye. Splotches of *metanduil* had hardened on her face and body, but ran like harmless drops of water from her armor. She seemed not to mind in the least. That smile grew wider, and darkness glittered in her cold, blue eyes.

Jaren screamed, aloud this time. "You will not take her—you will not take me! No!" he howled, moving between Morgaine and the Valir. Letting go of his reluctance and fear, he released all of the despair, anger, and hurt that had built within. Not only was the cry for Morgaine and himself, but for all of those who'd suffered, if not at Andraste's hands then at those of others doing the same master's bidding: at the hands of the False Sworn, in the service of the Deceiver. The faltering image of Morgaine's joyful sneer faded into the recesses of his mind, apprehension driven away by his anger and the urgent need to do something, anything, to stop the woman before him.

Andraste was hammered back by some invisible force, brushed aside by the irresistible wave of his raw emotion. Her talisman reacted with a white-hot burst of its own, though this energy was likewise swept aside by Jaren's irrestistible assault. He kept on screaming. He had to stop her. She would keep coming. She would keep coming until she had them. Until—

Power surged through him: unfettered power, unimaginable power. It coursed though him and gave life to his maddened cry, feeding it, making it unnecessary even to breathe. Deeper and deeper his scream became, until it was the primal voice of the very land itself. It was raw, searing. It was the energy of making and undoing, and he had unleashed it. The mountain shook with its awesome reverberations, huge slabs of rock dislodging from the canyon walls before him, crashing down to the base of the cleft. Fiery geysers of molten *metanduil* ore erupted from the stone all about.

Jaren screamed.

The *Valir* was buried in an avalanche of stone and streams of searing, liquid *metanduil*; his last glimpse of her was a feeble, raised arm attempting piteously to ward off the crushing weight of the onslaught. Then she disappeared under a growing, shifting mound of debris.

Jaren's anger remained unabated.

He screamed.

Lifting his eyes past the immediate destruction, he saw something familiar in the hazy fog of his vision, distorted by rising waves of heat, someone familiar. He willed his sight clear. It was Ver. He was crawling toward Jaren weakly, one leg dragging awkwardly behind.

Jaren tried to stop.

The primal cry continued, now a living thing over which he'd lost all control. It rose in pitch, responding to his dismay, but only in that small measure. It would not be ended. It could not be silenced. Not now. He tried to muffle himself with his hands, but it was like trying to hold back the winds of a great tempest. He dropped to his knees, clenching his hands into fists at his temples. Tears welled in his eyes.

A massive column of stone separated from the right cliff wall, tottering briefly before falling against the opposite incline and sliding deeper into the canyon, down toward the helpless avatar. Jaren closed his eyes once more. He could feel intense heat radiating outward. The brightness of the super-heating mass nearby reached even through clenched eyelids.

Stop! His mind shrieked silently, seemingly without effect. *Stop this! It's over!*

Slowly, Jaren felt the emotions within him begin to subside. Just as gradually, he was able to wrench control of the magic back to his own will. The scream ended abruptly once he was sure of his hold, separating himself from the magic. A dull roaring remained in his ears from the devastating release.

Even with the flow interrupted, he could feel the draw of the power, beckoning, calling. Waiting.

He was aware of Morgaine, staring at him. Her eyes reflected something beyond mere fear. Jaren saw utter horror within. He knew that look. He had regarded her in the same fashion after the encounter with the blacktongue. A hoarse groan escaped his raw throat. What had he done?

32

How long had they stumbled along the twisting paths? Two days? Four? Gray, endless days stretched on and finally ended with the siblings in collapsed heaps, neither fully registering the passage of time. Each was wrapped in their own, despairing thoughts. They wandered on in silence, the stretcher borne between them, hands blistered, raw and riddled with splinters from gripping the rough wood.

They had not been able to find the avatar, their futile scrabbling at the tons of fused rock and *metanduil* ore earning them nothing but scrapes and bruises. That, and the realization he'd caused Ver's death, that he could not control the power within him, left Jaren bitter and hollow. He would never willingly use his abilities again, ever. He could not be trusted.

Could he truly keep his vow? If they took him, Jaren could not be certain. They would try to force him to use the magic, make him face it again. A combination of coercion and the draw of the magic would render him utterly vulnerable, he feared. Under those circumstances, how could he not give in to the power once more?

Doubtless, if he was captured, the enemy would find a way to turn him fully to the darkness. He was probably more than halfway there on his own.

He looked across the prone figure of Llaw to his sister. Her hair was matted with sweat and dust from their journey, and her cloak hung ragged in more than a few places. She limped with each step, still favoring her ankle. He knew without seeing her expression that it was dark and introspective, as was his. She'd seen Jaren's face, contorted and twisted by the ecstasy of the magic. She knew that look had marred her own features before. No doubt she was fighting the same losing battle with her conscience.

Some time later, hours or perhaps only minutes passing, as the greater darkness of night engulfed the drab countryside, the glow of lights became visible. They came to the top of a rise that looked down into a wide valley. All along its length, lights flickered. *It must be Ghalib,* Jaren thought.

Past the valley were a few higher spurs of rock, then the country swept down into rolling hills and plains. They were through the Forge.

And yet, they were nowhere Jaren wanted to be.

The sight of the city shook Morgaine from her dazed state, at least for the time being. She led them down into the streets in search of an inn. Shadows played across the roadways, chased here and there by flickering lamplight from a window or firelight from a door propped open to let in the night's breeze, for the day had been warmer down in the vale.

Raucous laughter floated from not a few of the shabby, multistoried inns. Most, the siblings gave a wide berth. Llaw had warned them of the dangers of Ghalib. It was a mining city, built to supply the laboring masses in the tunnels with supplies for their work and entertainment for their brief stints of relaxation. All manner of characters populated the city, and no few among them were cutpurses, footpads, brigands, or simply rough miners out for a good time. Russet appeared to be the cloth of choice for dress here, the tough fabric suited to the rigors of mining work. Whether miner or not, everyone they passed, it seemed, was coated with rock dust from head to toe. Thankfully, Jaren and Morgaine fit right in.

They did receive a number of curious glances, no doubt due to their burden. Eventually, however, they found an inn where the music was quieter, if not soothing, and no commotion sounded from within. Jaren peered at the sign over the door. *The Golden Stalk*, it proclaimed. A full head of wheat upon a long stem was etched beneath the words on a dark green background, its golden paint as chipped and weathered as the rest. Morgaine warned him to remain out of sight nearby while she entered to arrange for their accommodation, which they would be lucky to purchase with money from Llaw's belt purse.

She emerged from the doorway a few minutes later and pointed to the stretcher. Two burly young men, nearly identical in appearance and dress, bounded down the stairs and took up the stretcher.

"This is Ulder and Ulam. They'll help us with our things," Morgaine said, then motioned for Jaren to follow her inside.

The rich scent of pipe tobacco floated on the air, and several patrons in finer dress huddled around a number of round wooden tables, though they, too, bore the same dust as everyone else. Apparently, even the wealthier travelers could not be free of it. The innkeeper, a portly woman with large hands and a round, kind face, gave him a sincere-looking, warm smile as he passed, brief though it was.

Their room was larger than he'd expected, with two fair-sized beds, a table, and several chairs. It even had its own washbasin on a brass stand. The bowl-haired young men moved Llaw's limp form from the stretcher onto the nearest bed and scurried out.

"How much did this place cost?" Jaren wondered aloud.

"Don't worry, Llaw brought a fair amount of money. Perhaps he knew we'd need to stay in the more expensive places to be safer."

"Gainey?" Jaren's voice was laced with uncertainty.

"Not tonight, all right? We'll talk tomorrow." The edge to his voice must have alerted her. She gave him a wan smile and collapsed on the second bed. He looked about. She'd left enough room for him to climb on as well, and he was thankful for that. Otherwise, he'd have to sleep in one of the chairs or share the bed with the unconscious Llaw.

He chose the first of his three options, and was asleep before his head hit the down-filled pillow.

⫘

He awoke to find Ensin Llaw's eyes staring into his own. Startled, he sat up with a jolt. "You're awake," Jaren said.

"So it would seem," the *Valir* exhaled weakly. "Might one of you tell me where it is exactly I've awakened to find myself?" He was still lying on his back, head propped on a pillow.

Morgaine stirred at the sound of their voices, and, after adding her own surprised acknowledgment, the two of them filled the *Valir* in on events since his injury. They began eagerly enough, spirits bolstered by his unexpected recovery, but, once they reached the point of the final confrontation with the *Valir* who had tracked them from Dal Farrow, both became quiet and despondent once more. Llaw tried to reassure and encourage them, mostly in vain, so he simply lay there and listened attentively.

Over the course of the next few days, Llaw's health improved markedly and his approach to their talents changed. He must have sensed their great fears regarding the magic, and instead of practicing at first, Llaw urged them to discuss both the expectations and apprehensions they carried. For Jaren's part, however, all he could coax was a return to the relaxation exercises, which came grudgingly at that. The younger Haldannon simply refused to try his hand at further summoning. Morgaine, however, slowly acquiesced.

The *Valir* told him of his thoughts on Jaren's use of magic, how the three selves—mind, body and spirit—appeared to require uniting in order for his ability to become manifest. He argued that it was the reason Jaren had only been able to wield the magic under adverse conditions to this point, only when, through dire need, he'd been forced to focus his entire being on what he was doing. It was a holistic approach. Because Jaren himself was the connection to the power and not *metanduil*, as in Morgaine's case, it seemed to follow that Jaren needed to train his thought not on the task or object of his summoning but on himself to channel the magic to useful effect.

All of that was well and good, Jaren thought, but it still didn't tell him how to control the magic. Still, having a better idea of what might drive his use of the power could be used to ensure it didn't happen again. He felt somewhat conflicted, accepting the *Valir's* information as if he were going to put it to use. And, in a manner of speaking he intended to. It was just going to be in the opposite fashion to what Llaw intended. He would use the knowledge to brace himself against summoning. He would make sure he never lost control of it again. If that meant forever abandoning his talent, so be it.

Jaren could almost have laughed at the irony of his predicament. So long searching within himself for and desiring the ability, only to find that he had it, more than anyone would have conceivably thought, and only to realize that the magic was far too dangerous for him to ever safely use.

That evening, while Llaw had stepped out to enjoy his pipe, Jaren approached Morgaine. She was sitting on the edge of the bed, apparently lost in thought. He joined her. "How are you doing?"

"Better, thank you," she replied after a moment. "Yourself?"

"Okay, I guess." Jaren hesitated. Better to just get it out. "Do you think it's safe to use the magic, Gainey? After what happened to both of us?"

"I've learned a lot over the past few days, Jaren. I think I can control it. Llaw has taught me how to see the warnings, and—"

"But that's just in theory. Look at what we did!"

"I know what we did!" she snapped, and then took a steadying breath. "But you and I are different, Jaren. Llaw knows exactly what I'm going through. All *Valir* have to deal with it."

He studied the floor for a moment. "What you said back there in the mountains, about what you felt, did you mean it?"

It was her turn to shift her eyes away. "No, but…it's all gotten so complicated since we left home. It used to be simpler."

"I didn't mean for any of this to happen, you know. I want you to be happy."

"I know, I know, and I'm sorry, Jaren. What I said…it didn't come out right. I was angry and afraid. I took it out on you."

"Forget it," he smiled. "But I just don't want anything to happen to you, now that I know what we're dealing with."

"What you're dealing with."

"We may be different, but the magic is still the magic. Don't tell me it doesn't call to you. While you're using it, it wants to be used, more and more." His voice had grown hushed, ominous.

"You're going to have to deal with it some time, you know. You can't avoid using it forever."

"Yes, I can," Jaren countered.

"And what if they catch you? And you've done nothing to prepare yourself? What then? You can find out how to control it, how to use it safely. You need to do that before they have a chance to—"

"To what, to turn me from the Truth? I'll beat them to it, if they do try." He could feel the gulf between them widening, their common bonds separating. "I won't let them turn me, and I won't use the magic again, ever. Even if I have to go, to leave—to run away for the rest of my life." He rose from the bed and stalked to the door.

"What kind of living is that?"

"Better than living with what I've done, and what I might do again." The door closed swiftly behind him. Morgaine let out a long, low sigh, her head falling into her hands.

🌱

All of this sitting around was driving Iselle crazy. Others were in danger of dying all about, and she was stuck in her room. Aldrain had not dared come near of late, knowing she was infuriated at being kept under guard. It was for her own good, he'd reasoned. She'd been so angry, she'd thrown a mug at him. At the king! Since then, he'd sent others, aides and servants. He used the excuse that he was busy tending to the defense of the Hold. She knew better.

Iselle moved to the arched window. It offered a fantastic view of the surrounding lands, but she cared little enough for scenery at present. She wanted to do something! Jaren and Morgaine surely needed her help by now, out there to the west, wherever they were.

Things never went according to plan. That was the wisest piece of advice she'd ever received from her father. *And always be prepared for when they don't*, he would add. Only, she could do nothing to aid them from here, hundreds of leagues away, she guessed.

A commotion in the corridor caught her attention. She turned and peered at the stout, oaken door. The latch worked softly, then it opened, and a cloaked figure ducked in, closing the portal swiftly behind.

Before she had a chance to demand the identity of the newcomer, the hood drew back to reveal Turan's face. His flat-topped hair appeared even darker in the dim light. A bright, mischievous smile flashed.

"Had enough moping around, yet?" he asked.

She stumbled over her surprise. "How…how did you get in here?"

"The guards at the end of the hall went to investigate something or other." He shrugged innocently. "I just happened to be nearby and thought I'd come visit." He winked.

Turan did that often, she'd found on their journey to the Hold. Iselle had several opportunities to converse with him, and he seemed quite likeable. He had a good sense of humor, too, just like hers.

His eyes grew more serious. "Actually, I'm leaving. Now that they're preparing to fight, they've left us more or less alone. I wanted to see if you'd come, too."

"You're leaving? How?"

He moved to the window and peered down. "The room below yours is empty. So is the hallway. All we have to do is get there."

Her eyes narrowed. "How do you propose we do that?"

He put a hand up to give her pause. Then, it disappeared behind his back with the other, into the folds of his cloak. He brought forth a length of corded rope, and smiled. "Beautiful night for a climb, don't you think?"

She threw him a flat look. "You have got to be kidding."

"Well, if that's a no, then I'll just be going by myself. If you wouldn't mind undoing the rope once I'm gone? It was hard to come by, and I'll probably find a use for it somewhere along the line." He looked about for something to anchor one end.

"You're serious, aren't you?"

"I'm tired of being held captive here, just like I was in Aendaras. Now I have the chance to be free, and I'm going to take it." He studied her. "You look like you'd rather be somewhere else, too, perhaps with your friends. We could go together." He winked again.

Under normal circumstances, Iselle would never have consented to such lunacy. But, then again, things had been far from normal since she had set out from home what now seemed so long ago.

"All right, let me get my things." She shot him a wary eye. "But if I fall to my death, I'll haunt you forever."

"Then I'll see you in waking and asleep." Winking again, he donned the most heartstruck of looks, "Because you already walk the land of my dreams."

"I think you have something in your eye," Iselle groaned.

Their descent was over quickly and without problems. He went first, hand under hand, slowly and carefully, until he disappeared into the darkened space that was the window below. His face peered up palely in the gathering gloom, and he gestured impatiently for her to follow. After one final glance at the anchored rope, she climbed on the ledge, turned about, and began to lower herself slowly. She'd held her eyes tightly shut at first, but then chanced a glimpse. What had seemed such a dizzying height before was not so bad now, mostly shrouded as it was in shadow.

Perhaps she didn't mind heights. There had been few enough to practice on in Dal Farrow. The tallest of the trees near the tiny village had seemed little challenge to her, but that was quite different than hanging from a slender rope one hundred paces above unforgiving stone.

Soon enough, she felt Turan's hands guiding her feet toward the ledge. Then she was inside, clambering down into the gloom of the small chamber, a feeling of exhilaration warming her after the chill breezes without.

"You're sure you feel comfortable with this?" he questioned.

"It's a little late to ask me now," she replied sardonically.

"I know, but I thought it was the polite thing to do."

She couldn't tell for sure, but she thought he'd winked once again.

33

THE WARWITCH IS TOYING WITH *us!* Aldrain's mind roiled. Three full days, her entire army had lain without. Lain without and done what amounted to nothing. Other than token actions, there had been no significant threat from her camp. Still no messages other than the previous demands had been conveyed, no further envoys or requests for parley sent.

He had conferred several times with the seven *Valir*—the Ergothani pair, a male and female, had arrived only minutes before the Witch's vanguard first appeared—and their moods darkened with every day. The Warwitch was shielding her presence somehow, so that they could not pinpoint her exact whereabouts. Until they were able, it would be impossible to confront her, until she chose to show herself.

All of it seemed to Aldrain as if she wanted to impress upon them the new manner of warfare she had ushered into the world. Her vast army could lay siege to the Hold for years, though he truly doubted it would come to that, considering her newest weapon. The feigned attacks, he assumed, were her way of keeping the rowdier elements among her host appeased. It was difficult, he knew from his father's recounting, to march men toward a battle and then deny them a fight. It made them restless and put them on edge. That was not a good recipe for proper, ordered discipline, a necessity with so vast a group. She was letting her generals launch insignificant, minor forays until she decided the game had gone on long enough.

But when might that be? And what would be her next move?

The news that the youths had gone missing only added to his sour mood. He did not think it a mere coincidence that the boy, Turan, had disappeared the same night as Iselle. The thought worried him.

Had he another choice at the time, he would have taken any other prisoner that appeared to be of Jaren's stature. But a chance riot in the dungeons had eliminated any other candidates. The boy hadn't caused any problems, though he had a troublesome smile, and there was something about him, an air that was not to Aldrain's liking.

He sat at the sturdy table, consumed by his thoughts, staring at something unseen beyond the maps and charts spread about. None of it mattered, really, until they knew what was to be the outcome of the struggle between the *Valir* and their nemesis. As if in answer, a flurry of knocks rained on the door.

"Enter," Aldrain commanded.

His runner gulped for breath heavily. "The *Valir* have requested your presence, Majesty."

⁊

The summoners had gathered within a large chamber several levels below their quarters. All seven were assembled, dark-robed, somber of face, their eyes full of hardened determination. They stood in a circle at intervals around a silvery metal outline, some fifteen feet in diameter, set into the flagstoned floor. It was engraved with runes and mystic symbols, none of which he recognized. Embedded in the center of the ring was a solid center circle, also *metanduil*, and similarly engraved. It was perhaps three feet across. Torches ensconced regularly along the walls cast the room in a warm, orange light that set their shadows to a haunting dance.

"Your preparations are complete, then?" he inquired.

Seven pairs of eyes regarded him at once. He felt them collectively, like a physical touch—a wary one, at that.

"We began these arrangements two days ago," Jhennain offered, "once it became clear that Rhianain had chosen not to show herself. At first, we were not sure we could work the ritual, but I believe we've succeeded."

"What exactly is it you've planned?"

Another answered, the woman from Ergothan. "The circle forms a portal. One can travel through it."

"I see," Aldrain responded. "And you can use it to go to her?"

"No, it will be the other way round," Jhennain said.

"I don't understand." Aldrain blinked. "You mean to bring her *here*?"

The Ergothani woman replied, "It is the only way, unless we would wait her out. That is becoming unbearable. We know she is out there, among her army. We cannot go to her without knowledge of her exact whereabouts, but we can draw her here. She probably believes us less than capable of the task." More than a hint of disdain touched the last.

Jhennain nodded. "You comprehend the nature of our undertaking, yes?"

Aldrain nodded, still unconvinced.

"The inevitability of what we are to sacrifice weighs heavily on us, each one. The longer that end is delayed, we fear, the harder it will become to remain committed. We must, each of us, be resolute when we confront the Warwitch. There is little room for doubt or regret." She shifted uncomfortably.

Was there something more that she wasn't telling him?

Jhennain peered at her compatriots.

Their eyes reflected what Aldrain saw in hers. There remained determination, but behind it lurked a darkness. Was it fear, or something else?

Regardless, he'd started to get a clearer picture of their circumstances. He knew it was likely a suicide mission they faced, but he hadn't considered the burden such knowledge must be to bear. He could understand their motivation. But still, bringing the Warwitch into the fortress? That was nearly handing victory to her if they failed, wasn't it? All she needed to do was unleash her power within the citadel, and it and everyone within would be doomed.

He thought of the crater that was once his home in Eidara and shuddered involuntarily. "Might she not just destroy us when she realizes where she is?"

"We will have her bound. That is the purpose of the disc. We are certain she will be unable to manage summoning of any significance," the Ergothani answered.

Her eyes belied the fact that she was actually less than certain—but how much so?

The Vetian spoke now, and for the first time Aldrain heard the grating, deep voice and its rolling accent. "We have not so much asked you here for your consent, as to inform you of our decision. It needs be so, or we must abandon this endeavor."

Aldrain considered a moment. Most likely, the Witch could unleash her weapon from without and cause nearly the same amount of damage. Either way, the result would be no different. "Very well, then. But let me have some of my men present. Perhaps we may find an opening during the struggle."

"That cannot be allowed," the Vetian said. "They might disrupt our concentration. You may attend, but that is all we can allow. You must swear not to intervene under any circumstances. You must do nothing. It is our battle, and ours alone."

Aldrain exhaled in wary acquiescence. "As you wish. When will you begin?"

"Within the hour," he answered. It was spoken with the final resignation of someone condemned to die. And so he most probably was—along with the others.

⚜

Jaren returned to their room late, to find Morgaine gone. Llaw sat at the table, chin resting on steepled fingers, peering distantly past the dusty glass of the chamber's lone window. He turned with Jaren's entrance.

"She left, looking for you. Some time ago," Llaw answered the unspoken question in Jaren's eyes after a moment's pause. "She mentioned something about needing space, and time to think. But, I believe she wanted to speak with you. I could read it in her eyes. She carries pain and anxiety there. I expected her back before now, or at least with you." Deep lines of concern creased his face.

"We need to go after her," Jaren announced.

The *Valir* nodded, taking up the walking stick he'd used since recovering. Even with it, walking appeared to be a laborious task for the old man.

Llaw placed a hand on Jaren's arm. "She does care for you—deeply. Like a sister should. Whatever has passed between you these past days, it can be overcome. You will see." His smile was genuine and warm.

Jaren returned it. "I know."

They had no sooner reached the bottom of the stairs than one of the twins came rushing in the main doors. Was it Ulam or Ulder? He couldn't tell the two apart. Whichever it was, the young man was clearly shaken up, and immediately went to the innkeeper. He leaned over the bar and whispered something to her. Briefly, his eyes met Jaren's. Just as quickly he looked away, and thrust a piece of tattered parchment at the innkeeper. She took it and, after some hushed words of her own, sent him off to the kitchens. Taking a steadying breath, she came toward the two of them.

"Someone left this with Ulder. Scared the life out of him, it did, too. They told him to bring it to you, straight away." She handed it to Jaren and wrung her hands.

He read the note:

We have your sister. If you would see her again, deliver yourself to the Warwitch. A vessel will await you in Thurssen on the river Tygar. It is named the Wave Hammer. Come alone, without the Valir. Our Mistress has no need of him. The boat will wait for the next full moon. If you do not arrive by then, your sister will die, and the Mistress will not again extend such gracious courtesies.

There was no signature. The letter was written in spidery and irregular script, as if penned by hands unused or unsuited to writing. Jaren could feel the color draining from his face as his stomach clenched tightly into a knot. He passed the note to Llaw.

The innkeeper's hands worked harder now, realizing it was truly ill news.

The next full moon was a little less than two weeks away. They took their leave of the plump woman, who still appeared nearly as vexed as they were, and retraced their steps to the room.

"You have more than enough time to make the boat, but you mustn't go." Llaw stepped through the doorway behind Jaren and closed it quickly behind him. "You are not yet ready. You have only just begun to realize your power."

Jaren ignored the words. He intended never to test the boundaries further. "I have to go. She's my sister."

"There is more at stake here than just her life," Llaw said in near pleading tones. "Should the seven fail, you are the last hope. You cannot simply hand yourself over to her."

"Morgaine will die."

"Perhaps, but perhaps not. However, there is little for you to do. She must face this struggle on her own. Even if you tried now, you would surely be too late."

"You don't know for sure. You don't know anything!" Jaren burst out. He closed his eyes and forced his breathing to slow. "I didn't mean that, *Valir* Llaw. It's just—"

"I know, my boy. I have been much less a mentor than you should have had, but we all do what we can with what we have. It may be that

Morgaine is strong enough to withstand the Witch herself, if it comes to that."

"But then, she'll be of no further use. She'll be killed anyway."

"There are worse fates than death, Jaren." Llaw sighed wearily. "Every struggle has casualties. Those who fight cannot control when or why their lives are given. It is only up to them to do what they feel is right. The rest is left to the will of the True One."

"What would you have me do, then?"

"Take the time necessary to become who you were meant to be. Keep away from the Witch until that time. Then, you can lead the people against her. Then, you will *win*."

"How many others will die before I reach that stage? If I ever do? Who knows how long it will take? Years, probably, and by then, what will be left to save? And who would rally to me? I'm no leader. I'm just a farmer's son."

"Before she became the Warwitch, Rhianain Othka was a potter's daughter." He paused to study Jaren's reaction. The resulting frown said he'd read little enough in it. "We are who we make ourselves to be, not simply what we are born into."

"Everything is changing. Nothing's the same."

"One age ends, and another begins. It is the way of things. But, it doesn't happen all at once. Please, take the time to consider everything that's at stake, Jaren. Then, make your decision." Llaw nodded with that. Wrinkled, leathery hands fumbled about his robes for a moment, then reappeared holding his pipe. "If you'll excuse me, I must take some time to relax, myself. A bit of leaf always helps." He limped to the door, the walking stick thumping hollowly on the floor boards. "You should rest as well, my boy."

The *Valir* returned to the darkened room barely an hour later. Jaren was lying on his back, staring through the darkness at a ceiling he could not make out. Hours after the old man himself lay in slumber, snoring lightly, Jaren remained gazing up at nothing, while at the same time, at everything he held dear.

34

THE BOWELS OF THE CITADEL were shrouded in darkness. There were few enough windows as they descended, and those were high above the floor and narrow, until eventually there were none at all. The immense weight of the place and the inky darkness pressed in on Iselle, allowing the torch only a few feet of illumination. It felt as if the whole of it might simply crush her on a whim.

Yet for some reason, Turan seemed unbothered by it all. He picked his way through the twisting corridors and passageways with relative ease. They'd only had to backtrack a few times. Soon enough, Turan found his way again. He must have done nothing but sneak off to explore the depths of the fortress since arriving.

Then, abruptly, they stopped. Iselle wasn't sure how long they'd been about their journey—half an hour, at the least—when Turan came up to what appeared to be a dead end. She was growing impatient, waiting for him to give the nod to turn around and head back, but he held the small brand nearly flush against the wall. What was he looking for? He reached forward with one hand and pressed a small joint of stone that appeared much the same as any other to her. There was a barely audible click from somewhere inside the rock, and then a deep, grating noise. The wall itself crept slowly sideways along a rusted track to the squeal of dirt being ground by metal.

"How did you know to look for that?" Iselle wondered aloud, half to herself.

"Quickly now, we're almost there," came the hushed reply.

As before, the small torch revealed their surroundings in only the tiniest of snatches. The sensation of pressure and utter darkness here was worse, if that were possible.

Something just wasn't sitting right with Iselle. *How could Turan possibly have had enough time to explore these passageways to move through them so easily?* It would have been nearly impossible for him to find that latch, if he didn't already know where to look.

Perhaps it was the faint, cool breeze wafting toward them down the corridor, replacing the enclosing warmth of the fortress, but now a chill ran the length of her spine. *Turan couldn't have had the time, and he wasn't old enough to be that good.* So what was she missing? She fumbled with her thoughts as they trudged on.

Worked stone now gave way more and more to rough, cavelike surroundings. The ceiling rose and fell unevenly, with the natural formations of conical stone becoming frequent, as was the sound of dripping water. The floor became moist as the flagstones were replaced by dirt and irregular rock.

There were occasional, larger expanses in the walls, side passages that formed part of the subterranean network, and these came and went silently with little more to mark their passing than the sensation of a greater emptiness or another cold caress of musty air.

Iselle's pace had slowed as her anxious thoughts swirled. Turan noticed, for he gave her a word of encouragement and took her hand, urging her forward.

"Not far now," he said, tugging.

How could he know the distance unless he'd traveled it already? Her inner voice had become more than vaguely skeptical. Now it was fully wary. He couldn't have explored the lower fortress and caverns sufficiently and gotten back without being missed. It was impossible. That reality left few explanations. Either he'd been in the fortress before, which she doubted, or he knew of it otherwise.

It dawned on her, then. She stopped abruptly. He was wrenched to a halt as well. Since leaving the upper levels, he hadn't once winked, even when he normally would have. She was aware of his gaze now, steady and intense, though his features were masked by shadow.

"How do you know where we're going?" Iselle demanded.

"What do you mean?"

"You've been picking your way along like you were raised in these tunnels. How do you know where we're going?"

Turan hesitated, then began in a tone of exasperation, "One of the prisoners in Aendaras, he used to be a soldier here in the fortress. When I found out I was coming here, I asked him, and he told me about them, told me the landmarks I needed to look for. That's all." Still, there was no flash of a smile or his accompanying wink.

"You mean, on the night before we left?"

"Yes. Iselle, why are you asking me all this? Don't you trust me anymore?"

"I heard the guards talking. There was a riot in the dungeon the night before we left. Everyone had to be separated. Everyone left alive, that was." Turan licked his lips nervously, as Iselle fixed him with a hard stare, hoping he didn't notice her hand inching toward the long knife at her belt. Though, she didn't know if she could use it on him. Anyone they'd fought had been a stranger. He was someone she'd gotten to know. He could have become a friend. "So, I want to know. How do you know where we're going?"

He didn't answer. A shuffling echoed from all about. Surrounding her, heavy, dark forms materialized from the gloom.

Turan offered a derisive sigh. "You've found me out, Iselle. I'm not who I seemed, I guess. It's hard to explain, really." Now he moved closer, just as strong hands gripped her arms with vicelike strength. She could see his face clearly. "But, believe me," and now, he winked, "you'll be safer here than up above. Please, don't try to struggle. There's no one but me and my ... friends, down here."

❧

The chamber was the antithesis of noise. Nothing moved, not a wisp of a draft stirred. Aldrain doubted if the *Valirs'* hearts were even beating. His was pounding in his chest as if it would burst free. He glanced to the closed door behind him. He wasn't to have soldiers inside, he'd been told, but he made sure to have several squads posted just outside the doors with instructions to storm the chamber on his order. Not that steel could do much, he guessed, if the ritual was unsuccessful.

The seven bordered the circle, statuesque in their concentration, heads lowered and arms raised slightly before them, palms outward. They had stood so for some time now. Aldrain was beginning to wonder if they were powerful enough to carry out the plan, though neither of the two possible outcomes was much to be desired. If they succeeded, the Witch would be present within his compound, and with only the *Valirs'* word that she could do no harm while so held. If they failed, however, the insufferable waiting might continue indefinitely. It was maddening.

The air above the metal disc began to shimmer. White and blue particles of light sparked into existence, rotating horizontally. More joined them, revolving about a center point scant inches from the surface of the floor. Hundreds of particles had formed now, and the slowly spinning mass took on the rough look of a seven-spoked wheel, each of the arms curving gently back from the direction of the rotation. The wheel of light rose gradually, widening in its ascent and then retracting again— tracing a spherical shape—until it was a pace higher than the tallest in the room. There, it hung suspended for a brief instant before descending once again.

A vague, mist-enshrouded figure was revealed as the slowly revolving plane of light proceeded downward.

At first, Aldrain could discern no details. Soon enough, however, haze and shadows departed, leaving the newcomer in clear view, or as clear as the smoky, amber glow of the torches allowed.

A woman stood casually upon the *metanduil* floor plate, one long, sensuous leg exposed by the high, side cut in the clinging dress she wore. Though covered by the gown, the remainder of her captivating figure was scarcely concealed from view by the sheer weave of scarlet fabric. She might have been beautiful once. Indeed, some might still find her … exotic. Straight, dark hair framed a chiseled, angular face, tight lipped and severe. Dark eyes peered about, wolflike, taking in everything at once. Those eyes said that everyone she observed, she saw as prey.

That was not the most alarming observation, by far. A familiar, silvery metal covered much of her form, but it was not simply worn. The *metanduil* was meshed with her body. Her flesh and the magic-metal were melded, fused. *By the Truth, how could she have done that? How could she have endured it?*

There was no mistaking the imperious set to her visage, the absolute air of confidence about her. This was surely Rhianain, the War-witch.

Her eyes flashed in challenge to the room, one from within a cold, metallic socket. It was disturbingly reminiscent of Angrill's eyepiece, except this still housed a functioning eye. Her expression changed to one of conciliation. "I beg you, forgive my absence," she shrugged, "but it has been such a taxing journey. And there have been so many tasks to oversee." Rhianain's tone was condescending. "May I ask, to what do I owe the pleasure of this invitation?"

"Enough of your games, Rhianain, you know why you are here: to answer to the council."

"You will be punished for your atrocities."

The Warwitch passed a cool eye over the speakers in order, first Jhennain and then the Ergothani woman. They seemed to shrink under that gaze. Then her eyes fixed on Aldrain.

"Yes, I suppose I need to do some explaining, though I had hoped it would be under more … relaxing circumstances." Her voice was less than apologetic. Extending her arm and taking a step forward, Rhianain poked a finger into the air before her. The faintest outline of an ethereal screen appeared at the tip of her extended digit, moving liquidly with her touch, fluid, but unyielding. Smiling as if amused, she traced her finger in a circle, watching feelers of light dance across the magic skin, smiling as if amused. Her eyes returned to the king of Carathon. "Your Majesty," she mocked with a nod, "I look forward to an era of good relations. Your father was an honorable man, however misguided in his beliefs. I trust you will prove more reasonable." She apparently noticed his reaction and put on an air of aloofness. "Things change, Majesty, as you will soon see."

Rhianain turned her attention once more to the *Valir* surrounding her. "As for the lot of you, wretched self-absorbed underlings, you will be lucky to perform on street corners for coppers soon enough, if you escape with your miserable lives." She glared at each in turn. "As I said, an explanation is due. Much has changed. Your pathetic council and the very guild to which you belong are obsolete. You will be allowed to continue in your chosen profession, so long as you swear fealty to me. You may be of some service, however limited. If you serve well enough, you may even be granted … the gift." She peered down at her left hand, the flesh completely replaced by *metanduil*, and flexed it several times open and closed. "You, and the governments you now serve, will bow to me. If not," she gestured toward Aldrain, "your fates will be sealed as others' before you. Think well on it, *brothers* and *sisters*."

"Silence, Rhianain!" Jhennain ordered. "You have been brought here in judgment, not to dictate terms."

"Oh, but my time has arrived, my precious Jhennain."

The latter's eyebrows rose in surprise, as did those of several of the others. What was happening?

Aldrain gripped the hilt of his sword absently.

"You thought you were so much my better, didn't you? While you and your parlor-trick lackeys played politics, judging who was and who wasn't of proper measure to be in control, I was studying. I was searching. I embraced my destiny. Who has need of your pitiful council? I wield more power than any other in the six realms, or any ten combined. Choose your next words wisely, council chair. They may be your last."

Silence answered. The seven bowed their heads once more. Before the faces opposite him angled downward, Aldrain could see the lines of concentration deepen, brows furrowing and eyes closing tightly.

The ethereal sphere that enshrouded the Warwitch began to glow bluish-white, pulsating with magical energy. She chortled. "So be it. You choose others before me once again, Jhennain, so now you will die with them. All of you will die!" Suddenly, she reeled as if struck, stumbling back. She straightened, concentrating herself, now. The shield contracted about Rhianain slowly. A horror-stricken look crossed her face. She gasped, a sound that turned quickly to a hiss of defiance. The Warwitch was forced into a crouch on the floor as the sphere continued its inward collapse. She screamed and held her arms above her, protectively.

It's working! Aldrain thought. *They're going to do it!*

Then, the Warwitch was laughing, the scream fading to nothing more than an echoing memory. She waved her hand over her head dismissively, and the shield simply vanished.

Rhianain stood, smiling cruelly. Her mirthless laughter echoed throughout the chamber.

35

JAREN RAISED HIS FACE TO the heavens but found no answer to his prayer in a silent, star-filled sky. He'd been responsible for the demise of the True One's defender. How much more aid had he a right to ask? The dancing light from the tiny fire he'd built threw ruddy yellow light and leaping shadows about the camp.

He stared into the flames absently, then tossed in another small limb. It didn't matter if he drew attention to himself, since he was heading to the Warwitch anyway. Any False Sworn he attracted would simply usher him there faster and probably without needing to stop and find their bearings, as he occasionally did. Surely, there must be hundreds of them, perhaps thousands, scattered throughout the six realms. Were they all connected? Or did they act in secret, isolated from each other until needed? Jaren rubbed his stinging eyes, the smoke drifting into them occasionally with the shifting breezes. His world had indeed grown larger on leaving Dal Farrow, and his view of it a good deal darker.

Just you focus on the task at hand, without thinking up new worries, he scolded himself. The words sounded like something his mother would say—or Morgaine. He scowled. Llaw had tried further to persuade him not to go, but Jaren had been adamant. Morgaine wouldn't abandon him to imprisonment, death, or worse without trying to help. He could do nothing other than the same. The problem was, he had made no real plan.

But he would break his vow—once. Just one time would do it. He needed to get close enough to the Warwitch for it to work, but he was sure it would. The swath of destruction he'd unleashed in the chasm assured him of that. And, there were the rumors. Stories had come to light about the rumblings emanating from Kerlain's Forge. He worked it back and knew it had occurred not only on the same day as his confrontation with the *Valir*, but at the same time of that day. It was him. The strength was there; it was more than willing to be released. And he would oblige it, one final time. All he needed was the opportunity.

A pocket of sap in the burning tree limb exploded with a loud snap, and Jaren was shaken from his reverie. He peered down at the last of the dried fruit sitting forgotten in his hand and finished it off. Only another few days of traveling remained before he reached Thurssen. He would be there well before the deadline.

A passing thought occurred to Jaren. Suppose they were taking Morgaine on the same vessel? That was unlikely, for the same reason they'd not simply taken him by force along with her. They feared his power because they had no knowledge of its limitations. On that, they were of one mind, he and the unknown author of the letter. Jaren gazed into the darkness. The Warwitch's followers were probably out there now, observing, following, and making sure he made his way as arranged.

No, Morgaine was probably taken as quickly as possible, probably even on horseback straight to Thurssen. They could at least have offered to get him a horse, too. He chuckled mirthlessly at the thought. Most likely, they needed time to arrange for his proper handling. That made sense if they feared his strength. So, they were being cautious, giving themselves time, and keeping the siblings as far apart as possible.

In the end, it didn't matter if he actually saw Morgaine at all, though it would have been comforting to see that she was safe and unharmed. It came down to being close enough to the Warwitch to be able to do what he must. As long as he succeeded, Morgaine would be all right, so long as no harm came to her beforehand. About that, he could do nothing.

He poked at the embers of the fire with a long, green branch. Though the flames burned low once more, he didn't feed it further. Instead, he pulled his bedroll about him and again stared aimlessly into the night sky, trying to recall better times, of Morgaine, Iselle, and home.

He failed to conjure the wanted images, so he practiced his focusing techniques instead, the only reliable way to ward his mind against the whispered temptations of the magic.

"Fools," the Witch uttered in contempt. "I sense your doubt, your fear. You cannot defeat me unless you are willing to sacrifice yourselves." She peered approvingly at Jhennain. "You are," she acknowledged. "But others here are not so dedicated. Even if every one of you were, there is a chance you'd fail." She cast glances about at the *Valir* as she spoke. "You, Belaine, daughter of Ergothani nobility, do you really want to die to stop me? And you, Vetian? Your anxiety wafts from you, like the fetid stench of a rotting corpse under the sun. You are all weak, vulnerable. You play at magic. I *am* the magic, now."

She admonished Jhennain once more, "I thought you might at least bring others talented or committed enough to challenge me. How disappointing." She waved her hand in an arc. Five of the *Valir* were flung from their positions, sent sprawling into the unyielding stone walls. They lay moaning or silent in heaps. Jhennain remained standing, as did one of the Jamnite summoners, though they were rocked as if by a mighty wave. Aldrain, too, was hurled backward into the door. He cried out in alarm, and thundering blows fell on the doors in vain answer. They were somehow barred. He rose gingerly to his knees, his head spinning. Then, he was held fast, he and the others. It felt as if the air had hardened to stone, for he could not move.

The Warwitch lowered her head, and an object materialized onto her outstretched hands. Through blurred vision, Aldrain tried to focus. It was a small box. *It's one of the weapons!* All that escaped his mouth was a low moan.

"You know what this can do, don't you, Your Majesty? Well, I suppose some lessons must be given more than once for the knowledge to stick. Remember what you have seen today. It is a new age. It is *my* age." She spoke pointedly to him, but eyed the others briefly as well. She set the box down and faded away into trailing mist.

It was only after his face struck the floor heavily that Aldrain realized he'd been freed from the magical bonds that held him. He tasted the coppery tinge of blood. Both doors flew open and dozens of soldiers rushed in, swords and spears brandished. They peered about in dismay, before several rushed to Aldrain and helped him up onto unsteady legs. The *Valir* were still gripped fast.

"Get everyone out!" he managed, though only a croaking whisper.

"Your Majesty?"

Finding his voice, he tried again. "Out of the room! Out of the tower!"

The chest started to pulsate with magical energy, emanating a deep hum that reverberated throughout the chamber.

❧

Hundreds of them, perhaps thousands, had marched past, heading to the citadel. *He betrayed you, and you fell for his ruse without a second thought!* These were not the dark-robed giants that had taken Iselle with such ease, but soldiers, armored and ready for battle. Blades glowed ruddily in the dim torchlight, the eyes of their bearers dark and grim. They filed through the corridor with the creak of leather bindings and the metallic clatter of plate and mail.

The defenders had no chance.

In futility, Iselle tried again to move an arm; the iron grip of her captors was unyielding. There were half a dozen of them, loosely ringed about her, off within the opening of a side tunnel, waiting, while the invading force passed by. Turan stood just to their fore, outside the formation. How could she have simply walked into his trap? She cursed silently. She should have realized earlier. She could have gotten away to warn them. Then, maybe, they would have had a chance. Not now.

After an agonizingly long time, the last of the troops thudded past, their glowing brands shrinking to the size of fireflies and then disappearing completely into the gloom.

Turan turned and delivered a hoarse command to Iselle's captors and their fellows. She was hoisted into the air and borne away. Iselle was but a feather to them, and their pace was swift. The ground slipped past beneath her. If not for the vicelike hold on her upper arms, she would have felt as though she were floating along in the dark.

Once her anger and frustration at being caught unawares began to subside, a new emotion surfaced. It was fear. Where were they taking her?

36

ALDRAIN EMERGED FROM THE ENTRANCE to the tower, followed by the foremost of his breathless soldiers, when the first of the breezes stirred. The men immediately scattered in all haste to the darkened reaches of the slumbering fortress to convey his orders of withdrawal. Aldrain knew this was no natural wind. It was pushing outward from the tower itself. And, carried on it was the same bass throbbing he'd heard once before.

It was happening again.

He bolted toward the dark bulk of the main turret as fast as he could. The breeze continued to pick up speed, and the ominous humming grew louder and higher in pitch, as he knew it would. Fine dust and sand cascaded into him, borne aloft by its strengthening force. It conjured dark recollection. He would never make it, he realized. Few of his men would escape, either.

Aldrain stopped. Slowly, he turned to face his demise.

Tendrils of electric energy began to snake from the tower, illuminating the night and buzzing with deadly power. More quickly now, like the tentacles of some ravenous beast, the feelers arced about, outlining the base of the structure and the surrounding outbuildings. The roaring, gusting wind stopped abruptly, and he steadied himself for his inevitable death.

A shockwave from behind pummeled him down, pushing him toward the tower. Everything seemed to blur and blend into one nightmare image; blue and white flashes of light raced inward, drawing everything of substance in with them. From several feet before him, and in the same spherical outline as the crater left in Eidara, everything simply disintegrated and collapsed in on itself —flagstoned ground, tower foundations, smaller buildings, metal, soldiers, all of it—simply coming apart into the tiniest of fragmented particles, collected into a white-hot glowing orb at the exact central point of the sphere, where it simply flashed out of existence with a deafening clap of thunder.

The entire base of the tower was erased from reality. It took scant seconds for the upper sections to tumble into the resulting void. Dust and debris shot high into the darkness, illuminated now only by the faint torchlight or fires nearby within the citadel.

It was a much more limited implosion than in Eidara. *But why?*

The doors of the main tower exploded from their hinges, fragments of wood and iron hurled outward. Several of these struck his legs and back, but armored as he was, they were little more than distractions. Aldrain whirled to see armed men—not his own—spilling forth from the entranceway, falling upon the stunned defenders.

He hadn't enough time to register the scene before he was fighting for his life, just as everyone else was, reacting initially on instincts of survival alone.

❧

The Wave Hammer was the largest ship Jaren had ever seen, and actually the first, although he supposed there were larger ones on the open seas. A few others of similar design were moored nearby. Probably, these were as large a vessel as could navigate so far upstream, though the Tygar, too, was a great, broad waterway, bigger even than the Marthuin.

Jaren stood motionless, hesitant, upon the dock, the sounds of lapping water and cries of gulls filling the crisp, morning air. Sunlight reflected across the water as thousands of scattered diamonds. Jaren wasn't certain of what to do now that he'd arrived.

The Wave Hammer's deck appeared deserted. Perhaps he was earlier than expected. He decided to take a seat on a discarded crate nearby when a harsh voice carried down to him from the ship.

"Look inside it."

Jaren did. Within lay a curious pair of manacles, wide, silvery circlets of *metanduil* attached to one another by joined links of the same material. Their entire surface was worked with intricate runes and symbols. Jaren frowned.

"Put them on," the voice echoed off of the water and the warehouses behind him.

Jaren hesitated.

"Jump to it, now!" came the impatient order. There was an edge to the raspy voice. "If you want to see your sister again, you'll do as you're told, when you're told."

Jaren shot an irritated look at the source. The figure peering over the deck railing recoiled slightly. Nevertheless, a repeated, fitful gesturing indicated he was to follow through with the order.

Reluctantly, Jaren placed the first of the cuffs on his wrist and closed it. There was no clicking of internal workings, nor did there appear to be a keyhole. The circlet had simply fused as one solid piece. He didn't relish the sensation of completeness it suggested. Awkwardly, he fumbled with the second. It closed with the same silent permanence. Immediately, a chill swept through him, radiating from his wrists to envelop his entire body. Just as quickly, though, the unpleasant feeling subsided. The urging whisper of the magic became muffled and distant. As much as he was grateful for that, it remained an unsettling experience.

Suppose he couldn't summon at all with the manacles in place? What chance did his plan have, then? Jaren steeled himself, recalling the awesome and seemingly limitless flow of the power. Nothing, it seemed, could withstand that. Still, a nagging doubt had planted itself stubbornly in his consciousness, all the louder now that the voice of his latent power was quieted.

The thumping of footfalls on the deck planking brought his attention back to the docks. The figure, the apparent source of the commands, drew near. He was stick-thin, clothing hanging from him like rags from a scarecrow, though he was a full foot shorter than Jaren. His hair was jet black though shot through with gray, scraggly and sparse, hanging to ear level uniformly about his head. A gnarled hand ran through the hair draped across his face, pushing it back to reveal deep-set, dark eyes. Trained off at an angle, they regarded the ground, not him.

"Don't make me repeat myself," the raspy voice squeaked at the same time as a rigid finger jabbed Jaren's chest repeatedly. "I'm not someone you want to upset."

Jaren peered down at the finger stabbing at him, his eyebrows raised, and the fellow nearly jumped back.

"And no tricks!" He attempted to make himself taller and advanced half a step. His eyes peered apprehensively at Jaren, then went back to their odd, downward angle. "Follow me, and be quick about it!" He spun on his heel and started back up the dock to the wooden planking that rose to the deck of the Wave Hammer, throwing nervous glances back over his shoulder. By his body language, it seemed he'd be just as happy had Jaren not followed.

"Are you the captain?" Jaren asked.

"I'm in charge of your sorry self," came the muttered reply, "that's all you need to know for now!"

Jaren vaguely heard something else mumbled under the other's breath, but couldn't make it out. The vessel appeared uninhabited, apart from the two of them, until he glimpsed several other cloaked figures moving about the deck. Immediately, he was ushered down a set of narrow, grooved wooden steps into the hold.

It took a moment for Jaren's eyes to adjust to the relative darkness. Soon, though, he saw that he was being led toward a large, blockish form. Momentarily, it became a square cage of shining metal—more *metanduil*, or at least its surface was gilded with it. The lone door stood ajar. His escort took up a position beside the opening and, in his twitch-motion manner, gestured impatiently for Jaren to enter.

Once more, Jaren hesitated. Magical bonds were one thing, but this seemed much more final, inescapable. The flattened bars of the structure were fully half an inch thick. A fleeting hope stirred within. He glanced down at the manacles. If she needed to keep him in so secure a jail, what did that say about the strength of the bonds? He sighed. If he were ever let out again, he might discover the answer. The look of the seemingly unassailable cell sent a shudder to his core. Were it not *metanduil*, it would have remained daunting enough.

"You don't listen very well, do you lad? In with you!" The gestures became yet more frantic. Resigned to his fate, Jaren slowly obliged. Just as soundlessly as the manacles, the door of the cage swung to. Similarly, there was no line of joints or hinges. The cage appeared to be forged of one continuous, unbroken piece.

A dry chortle jumped from the other's throat. "You'll learn to obey soon enough. Yes, the Mistress will teach you." His captor muttered to himself, still chuckling as he turned away and disappeared up the stairs to the deck.

The call of the magic grew completely silent, as if it no longer existed. The frequent creaks and groans of the ship were the only noises to replace it. Jaren sat for a good, long while, just listening, before he felt the first lurching movements of the vessel. He took a deep breath. He was on his way and didn't mean to come back.

They must have been magically silenced to have snuck up on her back in the caverns, Iselle reasoned, because they sure weren't moving quietly now. Every step landed heavily, thudding into the earth with enough force to leave a deep imprint. *What do these things weigh*, she wondered. By the feel of them—she was draped over a massive, un-yielding shoulder—they were made of stone. Their heads were cowled, their faces shrouded in dark shadow, even during the day. She hadn't glimpsed so much as a hair of their features.

It was some time since they'd emerged from the tunnels and con-tinued north over the plains. Her escort stopped only when Turan commanded them, and even so, they remained standing, motionless. The young thief gave her food and drink, mostly dried fruit and meat along with water, and unless he felt a few hours' sleep was in order, they started off again. She had puzzled over how it was he kept up with them, but then she'd awakened last night and seen Turan perched on the shoulders of the lead figure. Still, he did well enough to match their great strides for any length of time. He must be very fit, she thought. Maybe she couldn't have gotten away from him to warn the defenders of the citadel after all.

Iselle hoped not too many of them had died during the invasion, especially not Aldrain. As infuriating as he was to have kept her cooped up in her chambers, he was only doing what he thought was right. And, he seemed a kind enough and just man, the sort of person that should lead people, rather than the typical, snobbish lot everyone was usually stuck with. Even the Warwitch wouldn't kill a king, would she? But she already had: his father, and many others in the royal palace at Ei-dara. No, she would have needed him. If the Warwitch truly wanted to control everything, as Iselle had heard, would it not be better to have a legitimate king upon the throne? Then again, what did Iselle know of kings and politics? Still, she prayed that Aldrain was all right, he and as many of the others as the True One saw fit to protect.

A keening wail reached Iselle's ears. It built gradually over half an hour or so. At about the same time, she became aware of the briny scent of water. Beneath the shrill sound, too, rose a deeper, intermittent *whooshing*. Finally, they came to an outcrop of jutting rocks that heaved from the ground in a variety of angles and stark shapes. This was the origin of the wail. A gusting wind swirled and swept through the mass of rock, creating the eerie effect. Adding to it was the fact that Sholara, low on the western horizon, sent lengthening shadows creeping across the face of the escarpment.

Her captors continued forward through a narrow cleft in the great formations, descending rapidly. Their passage through the defile lasted several minutes, until, abruptly, they were out in the open, buffeted by the same strong winds that continued inland to howl upon the rocks.

Behind were jagged cliffs; elsewhere stretched a vast expanse of water, rolling waves as far as the eye could see, eventually meeting the darkening horizon. The waves crashed into the shoreline regularly with a low roar. An ocean. Which one, Iselle wasn't sure. Few in Dal Farrow had any reason to travel farther than the market of the nearest towns, but so much water in one place made this an ocean. Iselle knew that much.

They descended several dozen feet more, down a rocky incline to a short expanse of sand. There, pulled up onto the narrow ribbon of white, was a curious-looking vessel, though she admittedly knew as much about boats as she did the lands far from home. Still, it was different than the big ships mentioned in the recounted fables of traveling entertainers who passed though Dal Farrow from time to time. Their tales spoke of great, towering hulks with many sails and masts, and sailed by crews of a hundred men. This one was narrow and sported a single sail. It had notches along either side from which sprouted many oars. The bow of the craft was elongated and flattened, an inverted, roughly triangular shape, with a single red eye emblazoned upon it. The vessel hardly looked large enough to venture out into the vastness of the heaving waves surrounding them.

The wind's increased force finally drove the cowls back from a number of her captors' faces, and she was horrified at what she saw. They were most definitely not human. They appeared cast of solid metal, with inflexible, iron features forged into permanently blank expressions.

Iselle shivered as gusts of the cool sea wind chilled her all the more.

Heedless of her fears, they bore Iselle onto the vessel and launched it into the choppy water. She was placed immediately before the single mast. As each member of her escort climbed aboard, the small ship settled farther into the dark waters. There were half the number of them than the boat was meant to hold, but she feared if there had been just one more, the water would have begun to leak in through the oar notches, it now sat so low.

Behind her, Turan gave another sharp, guttural command, and they began pulling on the oars. Immediately, the small craft obeyed, sliding effortlessly over the waves, even loaded down as it was.

At least if the waves overtook them, her captors should sink and she'd be free of them. But, then there would still be Turan to deal with, and no boat. Her head was spinning, and her stomach had become unsettled with the tossing of the waves. *No, it's better not to think of going into the water.* She could consider her escape when she had solid ground beneath her feet once more.

37

SHE'D GONE SO NUMB WITH the cold press of the unforgiving stone that she nearly felt part of it, a continuation of the inert, unfeeling rock. It was a welcome sensation compared to .... Morgaine shuddered. The mere thought of that agony wracked the entirety of her being with utter dread. If only she would stop. *Please stop!* She had begged repeatedly, her voice gone raw and sobbing so hard that her words became incomprehensible. But the pain had endured. She could still feel the needles, the hot steel piercing her skin.

They were the source of the excruciating, lancing stabs of fire. The unbearable process was changing her. The Warwitch was transforming her. As much as Morgaine struggled and fought back, it was happening.

And the voice of the magic—during the struggle with the blacktongue, it had called to her, pleaded with her to be released. She had resisted its draw, honey-sweet and seductive as it was. It had only been that insistent, so close to overwhelming, that one time—until now. Now, the voice had free reign of her thoughts. It came and went as it pleased, teasing, testing. It waited for Morgaine to drop her exhausted guard. The Truth only knew how she'd managed to hold out for so long already.

Her mind reeled. She feared she was going mad with the exertions of the process. The process, the gift. Her shoulders shuddered, and it took a moment to realize she was laughing, though it sounded more like dry gasping in the brooding stillness. *Stay away, Jaren! Don't come here. Don't try to follow me!* But somehow, Morgaine knew he would. He was probably already on his way. It should have given her hope. It had just the opposite effect. What could he do against the Warwitch? She'd had time to hone her skills, to explore her abilities to their fullest extent. Jaren was no match for her, yet. He couldn't begin to challenge her mastery of the power.

But he could, a tiny voice sounded. *You saw what he did!* The voice was hollow, meaningless. It just meant Jaren had started toward the edge of the same dark pit into which she was about to topple. *You can't fight evil with darkness. That's what the magic is. It is dread.*

Mirthless laughter shook her once more.

Morgaine's vision came and went. Was she going blind, too? She tried to focus on her forearms, fastened to the armrests of the high-backed stone seat. To focus on the origin of the relentless, burning pain. As if through a haze, she observed them: pale, shot through with streaks of gray—liquid *metanduil* beneath her skin, injected into her flesh. Tears welled and then flowed down her cheeks. What was she becoming? Morgaine threw her head back against the unyielding stone to wail, but the only result was a hoarse squeak.

"Really, my dear, you should not struggle against it so. It could be much more pleasant."

That voice Morgaine feared equally as much as the echo of the magic. She moaned, all the protest she could mount in her ruined state. Still, she had to fight.

"If you only knew what it is you are denying, you would stop this foolishness and take the gift willingly." Rhianain stepped nearer, leaning forward to peer down at Morgaine. The Warwitch ran a cold, metallic hand across one pale cheek in a motherly caress, wiping away another tear. "It doesn't have to be this way, you know. It should prove much less uncomfortable than my own transformation. I've improved the process since then."

Morgaine flinched from the hand, turning her head away.

"Still, the fight lives in you." Rhianain straightened, frowning. "Your spirit will serve me well, willingly or not. You have such potential. You will be among the greatest of my servants." She sighed, pursing her lips. "But, it could be more than that. You could be…like a daughter. Just give in to the process. Let go. I know you've tasted the sweetness of the magic. Deep down, you want more. I can give you that. I *am* giving you that, but it doesn't have to be such a fight!"

Morgaine shook her head, her lips working in silent protest.

Cold rage flashed across Rhianain's features, and she roughly clenched a handful of Morgaine's hair. With an effort, she composed herself. The closed fist unfolded, became soft once more, stroking instead the locks it had seized. "In time, you will see. You will come to realize the beauty of what I am giving you. In time." She let her hand trace gently down the other's face, then turned and walked away, arms crossed beneath her breasts. Her retreating voice echoed through the vaulted chamber. "Until then, take what rest you can. Our next session will come soon enough."

No chains held him fast, no shackles constrained him. Yet, Aldrain, king of the Carathonai, was bound as surely as any prisoner. He rode absently, oblivious to the movements of the horse beneath him, staring blankly ahead. Not a full month had passed since the rule of Carathon had been thrust into his hands before he'd lost it in all but name. The enemy had known about the tunnels, tunnels about which none other than the royal family themselves, along with a handful of the most trusted subjects, were supposed to have known. He'd believed all knowledge of the passages, save for his and Ordren's, had been lost in the destruction of the palace. Again, he'd been wrong.

It seemed every decision he'd made since becoming king had been wrong, or, if not, simply undermined or anticipated and countered.

The Warwitch maintained him as the nominal ruler of the kingdom, he'd been informed, though he would have an advisor. Someone to whom he was to defer completely and without question, lest he should fall to some misfortune and his cousin Machim be raised in his place. It was beyond Aldrain why she'd allowed him to live at all. Probably, she reveled in the knowledge that he would suffer more from the arrangement than if simply put to death: Pacek was to be his advisor. She must have been aware of the bad blood between their families, between houses Draegondor and Pacek. It was a cruel and cunning machination. But she was capable of so much more.

Fully one-third of his soldiers had been summarily executed after the fall of the Hold, in addition to those who'd been slain in the short, but intense struggle. They were to serve as examples to others, that any who dared stand against her would be utterly crushed. The haunted eyes of every man who accompanied him home told Aldrain the message was not wasted. They reflected nearly as much terror as the eyes of the dead, staring from heads impaled on great wooden spikes upon the walls of Caren Hold.

Angrill's men had warranted a similar judgment, though their dead were lashed to the saddles of survivors' horses, to be dragged all the way back to Jamnar, or as long as the bodies held out against the terrain. Angrill's two sons had been officers in his company. The last Aldrain had seen, their corpses jounced brokenly behind their father's mount, tethered by their ankles. He doubted even the hard and grizzled Angrill, campaigner of so many years, would return whole from that experience. From the sunken look in his eyes to the defeated slouch, his fighting days were surely over, his spirit permanently crushed.

The walls of Eidara, usually inspiring from a distance, served only to deepen his despair. It rose within him with the looming ramparts. Soon, companies of his own men would ride forth from within, carrying the demands of the Warwitch to the other realms of Evarlund. Now, he knew, it was only a matter of time before they capitulated. With Jamnar's army destroyed and his nation fallen, they would all soon fall in line.

Aldrain furrowed his brow. Gibbets hung from the battlements. Never had such trappings of death been displayed before the city. Sudden rage swept him. He glared at Pacek, riding just ahead and to his left. Aldrain could faintly make out the partial expression. It was smug satisfaction. The traitor could barely keep from smiling openly.

Then, he saw it between the bars of the nearest suspended cage: Ordren's tortured face, or what remained of it, locked in a rictus of agony. His eyeless stare returned Aldrain's own horrified gaze; the crows had been feasting of late.

The king's anger intensified, until he feared he would explode. He would find a way to throw off the yoke of the Witch. And to deal out the justice that she and her followers so rightly deserved. Somehow, he would, he vowed to the Truth.

Pacek's face regarded him, reacting as if he could feel the heat of Aldrain's glare. The count returned a contemptuous sneer.

"I've taken the liberty of replacing your captain," he gestured with a self-pleased nod to Ordren's remains. "Seems he wasn't much use to us, after we got the information we needed."

Justice. The single word echoed in Aldrain's mind, all that could challenge the rising wail of anguish threatening to drive him mad.

38

JAREN SHOULD HAVE BEEN ASLEEP, but his prison didn't particularly lend itself to such a luxury. He had to struggle with an increasingly unpleasant, suffocating feeling just being within the jail. Even worse, when he laid his head down, the bare *metanduil* produced a thoroughly disruptive vibration. Jaren managed to doze uneasily for just a short time, despite the unnatural buzzing sensation, but then awoke with a scream from a terrible nightmare, cold sweat drenching his body.

In it, dark shadows pursued him. Formless, shapeless entities sought to trap and envelop him. He ran through a deserted town, the washed-out, dilapidated buildings and narrow streets reminding him of Ghalib. Racing through constricting lanes and alleyways choked with refuse and debris, he tried in vain to evade the hunters. Around every corner they stalked, down every avenue. Soon, they had him surrounded, hundreds of them closing in at once. Then, just as they reached out to him, he looked down at himself and froze with horror: he, too, was one of the shadow creatures! Their dark embraces beckoned in an eerie welcome.

It was at that point Jaren started awake, echoes of the haunting voices lingering in his mind as the stirrings above began. Several heavy thuds echoed through the hold, and he thought he could just make out a strangled shout. He sat up anxiously. What was happening? Were there brigands on the river? Jaren struggled desperately to think of what he should do, had the vessel been taken. He needed to get to the Warwitch. He needed to find his sister.

His swirling thoughts died to an anxious murmur as the hatch cover was hauled open. Slowly, cautiously, a dark form descended the stairs. Pale moonlight streamed through the opening, backlighting the cloaked figure and obscuring its face in shadow. The momentary, dim light had also revealed the sword it brandished, a sword stained dark with what Jaren feared was blood. It cleared the shaft of moonlight, becoming a vague shape among the shadows and seemed to float toward him, sitting helpless in his cell.

Jaren's mind raced. What could he do? Offer a bribe? He had little enough to barter with: a few gold crowns, the last of Llaw's money, which the *Valir* had insisted he take. That was all. Even so, there was nothing stopping whoever this was from just killing him and taking the coins. *He had to think!*

The figure paused several paces before the makeshift prison.

Plead with them! Beg if you have to! Jaren's mouth opened as the thoughts screamed in his mind, but nothing came out. In vain, he struggled against the paralyzing fear that held him as surely as the bars of his prison. *Speak! You have to get to Morgaine!*

"Did you think I'd abandon you so easily?"

It was Ver's voice. But that was impossible. He had killed Ver with his release of the magic back in the mountains. Jaren gaped.

"Come on now, no hard feelings. That's what it means to be friends, right?" The voice was warm, sincere. It was most certainly Ver.

"How did you ... but I thought I ... I thought you were dead!"

"You're not the first to have made that mistake. Though you did make an honest effort at it!" The avatar laughed.

"Ver, that was a mistake ... I never meant to ... to do all of *that!*"

"Easy now, Jaren, let's just see if we can get you out of here, first."

A short time later, the two of them sat on upended crates on the deck of the Wave Hammer. Apparently, the vessel had been enchanted to navigate on its own. It kept to the deeper waters of the river as an ample wind filled its sails. The two talked quietly as they watched the thickly forested riverbanks roll swiftly past on either side, swathed in various hues of silvery moonlight. The calm of the surroundings warred with the chaotic swirl of Jaren's thoughts.

"So you followed me all the way here?"

"Yes. I couldn't travel with you. It would have been impossible for me to hide from their eyes. I had to track you from a distance. Once you were on board, their network dispersed, and I was able to reach you."

Jaren's face became pensive. For some reason, he hoped the fellow who had taken him below deck hadn't been killed. He was the enemy, of course, but he hadn't seemed cruel or terribly unkind, like most of the False Sworn he'd encountered so far.

"You're thinking of the crew?" Ver successfully read his look. "I had to dispatch several, but the old man…he's probably still adrift in one of the lifeboats."

"Won't he get word to the Warwitch?"

"He won't remember anything for a while. And we'll reach the island by then. That is, if you still want to go there."

"I don't have any choice."

"You always have a choice, Jaren. Remember that free will I talked to you about? Well, it might seem that some options are more costly than others, but you still have the freedom to make your choice among them."

"What do you think I should do?"

"I think you should get some sleep." Ver chuckled lightly. "And, I think you should listen to your heart. It is there the True One speaks to us most."

"It's settled. I have to go. That's what my heart says."

"Then, I guess we don't have to abandon ship." The avatar peered about the deck. "I doubt we'd be able to alter her course, after all."

Jaren hesitated, but decided to ask the question screaming to come out. "Ver, why is the magic so…destructive?"

The avatar took a moment to reflect before answering. "Jaren, do you believe the True One is a kind, merciful being?" He waited for acknowledgment. The youth nodded. "Then how could a just and loving life source create anything that was merely destructive in nature?"

"That's what I was wondering." Jaren sighed.

"Even the Deceiver was not always evil. Did you know that?"

"No."

"Well, that's a story for someone else to tell at another time. What you must remember is that the magic itself is neither good nor bad, no more so than this ship might be used for right or wrong. It might be used by fishermen to feed a village, for example. Or, the same vessel might be sailed by pirates, to murder and pillage." Ver paused, gauging Jaren's reaction.

"But, isn't that a little different?"

"Not essentially. The boat—the lumber, rope, nails, cotton, and everything that goes into it—is created by the True One. Humans decide how it is to be put together and how it is used. Now, it may be a different sort of tool, but the magic is just that, a tool. The same goes for iron that can be fashioned into a hoe or a blade. It is the exercise of our free will that turns the use of any created material to good or evil purposes."

Jaren shrugged, still unsure. "That doesn't explain why its voice seems so ... dark."

"Voice? I don't believe the magic has a voice. Remember, it is only a tool. It's not alive, as such, though I suppose it has some lifelike properties."

"Then why do I hear a voice inside my head, telling me to use it, to use as much of it as possible?" Jaren cringed, as the memories of his ordeal with the magic surfaced briefly, then he pushed them away with an effort. "Or even more than that?"

"I think that's a question you'll have to answer on your own. But, as I said earlier, you should get some rest. You'll need your strength soon enough. We're not far from open water, and with luck, it's a short voyage to the Isle of Ice."

Again, Jaren nodded, though more sincerely this time. He glanced at his shackled wrists. Ver had not dared remove them, he said, because along with the ability to block his summoning, they greatly masked the aura of magic he radiated. Attuned to sense magic by nature, Ver informed Jaren that his aura was steadily growing in strength, for all his vows of halting it. Furthermore, with Jaren in the *metanduil* cage, Ver would not have been able to discern that he was on the vessel had the avatar not seen him taken on board. Though Jaren was free of his prison, he was still bound by the circlets of *metanduil*, and therefore it was possible to perceive his aura only in close proximity. Remove them, and the Warwitch would be forewarned long before their arrival that all was not as expected aboard the ship. Their landing would be decidedly different, then, Ver had advised.

Jaren sat, silently pondering the whisperings that would return with the removal of his bonds. If not born of the magic, then from where did the seductive urgings originate?

⚶

"Daughters, sit and speak with me. Until now, there has been no one to share my thoughts with, no one who could truly understand my existence. Now, sit with me."

Morgaine and Joselle came obediently on padded feet. Wordlessly, they lowered themselves onto the squat couch before Rhianain's luxurious chair and sat waiting, sunken eyes vacant. She smiled in satisfaction; the transformations were complete. Both were pale, near ashen in complexion; beneath their alabaster skin coursed rivulets of dark gray. Magic-metal glinted in their eyes, the retinas now pools of liquid silver, tiny veins of it shot throughout the whites. Living *metanduil*! She had done it! And they were hers to mould, to teach as her children. They were only the first, of course, the first of many.

It was to be the age of magic reborn in the six realms, an age that Rhianain would claim as her own.

Foolish men and their warring ways. A contemptuous huff escaped the Warwitch's throat. *What can their pathetic blades do against this? What use now, their vast armies?* Her time would be one of peace, of unity. She'd been given a vision, along with her gifts. If they refused her more than generous offers of allegiance, they would be made to submit by force. The ends justified the means. Hers would be a short campaign of violence, to ensure a lasting peace. It would be a necessary and final solution to the endless squabbles and petty conflicts among the nations of Evarlund, conflicts the *Valir* aided and sustained through their misguided meddling.

Yes, the guild had orchestrated a great many things, perpetrated much deceit. But she knew the truth of it. Now she would take control. Better her than a group of weak-spined *Valir* hiding behind secrecy and centuries of lies. Rhianain refused to skulk in the shadows. She would reveal to the nations what the age of the *Valir* had truly brought.

Rhianain looked upon her creations with a motherly pride. No longer would she need to make crude weapons of the magic-metal, sending them off to be used as mere bludgeons, consumed in the process. Her envoys could now wield the magic just as she did, again and again, and they could communicate her demands. Granted, the new procedure might require some adjustments. These two were rather less than articulate, presently. Perhaps they would come back to themselves with time. Possibly a lengthier, gradual development would have incurred less trauma. But these two were needed urgently. There had been no time for anything less immediate.

Rhianain's pride was tainted briefly by a sense of regret, as she continued to observe the two, silent and motionless as statues, their vacant stares seeing past her, through her. Just as briefly, the feeling was gone again.

It is necessary, the Warwitch reminded herself.

A wave of pain racked her body. Her hands clenched to fists atop the armrests of her gilded throne. Slowly, inexorably, it washed over Rhianain. She steeled herself against it, willing her mind to ignore it. After so long, the process of her own transformation still sent … reminders of the cost of her gift, both a blessing and a burden. Her vision cleared momentarily, and she regarded her young daughters in the magic once more. *No, there was no choice.*

Though she was certain the sibling would be manageable, there were always complications. Rhianain was still learning herself, though she would admit the fact to no one. It was inescapable, after a thousand years of years of ignorance, that there would exist a rather steep learning curve to the full secrets of *An'Valir.* While the boy could not possibly have developed his skills to the level she'd attained in so short a time, it was wise to take extra precautions. Her creations would be there with her, a committee of sorts, to welcome him, to introduce him to his place in the workings of things.

His was to be an equally exalted role, indeed. For, as much as she begrudged the fact, his potential might eclipse her own. His abilities were, after all, innate, and hers artificial, though no less a gift. Nevertheless, if she and the two silent figures before her could be described as powerful, he might well be next to omnipotent in the end.

The mere thought of harnessing such overwhelming strength sent ecstatic shivers through her. She steadied herself—one step at a time. The pieces must be set just so, in order to ensure his successful capture. Or, if not that, his demise. He was too much of a threat if not under her control.

Leaning forward in the ornate throne, Rhianain began her explicit instructions to the pair, as if speaking to small children.

39

SQUINTING INTO THE DISTANCE, JAREN could just make out the forms of the half-dozen or so cloaked and hooded figures nearing the vessel. Several lumbered up the wooden ramp and onto the deck of the Wave Hammer. Even from his removed vantage point, their movements were curious: rigid and unnatural.

Several of them, remaining on the beach, turned a large crank that worked a long-armed boom, running the great limb out over the hatch to the cargo hold. Two of the figures aboard the vessel disappeared into the hold. Jaren and Ver waited. Then, the figures ceased their activity and stood, motionless. Moments passed. Just as abruptly, they resumed their tasks as one. They opened the main cargo hatch and hoisted Jaren's prison cage with the beam. It was transferred onto a sturdy wagon and eventually led away by the nameless workers.

The pair waited for some time before stirring from their hiding place.

"Stay behind me, and keep an eye out for scouts," Ver said.

"Do you think she knows I'm here?"

"I couldn't say if she's powerful enough to know that yet or not, but I believe she'll assume you're here. I doubt she could stand to stay away if she was in your place, though I suspect for different reasons. She'll expect you to have done likewise, I'd wager."

Jaren was about to respond when the voice first reverberated through his mind. It definitely was not his own, inner self, speaking. And, it wasn't the magic either, or what he'd come to think of as the voice of the magic.

...Jaren...

He halted abruptly, causing Ver to stop as well, and the avatar cast a wary glance about them.

...Jaren Haldannon...

Immediately, he knew. It was her voice, the voice of the Warwitch. She knew he had come.

...Welcome to my home, to your new home, as well...to your true home, where you may finally find the answers you have so long sought...

The voice was warm enough, but there was a hint of a cold edge to it, a chill just beneath the veil of sincerity so earnestly attempted. It caused him to shiver.

... Welcome, and remember always that your powers are a gift, but a gift not without cost or personal sacrifice ... welcome to knowledge, to kinship ... I know how you have suffered, how you have yearned to learn of yourself ... to know your true nature and why you have heard the magic's call ...

He swayed on his feet and put a hand to his forehead. *She knows of the magic's voice! Maybe she can help, after all. Maybe ... no, it cannot not be. She is evil.* Everything he'd discovered of her and her followers had reinforced that fact. His gaze darted about as he wrestled with his thoughts. Ver tensed, but made no move. Jaren closed his eyes and attempted to steady himself, inhaling deeply.

... Come to me, Jaren ... come to me and start your becoming ... become who you were meant to be ... liberator ... protector ... brother in the magic ...

What did she mean, liberator, of whom? And who would need protection except against her? She wasn't making any sense or offering any of the answers he needed. *She's drawing you in,* his inner voice warned. *She's setting you up. Forget her words, and do what you've come to do!*

I am coming, he thought to himself, wondering if she was able to receive his thoughts as well as transmit her own. It didn't really matter. All he needed was to get close enough. That was all.

... I can sense your anger and confusion ... you have been misdirected and lied to ... but, fear not, I will help you ... just as you can help me, and help your sister ...

Morgaine! What had the Warwitch done to her?

... You have not come as I had hoped, but I admire your commitment, however misplaced ... but now you must put aside your own doubt and fear ... you must trust me, in order to save yourself and your sister ... you are both in great danger ... for all your potential, you are still at risk of being lost ... come to me and I will help you find your way ... come ...

Jaren waited for several moments, but the voice had grown silent. It took some time for the chill beneath her words to subside.

"Follow your heart," Ver offered simply.

The guarded chamber in the fortress of Caren Hold had simply been replaced by this prison on the island. At least there, Iselle had been allowed out, if infrequently and then only briefly. Now, she was a prisoner in every sense of the word. Except for the occasional visits from Turan, unsettling as they were, she had no contact with anyone. A tray shoved through a slot beneath her door twice a day provided her meals. Her chamber pot was removed only once, through the same opening.

Iselle gathered from Turan's bothersome ravings that she was being kept alive only because she might be useful in helping bring Jaren to heel. She was bait. Without Turan having said it directly, she realized it well enough. Turan had hinted that if she were not receptive to his advances, he could not guarantee her protection. A great intellectual leap was not required to discern the meaning behind his words and put a finger on her present worth. After Jaren was dealt with, her value depended on Turan's whim.

Iselle shivered. He was despicable. His casual wink, once amusing and almost endearing, now infuriated her. In a number of disgusting suggestions, sullied further by many sordid winks, he'd tried to describe his desires for her, but she would hear none of it. She would rather die. And, so, she probably would.

Iselle wished again that Jaren would be all right. Could he withstand the Witch? She didn't know. She wanted to believe he could do it, but he had just discovered his true nature a short time ago, and the Warwitch had been developing her skills for years. How could Jaren possibly be ready to face such a challenge?

The ominous, horrific screams had not inspired much hope. At various times of both day and night, the screams rose, bearing witness to unimaginable anguish. Distant though they seemed, their tortured echoes had been incredibly unnerving. She felt only pity for the poor, tortured souls who gave life to them. They must be driven mad with agony to cry out so. She hoped her own death wouldn't be like that.

Jaren would be hard-pressed to match someone as bloodthirsty and ruthless as the Witch, with the sheer power she must wield and the utter brutality she clearly employed in its use.

Maybe together, he and Morgaine could defeat her. Both were full of potential, both had the use of the magic. Maybe then—

The door to her cell creaked open, wide enough to admit a smiling Turan. He flashed a wink. Sudden revulsion drowned out all other concerns as her hand went of its own accord to the belt where she kept her long hunting knife. She frowned when she found only the folds of her tunic, recalling that her knife, like everything else, had been taken from her. She felt soiled by Turan's mere presence.

"Your boyfriend is coming," he said, and managed barely to mask a contemptuous sneer.

No, don't come here. Jaren, Morgaine, no! The sounds of the tortured cries echoed through her reeling mind. If he came, she knew somehow, he would die. Or worse, he'd live.

Observing her reaction with no small amount of satisfaction, he went on. "Now, don't be upset. The Mistress has planned a very warm welcome. You'll be able to watch, too." He relished in her disgust and grinned. "Once it's over, we'll have to decide what to do with you. There's still time." His smile turned vulgar.

She nearly leapt for his throat as she received another ingratiating wink.

40

JAREN AND VER PICKED THEIR way through the rocky landscape. It was a laborious trudge across the dark, rugged environment buffeted as they were by a frigid east wind, the first feelers of winter's icy touch probing and prodding. Its chill rivaled that carried on the Warwitch's voice, the cool malice hidden beneath a veneer of sincerity. At least this was a sensation of the natural world; it was flesh-and-blood cold and therefore not so disturbing.

Soon, Jaren's face and hands were numb. He hugged his cloak tighter about him as they ascended a series of jagged rises, only to find other peaks stretching away in all directions. Still, he felt they were nearing the Witch's lair. He could feel her presence more with every step.

His thoughts whirled about with the gusting winds. The Warwitch had tried to confuse him, to make his corruption an easier task. How far down that path had he put himself? She had spoken of *becoming*. He tried to push the images of the ordeal in the Forge away as they formed, but no sooner had he managed to dismiss one than another took its place. The Witch had done terrible things in her quest for power, but he too, was capable of great harm. What might keep him from suffering her fate? Could he really sacrifice himself? Could he control the power as he planned? Jaren stumbled on a sharp outcropping of stone and cursed, testing his foot gingerly. He wondered if they would traverse the entire, accursed island before finding her.

Eventually, just as he thought his mind might burst with the battling of his thoughts, a huddle of narrow spires became visible in the distance amid the jagged rocks. As they approached cautiously and with no little effort across the unkind terrain, the structure became more readily discernible, though it remained a curiosity all the same.

It was gradually revealed to be a palace, topped by angular, peaked columns stretching forth to the slate-gray sky. They appeared smooth and crystalline, and no less fragile, now and then sending a reflected glint of light their way, even with as little sunlight as there was escaping the leaden skies. A slightly wider, central column climbed from the midst of the others, a series of twisting, tubular channels entwining its length. At various intervals, vapors spewed from these, sinister-looking and hissing forth as they were released under pressure. From the top of this great chimney, similar wisps of smog vented.

The palace itself was fairly plain, a blocky keep of drab stone terminating in a sloped, inverted 'v', from which the spires made their ascent. Outer and inner curtain walls encircled the structure. Jaren doubted the Warwitch needed such protection. Was this some type of foundry or factory for *metanduil?* Jaren supposed it must be, seeing as the Warwitch developed her weapons out of the magic-metal. His eyes studied the battlements, finding them empty. Nothing appeared to move; no flicker of activity was apparent anywhere. Straining his ears, Jaren became aware of a distant thrumming, a deep, rhythmic vibration that seemed to come from the very foundation of the place. It was natural and otherworldly at the same time, much as he envisioned the Warwitch herself.

Ver looked questioningly at him, and Jaren nodded in response. The avatar immediately resumed his lead, heading for the main gates, which appeared to stand open. Jaren's scowl deepened. That was not a good sign, he decided. It was one thing to steal into the fortress, but to enter through an open door?

"Don't you think we should find another way in?" he whispered hoarsely.

Ver stopped and turned back. "The Warwitch knew almost the instant you stepped foot on the island." He shrugged. "Do you doubt she'll know when you enter her home? Or where you tread once inside?"

Jaren opened his mouth, but closed it as quickly.

"I doubt the fashion of our entry makes any difference at this point," Ver went on, after a moment's scrutiny of his companion. "If you wish a confrontation with her, then we might as well continue. Otherwise, why are we here?"

Jaren nodded wearily. "All right, after you."

The avatar took a final measure of Jaren, from head to toe, then nodded. Once more, he started off toward the gates. They loomed as the two neared, high overhead but barren of any signs of habitation. Wind swept the crenellations, producing a sorrowful moan that added to the feeling of isolation and emptiness about the fortress. Jaren lowered his head and strode onward, passing through the great, yawning portal.

They came to an outer courtyard, where a few stunted trees clung to their last dying leaves, the rest of which swirled in miniature whirlwinds about the paved walks and strips of overgrown gardens lining the enclosure. Their scraping dances echoed eerily about the place, underscored by the strengthening, bass reverberations from beneath the earth itself.

Ver led along a wide, paved path, apparently the main route to the entrance of the fortress proper. They reached an outbuilding, within which were set heavily braced, arched double doors. With a heave, they swung open, the hinges creaking with little resistance. Beyond stretched a long, empty chamber. At the opposite end, two darkened recesses beckoned, one in the corner and another straight ahead. Dozens of feet above the hewn-stone floor hung a series of gigantic candelabra, suspended from the arched ceiling by thick, iron chains. Tiny flames flickered wildly with the onset of the breeze from without. The scuffing of their footfalls echoed hollowly in the stillness.

Ver gave one last look back at Jaren. To go any farther now was to have no second thought.

Jaren met the avatar's eyes and then purposely directed his gaze ahead, across the chamber.

Ver wheeled and strode off, with Jaren following closely behind. He wasn't sure he would have needed the avatar's keen sensitivity even if the route were not evident, as he could sense the direction of the Witch himself now. Directly ahead, Jaren was aware, as if the needle of some inner compass had frozen in place.

Jaren almost bumped into Ver before he realized the other had stopped.

"I can go no farther," the avatar announced. "From here, you must go on alone."

Jaren had feared this moment would come. Feared it, and yet dared hope it would not. "Are you sure?"

"Yes, my young friend. It's up to you, now." A warm, though distant smile touched his lips. "I want to thank you for your companionship these past few weeks. It has been a long time since I was able to name anyone *friend*. It makes harder the things I have to do, and the things that are forbidden me, but, in the end, I would not have had it any other way."

"I'll see you again, surely," Jaren started, but then remembered himself. "Some time, anyway. I am grateful for your aid. I wouldn't have made it here if it weren't for you."

"Perhaps. Perhaps you would have come to the same point by a different route. Perhaps not, but the True One has had a hand in this and will continue to guide you, if you but listen."

"I think you've been the hand of the True One so far," Jaren replied.

Ver shrugged. "Remember our discussions, Jaren. Remember that the choices you make, and the reasons you make them, shape your destiny. Remember your free will." He placed his hand on Jaren's shoulder. "And remember, what the True One has made is supposed to bring balance and unity, not anger, fear, or revenge. Do not fear what is yours to use. Only beware the ends to which it is turned, and know the means will truly determine that outcome."

"Thank you, Ver." He cleared his throat as his voice hitched. "I—"

The other's head snapped to the side, eyes narrowing as he studied the nearby stairwell that ascended to darkness, listening intently. "You need to go now, Jaren. Through the door ahead. Go, and may the Truth guide you."

Jaren hesitated a moment, but the fire in Ver's eyes reinforced his words. "Farewell, Ver," he called back through the archway, heading into the darkened passage. He thought he could just make out the thumping of heavy, booted feet somewhere back the way he'd come.

41

RIBBONS OF LIGHT STREAMED IN through the murder holes lining the ceiling, so the darkness was not complete. Even so, as he stepped from the shadows of the corridor, Jaren's eyes took a brief moment to adjust. He was standing at the wider end of a broad, rectangular courtyard. A number of darkened, arched recesses lined either side wall. Several planters and strips of earth interrupted the otherwise flat stretch of paving stones before him. The trees and plants within were stunted and brown with neglect. Topping the far wall of the courtyard was a colonnaded balcony, wreathed in shadow.

Opposite him stood a figure he immediately knew to be the Warwitch.

He knew her simply by the commanding presence she exuded. The grand and intricate carvings adorning the walls about him faded indistinctly as his gaze was naturally drawn to her. The crimson gown she wore plunged to a low V at the neckline and continued down, hugging her figure to terminate at a tapered, narrow point just below her knees. A band of worked silver encircling her head swept back waves of long, dark hair that showed streaks of metanduil hue. What really drew his attention, though, were the patches of the silvery metal that covered parts of her body. It was definitely *metanduil*, though he had to blink to verify what his eyes were telling him. *It can't be possible, can it?* The metanduil didn't simply cover parts of her form. It was a part of her form. Not only the sight of her, but the reality behind her appearance was truly unsettling. What would she have endured to—

The Warwitch gave a slight nod. In answer, a loud, low rushing noise and a heavy crash sounded just behind him. A glance revealed the stout, flat, iron bars of a sturdy portcullis barring the way.

"I am so glad you decided to join us," the Warwitch began. Her smile seemed genuine enough, until Jaren looked into her eyes. There was no warmth behind them.

Jaren prepared his response as he strode forward.

He willed his shaking knees not to collapse. He had one goal, and he would not be denied. Here, at last, was the opportunity he had waited for. The scene had played out in his mind a hundred times. Welcoming the voice of the magic, he allowed it, even encouraged it to sing to him.

The Warwitch raised a concerned eyebrow. She considered a moment, then spoke in a louder voice, "Please, allow us to welcome you properly."

Jaren ignored her completely. He was halfway there. He could feel the anger and despair building within him. *She will not withstand me*, he promised, *she will pay for what she has done!* There remained only a dozen paces when something—a chance trick of the light perhaps—drew his attention upward. In that single instant, the welling rage within him turned to icy terror.

He had opened himself to begin the fatal release when he saw her. Morgaine.

Stopping abruptly, Jaren locked his mind shut, cutting off the source of the deadly power. *Don't let go of the magic! You'll hurt her!*

His sister stood on the balcony, mere yards above the Warwitch. Yet, something did not seem right. She was pale, drawn. Dark circles ringed her eyes and shadowy lines etched her skin. There was no warm smile, no sign of relief on seeing him. In fact, no hint of recognition showed in the least. He had not even time to consider the implications when he noticed the figure next to his sister. It was Joselle Banath. Or, at least it resembled her, as much as the other appeared to be his sister.

Then, the Warwitch was speaking again, her voice cutting through his frenzied thoughts.

❦

Hidden from view in a recessed archway, Iselle observed in helpless dismay as events unfolded.

No! She wanted to cry out to Jaren, but the hand over her mouth would not allow it. She tried to bite it, but that simply brought pain, as the hand clamped harder and the other arm about her torso cinched inward, making her exhale roughly.

Get away, Jaren, run! She screamed soundlessly, but Jaren remained there, as if frozen.

At least now, she knew why. Morgaine had just appeared on the balcony. But, even from this distance, she seemed strange, different.

"It looks like the Mistress will have an easy time of this," Turan's whispered taunt was hot in her ear. "No need to worry, though. I'm sure it won't last too long." An evil chuckle followed. "At least, not this part, anyway."

She collapsed against her captor, tears of angst streaming down her cheeks as she stared helplessly from the darkness of the sheltered alcove. Iselle's eyes rolled upward and she pleaded in silence for help, for anything that would save her friends.

Turan took her shifting as a sign of acceptance. "Good, that's good. Just forget about them and worry about yourself. Soon, you'll be with me. I'm all that's going to keep you from harm."

Iselle closed her eyes and continued her silent pleas to the True One.

⁊

The intruder below was an enemy, an enemy she must destroy, but not yet. Not until the Mistress ordered it. He didn't look dangerous. That was his greatest weapon, though, the Mistress had cautioned. He was going to appear harmless, a ruse meant to trick them into believing he wasn't a threat.

Morgaine would be ready. She had learned what to do.

Not so long ago... or was it? She couldn't remember, but at one time, she'd had to use a talisman to summon. She smiled. She knew it was true, but it seemed so distant now, like a memory from another lifetime. It was vague and hazy. Yet, she remembered the voice of the magic.

Now, it was a part of her. It was her voice. She no longer needed crude tools to summon, for she was of the power herself.

But something else bothered her. It nagged at the edges of her consciousness. Recalling something about the past had disturbed it, had set it to murmuring faintly, except that she couldn't quite make it out.

No matter, she breathed evenly. What mattered was her duty. She must serve the Mistress, with all of her newfound strength. Yes, this enemy would suffer, like any who dared oppose them. She had been made to understand that. She was a daughter. She was the hand of the Mistress, setting to rights all that needed tending.

Still, why did the feeling of disquiet return when she looked down upon the interloper? Soon enough, she knew, it wouldn't matter. He would be dealt with and forgotten.

❦

"You have come so far, dear one," the Warwitch coaxed, "surrender yourself and complete the journey. Join us and begin the new way of things, as it should be."

Jaren wrenched his eyes from Morgaine, or from the figure that looked to be her. "What have you done to my sister?" he demanded.

"I have awakened her. I have given her what she desired. Remade, she is at one with the magic."

"But she looks different. She doesn't look right."

"She has come a long way, as you have. Such a journey takes some rest. You will know her again, soon enough."

"But I already know her. She's my *sister*. I don't think she wanted this." He glanced at Morgaine once more, his expression hardening. "No, she didn't want this, I know it."

"Young one, you are not yet knowledgeable enough to understand. You must trust me. Let go of your anger and your fear. Let me guide you." The Warwitch offered a hand, smiling once more. Still, it did not touch her eyes.

"No," he replied simply. "If you want what's best for us, then you'll let us go. We're no danger to you."

"But you are a danger to yourselves, untrained and unknowing. You have no idea of the power within you." Her mouth drew to a thinly compressed line.

"I'm not using it anymore. Not ever. I'm going to forget it and go back home, with my sister."

She laughed then, a sound lacking warmth. "Jaren, you cannot go back home. You are changed, though you would deny it. I can see it in your eyes. There is no going back now."

"Then we'll just go away somewhere, far away. You'll never have to see us again. You'll—"

"Silence!" she cut in angrily. "You will do as I say from now on, *boy*. I have grown tired of your insolence. You will surrender now, or I will take you. The choice is yours; make it quickly."

Jaren flinched, startled by the abrupt change in the woman. Panic began to set in. What could he do? His only hope, his entire plan, had hinged on sacrificing himself to defeat the Witch. He couldn't do that now, with Morgaine at risk, but what other option remained?

"What is your answer?" the Warwitch demanded.

Jaren couldn't run back the way he'd come. The way was barred. Wide-eyed, he cast about for another means of escape, any other way out.

Seeing his panic-stricken searching, the Warwitch said, "So be it. Your choice is made."

She began to gesture, summoning, Jaren was sure, but he noticed something else immediately. She seemed to have suddenly become fuzzy around the edges, her movements blurred. It was as if parts of her were divided, out of time with the whole. She drew back both arms, palms outward. The blurring made it seem as though she were moving in slow motion, though she was surely not.

Jaren backed away guardedly, his mind racing.

The Witch thrust her hands forth. Instinctively, Jaren brought his own up in defense, and he was thrown backward. However, it was not as he had feared. Just as the would-be assassin's dagger had been thwarted back in Aendaras, the energy bolt slammed against a barrier inches from his outstretched arms, though it still bore him rearward. Moreover, instead of slamming into the unyielding wall himself, the barrier appeared to completely protect him, though he was jolted roughly within the shield as it impacted the stone.

Shaking his head to free the cobwebs that had formed, Jaren rose and steadied himself.

The Warwitch leveled her gaze, clearly irritated, and once more began gesturing. And again, Jaren noticed that she appeared out of synchronicity with herself. But what did that mean? He repeated the same warding posture of his own.

The shockwave of energy slammed into his shield with the renewed attack, driving it several feet into the wall and sending an explosion of broken rock cascading outward. This time, he remained on his feet, though it took some effort against the pounding blast.

Seeing him relatively unfazed completely unhinged the Warwitch. She screamed to the figures above her and began to weave her arms about furiously. The blurred movements were hypnotic.

Morgaine and Joselle began to work their own gestures.

Jaren gritted his teeth and settled into his guard once more. He hoped it would be enough. He raised his eyes to Morgaine. *Please, don't do this*, he nearly whispered. There was still no sign that he meant any more to her than a complete stranger. Worse, her twisted scowl had returned.

Thin bands of white-hot energy burst from the Witch's fingertips just as the other two finished their summoning. The result was a deafening explosion all around Jaren, and he was hurtled backward hard enough to knock the breath from his lungs.

His head swam, and dark spots appeared before his eyes. *No,* he screamed at himself. *You can't give up! Fight back!*

A stone clattered to the ground nearby, the sound muffled by the ringing in his ears. The air smelled of copper. He looked up from where he lay, sprawled in crushed and broken rock. He had smashed completely through the thick courtyard wall and come to rest on the other side. For the moment, the Witch was out of view behind the mound of debris and settling dust.

Should he run? He looked about, but saw no means of exit. He was in another open-roofed courtyard, much like the one he'd just been in. He couldn't flee. The Warwitch would surely just hunt him down within the maze of her own fortress. He doubted he could make his way back to the lifeboat of the Wave Hammer, either. No, there was nothing for it but to try to fight back, as hopeless as that seemed.

If only Morgaine would remember me!

42

MORGAINE HESITATED, CONFLICTED.

The enemy had been dispatched, clearly, and that had been the Mistress' wish. So why did she feel uneasy?

Perhaps because he was surely dead; they had been instructed to keep him alive at any cost, but to neutralize him all the same. That had proven difficult, even for the Mistress, seeing as she had called them to action so soon.

Didn't that mean his destruction was all the more necessary? He had been a greater threat than was believed. Still, even in her short time as a daughter, Morgaine had borne the costs of anything other than total submission to the will of the Mistress.

Again, a distant memory skirted just beyond thought. She had resisted ... fought against her becoming. That had brought pain, and a realization that she must embrace the inevitable. It had been for her own good, after all. Surrendering to the process did not alleviate the agony completely, but the pain of resisting, and the reprisals afterward, had been unimaginable. Perhaps it was the degree of suffering that allowed her to remember it at all, even hazily.

She was surprised as a twinge of sadness took her. Why did it have to be like that? Surely the Mistress would have spared her any unnecessary suffering. It must have been unavoidable, then. Even the Mistress still experienced her own manner of ... discomfort. A small price to pay for the gifts, she had told them.

But still, a nagging doubt remained. Pain and suffering were wrong, weren't they? Wasn't it wrong to hurt someone you cared for?

Morgaine shook her head, trying to dispel the nagging thoughts. What did that have to do with anything? The enemy was dead, and the Mistress could go on with her plans. Morgaine folded her hands upon the balcony rail and awaited the Mistress' call.

It came soon enough. Morgaine was directed to the wall that had buried the enemy. He *was* dead, wasn't he?

All the while, Morgaine tried to convince herself there was no lingering doubt, no elusive secret that danced just beyond her mind's reach.

⁂

Jaren forced thoughts of his sister aside. She could not help him now. No one could. He was going to have to survive on his own.

For some reason, the oddness about the Warwitch's appearance came to occupy his thoughts. Was it some weakness revealed? He recalled something Ensin Llaw had told him about the magic, about oneness. He had thought Jaren needed to be wholly committed—focused—in order to summon. Did the blurred movements of the Witch mean that she was not properly focused? Were their abilities somehow similar?

It made sense. Merging magic-metal with her own flesh could have made her into an *An'Valir* of a sort. If so, it would follow that she needed to summon in the same way he did.

But, even were that true, wasn't it was a stretch to think that was not simply the manner in which her summoning worked? As soon as that doubt arose, however, Jaren rejected it. Somehow he knew it had been neither intentional nor a natural occurrence. Nothing about the Witch was natural, now.

It was a gamble, to be sure. After all, Llaw didn't really know anything about Jaren's abilities. He was simply making logical assumptions based on his observations. Jaren had no choice but to do the same, to base his own guesses on the *Valir's* conclusions.

But the questions remained: whether or not he had sensed some weakness in the Warwitch's power, what could he do about it? How could he exploit it?

Jaren peered worriedly at the ruined section of the wall. They would be coming soon. He had to take the chance. Right or not, it was all he had. He assumed a posture of strength, one that Llaw had shown him some time ago to aid his exercises. Relaxation would be hard to manage at the present moment, but he had to try. His life depended on it, and perhaps Morgaine's, too.

If there was anything left of her to save.

Body, mind and spirit, the three selves: Jaren thrust all other thoughts away, as well as his mounting fatigue, and sought to balance himself.

❦

Turan half-dragged Iselle along.

"Come, my dear. We don't want to miss the spectacle, do we?" he teased.

Iselle had seen enough. Jaren was either dead—most likely—or near enough to it. No one could have survived the combined assaults of the Witch and the other two. *Morgaine had helped!* What had happened that she would strike at her own brother? Her racing thoughts ventured back to the horrible wails she'd heard since arriving. Had that been Morgaine? What under the Truth had been done to her?

Iselle was pulled roughly through an inner doorway and down a narrow corridor. Glimpses through open windows showed another courtyard, and she briefly caught sight of the partially collapsed wall. But the image that burned into her mind was the figure she saw standing just back from the rubble.

Jaren! He's alive! But how—

There was a sudden lurch, and Turan thrust her into a short passage that entered onto the square.

A surprised growl sounded in her ear as they stopped short of the opening, just far enough to peer around the rough edge of the archway. Turan had apparently not expected to see Jaren unscathed, either.

Iselle could not believe her eyes. Movement along the walls and at the crest of the rubble heap drew her attention. The Warwitch and the others were coming again. *Morgaine! How could you?*

Iselle let out a low moan. He may have survived by some miracle so far, but how long could Jaren hold out? She glanced up at Morgaine as she advanced. How long before Jaren became like that?

Turan chuckled evilly, obviously heartened at the reappearance of Jaren's assailants.

❦

The scowl that split the Witch's face was clear enough evidence that Jaren was not at all in the condition she'd assumed. By the expressions of the other two, though, standing to either side of the gap upon the wall, they could have been tending to the wash. Except that his sister meant to kill him, just like Joselle. At least that twisted smile of evil glee was gone for the time being.

The Warwitch again ordered them to strike. Each of them rained the white fire down at Jaren, but within his azure-walled cocoon, concentrating only on centering himself and holding the magic, he remained safe. The bolts of energy burst against his shield in vain or reflected dangerously away, boring deep holes into the stone of the courtyard.

He closed his eyes and was surprised that he could still see them, or images of them. Through his lidded vision, the image of the Warwitch appeared absolutely chaotic. Wildly surging flows of magic stormed about her, like some great maelstrom in miniature. The other two, similarly, were woven about by tempestuous streams of energy. In this surreal vision, the rest of his surroundings were dull and gray, more colorless even than the landscape of the Forge, but his three assailants stood out plainly.

Screaming in fury, the Warwitch barked orders to the two figures on the walk above. Their attacks once more became the hammering energies that had so easily borne Jaren through the stout wall. Except now, these, too, simply broke upon his barrier, dissipating into nothingness.

The Witch held up her hands, bringing the assault to an end. Despite the pause in her attacks, the chaotic whirlwinds about her increased.

"You are adept at learning the ways of the magic, Jaren Haldannon. But your cunning will not avail you. You cannot hold forever against me. Against us."

The words came from far away, as if across some distant land. *She's trying to distract you*, he admonished. *Don't listen to her!*

His focus wavered with these new thoughts and he shifted the slightest bit in his posture, bringing a crooked smile to the Witch's lips.

"Your sister knows—it is useless to fight your destiny. She can tell you what resistance brings: nothing but pain and regret. No, Jaren, listen to your heart. You know you need me. You need someone who can understand what you have experienced, someone who knows what it is like to be called by the magic."

It took a great effort, but Jaren locked himself away from her voice within his tiny refuge. Within his center, he drifted. The Witch pursed her lips, the temporary smile of satisfaction vanished. The voice returned, but this time it was as it had been on his arrival.

... The magic will destroy you if you do not seek my help ... you do not yet know its true nature ...

He squeezed his eyes shut and struggled to retain his focus. From somewhere in the recesses of his mind, Ver's voice echoed in seeming reply, "... Remember ... the magic itself is neither good nor bad ..."

The Witch's voice continued. *... I have faced the power and I now have control ... I can teach you how to do the same ...*

Echoing words of the avatar countered once more, "... It is the exercise of our free will that turns the use ... to good or evil purposes ... it is only a tool ..."

And, it came to him then, in sudden realization. It was *his* inner voice, *his* desire to use the magic, that was speaking to him all along. It was not the magic, but his very being, responding to the awareness of the power it could wield. That knowledge, the final truth of it, emboldened him.

He remained still, motionless as time.

Everything made sense. As Ver had said, the magic was a tool, though a natural, mysterious tool. In its awareness of the magic, his human nature had desired to connect with it, to use it. The whisperings were the voice of his own awakening, not the seductive call of a dark power. Using it was not corruption, but a natural extension of his being.

And he *could* control the manner in which he used it. He *would*.

The Warwitch exhaled impatiently, barely containing her rage. A flicker of movement off to one side pulled her eyes from the insolent youth before her. Another wicked grin sprouted, wide enough to flash teeth.

"Very well, boy. If you will not listen to words, another example is in order." She raised her voice, calling out to the recessed archway that had drawn her attention. "Bring out our other young guest," she ordered. "Have her bid Jaren welcome."

The words hardly registered with Jaren. He was aware of his inner serenity and of the Witch's forced grasp of the power. But the next sound hit him squarely, smashing through his calm and scattering his center.

Iselle's voice cried out in pain. She was here, too.

No!

No sooner had he dropped his guard than the white-hot band of fire lanced toward him. Jaren had time only to throw himself to the side in sheer panic, and the lacing strike moved in reaction, searing into his thigh. Pain exploded in his mind, and he reeled backward, writhing in agony. Jaren screamed as the pain engulfed him.

Iselle, too, cried out in terrified alarm.

The Warwitch's wicked grin widened, and she strode forward, picking her way easily down the piled rubble. She wanted to be closer when she took him. She wanted to look into his eyes as the realization of his doom struck home.

43

THE CRIES STIRRED RECOGNITION WITHIN Morgaine. She knew the voice, but how? Slowly, the memory came. *A brother, I have a brother, Jaren. But, what does that matter? He is ... he is ... here. Is he here? Did I really hear him?*

Then, there was the other. *A girl, a friend? No, she was Jaren's friend. What was her name?*

Morgaine shook her head, trying to clear her thinking. It didn't make any sense. The Mistress was her family now. She was a daughter of the magic.

But she had been part of a family before.

Morgaine leaned heavily against the balcony rail. *Jaren is here. How is that possible? He and ... Iselle—that is her name, isn't it?—are here. Why?*

She remembered being angry with him. He'd been up to his usual tricks, trying to steal all the attention, messing about in her business, getting involved where he didn't belong. But what had it been about?

The magic! A flood of anger swept through her. Jaren wanted to steal the magic. No, no, it wasn't that. It was something different. The swell of fury dissipated. *He was different. He was overshadowing her, again, taking all of the focus from her, leaving Morgaine ignored, forgotten. He was leaving her with the magic, but still, he was taking something else.*

The simmering thoughts frustrated her, and she looked about for Jaren. She would tell him to stay out of it, to leave well enough alone.

Then, her eyes found him. Jaren was lying on the paving stones below her. He was hurt, trying awkwardly to drag himself backward with one arm, the other holding his injured leg. But the Mistress had almost reached him.

The Mistress is going to hurt him again. Hurt him like ... like she had done? Yes, you helped do this to him, to your own brother. How could you have done that to Jaren? Morgaine gasped in horror. Movement to her side distracted her for an instant, and she saw the other.

After a moment, she recognized the girl standing there, too.

The anger that had moments ago stirred against her brother now welled up as rage. Rage at herself, at the Mistress, at this one beside her, whose deadly gaze now fell on her brother. She was Joselle Banath.

Morgaine remembered.

🜋

Iselle could endure no more of the torturous scene helplessly, while Jaren was about to die.

With all her might, she flung her head back, all too aware of where Turan's face was.

The result was a sickening crack and an alarmed grunt as his nose was shattered. Instantly, his grip fell away as he reached instinctively to his gushing face. Iselle stepped deftly away and rounded on him, pent-up frustration fueling her wrath. She kicked low, smashing his knee sideways. Turan cried out, now trying to hold both his nose and twisted knee at once, as he dropped. She punched him, hard, connecting solidly with his jaw, just below the ear, and the young thief toppled backward to lie still.

Iselle did not dare waste time. She whirled and ran to Jaren.

🜋

An explosion erupted above her, sending the Warwitch flying forward. She skidded on the rough, uneven flagstones, shielding her head as stone fragments rained down. Then, she peered apprehensively back at the wall, eyes wide with sudden wariness.

At the point on the wall where Joselle had stood mere seconds before, a smoldering, blackened gouge remained.

The Warwitch craned her neck farther, to take in Morgaine. Her eyes nearly popped from their sockets at the sight of her, already summoning again. This time, Morgaine was not focused on Jaren.

She means to attack me!

The Warwitch flung her hands up in a hurried warding gesture, just as Morgaine's release hammered outward. Though lying prone, her defense held.

Staggering to her feet, the Warwitch's snarling features matched those of her once-daughter. She prepared to respond in kind.

Back and forth, the two summoned, exchanging hammers of energy and white-hot bands of searing death. The True One himself must have guided Morgaine's actions, as she narrowly succeeded in blocking the Witch's attacks. Each time she seemed about to be destroyed, she somehow managed to throw up a barrier of blue energy. Miraculous as her achievements appeared, Morgaine was quickly becoming exhausted from repelling the other's potent energies. The swath of destruction widened.

Morgaine was rocked from behind. The strike flung her against the rail, which nearly buckled under the strain, as great chunks of stone dislodged and dropped to the ground in crumbled heaps. She staggered, close to falling from the balcony, catching herself with one shaking arm.

The Warwitch scanned about, looking for the source of the aid. It must be Joselle. *At least one daughter remains true.* Now, it was time to finish with the business at hand. Morgaine could be dealt with in time.

Then she, too, was struck. Not by a physical attack, but alarm. Wary apprehension followed the voice that now invaded *her* mind.

… You will not hurt my sister again … if you wish to avoid death, then flee; that is all the warning you'll get, Witch!

⚘

Jaren stood, at first leaning heavily on Iselle. Dark spots appeared across his vision once again, and he fought to keep conscious. Fortunately the pain wracking his right leg helped keep him lucid, though it was a struggle to concentrate on relaxing. Slowly, gradually, he felt the calm returning. Once he achieved his center, he stepped away from Iselle, ushering his friend behind him.

Focused within himself, standing in his renewed posture required no effort, only a fractional thought, as much awareness as he gave the far-off throbbing in his thigh. So far removed, it might have been a memory of pain experienced long ago. Still, he pushed that distraction away and attuned himself.

He didn't know exactly how he had spoken to the Witch, but the ability seemed to come naturally enough.

Jaren didn't close his eyes this time, but trained his attention upon her fully. He could still sense the roiling currents of magical energy that enveloped her. The streams continued to weave about her feverishly— the tumult even increasing—now that she had heard and turned to face him.

He was aware, too, of Morgaine's struggle with Joselle, for he could sense that the other still lived, even before she struck, but he could do nothing about it. It was Morgaine's fight, now. Detaching himself while balanced was becoming easier, his emotions coming fully under his control. The magical releases they cast at each other crossed as faint illuminations through his field of vision. He gave them no more thought than the glow of a lamp, or the light of a new day dawning. They simply existed, as did he.

Instead of simply shielding himself this time, he reached out toward the Witch. His hands worked of their own volition, powered by the mere thought. It was tentative, this first attempt, though far from soft.

The Warwitch took a step backward, as if pushed, eyebrows arching in surprise. Then her own hands rose, in a warding gesture. For the first time, she was forced to create a barrier against him. An expression akin to fear washed briefly across her features.

That realization itself nearly shocked Jaren from his focus, but he recovered before the Witch sensed anything. At least, she had not acted in response. Perhaps she was truly afraid now, afraid of *him*.

Renewing his center, Jaren attacked once more, much more forcefully. The result was the same as when their positions were reversed. Her barrier absorbed the damage, and she suffered no serious harm.

Several more times, Jaren tried, and she retaliated. To Jaren's surprise, he even managed several strikes with the white fire, somehow grasping instinctively the skills and mimicking her gestures, but to no avail. They were deadlocked.

A tremor shook his balance. This would go on forever, he feared, the resulting wave of dread sending a ripple through his focus. He had to find a way to end this, or he had to flee. He would have to take Iselle with him. His concentration wavered further as he hazarded a glance at Morgaine. What about her? Could he leave her behind, now that she appeared to recognize him again?

She had saved his life by distracting the Warwitch. He couldn't leave her, could he?

He was staggered backward by a great surge of energy. The Witch must have sensed his momentary lapse and attacked. He forced his mind to empty once more, with some difficulty, and recentered. Iselle's gasp of alarm sounded nearby, just before Jaren managed to seal himself off once more.

She was safe again, too, tucked away behind his shield. He couldn't include her in it. He hadn't managed to figure out how that might be done, if even possible. Then, the idea struck him.

His thoughts floated in the emptiness. Trying to shield both of them was attempting to force her into his own consciousness. He wasn't sure that was possible, and it didn't matter now. What was important was the resulting spark it had generated.

They were separate beings.

If the Witch was struggling to force her control, perhaps some inner division was the cause of her chaotic image. The swirling flows about her and the apparent lack of synchronicity might be related. Powerful though she was, her abilities had been created. She had seized hold of the magic by making herself into something other than human: part flesh and part *metanduil*, unnatural—off-centered, perhaps, *forcing* the magic?

Jaren had no other option but to try his theory. It was that or attempt to flee, and flight was too risky. He had been lucky enough, or blessed by the True One, to puzzle things out as well as he had managed so far. Trying to escape while still engaged against the Witch might prove too much. He wouldn't tempt fate any further before trying what seemed the more logical choice.

A monumental task lay before him.

Up to this point, Jaren had struck at her clumsily, wholly, and she had countered. But, if he struck at her differently—if he focused on a part of her, on one of her three selves, disunited as he suspected they were—then maybe he could get through to reach her.

To begin, he sensed outward with the magic. Perhaps he could gather some idea if he probed about. He let the energy flow toward her, searching, feeling.

He nearly recoiled at the sensations that returned: anger, loathing, fear, ambition. Then, he caught a hint of something else, something beneath. It was well hidden and the path was obstructed, but he probed more deeply. She had built walls and barricades within herself, within her own mind, to secret it away and keep it from her waking thoughts, to protect herself from it. But it was there, and he sensed it.

The Warwitch must have suddenly become aware of his searching, because he was abruptly blocked. She shouted out fiercely in dismay, as full realization of his delving hit home, and a great, impenetrable wall sprang up, sealing her mind from further attempts.

The damage was already done, though, Jaren hoped, the answer found. He summoned once more, differently again.

As her mind was closed to Jaren, he began with her body, sensing outward for the stray currents that led to her physical self. He found them, and began to summon. She screamed truly then, clawing at her head, staggering sideways.

The witch's guard dropped, Jaren seized hold of the channel to her mind as well. This time, his intent was not to search or investigate, but to suggest, to reveal. He used the same path as he had in sending his voice to the Witch, now delivering images of her true form, projecting an awareness of the unnatural construct she'd become. Of the vulnerability to the pain and suffering she still endured because of the process, because of the *gift*, because of her cursed existence.

Jaren had discovered Rhianain's innermost fears and doubts and channeled them against her.

"Noooo!" the Warwitch wailed. "It is not a curse! It is beautiful ... it is ... *power!*" She glared at him in hatred, willing him to believe her, and took an involuntary step toward him. Her clawed hands reached forward of their own accord.

Minutes stretched on. Jaren summoned an augmentation, an amplification of Rhianain's own rising emotions and physical scars.

Rage and frustration gave way to emptiness and despair, and the Warwitch fell to her knees, moaning, her voice coming in desperate sobs. "Please stop ... you don't understand ... it is only a fitting sacrifice for the gift!" A convulsion wracked her, and she pitched forward, supporting herself weakly with trembling arms. "I was promised! I was shown the future! I *am* the future!"

Rhianain looked down then, at herself. Recognition bloomed, horrible, awful recognition. It was as if she observed herself truly, and for the first time. Uncertainty and dread battered her mind, along with unbearable pain, the agony that was a constant reminder and consequence. She raised her left hand before her, turning it over, seeing it at last. Her mouth worked, spittle drooling from her tortured, maddened sneer.

Wrapped within himself, balanced in the knowledge that his actions were the only means of countering her dark abilities, Jaren continued feeding the power into the Witch, magnifying her own deepest fears and revealing the truth of her insufferable agony. He barely heard her strangled words.

Then she was gone.

He kept himself centered for several moments. It seemed seconds, and also days. Instantly, eventually, he glanced upward.

Morgaine was gone, too.

He was aware of releasing his focus, and of falling. Arms caught him, soft and warm. Darkness closed in, and he felt the embrace no more.

Epilogue

THE DOOR TO THE SHEPHERD'S Crook swung inward easily, admitting a young man and woman. Ather Haben blinked. The young man was little more than a boy, though he looked truly weary. His eyes were more … *aged*. He'd obviously seen much in his short span of years, and not all of it good. Still, he was too young to have that limp. The other, now, Ather had seen many like her: lively, full of mischief, if he knew anything. And after forty-odd years at keeping an inn, he'd seen enough to be sure.

They made their way through the packed house toward the bar. The young man leaned on his staff with every other step. The grimace on his face belied the pain he was feeling. It looked to be a recent condition, Ather thought. Most folks who were long used to such carried a resigned air of a sort when it pained them. This one's was still fresh, he'd bet. Probably the same incident gave him the dark look he sported.

Yes, he's too young for a look like that, too.

Ather hoped they wouldn't be trouble, but then again, he somehow knew they would not. That was another of his innkeeper's intuitions. He could, nine times out of ten, tell which ones were about to cause something and which weren't. That sense had kept his toughs very happy, and free of many scars that normally came with the job. It also kept them around longer than most.

Still, there was something about the pair. He was still trying to muddle it out when they asked for a room.

Ather started from his thoughts. *Well, that's a stiff shot.* He suppressed a chuckle. *No one's caught me daydreaming in a good while!*

"A double, if you have one," the young woman replied, with a curious look.

"Absolutely, young miss," he tried to redeem himself with a warm smile. "And will you be wanting to sup in your room or down in the commons this evening?"

She glanced aside at her companion. He was silent, still consumed in his thoughts. Very unsettling ones, too, if Ather read the young man's grim face right.

"In our room, please," she said.

"Very well, miss." Ather gestured with a nod. "The room's at the top of the stairs, third door on the right. When would you like the meal brought up?"

"In a few hours, thank you. We've come a long way."

Ather acknowledged with another nod. Distracted, he watched her ascend the stairs, assisting her companion with a supporting arm.

Raucous laughter at one of the tables set his intuition going. He turned and eyed the lot of them. Already into their fifth pitcher, they were. *Now, that bunch is going to be trouble*, he exhaled warily, gesturing faintly to get the lead tavern hand's attention. *Now, where has Jebba gotten to?*

⌘

Iselle watched the rise and fall of Jaren's chest as he slumbered deeply. The entire trip back to Colm, he had done little but sleep. Even on horseback for the journey here, he'd only been half awake. She could only sympathize. What kind of energy that battle had taken she couldn't possibly guess. She wished her own sleep would come as deeply and untroubled as his appeared.

She shivered uneasily. Jaren didn't know what had finally become of the Warwitch, nor did she. One moment she was there, the next, gone. It was a similar story with Morgaine and Joselle. They had all simply vanished, it seemed.

That made her more than a little uneasy, to say the least. So, while Jaren slept most of the time away, she'd been awake, if not alert, watching for signs of danger.

Still, if Jaren was so utterly drained, she reasoned, the others must have been even more so, especially the Warwitch. What she'd gone through—she appeared on the brink of madness at the last of it.

That small comfort had been all that allowed Iselle to take the few sparing moments of sleep she had dared along the way. Here, at least, they should be safe. They were among people once more, but two strangers in a large city.

Of Turan, she was not frightened in the least. If the wretch dared show himself again, Iselle would finish off what she had not had time to do in the Witch's hold. She almost hoped he would try to come after her. She would—

Jaren stirred, and Iselle regarded him.

"Where are we?" he croaked.

"In Nesmara, at an inn."

Jaren sat upright, stretching, and rubbed his eyes. "I'm famished. It feels like I haven't eaten in days."

"You haven't. Not much, anyway. You've barely been awake long enough to put a spoon to your lips. Or, for that matter—"

Jaren arched his eyebrows. "Never you mind," he said.

Iselle's mischievous look didn't fade in the least, until she feigned a hurt expression.

"I don't know what you were about to suggest," she began. "I was going to say you couldn't have stayed awake long enough to chew a proper mouthful."

"I'm sure," he responded, sardonically.

"Anyway, supper should be here soon. I told the innkeeper to bring it up after a while."

Jaren's eyes had drifted to the window that afforded a small view of the town to the north. Iselle frowned. He had that far-off look in his eye. It hadn't really left him since the isle of the Witch. *Who would it be this time?*

"Do you think he's out there, somewhere, keeping an eye on us?"

"Only if we need looking after."

"We just might, where we're going," he said.

"Jaren, I think your days of being watched over are … well, over."

He responded with a regretful look.

"Yes, I suppose so." He shrugged. "Then again, maybe not." He gave her a wink as a sly smile tugged at one corner of his mouth.

"Jaren Haldannon, I told you what would happen if you kept that up! I didn't tell you about that little weasel just to have you tease me to no end. You might yet need Ver to save you if you do it again!" If she were standing, her hands would surely have been planted on her hips.

"Careful now," he warned, "we're back in Carathon. You could be arrested for murdering me. I'm sure King Aldrain doesn't take kindly to that sort of thing. I know how much you enjoyed his … hospitality before."

"I swear on the Truth, Jaren, you're impossible!" She threw a pillow at him. "Besides, you shouldn't joke at King Aldrain's expense; he was in dire need from the last I saw."

The playful smile faded from Jaren's face, replaced by that distant look again, and his eyes sought the window once more. "He will have help, soon enough."

⁊

Alvarion Sanhaddan gestured in irritation to the white-robed servant holding the broad, feathered fan. That he couldn't keep up a steady flow of air was beyond irritating. Even rebuking the fellow hadn't worked. Perhaps he was from the islands to the south, and therefore unbothered by the cloying heat that lingered in Vetia well past the end of summer. Still, he had come cheaply, for a slave. Perhaps he would be better suited to other tasks, though he was marginally better than his predecessor.

That was a matter for later consideration. The item in his hands was not, however. Similar parchments had been delivered to the highest-ranking *Valir* across the six realms, or so the messenger claimed.

Alvarion broke the seal eagerly and began reading. The first of the passages came as little surprise. He had suspected as much. They had failed. Jhennain and the others were dead. Methas Kobol, then, was finally out of the way. Alvarion glanced up briefly. That meant he was the head of the guild in Vetia now.

He studied the painting on the far wall, as he frequently did. It depicted a great sailing vessel in the grasp of a crushing tempest. The waves threatened to overwhelm the ship at any moment, and lightning rent the sky in killing strikes. Why such a portrait seemed to calm him, he didn't know.

Alvarion read on. Slowly, ever so gradually, his eyebrows rose in response. By the time he'd finished, his hands trembled slightly, though whether from elation over his newfound position or apprehension to the final message, he was not entirely certain. He suspected the latter. Soon enough, he would have toppled Kobol in any event. It had simply been taken care of for him.

But the last of the note, that was ... unsettling. Rhianain was either missing or dead, though no body had been discovered. Her palace had been seized, and several *Valir* had arrived or were enroute to study the workings of her discoveries. They were promising, indeed.

By far the most alarming, however, was the information concerning the boy. He, too was gone, though it was expected he'd be located and properly handled soon enough. Yet, the message had borne strongly worded caution; the boy was believed to be extremely powerful and amazingly far advanced already, based on examinations at the scene of his struggle against Rhianain—too far along to be allowed free reign, or even kept in benign custody. Any word or sightings of the youth were to be reported to the guild heads and forwarded to the council at once.

The youngest Haldannon was to be found and placed under constant supervision at all costs. Ensin Llaw was spearheading that operation. Alvarion chuckled darkly. Llaw was a bit too academic for that sort of work.

Finally, five *Valir* of sufficient standing were required from each guild to aid in one of three endeavors: first, and foremost, the apprehension of the boy; second, the search for Rhianain, if it was determined she still lived; and, third, the further study of Rhianain's stronghold. They would begin using her island base as their own headquarters. The requested *Valir* were to make their way to the island without delay.

That was a first, or at the very least, a thing unheard of for an age. The *Valir* had not maintained an autonomous existence outside of other nations in centuries. Not since the guild war, when *Valir* loyal to an alliance of kingdoms aided in the destruction of the sovereign city of Ketarra, the *Valir* stronghold. They had believed the council of Ketarra too concerned in its own matters, and therefore not concerned enough in keeping with the wishes of the six realms.

Ironically enough, Ketarra had been established on the Isle of Ice.

Alvarion sighed: so much for ancient history. The past was becoming the present, it seemed. He stood, gathering parchment and ink for his own dispatches.

He felt a growing sense of exhilaration. Perhaps he was excited to begin his duties as guild head, after all. He had already begun formulating the list of *Valir* he would send on Vetia's behalf, and their instructions, were they part of the group that took the boy. In all truth, they weren't the best or most trusted he had to call on, but they were close at hand and time was definitely of the essence. They would have to do.

Alvarion was so engrossed in his thoughts that the slave's apparent neglect of his duties was forgotten for the moment. Neither did he pay attention to the fellow's eyes, which followed his master's every move, missing nothing. Cold and calculating eyes.

LaVergne, TN USA
01 October 2010
199282LV00003B/2/P